f

HA'PENNY CHANCE

Ivy Rose Murphy dreams of a better future. For years she has set out daily from the tenements known as 'The Lane' to beg for discards from the homes of the wealthy. Her fortunes take a turn for the better, but there are eyes on Ivy and she is vulnerable as she carries her earnings through the dark winter streets. Jem Ryan, who owns the local livery, longs to make Ivy his wife, but she is reluctant to give up her fierce independence. Then a sudden astonishing event turns Ivy's world upside down. A dazzling future beckons and she must decide where her loyalties lie.

HA'PENNY CHANCE

by

Gemma Jackson

Magna Large Print Books
Long Preston, North Yorkshire,
BD23 4ND, England.

British Library Cataloguing in Publication Data.

Jackson, Gemma
    Ha'penny chance.

    A catalogue record of this book is
    available from the British Library

    ISBN   978-0-7505-4096-4

First published in Great Britain in 2014 by Poolbeg Press Ltd.

Copyright © Gemma Jackson 2014

Cover illustration © Stephen Mulcahey by arrangement with
Arcangel Images

The moral right of the author has been asserted

Published in Large Print 2015 by arrangement with
Gemma Jackson whose agents are Edward Fuglewicz

Magna Large Print is an imprint of Library Magna Books Ltd.

Printed and bound in Great Britain by
T.J. (International) Ltd., Cornwall, PL28 8RW

Acknowledgements

It's amazing how many of my family and friends felt insulted that I didn't mention them in the acknowledgement page of my debut novel. If I listed everyone individually I'd need to put an addendum to the book! So, hopefully it suffices to say... Family and Friends. Does that cover it?

I have two brothers and four sisters and a delightful supply of nieces and nephews. Special mention goes to my parents' first-born, Renee (the one we were all compared to!), my mother's shining star who manages to travel the world while looking impossibly glamorous as she battles the cancer eating at her. Also to my brother Seán, who according to family legend has been feeding the family since his first day of work on a backstreet Dublin farm at the age of two! I wasn't alive at the time but my mother extolled his virtues and I've been one of the hungry he fed. And my brother Patrick, the baby, who greets me with a beaming smile and a rib-tickling hug whenever he returns home to find my tent erected in his fabulous garden.

I have to mention my daughter Astrid. She has threatened to cut off my supply of tea if I leave her out. That woman knows my addictions.

I'd like to give a nod to the people who work in

radio. I was fortunate to meet smiling charming people working in radio as I promoted my book *Through Streets Broad and Narrow,* so thank you to those unsung heroes and heroines. But I want to thank also the people who accompany me as I work away at my computer. The radio plays constantly and sometimes when I'm searching for an idea or a word the music playing in the background supplies just the hint I need. Thank you.

For all the nurturing, wise, wonderful, strong, courageous women who populate my world. I've been truly blessed to know you.

Chapter 1

'Wait up, Ivy Murphy, will yeh?'

Ivy looked over her shoulder and grinned at the little urchin calling her name. The boy didn't even come up to her hip but his brow was furrowed like an old man's. His little body was enshrouded in a badly frayed, cut-down, adult sports jacket which was held in place by a length of fraying hemp rope wrapped several times around his waist. His two hands were clenched around the neck of a burlap sack thrown over his shoulder. His bare, blue-tinged feet slapped the muck accumulated on Dublin's Grand Canal walkway. Under his perpetual layer of filth it was difficult to make out the boy's features.

'I've been calling yeh for ages, woman. Are yeh deaf?' Seán McDonald panted, his little legs moving like pistons as he hurried to catch up with Ivy.

'Have you been working at your farm this fine October morning, Mr McDonald?'

Ivy was wrapped against the weather in an old army coat that covered her from neck to ankle – it had been green at one time but after years of hard wear it was now a bilious colour that defied description. Her head and shoulders were covered by her black knit shawl. She was reluctant to stop her heavy pram rolling forward. She was tired, cold, wet and hungry. The wind coming off the water of the Grand Canal sliced and bit into any

11

exposed flesh – but at least it had stopped raining. Sighing, she halted, waiting for the young lad to catch up with her.

Seán and his multitude of relatives lived at one end of the tenement block that housed Ivy's basement home. The first time young Seán heard Old Man Solomon's gramophone playing 'Old McDonald Had a Farm', he had adopted the name as his own. The lad had been working since he was two years old on one of the many back-yard farms that littered Dublin city. He'd earned the name McDonald; at six years old Seán was a veteran farm worker.

'Can I put me sack on your pram, Ivy?' Seán tried to rearrange the string-tied burlap sack over his shoulder. The sack was long and weighed down by its contents. The weight belted Seán across his thin bare ankles every time he moved.

'What's in it?' Ivy asked, buying time. She could see the weight was too much for the lad but she didn't want anything that might leak unpleasant matter into her pram.

Ivy had spent her morning visiting the back doors of the houses on Merrion Square and Mount Street. It had been a good morning for her. She'd returned to her two basement rooms twice already to unload the items she'd scavenged from the homes of the wealthy.

'I've pigs' cheeks and four crubeens.' Seán worked on the Widow Purcell's little back-yard farm. The woman did the best she could to see the young boy was fed. 'The widder woman doesn't care for 'em.'

'Your family will be well fed tonight.' Ivy pulled

12

a load of newspaper from the bottom of her pram. They hadn't far to go. The paper would soak up any spills.

'I'm not taking them home.' Seán sounded completely disgusted. 'There's never a fire going in our place, Ivy, not unless I bring something in that burns. I wouldn't give them to that lot to cook anyway. They'd ruin the things.'

'Going to sell them?' There was always a demand for any kind of foodstuff going cheap.

'You've met yer one that took over Granny Grunt's place?' Seán said, referring to an old neighbour who had passed away recently.

'Yeah, I sold her that stove of Granny's.' Ivy had inherited the contents of old Granny's one-room basement home next door, and Granny had been the proud owner of the only freestanding cast-iron stove in the tenements known locally as The Lane.

'Oh, yeah, I remember her saying something about that.' He didn't mention yer woman ranting on about Ivy robbing the thing: that was between the pair of them. 'That stove's mighty – yeh must have got a fair few bob for that thing.' Seán's eyes gleamed at the thought of all that money. 'I wish we'd been able to buy it off yeh. Yeh wouldn't know yerself with somethin' like that in yer rooms.' He shivered in delight at the thought of the heat.

'What has yer one to do with the price of eggs?' Ivy had met her new neighbour only briefly. She didn't seem a friendly sort. Someone had mentioned to the woman that Ivy had removed the stove, with its stand and chimney, from Granny Grunt's back-basement room. The woman had knocked on Ivy's door to demand the return of

13

what she'd believed was an integral part of the room she'd rented.

'Do yeh know she's been to America?' Seán's voice held tones of complete amazement. The poverty-ridden tenement block, hidden away from its more upmarket neighbours, didn't normally attract world travellers.

'Where did you hear that?'

'She told me so herself.' Seán puffed out his chest importantly. 'Yer one buys all the sticks off me I can find or cadge – I think she likes me.'

'That's nice.'

'She was on the *Titanic*.' Seán almost bounced in place with this impressive announcement. The sinking of the mighty ship was still considered important news even after more than ten years.

'Go 'way!' Ivy stopped walking to stare down at the frantically nodding young boy.

To the people of Dublin, a people very aware of the living to be made from the sea and river-going trade, talk of the Titanic disaster still sent shivers down the spine. There was many an Irish life lost when that great ship went down. Ivy's own father had lost a sister in the disaster.

'Honest to God.' Seán opened his pale-blue eyes wide. 'I swear.' He held one dirty hand to his chest.

Ivy tried not to notice the threadbare state of the oversized adult jacket Seán wore. The cutdown man's jacket fell to his calves. She didn't want to think about what he might or might not be wearing underneath.

'The woman told me all about it herself,' he said. 'I got the whole story – from her very own lips.'

14

'That's a turn-up for the books. Do yeh think yer one would be willing to tell her tale at a story night?'

Story nights were a source of entertainment to the inhabitants of the Dublin tenements. Tall tales and true were told to fascinated listeners gathered in the long, wide hallway of one of the tenement houses and everyone was welcome.

'I wouldn't know,' Seán shrugged.

'That's a story everyone in the place would love to hear.'

'I'll tell her about story night when I see her, Ivy. I'll be going to her place later because she promised to teach me a new way to cook pigs' cheeks and feet.' Seán nodded towards his sack sitting high on Ivy's big black pram.

'Be sure to let me know what she has to say. I wouldn't want to miss that story.' Ivy didn't find anything strange about teaching a six-year-old to cook the food he'd managed to gather for himself. There was no childhood in the tenements. Survival took every hand to the pumps.

'She said she'd show me how they cooked pig in America,' Seán went on, addressing the most important point as far as he was concerned. His stomach came before stories. He strutted along beside Ivy, his little legs pumping to keep up with her longer stride. 'Yeh can get crackle from feet and cheeks, she says.'

'What's crackle when it's at home?' Ivy let the subject of story night drop.

'Haven't a clue but yer one says I'll love it.' Seán was willing to try anything if it would plug the constant pains of hunger in his stomach.

'Yeh'll have to show me how yeh make it.' Ivy grinned down at Seán. 'Yeh'll start a new fashion all on yer own.' She was glad they'd almost reached the tunnel leading into their tenement block. She'd been aware of Seán's struggle to keep up with her. She'd have offered to let him ride on the pram but she knew his pride would be mortally offended at that.

'Ivy,' Seán's smile disappeared at the sight of the entrance to The Lane, 'can I ask yeh a favour?'

Ivy had been instrumental in sending Seán's abusive grandfather to jail. Tim Johnson, a thoroughly unpleasant man, had stepped outside the law in his efforts to force Ivy into his clutches. He'd been taken away by the local Garda. In Seán's eyes Ivy was a hero.

'What is it?' Ivy had noticed the change in the lad at her side. She understood. Seán's home life wasn't exactly ideal.

'Will yeh keep me takings with yeh?' Seán almost whispered, his head shrinking into his narrow shoulders. 'I'll come and get them later.' Then he added, to underline the secrecy of the matter, 'Out the back yard.'

'No problem.'

'Thanks!' Seán shouted over his shoulder as he ran down the tunnel leading into the hidden square that housed the tenement block. He didn't take any notice of the horse and carriage making its way slowly into the long tunnel. The trainee driver, holding the horse's reins in his sweating hands, shouted curses at the young boy but Seán didn't care. He didn't want anyone to see him with Ivy Murphy. He'd take the beating he'd get for

16

returning home without food for his aunts and uncles. He'd learned how to look out for number one. His mouth watered at the thought of the food he'd stashed away with Ivy. There'd be wigs on the green if he was found out but he'd risk it.

Chapter 2

'Ivy, I've got the kettle on.'

'Jem, yer blood should be bottled. I'd murder for a cup of tea.'

Jem Ryan, the local jarvey and Ivy's friend, was standing in the open doors of his livery building. He was holding the reins of the returning carriage in one hand, gently rubbing the standing horse's head with the other, while listening to the report from the driver and his trainee.

The livery, a long barnlike building, was brilliantly white with black trim. Jem and his crew of lads had freshly painted the exterior over the summer. It formed one side of The Lane and was directly across the cobbled square from the row of Georgian houses that were the tenements. A block of squat-looking two-storey houses sat at one end of the square, seeming to march across the space that separated the tenements from the livery. The fourth side of the square was formed by a high wall that blocked the rear gardens of the houses on Mount Street and the rear of the pub there. In that high wall was the tunnel that was the only entrance and exit to The Lane.

Ivy stood, half-listening to the talk between the men while examining Jem's handsome figure. There was such a difference in the way Jem carried himself these days. He stood tall, his broad shoulders pulled back, chest out, head high. Ivy let her eyes roam down his strong masculine body. With his mahogany hair gleaming in the pale winter sunlight, green eyes smiling, clean-shaven chin held high while he listened to his returning workers, Jem Ryan looked the king of all he surveyed.

He directed his next comment to the experienced man on the box. 'Put this horse away. She's done enough for the day. I'll want you to change horses, clean out the carriage and take it back to the rank at Stephen's Green.' Jem kept a number of carriages waiting at the horse-drawn standing rank around Stephen's Green, convenient for passing traffic. When a telephone call came through the livery exchange asking for a pick-up, Jem sent one of his lads down to the rank on a bike with careful note of the details in hand. If one of Jem's own horses wasn't available, for a small fee the lad passed the information to the nearest jarvey.

'Fair enough, boss.' The driver clicked his tongue against his teeth and the horse started to walk slowly forward.

'Conn,' Jem said, referring to one of the lads who worked for him, 'is bringing a bucket of food, enough for everyone, from the Penny Dinners. By the time you have the horse groomed and fed and the carriage cleaned out, there'll be a bite waiting for yeh.'

18

The Penny Dinners, set up to serve the Dublin poor, seemed to constantly serve stew but it was a welcome addition to the diet of the hungry. The nuns nearby ran a Penny Dinner service from the rear of their convent.

'I wish you'd told me you had food coming before I let young Seán run away,' Ivy said. 'The only thing he'll get at his place is a thick ear.'

'Yeh can't save everyone, Ivy.' Jem kept a careful eye on the carriage being driven through the open livery doors. 'No matter how hard you try.'

'Seán seems to be making a friend of yer one that moved into Granny's old place.' Ivy pushed her pram into the stable. She left it standing outside one of the newly filled stalls, well out of the way of the stall's inhabitant, giving the curious bay mare a quick caress when she put her head over the half-door.

'I'm going to close these doors.' Jem pushed the big double doors closed. 'Keep the heat inside. God knows there's enough hands around here to open and shut them as needed.'

Jem Ryan was investing a great deal of money in his livery business. He'd bought young horses to pull the traps and carriages he was refurbishing. Jem's uncle had been a magpie when it came to picking up cheap, out-of-fashion old vehicles of all sorts. The man had had great plans for his business when he'd invited Jem to leave his home in Sligo and join him in Dublin. Time and a debilitating illness had put paid to his grand ideas. While nursing his uncle through his long final illness Jem had allowed the business to fail. He'd sold off all the horses except his favourite, Rosie.

He'd worked only enough to keep food on the table and the bills paid.

'Pete Kelly, you're not in your mother's now!' Jem shouted at a young lad half-heartedly sweeping out one of the long aisles that divided the stables. 'Put your back into cleaning that floor!' Jem employed a number of local lads. He fed them and paid them pennies to put their hands to the work that needed doing – it kept them off the streets.

The year 1925 had started with a bang for both Jem and Ivy. They'd barely survived the shocks that had been in store for them during the year. Now the year was dying and Jem was pushing forward with his plans for expansion. He had a chance now to make something of himself and he was going to take it.

'I hear yer one that took over Granny's place has a radio.' Jem walked over to a part of the stable which he'd got the lads to clear of trash and set up as a rest area.

'What do you mean, a radio?' Ivy strolled over to join him. She watched him pull the steaming kettle from the top of the cast-iron closed fire the local blacksmith had made and installed. The fire stood on a thick sheet of metal. The wall behind it was also protected by a metal sheet. The exposed metal chimney climbed the interior wall, adding to the heat generated by the fire.

'Just what I said, Ivy Murphy – a radio.' Jem gave the little stove a satisfied grin. He'd been terrified at the thought of putting a fire into his building but the blacksmith had done him proud and the heat source was welcome on days like this. 'Sit yourself down here, Ivy – there's great heat from the stove and you're soaking wet.' He pulled up a rickety wooden chair and Ivy gratefully sat down.

'Why would your woman need one of them radio contraptions?' she asked as Jem opened a little freestanding cupboard and took out one of the cups and saucers he kept on hand for Ivy. His lads, she knew, were a mite hammer-fisted and enamel mugs lasted longer in their hands. Jem took an enamel mug out for his own use. 'Don't soldiers and sailors use them things for talking to each other?'

'They're making them radios now so you can hear music, all kinds of music they say, played by professional people, and you'll be able to get news from around the world.' Jem shook his head in astonishment.

'Go 'way!' Ivy had heard everything now.

'Honest to God.'

Jem was unaware of the thrill he gave Ivy every time he served her tea. He'd been looking after himself for years and thought nothing of mucking in to any chore that needed to be done. Ivy was more accustomed to men who believed women were put on this earth for their convenience. Her father and three younger brothers wouldn't be caught dead making a cup of tea for themselves, let alone for a woman.

'I went into Piggotts' and had a look at these new radios.' Jem handed the filled cup on its saucer to Ivy. He pulled over another chair and sat across from her after checking the chair to be sure its legs were even. He took a big swig of tea before saying, 'By God, Ivy, them radios are mighty.' He shook

21

his head in wonder. There were so many new marvels being invented every day. It took a man all of his time to keep up.

'Yeh weren't thinking of buying one, Jem Ryan, were yeh?' Ivy sipped the welcome brew while looking around the open space. Jem had created a decent-sized room that held a wonky-looking table, a couple of freestanding cupboards and a load of old wooden chairs.

'I wanted to.' Jem gulped tea from his mug. 'I really did, Ivy. The radio itself isn't such a big deal. I could make one meself if I had the bits. It's the earphones.'

'The what?'

'Earphones,' Jem repeated, lifting a hand to cover his ear. 'Yeh need them to be able to hear the radio. They cost a fortune, Ivy, and only one person can listen at a time. That's no great shakes, I'm thinking.'

'But still, Jem,' Ivy marvelled, 'imagine being able to hear music any time yeh wanted! It beats believin'.'

Ivy loved listening to Old Man Solomon's gramophone. It was the talk of The Lane. The old man always brought the machine down for the summertime street parties and played it for the entertainment of his neighbours and friends. He allowed the children to turn the chrome handle to power up the machine. However, no one else was allowed to touch the delicate black records he kept carefully packed in their brown-paper sleeves. The magical 78 records produced wonderful music that blasted out of the tall wide-mouth megaphone. That machine was a marvel –

and now, radio. What was the world coming to?

'There's talk of a radio station being set up right here in Dublin, Ivy. I read about it in the paper.' Jem's green eyes gleamed with delight over the rim of his enamel mug. He took a gulp of tea, 'Can you imagine such a thing?'

'The world is changing in leaps and bounds, Jem. Remember when yeh picked me up outside the morgue?' Ivy had been coming from viewing her da's body when Jem happened to pass. 'You talked then of the changes taking place in the world. Do you remember?'

'Of course I do.' Jem sipped his tea.

'I suppose it was kind of hard to forget.' Ivy held out her empty cup on its saucer for a refill. 'For me anyway. Me first carriage ride.'

'We're only talking ten months, Ivy.' Jem stood to refill Ivy's cup. 'Who would have believed so much could happen in such a short space of time?'

'Well, at least we're living in those exciting times you talked about. God knows, no one can say we're not willing to move with the times.' She took the cup and saucer Jem held out to her.

'You and me, Ivy, are moving so fast ahead there are days I'm dizzy.' Jem took his seat again.

'Jem, are yeh about?' Conn Connelly's voice came ahead of his body as he opened the people-door cut into one of the livery double doors. The smell of the stew he'd picked up from the Penny Dinners wafted into the room. He stepped over the lintel and into the livery, closing the door quickly behind him. 'I don't know – here I am, out searching for food to feed the hungry while me boss is sitting in front of the fire with a good-looking woman. Some people have all the luck.' He set the bucket of stew he carried on top of the fire before removing his heavy jacket. He shook the droplets of rain from the jacket and beat his cap against his knee before draping both items over a nearby chair.

'How's it going, Conn?' Ivy thought the changes in her young neighbour's appearance since he'd started working for Jem were astonishing. The lad was filling out, his long skinny body beginning to develop muscle. His skin glowed with health and vitality, his blue eyes framed by long, thick, black lashes were clear and sparkling, and there was a shine of health to his thick black hair. Conn was growing into a handsome young man.

'Can't complain, Ivy.' Conn began to rummage in the freestanding cupboard for mugs. 'How's yerself?'

'Getting by, Conn, getting by.' She nodded when Conn held one of the mugs aloft. She'd enjoy a mug of stew. 'Jem, remind me – who built the cupboards you've got in here?' She glanced at the sturdy, obviously homemade pieces of furniture that decorated the space.

'One of the lads we trained up to answer the phones,' Jem answered absentmindedly.

'Jimmy Johnson,' Conn said, handing Ivy her mug of stew. 'He makes the stuff when he has a minute free. He's working on a table and benches now. We won't know our luxury when he finishes.'

'Jimmy Johnson,' Ivy sighed. Tim Johnson's son, one of little Seán's many uncles. 'He not here now, is he? On the phones?'

'No,' said Jem, looking at her questioningly.

24

'He'll be over later.'

'When you've finished your stew, Conn,' said Ivy, 'will yeh run over and give Jimmy a knock for me?'

'Aw, Jaysus, Ivy!' Conn pulled a chair over to the table, before dropping into the seat. 'Me ma would do her nut if she saw me going down them stairs.'

'What are yeh talking about?' Ivy snapped.

Conn shifted his eyes sideways towards Jem, hoping he'd help him out. Conn didn't like to badmouth neighbours.

'I pass their building when I bring me pram around the back,' said Ivy. She usually pushed her heavily laden pram around the tenement block into the back yard and down to her rear entrance. 'The place is a bit whiffy, I admit, but everyone knows the Johnsons are a lazy lot.' Ivy didn't admit that she ran past the house where the Johnsons rented the basement flat. She didn't want anything to do with that family.

'It's stinking, Ivy,' Jem said. 'The neighbours are always complaining to the rent man. The lads seem to use the stairs down into the place as a privy. I don't blame Conn for not wanting to go down there. I wouldn't fancy it myself.'

'So what d'yeh want Jimmy for, Ivy?' Conn was using his fingers to scoop up the potatoes, peas and carrots sitting in the bottom of his mug.

'I want to have a word with him about making something for me.'

'What do you need?' Jem asked.

'I want something to sell me Cinderella dolls from.' Ivy and the family she'd employed to help her – the Lawless family – were frantically dressing

25

a consignment of small rubber dolls she had bought from Harry Green's warehouse. They were using the accumulation of high-quality materials Ivy had collected over the years to dress the dolls. She planned to sell Cinderella dolls outside the Gaiety Theatre during pantomime season. 'I thought I could use something like them cinema usherettes use to sell ice lollies and chocolates during the interval.'

'What, a tray thing with straps that go around your shoulders?' Jem asked.

'Yeah, just like that.' Ivy nodded. 'I don't want to sell the dolls from me pram. The auld pram wouldn't create the right impression. I'm going to charge a lot of money for those dolls. I have to think about presentation.'

'Listen to your woman!' Conn stood to refill his mug, at a nod from Jem.

'Conn, a good friend of mine told me times were changing.' Ivy nudged Jem with the toe of her boot. 'We have to change with them.'

'No one could accuse you of not moving with the times, Ivy,' Jem remarked. 'It seems every time we turn around you have some new plan or scheme you want us to go along with.'

'Just planning ahead, Jem.' Ivy shook the last of her stew from the bottom of her mug into her mouth. She could have used her fingers like Conn but she hated dirty hands. She passed the empty mug to Conn and shook her head when he offered her a refill. She finished the tea cooling in her cup, then stood to refill the cup from the teapot sitting on the stove. 'How are your brother and sister doing, Conn?'

'I've a load of them, Ivy.' Conn was on his knees taking an enamel bowl out of the cupboard. He wanted to fill the thing with warm water – then the lads would have no excuse for not rinsing out the cups they used. Conn had no intention of becoming the general dogsbody for some of the lazy lads too used to their mothers doing everything for them. 'Which ones do you mean?'

'Did anyone ever tell yeh yer a cheeky bugger, Conn Connelly? Yeh know very well I mean Liam and Vera. It's not often two of our own take to the stage.'

'There's been a bit of excitement there. Hang on – I need to get a drop of water.'

Conn took an empty bucket over to the standing tap. He appreciated having an indoor supply of water – it was great not to have to stand in line. He was back in no time and put the freshly filled bucket on the stove to heat.

'So what's happening with Liam and Vera?' Ivy sipped her tea.

'I'll tell yeh about Liam and Vera in a minute.' Conn decided to have a mug of tea himself. He bent to get a fresh mug out of the cupboard. 'I overheard a bit of gossip when I was standing in line at the Penny Dinners.' He looked over his shoulder to be sure he had their full attention. 'It seems yer man – the one everyone is talkin' about – that variety headliner fella – had a bad accident and won't be able to go onstage for a long time.'

'No! The fella that was to play the Prince in the panto?' Ivy asked in tones of horror.

The pantomime was a huge occasion to Dubliners. The newspapers carried stories and gossip

27

about the show and its players for months before the big event.

'I caught our Liam on his way out with his dogs.' Conn took his seat again. 'To hear him tell it, they were lucky enough to get another fella in at the last minute – some real big noise by the sound of it. He's going to be top of the bill at the variety but he hasn't agreed to stay for as long as they need. And Liam said yer man doesn't want to play Prince Charming!'

'I didn't read anything about an accident in the papers. How would your Liam know all about it?' Ivy asked.

'Wait for it...' Conn put his mug down and used both hands to beat out a drum roll on the table. 'Liam, his ruddy dogs and our Vera have been booked for the Gaiety variety show that's running right now! And they're going to be in the panto-mime too. They've started rehearsing their parts.'

'Go 'way!' Ivy kicked at Jem's feet. 'Did you know about this, Jem?'

'First I've heard, Ivy.' Jem pulled his feet out of Ivy's range.

'Me da nearly fainted when Liam told him how much they're going to be paid.' Conn grinned. 'As you know our Vera and Liam have been making a few bob from their appearances around the town at Amateur Night. They've been mostly winning lately.' He knew his brother and sister had worked very hard to perfect an act they could take to the big bosses of Dublin theatre life. 'Some big noise saw them and he approached them about appear-ing at the Gaiety. So, put that in your pipe and smoke it!'

'Well, if that wouldn't make the cat laugh!' Ivy grinned – it was good to see someone achieve their dream.

'We'll go and see their act one of these evenings, Ivy,' Jem said softly. 'Get to see them before they become famous. We'll be able to say we knew them "when".'

'Jem, I'd love that.' Ivy stood suddenly – she had to get home. 'You tell me where and when and I'll be ready.' She loved the time she got to spend with Jem on their rare public outings. 'I'm off. If you'd give me a shout when Jimmy gets here for work I'll come over and talk to him about that carpentry job.'

'I'll walk out with you.' Jem stood and picked up Ivy's coat, holding it open for her to shove her arms in. 'There's grub up for any who want it!' he shouted loudly. 'Come on, Ivy – we'd better get out of the way of the stampede.'

Chapter 3

'I can find me own way home, you know, Jem Ryan.' Ivy appeared to pay no attention to her surroundings as she pushed her pram at speed around the block of houses that formed one arm of The Lane. She was, in fact, keenly aware of everything around her. She'd been feeling eyes following her lately and it was making her nervous.

'I wanted a word with you.' Jem's long legs easily kept pace with her.

29

'Oh, aye, what's up?' Ivy glanced around. You were never truly alone in The Lane. There was always someone hanging around. She'd been forced to become more careful since her da's death. The kind of people who made their living by taking advantage of others knew Ivy's da was dead and her brothers had left home. She would seem fair game to them.

'Not here and now.' Jem was aware of the eyes and ears paying close attention to them. 'I'll come over to your place tonight when Emmy's in bed.' His 'adopted niece' lived with him at the livery.

'Give us a clue, will yeh?' She didn't want to worry and wonder for hours.

'We need to talk, Ivy.' Jem stopped walking when they reached the area that opened onto the back yard of the tenement block, and stared down into Ivy's violet eyes. 'There's been a lot happening around here you don't know about,' he whispered. 'You're running around the place like a chicken with its head cut off. It seems to me that you're not giving yourself time to breathe lately. I'll be over later.' He bent down and pressed a demanding kiss into her pouting lips. He knew he shouldn't. People were beginning to talk about them. He knew he'd be forgiven for any dalliance but Ivy would be crucified in gossip.

'I can't think when you do that!' Ivy's head was spinning, her breath coming in gasps.

Jem pressed a firm kiss into her blushing cheek and turned to leave. 'See you!' he called over his shoulder.

'Yeah, see you.' Ivy's knees were knocking. Jem's kisses took all the strength from her legs.

She grabbed the handle of her pram, glad of its support, and continued on her journey to her own basement rooms.

Thankfully, the cold and wind were keeping people away from the freestanding tap in the back yard. Ivy didn't want to stop and chat. She wanted the chance to dry out in the comfort of her own rooms.

'Ivy! *Pssst!* Ivy Murphy!' Seán McDonald crept out of the single water closet that served the entire tenement block. He'd been keeping out of sight, shivering in the dark, cold, smelly little space. He checked the area carefully. He didn't want to get caught again. 'Have yeh got me sack?'

'Of course I have.' Ivy stood waiting for the boy to cross the weed-choked slabs. 'Didn't I promise yeh?'

'I'll take it off yeh when we get closer to your place.' Seán used the bulk of the old pram to hide behind while they walked towards Ivy's back door.

Ivy was firmly biting her tongue to stop the questions that longed to explode out of her mouth. Seán's face was sporting a fresh collection of bruises. She sighed sadly. There was little she could do at the moment to help the young lad.

'Here we are,' she stated unnecessarily, stopping outside the door of what had been her old mentor's home. 'Do you want me to wait, make sure yer one's home?'

'Nah, I know she's in.' Seán grunted with effort as he removed his sack from the pram. 'I saw her going in a while ago. I'll be fine – you get along home,' he advised like an old man.

'Take care of yourself, Seán.' She shrugged off

the depressed feeling that was weighing her down. There was only so much you could do to help your neighbours. She took the few steps necessary to reach her own door.

With a sigh of relief she opened the door and pushed the pram inside. She locked the door quickly and decided to leave the pram standing just inside it for the moment. She removed her wet shawl before undoing the buttons of her old coat. She let both articles fall to the floor and with a sigh dropped into one of the stuffed chairs in front of her glowing black range.

'At least me new second-hand boots protected me feet from the wet, Da.' She'd fallen into the habit of talking aloud to her dead father when she was alone.

She bent to unlace the heavy boys' work boots she wore, then dragged them off. She pulled her long knitted socks off before wriggling her toes blissfully towards the barely glowing fire.

'I'll tend the fire and put the kettle on.'

She jumped to her feet. The hem of her black skirt beating uncomfortably wet against the back of her bare ankles made her stop. The ends of her jumper sleeves were wet too. She'd better change her clothes. She'd tucked the boys' trousers she wore under her skirt into her socks so they'd re-mained dry and warm. At least she had something to change into nowadays. Gone were the days when she only possessed what she stood up in. She dropped to her knees and, strictly by feel, rooted under the big bed and pulled out her old black skirt and a carefully wrapped cream twin set. Jem was coming over later and she wanted to look decent for him. She shivered while she changed. The room was cold away from the heat of the range.

With her damp clothes in hand, she walked over to fetch one of her two wooden chairs and pulled it closer to the range. She spread her skirt and jumper over the arm of one of the soft fireside chairs before picking her shawl and coat up from the floor. She draped the shawl over the seat of the wooden chair. The heavy old coat was put over the tall wooden shoulders.

With a sigh she knelt to rake out the cooling ash from the grate before dropping dry kindling and small nuggets of coal onto the remaining burning embers. She watched carefully to make sure the fire took before adding more fuel.

'I don't know where the time is going,' she remarked absently while preparing a pot of tea. 'Thank God Halloween falls on a Saturday this year. This year has run away with me. I've only ten days to come up with a costume for Emmy.'

When Emmy first came to live with Jem, Ivy had helped out by minding the child after school while Jem was out driving his hackney carriage. Then Jem decided to improve his business and employed men to help with the process. He was home for Emmy nowadays and Ivy didn't see as much of the little imp as she'd like.

'I suppose I could make a little black cat and a tall hat and dress Emmy as a witch.' Ivy took one of her precious cups and saucers from the shelf. 'Emmy's black hair and green eyes would suit a witch costume, I think.'

The children of the tenements loved Halloween. They could pass their usual rags off as costumes, black up their faces and travel around Dublin taking up a collection. The cry of 'Help the Halloween Party!' echoed all around Dublin on the 31 of October. The children collected fruit – apples and oranges and, for a lucky few, grapes – and assorted nuts still in the shell from the people they met around the city.

'I've that much to do I don't know if I'm coming or going. I don't know where I'd be if the Lawless family didn't do most of the busy work for me these days. The money I made from the sale of them baby dolls is still a shock to me.'

Ivy and the Lawless family had dressed a batch of naked baby dolls Ivy had purchased on spec. She'd hoped to make a few bob profit from the dolls but, thanks to a surprise development, the darn dolls had sold for what Ivy considered a small fortune.

'I'm going to drink this pot of tea like a human.' Ivy poured the tea and added sugar and a drop of milk from the tall metal can she'd had filled that day at the local creamery. Then, carrying her cup and saucer carefully, she went and sat in one of the chairs in front of the range. 'I went by the creamery today, Da. Isn't that a kick in the grass? I never did anything like that when you were alive. Yeh had me convinced I wasn't fit to be seen in public. Well, now you're gone, if I don't do things for meself who's going to do them for me? Answer me that if yeh can, Da.' She sipped at her tea, enjoying the luxury of fresh milk.

Since Éamonn Murphy's death, life had opened up for Ivy. She had far more cash than she'd ever had in her life before. Éamonn had watched her every move and had been quick to take every penny she made out of her hands. If Ivy hadn't fought him all the way there would have been no money to pay the rent-man. Ivy's mother's motto of 'You can eat in the street but you can't sleep in the street' had been engraved onto Ivy's soul. She never missed paying the rent – never.

Ivy stood to pour herself a fresh cup of tea. She dropped back into her chair and raised wide violet eyes, eyes shadowed by long, thick black lashes and naturally pencil-slim brows, towards the ceiling. 'Hey, Granny, are yeh with me?'

Ivy didn't find it strange to be talking to the dead. If they answered her back, now that would be strange. Granny had been Ivy's mentor and friend. The old woman had passed away peacefully of old age. Ivy missed the old woman but it was difficult to grieve. Granny had been ready to meet her Maker.

'I wanted to thank you for making me take care of me hands.' Ivy laughed, looking down at her pale white skin. Her hands were soft, the flesh creamy white, the fingers long and elegant, the nails trimmed and spotlessly clean. Granny would accept nothing less. She'd insisted on teaching Ivy everything she'd learned over a long lifetime. Granny knew more about the various needlecraft skills than most people would ever know. The old woman had been a talented lace-maker and much in demand by the designers and shop owners of Dublin. She'd been paid a pittance for the exquisite work that sold for guineas in the upmarket shops around Dublin. Granny had taught Ivy, by

35

means of a strong clip around the ear, to always look after the skin of her hands. Ivy must never allow her hands to be blemished.

'I've shaken more hands since I started palling around with Ann Marie than I ever have before in me life.'

Ivy's friend Ann Marie Gannon was from a different social class altogether but the two women had formed an unlikely friendship.

'When you were alive, Da, and the boys at home, it was all I could do to keep body and soul together.' Ivy had been the main breadwinner of her family from the age of nine. She'd raised her three younger brothers until each had left home at sixteen, never to be heard from again. 'Now I have options.' She smothered a sob. 'Wouldn't that make the cat laugh? I ask your sacred pardon – "options". Who ever heard the like?'

She drank the rest of her tea while her head spun with ideas about all of those options. She would admit, only to herself mind, that there were days when the thought of all of those options scared her silly.

'Well, this won't get the baby a bonnet.' She left her cup and saucer on the hearth to be washed later and jumped to her feet. 'I need to get doing.'

She banked the fire in the range then left the comfort of the heat with a sigh. She went and brought her pram through to the front room, pushing it over to the work table. She stood and examined the goods resting on her work surface. With quick movements she arranged a row of orange packing crates along the outer rim of the worktable. She sorted through the items she'd

36

collected that day, examining them with experienced hands.

It didn't take her very long to sort the articles into different crates. Some things, like the cracked and chipped ornaments, she'd take directly to her market contacts, others she'd wash and repair. In some cases she'd refashion or reuse materials. But in every case there was a profit to be made.

Ivy then arranged the orange crates one on top of the other, noticing a layer of dust on the floor as she did so. Something else she needed to take care of: she grabbed a broom and began sweeping out her two rooms while she continued to talk aloud to the dead.

'I'll have to light a fire in this room if I'm going to work in here – it's freezing. I'm going to bring a branch of candles over to the work top – it seems to get dark so bloomin' early these days. I suppose it doesn't help living in a basement but since that's all I've ever known – well, mustn't grumble. I'll get a bit of work done on my first bride doll. Although, if I'm honest with meself, I think it'll be me first and last bride doll. I can't see meself making any money off the thing, what with all the bits and bobs I've had to buy, not to mention all the work I'm putting into the ruddy thing.' The work she was doing on the tiny doll outfit was time-consuming and exacting. It left her with aching shoulders and a headache. She dreaded having to attach all the tiny beads to the gown but could only be thankful she wasn't one of the women sewing ten thousand beads onto an actual bridal gown.

'I'll have to talk to the Widder Purcell about getting a goose. I'm nearly out of that goose-fat cream you made, Granny.' Ivy dumped the dust she'd collected into the old biscuit tin she kept for household waste. 'I found your little recipe book though. Can yeh believe I can read it for meself? Honest to God, Granny, there's days when I don't know meself.' She put her broom away. 'The nuns across the way make a hand cream like yours from goose fat. Did yeh know that, Granny?' She didn't expect a response. 'Yeh'd never believe the price they want for the thing. I'd rather make it meself, thanks very much.'

Ivy filled her second-best enamel bowl with hot water from the reservoir in her black range. She'd only had the use of the range since her da's death and couldn't imagine ever taking the comfort of instant hot water for granted. With a contented sigh, she shaved curls from a bar of Ivory soap, adding them to the hot water. She dunked two rags in the hot soapy water, tied them to her bare feet and began to dance around the two rooms to clean them.

'Just think, Granny, for the price the nuns are asking for their cream I could buy me own goose. Wouldn't that be something, Granny, a goose for Christmas? I wouldn't know meself. I'd get the goose flesh to eat, the fat I need for lots of hand cream, plus the feathers to sell and the bones to make a stew from. Yeh can't beat that for value, Granny.'

Ivy imagined music playing as she danced elegantly around the room.

'Did yeh hear what Jem was telling me about the radio?' She giggled, amused with her own imaginings. 'The state of me and the price of best but-

38

ter!' She had a mental image of herself waltzing around the two high-ceilinged rooms, feet covered in wet grey rags. Her black second-hand skirt was shiny with age and touched the top of her toes and her hand-knit twin set didn't match any ball gown she'd ever heard of. 'I don't care.' She shrugged away her dowdy outfit. 'I can fancy me chances, can't I? Imagine being able to listen to music all the time, hearing news from around the world? The wonder of it all, what would it be like?' She grinned broadly, thinking of Jem's face when he was talking about the radio. She'd be willing to bet the man would buy himself a radio before too long. Jem was losing the run of himself. She shrugged off the thought. There's many a one would say the same thing about her.

Ivy pulled the wet rags off her feet and threw them into the enamel basin. She crossed to the front-room fireplace, knelt, and with quick experienced moves soon had the fire set. She grabbed the box of matches she kept on the mantelpiece and lit the scrunched paper.

With a tired sigh she stood upright. 'The floor needs to dry and I have to wash meself and get out me white apron.'

Ivy wasn't aware she was still talking aloud. The two rooms echoed around her.

Ivy, her parents and three brothers had lived in these two rooms. One by one everyone had left. Ivy's mother Violet had been the first to leave. She'd taken the mailboat to England when Ivy was nine years old, never to be heard from again. Ivy's brothers too had taken the mail boat. She sometimes dreamed her family were living together somewhere else, without her. When her father died Ivy was alone.

She took two potatoes from the orange box shoved into the high cupboard Granny had insisted on giving to her before she died. She scrubbed the potatoes before pushing them into the hot ashes sitting in the grate. Two apples joined the potatoes. Ivy grinned, brushing off her hands. The food would cook slowly while she worked. The grub would see her through till tomorrow. She washed her hands, carefully removing every speck of grime.

With everything she needed to hand, the fire she'd just lit in the front-room grate burning brightly at her back, Ivy sat in her front room, now covered from neck to ankle by her pristine white apron, just like Granny had taught her. She'd pulled one of her two hard chairs into the room and up to the long bench that served as her work space. She'd a brace of candles close to hand. She also had her best basin filled with hot soapy water nearby. She could not afford to stain the tiny white garment. A simple pinprick could cause blood to soak into the delicate fabric. She'd had a headache for days embroidering the tiny white stitches onto the white fabric. It looked wonderful, she couldn't deny it, but she'd prefer not to have to do the work all over again, thank you very much.

She slowly unfolded the white fabric that wrapped the skinny rubber doll. The tiny dress she kept wrapped up with the doll was an actual copy of the gown that a society bride, Miss Bettanne Morgan, would wear to the wedding that was already the talk of the town. Ivy had gone hat in hand to the hoity-toity designer of the bridal gown and begged to be allowed to copy his design. She'd thought the limp-wristed designer would faint at her daring. She'd had to promise to keep the design secret. It was only her closing argument that she did not mix in the same social set as the future wedding guests that clinched the deal. It was ironic, Ivy thought – the Morgan twins, two women who lived in the splendour of Merrion Square surrounded by servants, had been contributing to Ivy's household funds for years. They just didn't know it.

'Who would have thought me round would lead to this?' She turned to the fire and made a long paper spill from the stock of newspaper she kept in an orange crate by the side of the fireplace. She lit the spill from the fire and used it to light the candles she'd placed on the table. She needed the additional light to clearly see the intricate white-on-white needlework.

She'd already cut the white satin fabric for the doll's dress – sewing the gown together would be the last thing she did – and the embroidery that mantled the tiny gown was complete. She still needed to embroider the tiny copy of the veil that would trail behind the bride. She intended to sew the miniature beads onto the dress that evening – work that was intricate and time-consuming.

Time passed as Ivy became absorbed in the intricate work. At a hard rap on the outside door she screamed in fright and threw her arms in the air. The chair she'd been sitting on wobbled at her sudden jerk. She'd nearly stabbed herself with the needle.

Chapter 4

Ivy's heart was racing, her body shaking. She'd been so intent on her work she hadn't been aware of time passing.

She looked around the room, blinking in surprise. Outside the range of the now-sputtering candles it was black as pitch. How long had she been sitting here working? She sniffed the air. She must have burned her food to a cinder.

'Just a minute!'

She couldn't see her hand in front of her face outside the light from the candles. The fire she'd lit to keep the room warm was almost out.

She crossed the room carefully, following the light from the dying fire. With quick efficient movements she took another piece of paper from her supplies, put it in the fire and set it alight. She removed the gas globes from the two gas-light fixtures set into the fireplace mantel, then pulled the chain releasing the gas into the two lamps, touched the burning paper to the wick and immediately had the blue flame hissing and burning brightly. She replaced the glass globes over the blue flames with a sigh of relief. Now she could see what the heck she was doing.

She carefully blew out the candles before walking over to the single window that overlooked the cement well at the bottom of the stairs that led down to her basement rooms from ground level.

'Jem, you scared me out of me growth!' she shouted before opening the door to her friend. 'Me heart is still somewhere around me mouth.' She stood holding open the door, glaring.

'I told you I'd be calling in to see you.' Jem ignored Ivy's dramatics. He pushed her gently back into the tiny hallway and back into her own front room. It was impossible to close the front door with Ivy standing in the way.

'Give me a minute.' She removed her white apron as she walked, taking the time to drape it carefully over her work. 'Wait till I get the lamps lit in the other room – then you can put out the lamps in here for me.'

She grabbed the precious box of matches from the mantel and hurried away.

'Where's Emmy?' she shouted while lighting the two gas lamps in the back room. 'I thought she'd be with you.' She grabbed her damp clothing from the chairs and threw everything onto the big bed pushed against the wall dividing the two rooms.

'Asleep in bed.' Jem pulled the chain on the gas lamps in the front room. He blew gently behind the glass globes to extinguish the flame. He stood for a moment checking the lamps were safely extinguished. 'The lads know I'm over here – they'll keep their ears open for her.'

Ivy picked the wooden chair up and with a few strides had it pushed under the kitchen table.

'What time is it?' she called.

'Late.' Jem walked into the back room, closing the door between the two rooms behind him.

'I'll put the kettle on. I'm spittin' feathers.'

43

'You better eat whatever that is I can smell.' Jem looked at the two big soft comfortable chairs placed in front of the range. He wasn't about to sit there – there would be too much temptation to pull Ivy down onto his knees and forget the world outside.

'Oh, me dinner, it'll be ruined.' Ivy became a whirlwind of activity while Jem strolled back into the front room to fetch the second wooden chair.

He put the chair by the table and sat, waiting patiently while Ivy set the table for her seemingly ever-present tea. He watched as she pulled the charred potatoes and apples from the grate. She brushed the ash carefully from the potatoes, halved them and put them on a small plate, then scooped the soft apple onto the potato and carried the plate to the table. His green eyes followed her as she made the promised pot of tea, her movements quick and deliberate. The tender smile on his face turned into a grin when she dropped into the chair across the table from where he sat.

'I think it might be a good idea for you to start eating with Emmy and me over at the livery every evening, Ivy.' Jem hadn't really thought about it before but the good Lord knew he of all people should be aware that it was no fun making a meal for only one person. He'd eaten a lot of meals at the men's clubs dotted around the city – it was only since Emmy came to live with him that he'd begun planning meals for the pair of them.

'I seem to eat with you often enough as it is.' Ivy stopped shovelling the soft food into her mouth and looked across at him.

'So you do.' He stood to fetch the teapot from

the black range. He'd things he needed to say to her and he'd better get them said before he got lost in the temptation offered by having her all to himself behind closed doors.

'You're in an unusual position, Ivy.' He put a hand on her shoulder, gently squeezing, while he leaned forward to pour the tea. 'A young woman living alone, it's practically unheard of – you know that yourself.' He carried the teapot back to the range, setting it carefully to the back out of the direct heat – the residual heat in the cast-iron range-top would keep the tea hot.

'It is what it is.' She forced the food past the lump in her throat.

'Ivy,' he took his seat again and stared across the table at her, 'you can't go on like this.'

'What...?'

'You lock yourself away in these two rooms, beavering away while the world goes on around you.' He hated to be the one to put a halt to her gallop but there were things she needed to know.

'I know what's going on.' Ivy's head almost disappeared into her shoulders as she sank down in her chair.

'If you knew the half of what's going on around here you'd never have asked Conn to knock on the Johnsons' door. Declan Johnson has taken over the rent book on his da's place.'

'*What!*'

'It's a fact.' Jem wanted to punch something. 'He walked into The Lane bold as brass ... moved back in bag and baggage.'

'I thought he'd gone to America or Australia or something.' Ivy gaped at Jem. 'Has Declan John-

45

son lost what little mind he has? That Madame Violetta,' she named a well-known local brothel keeper, 'still has a price on his head, for the good Lord's sake.'

'Nonetheless, the man's back and by all accounts up to his old tricks.' Jem felt embarrassed colour stain his cheeks. Declan Johnson kept a stable of 'wives' he made money from. The local brothel keepers didn't look kindly on anyone taking business away from them. 'He'll bring trouble to The Lane, Ivy. You and I both know that.'

'Declan Johnson is the last thing any of us need.' Ivy felt the food she'd just eaten roil in her stomach. 'Are the men not going to do anything?' The men of The Lane used their fists and hobnail boots to make troublemakers see reason.

'He's got a couple of big bruisers he's paying to protect him.' Jem stared at the table top. In this day and age, it was every man for himself. 'You need to talk to Billy Flint, Ivy.'

'Jem, I can't believe it's you saying that!'

'You think I don't notice you checking over your shoulder every two minutes? You think I don't know the danger you're in walking around the streets of Dublin with money rattling in your pocket?' He forced himself to remain seated even though he wanted to shake the stubborn woman until her teeth rattled. 'You can bet that Declan Johnson is keeping a close eye on your comings and goings.' He waited but Ivy remained silent. 'I can't be everywhere, Ivy. You need to talk to Billy Flint.'

'I'm not going to pay protection money and that's that, Jem.'

Billy Flint was rumoured to control certain aspects of the Dublin street trade. It was said that he had his hand in the pocket of every man in Dublin.

'I'd like me job paying that man for doing nothing.'

'You're a hard-headed woman, Ivy Murphy.' Jem pushed his hands through his hair. He bit his tongue on the words that wanted to come out of his mouth. She'd been paying her da for doing nothing most of her life. But he knew if he said something like that to her she'd be over the table trying to scalp him. 'You have to take better care of yourself. There are a lot of people who care about you. We wouldn't want to see anything happen to you.' He took a deep breath for courage. He'd been thinking about this ever since Declan Johnson showed his ugly face back in The Lane. 'We've been walking out for a while now, Ivy. You know I think a lot of you. We get along okay. The thing is, if we were to marry, I'd have the right to take care of you ... protect you.' He could almost taste the silence that followed his words.

'Ah, Jem, I'm an unnatural woman.' Ivy reached across the table and took his two hands in hers as she admitted to her failing. Her large violet eyes were shadowed and serious as she stared into his green ones. 'It's usually the man dragging his feet when the word marriage is mentioned. Any woman in her right mind would be trippin' yeh up and dragging yeh before the altar of God. I know that, Jem.' She squeezed the hands she held. 'I appreciate yeh, honest I do. I would never be tempted to marry any man but you if that was me

47

hope. It's not you, Jem, it's me. I don't think of a new frock and cake when you mention weddings.' She shook her head, fighting tears. 'I just see problems.'

'Ivy, being married means facing your problems together.' He gave her hands a gentle squeeze. From his own point of view it wasn't an ideal time to mention marriage. He hadn't everything in place yet. He'd wanted to have more to offer her before he mentioned getting wed.

'Where would we live for a start?' She was enjoying having her place to herself. She was able to leave her stuff sitting out around the place. She could allow the dust to gather while she took care of her business. Did worrying about something like that make her even more of an unnatural woman?

'Ivy, six people lived in these two rooms,' he said quietly. 'I could build extra rooms under the eaves in the livery if it came to that. It's not what I wanted to offer you, I admit that, but something has to be done. It frightens the life out of me watching you walk around the town unprotected.' He knew it was unfair but when Ivy married him she would be seen as his property, and a man would think twice before touching a woman known to have a strong man to protect her.

'You have Emmy to think of...'

'You know as well as I do that Emmy would be thrilled if you were to marry me,' Jem interrupted. 'You can't use her as an excuse.' He felt his heart sink. Had he made a mistake? Did Ivy not want to marry him?

'Jem!' Oh, God, she'd hurt his feelings. The last

thing she wanted to do. He was a good man, one of the best, but she'd so much to think about, so much to get done. She had plans for her own life, stuff she wanted to do while she was free to do it. Was that too much to ask?

'I have to get back over the road.' Jem released her hands, pushed back his chair and stood. He'd said what he'd come to say. If the woman didn't want to marry him, well, there was nothing he could do about that. He wasn't going to sit here and beg.

'I don't want us to fight, Jem.' She too stood and simply waited to see what he would do. Had she ruined their friendship?

'Ivy,' Jem sighed deeply while stepping around the table and pulling her into his arms, 'I don't know what to do with you, woman.' In a lot of ways he agreed with her. Neither of them was ready yet. It would be better if he had more time to build up his business but life went on no matter how hard you tried to plan your way.

'Give me a bit of time, Jem.' Ivy stared up into his eyes. 'Please!'

'You can't take too long, Ivy.' Jem bent his head towards her lips. 'I'm only human.' He took her lips in a deep, devouring, kiss. The passion that flamed between them almost singed his skin. He couldn't continue to hold and kiss her like this then turn to walk out the door. It hurt too much and he was afraid that one of these days the temptation to throw her down on the nearby bed would overcome him. He would not dishonour Ivy like that. She deserved better.

Chapter 5

Ivy turned over in bed and slowly awakened to the muted sounds of the tenements around her coming to life. She felt as if she'd only just closed her eyes. She'd tossed and turned half the night again. Every time she closed her eyes lately she'd see Jem's hurt face when he made his offer of marriage. It had been almost a week and she still hadn't come up with an answer. Why wasn't she dancing in the streets with joy? What was wrong with her? She sighed deeply, wanting to just pull the covers over her head and escape her problems by falling back asleep.

She lay there, reluctant to take that first step out of her warm cocoon and into the cold she could feel biting at her nose. She imagined she could hear women shouting at their menfolk and older sons, trying to get them out of bed. The women employed by the local factories would be yelling abuse and threats as they tried to prepare for the day ahead. She knew the younger children in the family managed to somehow sleep through the noise around them. They too would be awakened soon to get ready for school. For the fortunate few the sound of raking coals would mean heat and perhaps a bowl of oatmeal gruel to start the day.

The tenement day began in relays. First the men, on their way down to the nearby docks hoping to find some kind of work, would march their hobnailed boots out of the cobbled court-yard. The female factory workers crept around the place. The homeless men sleeping rough, wrapped in newspapers on the inner staircases, would start to scratch and stretch, hoping for a cup of tea and perhaps a chunk of bread to fill their aching stomachs. There were very few gainfully employed men living in the tenements.

Ivy looked through the almost pitch darkness of her room over at the glowing embers of the coals in her black range. She was living high on the hog in comparison to most of her neighbours. She had a sheet on her bed and even though she'd felt guilty she'd kept the last lot of torn and tattered blankets she'd collected on her round. She'd repaired the holes with the invisible mending Granny had taught her. She didn't know herself these cold mornings. Too many mornings she'd awoken to ice forming from her breath through the night. To be able to afford to keep the fire burning night and day was an unimagined bless-ing she'd never take for granted.

She threw the blankets back and sat up shivering – even with the fire burning low all night the room was cold. She searched under the bedclothes for her knitted slippers. Keeping articles of clothing in bed with you through the night kept the items warm at least. She pulled the slippers over her feet and bravely stepped out of bed onto the freezing cold floor.

'Right.' She rearranged her 'poor man's pyjamas' over her shivering body. The long loose hand-knit jumper she'd pulled over her head was still in place

51

but the bottom jumper, her legs forced through the arms, was adrift. She settled the bottom jumper as well as she could. It was uncomfortable with the neck opening hanging between her knees but she needed the heat.

She trembled her way by touch and familiarity to the big black range. Her seeking fingers easily found the twisted paper she'd formed and laid out the night before. In almost total darkness she crossed to the glass-covered gas lamps set in the wall. She removed the glass domes from both lamps before returning to light the paper from the glowing embers of the fire. A quick flick of her wrist on the chain-pull released the gas and soon both lamps were burning brightly.

With a relieved sigh she crossed to the tall, blue flower-decorated porcelain chamber pot that stood in one corner of the room, concealed by a curtain hung on a string. She'd spotted the chamber pot or 'po' on her round. It had been dumped in a backyard and ignored for years. The tall po's had fallen out of fashion after the Merrion Square houses had changed to indoor plumbing. She'd brought the po home on her pram then spent hours scrubbing it clean. The heavy knee-high porcelain chamber pot made a nice change from a metal bucket. She took care of her bodily functions while frantically trying to plan her day.

'I'll have to try and get a load of stuff ready for the market tomorrow. At least it's a Thursday and I have the whole day to meself to get things sorted. I'll have to try and shift as much stuff as possible at the Tuesday and Friday markets next week. I don't know how I'm going to get everything needed done. The dealers round the markets will be looking for stuff they can sell for Christmas. I'll be able to get rid of most of the stuff I have ready to shift. God alone knows when I'll be able to get back to my usual routine. It won't be long before I'll be out selling those Cinderella dolls.'

She stood with a sigh and drifted over to her bed, picked her black-knit shawl from the bottom of the bed and threw it over her shoulders.

'I've that much to do,' she sighed.

She filled the black kettle with warm water from the reservoir on the range and set it to one side on top of the still-warm range. She dropped to her knees and began taking care of the most important morning chore, cleaning out the fireplace and getting the fire burning brightly. She did it with relish, remembering all the mornings she'd shivered with cold and hunger. Those days were in the past. If she had anything to say about it she was never going back there.

'I can't be neglecting me own little world, no matter what Jem Ryan says.'

She scooped the hot, red-sprinkled ash out of the range pit, dropping it into the old biscuit tin she kept for that purpose. She was making a conscious effort not to think of Jem. If she just kept herself busy maybe everything would turn out all right. She ignored the little jeering voice in her head whispering that hiding her head in the sand exposed her rear end for a swift kick.

The fire was burning brightly in the grate when Ivy pushed the big black kettle into place over the flames. She was worthless until she'd had her first pot of tea of the day. She filled an enamel bowl with water and took a large cake of kitchen soap sitting on a cracked side plate from a shelf on her kitchen dresser, then carried both over to the table sitting against the wall leading to the back door.

She stepped over to the big iron bed and pulled the well-worn long black skirt and hand-knit twin set she'd worn yesterday from under the bed-clothes. The outfit would do her well enough for the day. She'd cover everything with the apron that was almost a uniform for the women of Dublin. The apron, a long dark cotton sleeveless wrap-around affair would cover her from neck to ankles.

The big black kettle was spitting steam from its spout when she turned back with her chosen clothes over her arm. She dropped the clothes on one of her kitchen chairs and hurried over to fill her metal teapot and sit it back on the warm range top to brew. 'I'm losing the run of meself,' she said, pouring the rest of the water from the kettle into the enamel bowl sitting on the kitchen table. She refilled the kettle before sitting it well back on the range. She moved her teapot away from the hottest part of the range and left it warming on the back of the range top.

In an automatic gesture she took the special tool hanging by a string over the range and lifted the hot cover from the water reservoir to check the water level. She replaced the top with a sigh. She needed to fetch more water from the single freestanding outdoor tap that was the only water supply for the tenements.

'This getting washed and dressed every morning doesn't half use up me water supply.'

54

Ivy had only recently been able to wash and dress herself in comfort every morning. Unlike the majority of the people living in the tenements she no longer slept in her clothes. Having lived most of her life with her da and brothers underfoot, privacy to take care of her bodily needs was a newly treasured gift.

She took one of her precious teacups and a saucer from the tall dresser and set them on the table. Then she carried the matching milk jug into the front room to fill it. She noticed that the level of milk in the metal can she kept standing in cold water in her icy workroom was getting low. She'd have to make a run to the creamery and refill the can, maybe pick up a bit of cheese. She hurried out of the freezing cold room, slamming the dividing door at her back, wanting to keep the heat in the back room.

She quickly filled her cup and, still standing by the range enjoying the heat, she took the first sip of the tea that was her lifeblood. With a contented smile she stood and emptied the china cup in minutes. She refilled the cup before walking over to the kitchen table.

Taking a knife from the drawer under the lip of her kitchen table she shaved the large block of kitchen soap into the steaming water and swirled it around with her hand. With a grin she made bubbles in the space between her thumb and fist, blowing the bubbles away and admiring the rainbow of colour that danced around the room. Her da would have given her a thick ear for messing but he wasn't here and she did love to make bubbles. She dunked an old rag into the warm soapy water and prepared to scrub herself clean.

By the time she'd washed and dressed Ivy had emptied the teapot. With her warm clothes in place, her long knitted stockings pulled up her legs and her boys' work boots on her feet, she was ready to face whatever came her way.

'Right, I'll make meself another pot of tea and this one I'm going to drink like a human – sitting at the table.' She hustled around, getting ready to prepare the second pot of tea of the morning. She moved the big black kettle over the flames and while the water was boiling carried the enamel bowl to the back door. She unlocked the door and flung the dirty water out onto the weed-choked cobbles of the back yard.

Ignoring the untidy state of her room, Ivy prepared a fresh pot of tea. She removed another cup and saucer from the dresser, carrying the set over to the table. She had things to think about, plans to make.

'Well, the state of me and the price of best butter!' She was seated with her back to the wall, a cup of tea in hand. 'Is this me lot in life then?' she asked of no one in particular. 'Am I going to refuse to marry one of the best men I've ever met to spend me days sitting here all on me lone-some?' With her elbows on the table and the cup of tea pressed to her lips, she examined her surroundings. 'Is that really what I want for meself?'

The life she was living now wasn't perfect but it was a heck of a lot better than anything she'd ever known before. There was no one to take and spend her earnings. She could burn the gas lamps without fear of them sputtering out because she hadn't a penny for the gas meter. The fire burned in the big black grate day and night.

With a silent huff she visually examined her unmade bed. She had sheets, blankets and pillows – who else in The Lane could claim that kind of luxury? Sheets and blanket gift packages were used as currency by the women in The Lane. A popular wedding present, sheets and blankets were beautifully packaged with satin ribbons. The women knew better than to open the package. The pawn shops paid good money on a set of sheets or blankets. In really hard times women borrowed the packaged sheets and blankets from one another. The money you could get from the pawn shop for several sets of sheets, with careful planning, would keep a family fed for a couple of weeks. It wasn't unheard of for the women to bunch together their sheet packages to help a neighbour out with the rent. To the people of The Lane good sheets and blankets were currency. They were not to be used as bed covers.

The noise coming from the back yard dragged Ivy out of her wool-gathering daze. She'd been reliving Jem's words, trying to find a way of dealing with a situation that scared her so much it rattled her bones. She hadn't bothered to check the time yet this morning. It didn't seem that important. She sighed deeply as the music of many women chatting carried into her room. It must be a lot later than she'd thought.

She reluctantly pushed to her feet. She needed water and it seemed from the sounds outside that she'd have to join a long queue of women waiting to use the tap in the yard. She emptied the dregs of water sitting in her two galvanised buckets into the water reservoir of her range and with a bucket in each hand turned towards her back door.

Chapter 6

'Ivy!' Bitsy Martin yelled from her position at the end of the line of women and children waiting to use the tap.

The long line of women and a scattering of old men turned to look in her direction. It was difficult to make out individual features as everyone was wrapped up against the cold damp weather. Some of the old men had newspaper under their threadbare jackets and threadbare, torn old blankets around their shoulders like shawls. The children, huddled against the nearest person for warmth, seemed to ignore everything around them.

'If you've the makings of nappies about the place, my youngest is up the spout again!' Bitsy called.

'Lock that door behind yeh, Ivy,' Marcella Wiggins shouted from her place in line.

Ivy didn't usually lock her door when she crossed the yard to fill her buckets. She shrugged her shoulders and reached into her deep pocket for the keys she'd picked up automatically. She locked the door as ordered, the habit of obeying your elders as natural to her as breathing. With her buckets swinging from her hands she walked over to join the women.

'Yeh should tell yer daughter about the "fiddler's elbow"!' Jenny Black shouted at Bitsy Martin while kicking the buckets at her feet forward a few inches as the line progressed. 'If your girl knew what caused all them babbies she might not have so many. She'd be a lot better off with less childer. What with that man of hers being sickly and always out of work.'

Marcella drew Ivy carefully off to one side. She wanted a word. With the two women entertaining the line of people waiting at the tap, no one paid any attention to them. It wasn't unusual to see two women throwing off their shawls to batter each other. A fight between women was far more interesting than a little private chat between two people.

'Keep yer nose out of my business!' Bitsy Martin shook her fist in the air. 'I'm only asking Ivy to keep her eye out for the makings of nappies for us. What's it to you, yeh auld cow?'

'Amazing how he's never too sickly for some things,' Peggy Roach sniggered.

'Ladies!' Old Man Russell barked out from his place in the line, his seamed face barely visible between the folds of the blanket bits wrapped around his head and shoulders. 'There are children present.'

That shut the line of women up – for a while – nothing could keep these women down for long. When Lily Connelly came along with her empty buckets the line exploded with shouted questions and exclamations. The news of Lily's son Liam and daughter Vera appearing at the Gaiety and being booked for the upcoming pantomime had made the rounds. This was the chance to get all the latest gossip.

'Ivy, I wanted to ask yeh...' Marcella Wiggins was in no hurry. She was one of the lucky ones. Her menfolk were in work. She enjoyed the company and gossip to be found around the tap. Marcella's whisper was lost under cover of the shouted questions and demands being tossed at Lily Connelly. 'Are yeh thinking of moving out of them two rooms anytime soon?'

'Mrs Wiggins,' Ivy gaped at her neighbour, 'why would you ask me something like that?' She stepped back into the moving line for the tap. She couldn't spend all day out here gossiping.

'You've been walkin' out with Jem Ryan.' Marcella's many chins shook as she nodded her head for emphasis. 'There's neither of yeh getting any younger. I don't know if you're planning to stay in them two rooms when yeh marry but I wanted to get me spoke in before anyone else.'

'You'd move into basement rooms?' Ivy was astonished. The Wiggins family had one of the two front flats in a nearby house. The large front room with its wide window and the inner back room that was protected and private was considered a prize location. A basement would be a big come-down for this woman, quite literally.

'Ivy...' The big woman with a heart of gold and a helping hand for her neighbours looked heartbroken as she stared down at the weed-infested ground. 'I can't put up with living over the Johnsons any longer.'

'Oh.' Ivy ignored the noise around her. The crowd seemed to be enthralled by everything Lily

60

Connelly had to tell them. Ivy kicked at her buckets, trying to think of something to say.

Marcella too kicked at her buckets. 'Me husband was all ready to get a few of the lads together. He was going to teach that Declan Johnson manners. Then we heard that that reprobate Declan is paying protection to Billy Flint. Me man's no coward but he couldn't go up against Billy Flint. I understand that but I can't turn a blind eye to what's going on under me very nose.' There was a break in the big woman's voice. 'I thought we'd have a bit of peace with the auld fella locked away but that Declan is ten times worse than his auld man ever was.'

'Are yeh telling Ivy about them Johnsons?' Tilly Fletcher, six months pregnant, and with four of her six snotty-nosed tow-haired youngsters clinging to her long skirts, shouted aloud as she approached the standing group. 'Something has to be done about him. I had the relievin' officer in.' Members of the Saint Vincent de Paul charity were known locally as 'relievin' officers'. 'Declan Johnson was up them stairs like a light. He's wantin' a cut of any money I get for me childer.'

Ivy felt her heart almost hit her feet. Tilly was the same age as herself. They'd grown up together. The sight of the woman old before her time with frown lines and a perpetually turned-down mouth sent shivers down her spine. The crowd went eerily silent. You could hear the water hitting the end of someone's bucket.

'In the name of Jesus,' Marcella blessed herself while taking the Lord's name in vain and glared at the younger woman, 'who needs the *News of*

61

the World with you around?'

'That Johnson family are a bloody disgrace,' Bitsy Martin shouted. 'It's shameful enough having to ask them fellas for a hand-out without having to put up with Declan Johnson as well! That blaggard was up with Nelly Kelly as well. He told her he wanted money off of her and he explained the matter with his fists. Nelly had a black eye, which is bad for her business. Have yeh heard about that, Ivy Murphy, Nelly being such a good friend of yer da's and all?'

'I try to mind me own business, Bitsy.' She didn't know why Bitsy was picking on her today. She wouldn't be doing business with Bitsy Martin. The woman had a way of forgetting to pay. It was a well-known fact around The Lane that Bitsy Martin and all belonging to her would 'live in your ear and charge rent for the eardrum'. She could get old torn sheets for nappies from someone who didn't know her.

'Well–' Bitsy took a deep breath, delighted to be the one to pass on the latest gossip.

'Will you hold your whist, Bitsy Martin!' Marcella roared. 'We don't need to be talking about such things out in plain sight.'

'Maybe Ivy can have a word with that Franciscan Friar that's always popping in to visit her,' Tilly Fletcher said sourly as she administered a quick flick of her hand around the back of one of her children's ears.

Ivy's friendship with Brother Theo was a constant subject for discussion around The Lane. The holy man's visits were counted and remarked upon around the tap and courtyard. It was a strange friendship to the people of The Lane since their sainted Parish Priest Father Leary hadn't a good word to say about Ivy Murphy.

'You'd bring the do-gooders down around our ears,' Peggy Roach gasped. The woman stood with two full buckets of water at her feet. She hadn't wanted to miss any of the news being bruited around the place.

'Something will have to be done before the situation around here gets much worse,' Lily Connelly offered quietly. 'We'll all have to start locking our doors soon. That Declan always did believe that what's yours is his. If Father Leary wasn't away on that retreat he'd soon have that lot sorted out.'

'I don't want any do-gooders putting their nose around my place,' said Tilly Fletcher.

'That's because you know they'd be around to fumigate the ruddy room,' Peggy Roach muttered, not quite under her breath.

'Someone needs to go have a talk with Billy Flint,' a voice offered from the crowd.

'Who said that?' Marcella shouted.

No one answered. It was all very well to suggest that someone should talk to Billy Flint but no one was brave enough to offer to be the one doing the talking. The man was said to be a terror for his privacy. He didn't welcome people sticking their noses into his business.

Ivy was relieved to finally be in front of the tap. The crowd would continue to stand here and discuss options. If they came up with a plan someone would let her know. She filled her two buckets and with a sigh picked up one in each hand. She made her way carefully, trying not to spill the precious liquid, over to her own back door, hoping she could get inside while the crowd was occupied with shouting out suggestions for solving their problems with the Johnsons. She had to put the buckets down to reach into her pocket for her door key. She ignored the sharp ringing sound of the slap of naked flesh against flesh and the outraged cry of a child.

'Sweet Jesus!' Ivy was indoors, the back door safely locked. She carried her buckets over to the range. She was shaking. She used the handy tool to open the top of the range and emptied one bucket into the reservoir. She'd keep the second stashed in the alcove by the range. She needed more water for her day's chores but she wasn't willing to step back out into that yard. She'd keep an eye out and hopefully run out when there was less of a crowd.

'I don't want to end up like Tilly Fletcher.' The image of that woman was burned inside her head now.

She opened the floor cupboard of her tall unit and began pulling out the ingredients for griddle cakes. She needed to eat something. 'That's the real reason I'm afraid to marry Jem.' She whipped egg and water together. She hadn't enough milk to add to the batter. She preferred to keep the milk for her tea. 'I've been making up excuses because I'm afraid to admit to him that I don't want to have a gaggle of snotty-nosed childer clinging to me skirts.' She shivered wildly, hearing her own words almost echo back to her, and her stomach roiled.

'I can't admit that aloud to Jem. It's a sin against

God and man to even think something like that. He'd be ashamed of me.' She'd been listening to the women of The Lane heap verbal abuse on her own mother's head all of her life. Violet Burton hadn't wanted to be constantly pregnant. She'd been very vocal in her opinion. Her outspoken opinion had been fodder for the old biddies to gossip over – forever, it seemed to Ivy. Was she too an unnatural woman? Was something like that passed down through the blood?

She assembled her meal without thought, going through the motions of making the griddle cakes and a pot of tea. When they were made she carried everything she needed over to her kitchen table and almost collapsed into one of her chairs. She leaned her elbows onto the table in front of her and dropped her aching head into her hands.

'The rich are different.' She pushed back in her chair and began to pick at her meal. She did a mental recap of the houses she visited on her round. Those houses weren't bursting at the seams with children. 'They must know something we don't.' Ivy felt as if she was on the verge of a big discovery. Her friend Ann Marie was an only child; her uncle had only the two children. How did they do that? 'Who can I ask?' She remembered the arguments that resulted between her parents when her da had asked Father Leary for advice. She couldn't go to a member of the clergy with this question. Did she dare broach the subject with Ann Marie? The friendship between the two women was precious to Ivy. Did she dare discuss something so private with her friend?

She stuffed the food in her mouth, gulped the

pot of tea and, with her mind whirling with questions she longed to find the answer to, she stood to take care of the business at hand. She'd bought a rabbit ready for the pot from a local lad who'd managed to trap several. She'd been lucky to get the last rabbit the lad had for sale as she came home yesterday. She'd put that on the range with a load of bruised vegetables, handfuls of lentils and barley, cover the lot with water and she'd have a meal fit for a king that would keep her fed for days. She'd work to do that wouldn't wait for her.

Chapter 7

Ivy used one of the tea chests that served as the base of her work table as a lever and pushed herself to her feet with a groan. She pressed her two hands into the small of her back and tried to push herself into a standing position. She'd been crawling around the ice-cold floor on her hands and knees for ages, checking out her supplies. This day seemed to be running away from her and she still hadn't been out to get more water. In spite of being wrapped up in her outdoor clothes she was freezing. She could almost see her breath in front of her face.

She gave her stuffed pram a happy slap. She had it almost full with items she'd take to market in the morning. She'd made a mental note of the market layout, planning her day, as she'd carefully packed the goods. She liked to have everything she needed close to hand as she approached each stallholder. There would he no foutering about and letting them get an eyeful of her goods. This time of year they were eager for anything they could get their hands on for the Christmas trade. She had her preferred group of stallholders she did regular business with all year.

'I'll iron these sheets and bits dry.' She crossed to the damp laundry hanging from a rope line she'd stretched across the room. The line was tied to hooks set into the walls of the room. It could be removed easily but it was a blessing when you were trying to get items dry in this weather. The clothes and small items could drip onto the floor in the front room before being ironed dry.

'I'll do me ironing in the back room.' She examined the three sheets she'd been lucky enough to get on her round. There were a lot of bald places and tears but there was enough good quality material left intact. She'd drunk her sweat hauling water for this lot, not to mention walking on them in her tin bathtub. The money she'd make would make all the work of getting them bleached white worth her while. The bits of lace and fancy fabric she'd pulled off well-worn clothes, washed and stretched would fetch a few coppers.

'I'm going to push the Singer sewing machine Granny left me into the back room,' she decided as she stood planning. 'I'll not waste me coal lighting the fire in this room. The range will serve to heat the irons.' She grabbed the damp, cold sheets from her line and, with them folded carefully over her arm to protect them from the floor, she hurried into the back room.

The heat that welcomed her when she opened the door dividing her two rooms almost made her purr. She stepped in quickly, closing the door firmly at her back. She stood for a moment, enjoying the heat, trying to warm herself before removing her outdoor clothing.

She dropped her armload of sheets onto the kitchen table she'd scrubbed clean earlier in the day. She removed her shawl and heavy coat and threw both on the foot of her bed. The smell of the rabbit stew she'd put on the back of the range to simmer almost brought her to her knees. She hadn't realised how hungry she was.

'Right.' She stood by the bed and stared around her room. 'I need to get organised. I want to turn those sheets into handkerchiefs this evening.'

She intended to cut the sheets into three different sizes. She'd use the Singer sewing machine to hem around the edges. Handkerchiefs were a popular Christmas gift. The women of Dublin would buy plain white handkerchiefs at this time of year and those that had the skill would embroider some for their men and add a bit of lace or a few fancy buttons to smaller squares for their daughters.

The nuns and priests checked every child's hands and nails when they arrived for school in the morning. Woe betide any child who didn't have a clean handkerchief to show. She knew these handkerchiefs were more ornamentation than anything else – most childer used the threadbare cuffs of their jumpers or jackets to swipe their runny noses.

'I'll keep a few of the handkerchiefs back for Jem and Emmy.' She was on her knees, rooting under the bed for her two black flat irons. She'd put those to heat on the range top while she had some of the rabbit stew. 'I'll do white-on-white embroidery for Jem and add a bit of colour and lace to the ones I'll make for Emmy. She'll be thrilled.' She backed out from underneath the bed, dragging her two heavy black irons along with her.

She put the irons on the back of the range where they would heat slowly. Her mind was spinning, thinking of everything she needed to get done. She had a sugar solution to prepare, she reminded herself, but that could wait until she had the handkerchiefs made up. She'd use the sugar solution to starch and stiffen the handkerchiefs when she gave them a final belt of the iron. If she'd any strips of good material left over she'd hem it. She had a woman at the market who would buy all she had to make into collars and cuffs.

'It gets dark so early these evenings,' she muttered, looking out of her window into the back yard. 'I need more water, but that will have to wait until I have the time.' She poured a small quantity of hot water from the brass tap of the reservoir into an enamel bowl. She'd give her face and hands a quick wash. She loved her fire but the dust and ash got everywhere. She felt filthy from crawling around the place.

'Brother Theo!' Garda Barney Collins stared at the familiar brown-robed figure strolling along Stephen's Green. The man was an answer to a prayer. 'Are you on your way to The Lane to visit Ivy Murphy?'

'Good afternoon, Garda Collins.' Theo's hands

were pushed inside the wide sleeves of his habit. 'There's a fair old bite to the day.' He stopped walking. 'To answer your question, yes, I thought I'd stop in and visit Ivy. This being Thursday I know she'll be at home.'Theo enjoyed visiting Ivy. The Lane was a microcosm of a life he was unfamiliar with; he was learning a great deal about the human condition from his frequent visits.

'There's the problem.' Barney Collins clenched his huge fists in frustration, 'Right there, in a nutshell.'

'I beg your pardon?'

'Everyone knows the woman's movements.' Barney Collins waited to see if the holy man understood his meaning. When he found himself simply waiting, he continued, 'There's trouble in the air. I can smell it.' He didn't know how to explain the situation any better than that. 'Look, it's too cold to stand here talking.' He reached out to take the other man's elbow and stopped, almost blushing. He'd nearly laid hands on a friar. 'I'll walk with you, if you don't mind.' He'd been walking his beat. It didn't make any difference if he turned around and went back over the ground he'd just covered.

'Glad of the company.'

The two men stepped out together, heading in the direction of the Grand Canal. Theo waited patiently. He could practically feel the frustration pouring off the other man. They strolled along the busy street, passing shawl-cloaked women pushing prams and pulling youngsters along with them. Uniformed nannies too, with their charges well in hand, strolled along. The women bowed their heads and muttered greetings as they passed. The men raised their hats or cloth caps in greeting but no one stopped to chat with the pair.

'What is the problem?' Theo broke the uneasy silence. The Lane was steps away – if this Garda officer had something he needed to speak of, now was the time.

'I wish I knew,' Barney Collins blew a frustrated sigh through his nostrils, sounding for all the world like a horse. 'I can feel something, something wrong, but I can't put my hand on whatever it is.'

Barney stopped walking when they reached the final crossroads before The Lane. He took his uniform hat from his head and ran the fingers of one hand through his cropped grey-streaked hair before replacing it. 'Something just isn't right about The Lane.' He paused to stare into Theo's eyes. 'I can't put a name or a finger on whatever it is that is wrong but there are too many strangers around The Lane. Too many conversations break off whenever I stroll by the public house – something is going on in there and, if I can't get a hold of it, it may blow up in our faces.'

'You believe this trouble has something to do with Ivy?' Theo didn't know what this man thought he could do about the mystery situation. He liked to believe he was a man of God but he had no mystical abilities.

'It might, then again it might not.' Barney stared at the other man. It seemed he was going to have to explain some of the facts of life to the man. 'Ivy is a well-known local character. It worries me that everyone seems to be aware of her movements.

71

Look at yourself,' he waved a hand at Theo, 'you know she'll be at home today, probably alone. How many other people know that?'

'I fail to understand the problem.'

'That woman walks around this town on her own. According to her late and unlamented father Éamonn Murphy, she makes money left and right. He loudly boasted to his drinking cronies about the soft life he lived thanks to his daughter's takings. There's many a man would like to be kept in style by Ivy Murphy. The fact that the woman is not hard on the eyes is beside the point to these fly boys. It's drinking money and a soft life they're after.'

'You believe Ivy to be in danger?'

'She strolls around the place with a target on her back.' Barney sighed. 'I try to keep an eye on her but there is something else going on, a bad smell in the air. I need to get a handle on it and I thought, since you're a welcome visitor to The Lane, you might be able to see something I've missed.'

'I'll certainly keep my eyes open.' Theo started walking again. It was too cold to stand here with the icy wind blowing up under his habit and freezing his winter woollen bloomers. He noticed a ragged urchin peeping out of the tunnel that led into The Lane but thought nothing of it. There were always runny-nosed children somewhere around the place, although this one at a glance seemed clean at least.

Seán McDonald was shivering, his bones rattling. It wasn't only the cold – he was scared. Mrs Wiggins had ordered him to run and find the

Garda that walked up and down these streets. His family didn't have anything to do with the Garda but when Mrs Wiggins ordered you to do something you jumped to obey. I'm petrified, he thought with a sharp nod of his head. He liked that expression – he'd heard it in a story. His body hurt from the blows his Uncle Declan had given him for not bringing home the goose he'd ordered him to steal. He wouldn't steal from the Widder Purcell. His ma was missing too. She'd tried to stop Declan punching him, but the so-an-so had turned his fists on her. Seán sobbed softly – he didn't know where his ma was.

He darted out of the tunnel, his bare feet slapping the pavement as he ran towards the two men. He knew if anyone told his uncle about him talking to a priest and a police, he would kill him – but he had to do it. Mrs Wiggins said so and she was more scary to Seán than his uncle.

'They want yeh,' Seán whispered when he reached the two men. He tried to hide his body behind the bulk of the two men, hoping the friar's habit would conceal him from passersby. 'Yeh have to come. They said.'

'Who said what?' Barney Collins took the young lad by the shoulder. He noticed the wince of pain on the lad's face and quickly released his grip.

'The women,' Seán offered with a shrug that threatened to expose his tiny chest. 'They're on the warpath.' That explained everything as far as Seán was concerned. 'They want yeh to wait in the livery. They said try not to make a show of them.'

'It would appear your sense of smell for trouble was not off,' Theo offered, fascinated by this latest occurrence.

The two men and the young boy, each for their own reasons, aware of the stares they were receiving from the men congregating in front of the nearby pub, hurried towards the tunnel that led into The Lane.

'Thanks for coming, Garda Collins.' Marcella Wiggins grabbed hold of Seán as soon as the threesome put foot onto the cobbles of The Lane. 'It's good yer here, Father Theo. I beg yer pardon but I haven't the time to talk to yez right now. If you wouldn't mind waiting in the livery, please. I'll be along to explain.' With her hand firmly on the back of Seán's head Marcella hurried away. She'd things to take care of.

'It would appear we have our orders.' Theo was accustomed to being addressed by the people of Dublin as 'Father'. 'Let us see if Jem Ryan has the kettle on.'

'You've been around Ivy Murphy too long, Brother Theo.' Barney Collins wondered what was going on but he'd bide his time. He knew Marcella Wiggins and the woman was a force to be reckoned with.

Chapter 8

A frantic knocking on her front door stopped Ivy in her tracks. She'd been about to open the back door and fetch fresh water. She put her two buckets to one side and hurried through her two rooms to see who had come calling.

'Ann Marie!' Ivy shouted at the sight of her posh friend standing outside her front door, 'Come in out of the cold, quick.' She stepped back to allow her friend to enter. She closed the door with a snap, turned the key in the lock and for reasons she couldn't explain pushed the heavy bolt across.

'What's going on, Ivy?' Ann Marie Gannon knew her way about Ivy's two rooms. She stepped into the front room and waited. 'Jem almost pushed me down your steps and the man ordered me, there is no other way to describe it, he ordered me not to move again until he came to get me.' Shorter than Ivy by several inches, Ann Marie was wearing the black second-hand suit Ivy had purchased for her to wear whenever she visited The Lane, with a black shawl draped over her head and shoulders. To Ann Marie the outfit she was wearing was a costume, a way to fit in. She loved it. Her pale-blue eyes sparkled behind the gold-rimmed glasses perched on her nose.

'I haven't a clue.' Ivy shrugged. 'I was out and back to the creamery earlier – everything seemed fine then.'

'I have another ten Cinderella dolls here from the Lawlesses.'

The Lawless family lived in the servants' quarters of Ann Marie's house, the house she had bought on the banks of the Grand Canal, only minutes away from The Lane. She'd wanted to be within walking distance of her friends and at the same time have a home of her own without servants constantly hovering over her shoulder. She and the Lawless family were learning to live to-

75

gether in an unusual arrangement that they hoped would suit all concerned.

Ann Marie held an orange crate on her bent arm. 'I feel I haven't seen you in ages.' She walked over to the board-covered tea chests that formed Ivy's work table, wondering if she should just leave the orange crate on top.

'Thanks.' Ivy took the crate from her friend. 'I'll put these away with the others.' She walked over to the shelves Jem and some of his lads had built into the alcoves at either side of the fireplace. She pulled back one of the curtains that protected the area from the dust generated by the fire and pulled out one of the stack of orange boxes she kept on the shelves. She took off the custom-made cover and carefully placed the newly dressed dolls inside with the others. The box was almost completely full now. Ivy sighed in satisfaction. The Lawless family were really pushing these little dolls out.

'Come into the other room,' she said when the dolls were stored. 'It's freezing in here.'

'Ivy, you need to have a telephone installed.' Ann Marie worried about her friend. Ivy was fiercely independent but Ann Marie had been present when Tim Johnson led a crowd of drunken men into The Lane, a crowd of louts intent on harming Ivy. The sight would never leave her. The fear she'd experienced was something she'd no wish to experience again.

'Would yeh get up the yard, Ann Marie!' Ivy laughed over her shoulder as she led the way into the back room. She decided to light the two gas lamps as it was getting dark. 'Jem is already the talk of the town since he had the telephone put in.

I'd never be able to face me neighbours. They'd think I was stepping above me station in life.' Not to mention the cost of having a telephone installed and the charge for the line. The woman hadn't a clue.

'You can't continue like this, Ivy.'

'I'm fine. Listen, you caught me in the middle of something – sit yourself down while I get organised and then I'll put the kettle on – fancy a cup of tea?'

'You and your tea, Ivy Murphy!' Ann Marie shook her head. 'If you are ever opened up the doctors won't find blood – they'll be awash in tea.'

'Me tea keeps me going.' Ivy scooped the handkerchiefs she'd cut and the loose material into a bundle, with a sigh at the interruption. She carried the armload into the front room and placed everything carefully into one of the tea chests under her work top. The sewing machine she'd pushed into the back room could stay where it was. She took the time to replace the wooden cover over the machine but otherwise left it alone.

'Go on then,' Ann Marie smiled, wondering what all the bits of white were for, 'put the kettle on. I know you want to.' She marvelled at the position she found herself in. Who could have imagined that a chance meeting in the Dublin morgue would lead to this strange friendship? Ivy Murphy had changed Ann Marie's life in ways she couldn't even begin to count.

'Fancy a biscuit with your cup of tea?' Ivy grinned, delighted that she was able to make the offer. To be able to offer someone a shop-bought biscuit was a step up for Ivy.

'Thank you.' Ann Marie didn't really want tea and biscuits but she did want Ivy to sit down.

'How come you're delivering the dolls?' Ivy put the kettle on. She used a damp cloth to give the kitchen table a quick wipe down. 'John Lawless usually drops them off here when he comes to work at the livery.'

'I wanted the chance to visit with you,' Ann Marie said. 'What with moving into the new house, not to mention the work I've undertaken for the livery we haven't had much of a chance to sit down and visit lately.'

Ann Marie was serving as financial consultant and business advisor to Jem Ryan. She had a financial stake in the success of Jem's new business venture. She had faith in Jem and she hoped the money she'd invested would indirectly help the people of The Lane. It gave her a warm glow to observe the improved health of the young lads Jem employed.

'How are you getting along with the Lawless tribe?' Ivy was curious. She tried to keep her nose out of others' business but Ann Marie and the Lawless family were special to her.

'It's early days yet.' Ann Marie was excited by the new opportunities opening up to her. 'We are sure to have some problems but we'll solve them together.'

'How's your uncle and his family dealing with all of this?' Ivy carried two filled cups to the table. She set the delicate china teacups carefully down onto the matching saucers and put a plate of biscuits on the table before almost collapsing into the chair opposite Ann Marie at the table.

She'd been working hunched over for a long time and was suddenly tired.

'I'm worried. My aunt is talking of reducing the number of staff she employs.' Ann Marie hated to think that her move from her uncle's home was responsible for people losing their livelihoods.

'I can't believe that your presence in Number 8,' Ivy always referred to the houses on the Square by their number, 'increased the number of staff needed to keep the house running.'

'It would appear my aunt disagrees.' Ann Marie had made a monthly financial contribution to her uncle's accounts while she'd lived in his home.

'Has your aunt mentioned which members of staff she's thinking of laying off?' Ivy knew all of the people employed in and around the Square. It was a tragedy for a house servant to be let go. The person lost not only their post but the roof over their head, the clothes on their back, and the food that formed part of their wages.

'I haven't dared to ask her.'

'She'd hardly let auld Foster,' Ivy was referring to the Gannon butler, 'or Mrs Reilly go. Mrs Reilly is one of the best housekeepers on the Square. She could walk into another job tomorrow.'

'I doubt my aunt would dismiss the top members of her staff.' Ann Marie was more aware of the hardship people faced, thanks to Ivy. 'Oh, Ivy,' she almost sobbed, 'what if I've caused Mary Coates to lose her position? She is such a pleasant, obliging young woman.' Mary Coates was one of the upstairs maids working in the Gannon household.

'Why don't you employ Mary Coates yourself?'

Ivy suggested. 'The woman has been taking care of you for the last couple of years.' Ann Marie had moved into her uncle's home upon the death of both her parents in a flu epidemic.

'Ivy,' Ann Marie shook her head, 'I don't wish to be surrounded by servants any longer. I want to be able to sit down in my own home without having someone appearing at my elbow to ask if they can serve me. Surely that is not unusual.'

'Never having been surrounded by servants I wouldn't know.' Ivy grinned, knowing her answer would annoy Ann Marie.

'Ivy, I'm serious.' Ann Marie grimaced. 'I hate to think I'm responsible for someone losing their position.' She sipped the unwanted tea.

'What about your family estate in Dalkey?' Ivy had been taken to see the estate by Ann Marie. The house looked like a castle to Ivy's eyes. The house was huge, sitting high on top of a cliff over-looking the ocean. The house had stood empty while Ann Marie rented rooms from her uncle.

'What about it?' Ann Marie didn't want to admit aloud that she wished to remain in the centre of Dublin because of Ivy and the motley crew of interesting people she'd introduced her to. She didn't want to be sequestered on her own in the country. She wanted to be a part of the life Ivy was building. She found the whole experience fascinating. She was observing life in a way the people of her social set could never conceive of.

'I've been thinking,' Ivy almost whispered. Sitting alone almost every night doing handwork left her with a lot of time to think.

'As Jem Ryan would say, "Look out!"' Ann

Marie laughed aloud.

'That estate of yours in Dalkey is something else.' Ivy's eyes had almost fallen out of her head when Ann Marie turned her motor vehicle in through the enormous iron gates that guarded the entrance to the estate and she'd bit her lips until they almost bled trying to keep her opinion to herself. 'You can't let it fall into disrepair, Ann Marie. What would your parents think?'

'I have a team of grounds men who look after the place,' Ann Marie said. The estate had been in Ann Marie's mother's family for generations. She was the last of that line and very conscious of her responsibilities.

'It's not the same thing, Ann Marie, and you know it.' Ivy couldn't imagine paying people to look after an empty house.

'You think I should visit the estate more?' Ann Marie took her beige leather clutch-purse from one of the deep pockets of her skirt, opened it and removed her solid-gold cigarette case. 'Will you have a cigarette, Ivy?' She took out and assembled the pieces of her long ivory, gold and ebony cigarette-holder. She took a cigarette from her gold case and inserted it into the holder before looking up at Ivy who'd stood to fetch yet another cup of tea.

'No, thanks.' Ivy had never taken up smoking. Cigarettes cost money she didn't have.

'Do you have something I can use as an ashtray?' Ann Marie looked around as if expecting the ashtray to appear from thin air.

'Here.' Ivy put a chipped saucer on the table. 'Ann Marie, I understand that the estate is too

81

far outside the city for you.' She knew just how awful it was to live alone. She was surrounded by people and knew she could knock on any of the neighbours' doors and be invited inside to visit. The regular story nights too helped keep loneliness at bay. She couldn't imagine living in the country with only the wind and the sound of the ocean for company.

'What were you thinking about?' Ann Marie allowed Ivy to top up her tea. She knew Ivy had a plan of some kind. The woman seemed to be constantly dreaming up new ways of doing things. Ivy had been left alone and responsible for her family at a young age. Ann Marie believed the lack of ground rules had liberated Ivy in a way that was difficult to understand.

'Your estate in Dalkey is the most magical place I've ever seen,' Ivy said. 'It's like something out of a story. The grounds look like a park, the fruit trees and gardens are out of this world.'

'And?' Ann Marie knew there was more to come.

'Well...' Ivy sipped her tea, trying to organise her thoughts. The ghost of an idea was beginning to nibble on the corners of her mind. She needed more time to think about the situation. Ann Marie dropping in to visit plus seeing young Seán the other day had put an idea into Ivy's head but she hadn't had time to work it all out yet.

'Spit it out, Ivy.' Ann Marie sat with a gold lighter in her hand. She hadn't yet put a flame to her cigarette. 'Whatever it is you've got brewing in that head of yours.'

'Well,' Ivy could give her friend a hint, 'the

charabanc goes from the city centre to Dalkey now, you know. I was just thinking some of the women and childer of The Lane would enjoy seeing those grounds of yours and playing on your strand.' She watched Ann Marie play with the idea. She knew her friend would want to think about her suggestion. They had time: it was too cold and wet for day trips at this time of year.

'I'd have to look into matters before I could comment.' Ann Marie imagined the ragged children she'd seen in The Lane running around her family estate. The image gave her a warm glow of satisfaction.

'Are yeh waiting for someone to light that feckin' cigarette, Ann Marie?' Ivy remarked.

'Oh.' Ann Marie looked at the lighter in surprise. She had been sitting there expecting someone to light the cigarette. 'I forgot it.' She lit the cigarette. She wasn't going to admit to Ivy she'd been sitting here like a lump on a log waiting for someone else to perform the chore. She'd never hear the end of it. Then she thought of something she needed to let Ivy know. 'Before you start lecturing me again, Ivy Murphy,' she said, blowing a plume of smoke into the room, 'I should mention I asked Mrs Jones, my aunt's cook, to stock up on fruit and nuts for Halloween but I'm sorry to say that Foster plans to remove the front-door knocker that evening.'

'That's just like that miserable auld geezer.' Ivy wasn't surprised. It was something a lot of the houses on the Square did. 'You'd think he was paying for the stuff himself. Halloween is one of the best street parties we have here in The Lane.

You're welcome to join us if you want to.'

Ivy was sure Ann Marie had invitations to fancy parties around the city but for some unknown reason the woman preferred the company of the people of The Lane. She'd always known the rich were different but to Ivy's mind Ann Marie was in a class all of her own.

'Will I have to brush up on my party piece?' Ann Marie had been to several impromptu street parties this past summer in The Lane. She'd been astonished at the level of talent for entertainment displayed by the entire population of The Lane. She'd even been forced to perform a little ditty of her own.

'Depends on how long you plan on staying.' Ivy shrugged. 'The early evening is for the childer. We have bobbing for apples, games, scary stories and apples on a string. Old Man Solomon brings down his gramophone and some of his records. He plays them while the childer dance and sing.'

Later in the evening the older children would gather in one of the tenement hallways and amuse themselves telling banshee stories and trying to crack the shells on the nuts and coconuts they'd gathered.

'That sounds like fun,' Ann Marie said – far more fun than she'd experience at her aunt's formal evening of entertainment. 'I'll send some fruit and nuts to you as my contribution but this year I'm afraid I feel obliged to show my face at my aunt's elegant soirée.'

'That's a shame.' Ivy shrugged. 'You would have enjoyed yourself. It's a great party. Right, while you're puffing on that cigarette I'm going to go out and get water. I was on my way out when you knocked. I shouldn't be too long, but I'm going to lock the back door behind me. I want you to push over the bolt inside the door when I go out.'

'What's going on, Ivy?' Ann Marie stood. 'Jem almost shoved me down your outside steps and ordered me to stay put. Now, you're going to lock the door when you're only stepping out to the tap. What's wrong?'

'I won't be long.' Ivy ignored Ann Marie's question, grabbed her two buckets and stepped outside. She turned and locked the door at her back with her key. She waited until she heard Ann Marie slide the bolt home before walking away.

Chapter 9

Ivy walked down the yard, swinging the buckets. There was no one standing in front of the tap, she was glad to notice. The place seemed deserted which was unusual enough to have her checking over her shoulder. Something wasn't right. A soft sobbing sound caught her attention. She thought it came from inside the toilet cabin. She filled her two buckets quickly, glancing frequently over her shoulder. The noise continued – she couldn't just walk away. She left her buckets on the ground by the tap and crept over to the toilet.

She pulled the cracked wooden door of the single toilet open and bit back the scream that jumped to her lips. Ginie Johnson was against the back wall of the toilet, her shoulders shaking. She turned her painted face towards Ivy. The fear in the bruised, swollen face was heartbreaking. She was crouched on the dirty floor, her knees pulled up to her chest, sobs shaking her body.

'Ginie,' Ivy whispered with a fearful look back over her shoulder, 'what are yeh doing in here?'

'Have yeh seen our Seán? I can't find him anywhere.' Ginie ignored Ivy's shocked reaction. Her son was missing – that was all that mattered. She knew this place was one of Seán's favourite hidey-holes but he was nowhere to be found.

'Yeh can't stay in here, Ginie.' Ivy took her by the arm and pulled her to her feet. 'Come into my place – we'll have a cup of tea and sort something out.' She thought Seán was probably with the woman in Granny's old room but the little lad was skilled at finding places to hide – if Seán didn't want to be found it would take them ages to lay their hands on him. 'Let me get sorted and we'll see what's what.' Ivy practically pulled Ginie along with her. 'I need to get me water buckets.' She grabbed a bucket in each hand and with Ginie trailing like a lost dog after her she made her way to her own back door.

'Ann Marie, open up.' Ivy used the toe of her boot to rap gently on the door.

Ann Marie unbolted the door then stood back as Ivy and a woman unknown to her almost exploded into the room.

'Bolt the door, Ann Marie!' Ivy carried the two buckets over to the range. 'I've a feeling we're going to need an ocean of tea.' She emptied one of the water buckets into the reservoir then hurried to fill the kettle. 'Ann Marie, meet Ginie Johnson. Her son Seán has gone missing. I'm going to give her a hand looking for him.' Ivy kept her back to the other two. She wondered how Ann Marie would react if she explained that Ginie was the eighteen-year-old prostitute mother of six-year-old Seán. On her eleventh birthday, Ginie Johnson hadn't got a cheap card and a biscuit. Her eldest brother Declan had taken her down to Monto and sold her.

Ivy looked over her shoulder. The two women were standing frozen, Ginie with her back to the door as if she wanted to run back into the night. She suddenly remembered Ann Marie's expensive bag and gold case sitting out on the table. Ginie would have them in one of her pockets before you could blink. Ivy didn't care how rude it appeared. She crossed to the table and with a quick flick of her hand shoved everything back into the bag and the bag into the deep pockets of her worn skirt. No point in leaving temptation lying around.

Ann Marie was incapable of speech. She stared down at the tiny child-sized woman standing in the light cast by the gas globes. Ginie didn't even stand five feet tall and her body was thin and undernourished. The bird-boned wrists sticking out of the torn dark garment she wore were marked by black-and-blue bruises in the shape of thick fingers.

'Ann Marie is a friend of mine, Ginie,' Ivy said. 'Sit down and I'll get yeh something to eat.' No point in asking if Ginie was hungry.

'I only wanted to know about my Seán.' Ginie looked around like a trapped animal.

Ann Marie thought she was probably scaring the young woman. She hurried back to take a seat at the table with a sigh of relief. She had noticed Ivy removing her belongings but said nothing. This was Ivy's world.

'Sit down, Ginie.' Ivy ignored Ginie's obvious reluctance. 'I'll dish yeh up some of me rabbit stew.'

She'd said the magic words: Ginie's stomach rumbling could be heard and she walked slowly over to sit across the table from Ann Marie.

Ivy got busy, preparing the tea and dishing up an enamel plate of her rabbit stew. The silence between the two women sitting across the table from each other almost hurt her ears.

Ginie glared at the uppity bitch sitting at the table with her. She didn't know who Ivy Murphy thought she was fooling. Your one might be dressed in a second-hand suit now but Ginie had seen her driving around Dublin in her fancy automobile. Ginie wanted to jump to her feet and run out of this place but the smell of food kept her feet almost nailed to the floor.

'Here.' Ivy put an enamel mug of tea and the brimming plate of stew on the table in front of Ginie. She felt hard-hearted but there was no way she'd allow Ginie to break any of her delicate china dishes. 'Get that inta yeh.'

'Ta.' Ginie slurped the tea like a dying camel. 'Jaysus, Ivy Murphy, there's milk in here, fresh milk.' She wiped her bruised and bleeding mouth carefully with the back of her hand. She moved to shove the grain-rich stew into her mouth using her fingers but Ivy stopped her, slapping a spoon into her hand before she could blink.

'I went by the creamery this morning.' Ivy grinned. It did her heart good to be able to serve little luxuries to her guests. 'Molly Chivers,' she was referring to a neighbour who worked at the local creamery, 'gave me a pint extra when Old Man Ivors wasn't watching.'

'That's the ticket.' Ginie grinned then winced when her split lip objected to the movement. 'If we don't help each other who will?'

'If that isn't the God's honest truth, what is?' Ivy turned back to the black range.

'Merciful Jaysus, this stew is mighty, Ivy!'

Ann Marie had to look away as the young woman crammed the food into her mouth.

'Yeh mustn't know yer luxury since yer da died.' Ginie opened her mouth wide, displaying the half-mashed food inside.

Ann Marie felt her stomach turn.

'I'll get yeh more tea,' said Ivy.

Ivy was amused by Ann Marie's obvious reaction to Ginie's table manners. What had she expected? Ginie Johnson was one of seventeen children living with a bad egg of a da and a changing flow of ma's in two rooms. It was every man for himself. You fought to get every little bit and then had to cram it into your mouth fast or lose it.

'Yeh need to slow down, Ginie,' Ivy cautioned. 'That food is going to meet itself coming back up if yer not careful.'

'Yer right, Ivy.' Ginie forced herself to stop shovelling the food into her mouth. The last time she'd been able to eat slowly and savour the taste was the time leading up to Seán's birth when the women of The Lane had passed her from house

89

to house and nursed her.

'You're among friends – enjoy the feckin' food,' said Ivy and threw a damp rag at Ginie. 'Wipe your face and hands.'

Ivy reluctantly joined the other two at the table, pulling one of her supply of wooden orange boxes to the table. She turned the box lengthways before sitting down. She wasn't any more fond of bad table manners than Ann Marie but she understood Ginie's desperation. Hunger was a demanding master.

'Ginie,' Ivy dared to say when Ginie had made a decent dent in the food on her plate, 'do yeh not earn enough to get a room somewhere for yourself and Seán?' Ivy knew Ginie went out on the stroll every day God sent. Surely the money she made could be put to making a better life for herself and her son?

'It's well for yeh, Ivy Murphy,' Ginie snapped, 'sitting here in yer little palace judging others.'

Ann Marie looked around the room she considered little better than a hovel in spite of Ivy's best efforts. The room was a bare shell. There was no art work on the whitewashed walls, no covering on the bare black stone of the floor, no touches of comfort. The big iron bed pushed into the corner by the wall that divided Ivy's two rooms was a monstrosity in her opinion. The tall freestanding wooden cupboard pushed up against the far wall was functional. The open shelves of the top held Ivy's meagre supply of dishes. Ann Marie knew Ivy sometimes used the central flat surface of the tall unit as a work surface. She couldn't begin to guess what the closed doors of the bottom cupboards hid. The table they sat at was ancient and well used. Ivy was sitting on an upturned orange crate for goodness sake. The two decrepit old chairs sitting in front of the black range completed a picture of abject poverty as far as Ann Marie was concerned. She wondered what kind of home this young woman had that she'd consider Ivy's bare little room a palace.

'I notice yeh gave me a cheap muggin – but yer woman gets a fancy china cup,' Ginie snapped. 'Getting above yer station, aren't yeh, Ivy Murphy?'

'You can be a contrary bugger, Ginie.' Ivy shrugged. 'These china cups were a gift – they mean a lot to me. I wouldn't put it past yeh to get in a strop and break them just to upset me. Do you blame me, Ginie?'

'No.' Ginie shook her head sadly, sometimes she just had to hurt the people around her, share the feckin' pain.

'Ginie,' Ivy persisted, 'could yeh not afford a room for the two of yez?'

'Who's going to rent a room to me and me son?' Ginie snapped bitterly. Did the woman think she hadn't tried to get Seán out from under the rule of her family? It was all she could do some days to put one foot in front of the other.

'Yeh could say Seán was yer brother,' Ivy suggested.

'Seán might have been born a bastard but I'll not deny him, Ivy Murphy,' Ginie snapped with an indignant glare. Seán was the only child she'd ever have. Those men she'd been sold to in the Monto brothel had damaged something inside her. The wise woman had told her so. Ginie shoved the rest of the grub into her mouth, thinking of running out of the place. She didn't need these two uppity bitches telling her how to live her life.

'I worry for yeh, Ginie.' Ivy had been there when the women of The Lane mounted an attack into the heart of the Monto. They'd gone in armed with rolling pins and iron pots, and they'd managed to find Ginie and drag her out of a nightmare. Unfortunately, by the time the women had learned of Ginie's fate it had been too late to save her body from injury. They had rescued Ginie from the brothel in Monto, but the damage had already been done. It was a day she'd never forget. She sighed sadly now, knowing there was nothing she could do to change things. Ginie had to make the move herself.

'It's well for yeh, Ivy Murphy,' Ginie gulped her tea. 'Sitting here, having all this space to yerself. What do yeh know about the rest of us? Pallin' around with this fancy piece – is she the one givin' yeh ideas above yer station?' She waved a still grubby hand in Ann Marie's direction. 'Keep yer feckin' worry to yerself – me and Seán are doing all right. We don't need you sticking yer nose into our business.'

Then Ginie jumped in fright when a sharp knock sounded on the back door.

Ivy jumped to her feet and crossed to the window overlooking the door. Pulling the lace curtain aside she looked out. 'It's Mrs Wiggins,' she said, looking back over her shoulder at the other women. 'I wonder what she wants.'

She pulled the bolt open and unlocked the door.

'Good.' Marcella Wiggins didn't give Ivy a chance to speak. 'You're locking your door, keep it that way.' The big woman pushed the door open so she could see into the back room. 'There yeh are, Ginie – I was looking for yeh an' you're here, that's good.' She turned and made a wide gesture of her arm to somebody outside. Ivy stuck her head through the doorway and saw Seán McDonald exploding out of the dark and running towards Marcella.

Ivy stood with her mouth open, wondering what was going on.

'I've not got time to stop.' Marcella gently pushed Seán into Ivy's back room. 'Ivy, if you've a curtain, you need to pull it over that window. Anyone could look in on yeh.' Without pausing for breath she continued: 'Jem will be knocking on yer front door in a minute. He's leaving young Emmy with yeh. Be ready.' Without waiting for a reply the woman turned away. 'Don't any of yez step foot out of them rooms until we tell yez to,' she shouted back over her shoulder.

Ivy forced her mouth closed and in a daze moved to pull the thick tablecloth she'd turned into a curtain over the back window, as ordered.

'Ma, is yeh okay?' Seán ran towards his mother. 'I was so scared, Ma.'

'I'm okay, son.' Ginie grabbed Seán into her body, holding the little boy tight and rocking her body in relief.

'I did what yeh said, Ma.' Seán patted Ginie's bruised cheek with one little hand, a hand calloused by years of hard work. He was still wearing the cut-down jacket tied with string but his skin and hair looked as if they'd been well washed recently. 'I was so scared. Yeh were asleep and yer head was bleedin' but yeh told me, Ma, didn't yeh always tell me to run away from trouble?'

'I did, son, and I'm that proud of yeh!' Ginie pressed a kiss into his soft cheek, an embarrassed blush staining her painted one. She was being soppy in public but she'd been so worried. 'Did yeh get something to eat?' She felt guilty for the food she'd gobbled up without a thought to what Seán might be getting.

'I had me cracklin' in me pocket and I ate some of that. Then, Mrs Wiggins took me into her place and scrubbed me within an inch of me life, Ma.' Seán shrugged. 'She gave me a big chunk of bread and drippin', but she said she'd no time to feed me proper, she had things to do. I had to run around the place doing messages for her, Ma.' He didn't mention the police and priest he talked to – he'd tell his ma later. Seán wriggled to be free of his mother's arms. He glanced around the room, taking careful note of the exits. It was best to be prepared to run – his ma had taught him that.

'Yer among friends, Seán,' Ivy said gently. 'Sit yourself down by your ma and I'll get yeh a plate of food.' She pushed her own orange crate close to Ginie's chair for him. She knew what the young boy was thinking and it saddened her that one so young should have to be so aware of his surroundings.

'I'm okay, I said, didn't I? I had a bit of chuck and some of the cracklin' yer one next door showed me how to make.' He was pulling open the jacket that was all he owned. His little chest was

94

exposed, bruises shining on the white flesh. 'She sewed me a pocket, Ivy,' he beamed. 'A hidden pocket. Can yeh credit that?'

'That was nice of her.' Ivy grinned down at the boy. 'You keep hold of your cracklin' – I've a pot of rabbit stew on the go. You sit down and I'll give you some.'

'Look!' Seán pulled long strips of burned pig fat from his hidden pocket. 'This is it. Yeh have to boil the stuff like we always do. Then,' he took a deep delighted breath, 'then yeh put the fat on top of the stove to sizzle and burn. Yer one says if you don't have a stove yeh can hang it over the fire. Do yeh want a taste?' Seán generously offered his prize.

'Give yer ma a taste.' Ivy smiled gently. 'I'm only after me dinner.' She turned back to the stove.

Ginie had already seen, tasted and heard all about the wonder of cracklin' but she wouldn't hurt his feelings for the world. She bit a small amount off the long strip of seared fat Seán held in his fist. Her teeth biting into the hardened fat made a loud crunching noise.

'Merciful goodness!' she said, causing Seán to giggle with delight. 'That's something, that is, and now yeh know how to do this we'll be laughin',' she said, not for the first time. She pushed the little hand away from her mouth.

'Would yeh like a mug of milk, Sean?' Ivy put an enamel plate of stew on the table in front of the child. She put a spoon into the stew and stepped back.

'I'm going to have a feed and a mug of milk. Isn't that the business, Ma?' Seán examined his mother's face with worried eyes. He could see the bruises where his uncle had hit and kicked her.

'It's a livin' wonder, son.' Ginie smiled gently down into the worried face, her heart breaking.

'Eat your food, Seán,' Ivy said softly. She suddenly remembered the packet of biscuits sitting in her cupboard. 'When you've eaten it all up, would yeh like a biscuit and another mug of milk?'

'A biscuit!' Seán's eyes opened like saucers. 'Did yeh hear that, Ma? I'm going to get milk and a biscuit after I eat all me food up. Isn't this the best day ever, Ma, isn't it?' Seán was happy as a sandboy. His ma was sitting here with other women smiling at her and he was going to have milk and a biscuit. It just didn't get better than that in his world.

Ann Marie was watching the scene around the table with what felt like a block of ice in her chest. The people of The Lane touched her in a way that nothing else ever had in her life. 'I haven't a penny' wasn't an expression to these people. It was a way of life. She had so much and watching these people made her appreciate her own advantages more than ever. She wondered what new crisis had brought these people to Ivy's door but she could wait to ask until an obviously starving child had a meal.

'I'll put these here for later, Seán.' Ivy pulled the untouched plate of biscuits from where it sat on the table in front of Ann Marie and set it in hand's reach of the boy. 'If yeh can't eat all of them put some in your "secret" pocket. I won't mind.'

'It's the business.' Seán picked up the mug of milk by his plate carefully. He didn't want to spill any of this special treat. He'd never had a full mug of milk to himself before and now there was the promise of another mug of milk and a plate of biscuits. He was really getting treated like the bee's knees today. 'Isn't it, Ma, isn't it the business?' He didn't wait for his mother to reply.

'What's going on, Ivy?' Ann Marie ventured to say.

'I've no idea.' Ivy marvelled at the speed the food on Seán's plate disappeared. She was about to offer him more stew when he raised his eyes to stare around the table.

'Mrs Wiggins had the men carry out the tin bins and light fires.' He offered that bit of news then took one of the biscuits sitting so temptingly before him and with a smile that blessed the world bit into the first shop-bought biscuit he'd ever tasted.

The tall tin bins with holes punched out of their sides were filled with coal nuggets and scraps of wood and used to warm the courtyard when The Lane had one of its parties.

'What's going on, Ginie?' Ivy had noticed the worried frown on Ginie's face before she lowered her head to stare at her son.

'I don't know what yer talkin' about.' Ginie held up her enamel mug. 'Any more of that tea?'

Ann Marie had opened her mouth to question the situation again when a sharp rap sounded from the front room.

'That'll be Jem with Emmy.' Ivy shared a look with Ann Marie and shrugged. 'I'll let them in.' She walked towards the door that separated the two rooms. Jem would be able to tell her what the heck was going on around here. She closed the dividing door at her back, wanting to keep the heat in the back room. That left the front room cloaked in gloomy shadow.

She pulled open the front door with a smile on her face and a determined tilt to her chin. She wanted answers.

'Auntie Ivy,' Emmy Ryan, her blue-black hair bouncing on her back, threw herself forward to clasp her arms around Ivy's waist in a tight hug, 'they're lighting the party fires.' Her green eyes glistened with excitement as she stared up at one of her favourite people. 'Did you know?'

'I know nothing.' She glared at Jem who simply grinned and shrugged.

'I can't stop.' Jem looked over Ivy's shoulder towards the cold grate in the front room. 'If I were you I'd light that fire.' He nodded towards the grate. 'I've a feeling you'll be spending a lot of time in that room tonight.' He escaped Ivy's grasping hands with a wriggle of his shoulders. He pressed a kiss on her mouth, dropped a quick kiss on Emmy's head and turned to run back up the outside steps. 'I'll fill you in later!' he shouted over his shoulder as he left the two females staring after him.

'Well!' Ivy stood with her hands on her hips, staring up at Jem locking the gate at the top of the iron steps leading down to her door.

'Get indoors, woman!' Jem shouted down at her. 'I want you and Emmy behind locked doors. Use the bolt – go on now, get inside.' He turned around and left, not waiting for Ivy to take it into her head to follow him.

'It seems we have our orders.' Ivy took Emmy's little shoulder and pulled the child with her deeper into the hallway. She locked and bolted the door before walking with Emmy at her side into the front room. 'Ann Marie and some people are in the back room,' she added, hoping to distract Emmy with the promise of company. She could see the questions on the little girl's face and she simply didn't have any answers ... not yet.

Emmy ran towards the closed door; she never doubted her reception in any situation.

'Ann Marie!' she screamed, throwing herself against the seated woman. 'The party fires are being lit!' She stared at the little boy sitting at her Auntie Ivy's table. She knew who he was of course – everyone in The Lane knew everyone else.

'Ivy?' Ann Marie asked as soon as Ivy appeared in the open doorway.

'I'm none the wiser, Ann Marie.' Ivy shook her head. 'Jem dropped Emmy off and disappeared, almost in a puff of smoke – he was that quick, here and gone.'

'May I please have a jam jar of tea, Auntie Ivy?' Emmy had spotted the plate of biscuits sitting on the table. Emmy loved the milky concoction Ivy poured into a glass jam jar especially for her.

'I'll make a fresh pot of tea.' Ivy didn't know what else to do or say. 'I'll put the kettle on.' She turned to fill the big black kettle.

'Do you want to play?' Emmy stared at the boy. 'We can use my coloured chalk to draw pictures on the floor,' she tempted him. 'My Auntie Ivy allows me to do that – do you want to?'

Seán stared over at his mother. He couldn't

99

imagine being allowed to make a mess on the floor. Was the girl trying to get him into trouble? Ivy had fed him – she'd even given him milk and biscuits. He didn't want to upset her.

'Go on, son.' Ginie gave him a gentle pat. If she had to talk to these women she'd prefer to do it without little ears listening.

'Come on.' Emmy walked around the table and attempted to pull Seán off his perch on the orange crate. 'Take off that ugly old coat and come play with me.'

With her back to the room Ivy closed her eyes and sighed: leave it to a small child to say what everyone else was thinking.

'Can't.' Seán shook off her hands and lowered his head.

Ivy turned around quickly. 'Seán doesn't want to get chalk all over his coat.' She had already decided that she was going to do something about the state of Seán. Ginie could give her all the evil looks she liked. She held out her hand to the child and smiled. 'Come with me, Seán – we'll soon find something you won't mind getting dirty.' She had an outfit she'd fixed up the other day after seeing him. The little shirt and jumper were well worn and mended. She'd replaced the seat in the short trousers. The articles were worn enough to prevent the boy's family from pawning them.

Ginie opened her mouth to object but the glare Ivy gave her shut her up.

'Come along, Seán.' Ivy still had her hand held out to the lad. 'Come with me.'

'Go ahead,' Ginie whispered.

'I'll be a while.' Ivy pulled the reluctant child

along with her towards the front room. 'Emmy, get out the box of chalk while I'm away.'

The back room remained silent while Emmy fell to her knees to root under the big bed for her very own orange crate. Ivy kept Emmy's supplies in a special box the child was familiar with. She took her rag doll, a twin of the one she had in her own room over the livery, out of the box and shoved it under the bedclothes. She knew little boys sometimes made fun of girls with dolls. She didn't want her doll hurt. She withdrew the box of coloured chalk and settled quietly to making matchstick figures on the black slate of the floor. She kept glancing over her shoulder. She wanted her Auntie Ivy to come back.

Chapter 10

'Where are yez?' The angry masculine shout coming from the back yard caused all three people in Ivy's back room to jump. *'I don't care who's hiding the buggers! Yez better send them out here, do yez hear me? I said all of yez get out here right now!'* A rattle of metal rang like a loud bell. *'Do yez hear me, ye shower of useless little fuckers?'* The sound of a heavy fist and what for all the world sounded like steel-toed boots being applied to doors echoed around the yard. The rattle of metal was added to the din.

Emmy jumped up from the floor in fright and ran over to huddle against Ann Marie who cuddled the child close although she wasn't feeling exactly brave herself. With Emmy held close she stared across the table at the young woman who was turning an interesting shade of green. Ginie certainly seemed to have some information as to what was going on around here.

'Right.' Ivy appeared in the open doorway between the rooms. 'That is it, Ginie Johnson. What the heck is going on?' She had to shout to be heard over the noise coming from the back yard. If she hadn't sussed it already, now she knew there was something unusual planned for The Lane, because no one was shouting at the noisy bugger to shut up!

Seán, dressed in his new, well-worn outfit, sidled around Ivy's figure and hurried over to huddle close to his mother.

'Emmy – Seán,' Ivy walked over to the table, took both little children by the shoulders and pushed them gently towards the abandoned chalk on the floor, 'you two play quietly for a while.'

'But–' both children objected.

'I'll make yez jam jars of tea in a minute and yez can have a tea party on the floor,' Ivy promised while staring bullets at Ginie.

'Declan has big plans to turn our two rooms into a shebeen,' Ginie offered quietly while the noise continued outside.

'I beg your pardon?' Ann Marie moved her chair closer to the other two women. She didn't want to miss any of this and it was hard to hear over the noise outside.

'A shebeen, Ann Marie,' Ivy snapped. 'An illegal pub.'

'He has the other lads brewing up poitín day

and night,' Ginie went on. 'He's goin' to offer other things as well.' She looked towards the two children and shrugged.

'In the name of God!' Ivy pushed her two hands through her hair and pulled. She spun and removed the kettle, which had almost boiled dry, from the range. She set it in the grate. The tea could wait for once. She wanted to hear this. She pulled the orange crate close to the table and the three women huddled, heads bent close together.

'That's Declan out there, isn't it?' Ivy said.

'Yessss,' Ginie almost hissed. 'Him and his two neckless wonders – they'd be the ones kicking doors. Declan loves using an old tin pot and spoon to make as loud a noise as he can. Yeh ought to hear that bloody racket inside, it fair rattles yer brain.' She fell silent, her head almost disappearing into her thin shoulders.

'And? Come on, Ginie, there's more going on out there in The Lane than you're telling.' Ivy slapped the table top.

Ann Marie wanted a cigarette, quite badly.

'Declan has been talking ever since he came back about his big plans to make money. He told the men in the pub and all his old cronies that he'd be in business, starting tonight.' Ginie had been at her wits' end trying to think how she could stop him. 'I told Mrs Wiggins what was going on. I'm not going to let him do to me brothers and sisters what he did to me.' She crossed her arms over her chest and gave a sharp nod of her head. She wasn't sorry for what she'd done.

'What's happening now?' Ivy and Ann Marie asked together.

103

'I don't know.' Ginie glared at the other two women when they gave her looks of disbelief. 'I really don't know. The childer are hidden around The Lane, two each, an older and younger one together in each house. I know that much. Mrs Wiggins told me to keep me nose out of it. I was ordered to hide meself and Seán. She said she'd take care of the rest.'

'I'll make a big pot of tea and we can drink it in the front room,' said Ivy.

'Ivy,' Ann Marie held out her hand, 'give me my cigarettes.'

'Here.' Ivy took Ann Marie's items from her pocket and passed them over. 'You two go into the front room and see if you can figure out what's going on outside from there. I doubt it but you never know.'

The two children stared with big eyes as the three women almost jumped into action.

'Leave the door open,' Ivy called over her shoulder. She took five jam jars from her supply at the back of one of the bottom cupboards in her dresser. They could all drink their tea from jam jars. She wasn't about to risk her tea set.

'It's impossible to see anything from your window, Ivy,' Ann Marie shouted while assembling her cigarette and holder. The window in Ivy's front room overlooked the concrete cage directly outside Ivy's basement door. The courtyard was on ground level. 'We could open the window and perhaps hear what's going on.'

'To heck with that!' Ivy had refilled the kettle from the reservoir and returned it to the range top. 'Ginie, come watch this kettle for me.' She waited until Ginie stepped back into the room before grabbing her shawl from the end of the bed.

'Right. Everyone keep quiet now. I'm going to have a peek outside.' She pulled her black shawl around her head and shoulders. She hurried through her rooms.

'What are you planning, Ivy?' Ann Marie was standing by the closed window, puffing out clouds of smoke.

'We'll learn nothing from down here.' Ivy pulled open the inside door. 'I'm just going to see if I can see anything.' She opened her outside door and crept silently up several steps. There were a lot of people rushing about but without exposing herself Ivy couldn't make out what was going on. She sighed and turned back towards her rooms.

'Your kettle's boiling!' Ginie shouted from the back room as soon as Ivy entered.

'Coming!' She was going to have to make the tea in the big black kettle – her metal teapot wasn't big enough for all these people. She'd sold the big family teapot down the market years ago.

'We're going to have to go outside and wait to see what's going on,' Ivy said as soon as she'd made the tea. She moved the heavy kettle to the back of the range. She'd guessed at the amount of tea leaves needed to make a good cup of tea. She'd give it a few minutes to brew. 'You two need to put on your outside clothes.'

'Ahh,' Ann Marie's voice carried from the front room, 'we're going to pop our heads over the parapet.'

'Now's not the time to be confusing us with your fancy words, Ann Marie,' Ivy snapped, 'but if I've understood yeh that's about the gist of it.' She turned her attention to the children. 'Right, kids, it's time to clean up me floor.' She wet a rag and offered it to the fascinated children. 'Get all that chalk washed off me floor then hop up on the bed. That floor's too cold to sit on for long.' She picked her long coat up from the bed and put it on while watching the two children crawl around. Emmy was picking up her chalk and packing it away, Seán was scrubbing the wet rag over the chalk decorations on the floor.

She grabbed one of her wooden chairs and carried it over to place beside the bed. She put the plate which still held a few biscuits on the chair then prepared two milky jam jars of tea. She pulled an old deck of cards belonging to her da from the back of one of her dresser drawers and added that to the items on the chair.

'Right!' Ivy slapped her two hands together and looked around. 'You two, up on the bed. Yeh can have yer tea and biscuits then play a game of Snap with them cards. If you get cold climb under the bed covers.'

While the children jumped to obey Ivy prepared three jam jars of hot tea. 'We'll be just outside if yez want anything but I want yez to play nicely here while we're busy. Understand?'

'Yes, Auntie Ivy.' Emmy nodded her head frantically. There was always something exciting going on in this new life of hers.

'Yes, Ivy.' Seán wasn't bothered about anything happening. He was fed, warm and dressed like all the other boys. He was happy as a sandboy – he'd heard Mrs Wiggins say that and he liked how it sounded.

'Right.' Ivy had to make two trips to carry the tea into the front room. 'I'm the tallest so I'll stand on the lowest rung of me outside steps. We'll have to be careful not to be seen – I think if we pop our heads up over ground level out there we should be able to see what's going on.' She opened the two doors leading outside and, grabbing her hockey stick in one hand and with her tea in the other, began to lead the other two out into the night.

'Ivy, is this wise?' Ann Marie desperately wanted to know what was happening in the courtyard but they'd been ordered to stay behind locked doors.

'I want to know what's going on,' Ginie sipped at the hot tea. She knew the men of The Lane wouldn't let her brother lay a hand on her, not now at any rate.

'Come on.' Ivy wasn't waiting. 'Be quiet as you can.'

The three women crept almost silently out of Ivy's home. They walked carefully up the outside iron steps, each woman choosing a rung that would allow her to see over the rim of the ground level and onto the courtyard. Ivy had to bite into the cloth of her coat to block the gasp that almost escaped her when she saw Brother Theo and Garda Collins standing large as life around one of the four bins that had been lit around the cobbled courtyard. She didn't think she'd ever seen so many people gathered in the courtyard when there wasn't a party going on.

There were crowds of women of all ages wrapped up tightly in their shawls, their white faces barely visible as they grouped around the

107

fire-bins. They were holding their hands out to the flames but there was no sound of the usual talking that should be taking place when a group of these women got together. The silence was almost eerie; no men were visible and no children ran around the place.

Ann Marie turned, a silent question on her face as she looked at Ivy. Ivy simply shrugged and gave a jerk of her head towards the scene in front of them. She hadn't a notion of what was going on out there. They'd just have to wait and see. They stood sipping at their jam jars of hot tea and waited.

They didn't have long to wait. The noise of men making their way down the tunnel and into The Lane could be heard. The women standing in the courtyard straightened but nothing was said until the men emerged from the tunnel.

'Eddie Campbell,' Marcella Wiggin's voice sounded unnaturally loud in the silent courtyard, 'is that yerself? Shouldn't you be going home to yer wife and childer?' The man she'd addressed aloud almost tripped over his own feet. 'Shay Heffernan, what are you doing down this way? Does your mother know yer out?'

It seemed Marcella's voice broke the silence and more women started shouting out men's names. The women added notes of warning and advice for each man they named. The happy crowd of males that had been strolling along with purpose suddenly got a hitch in their stride. Those named by the women dropped their heads and tried to disappear into the crowd, many of them turning around and leaving. Some brave souls continued on into the main body of the courtyard. They'd been promised cheap booze and floozies. They weren't going home until they'd got what they were promised.

Brother Theo held his hands out to the flame of the fire and watched fascinated as the women of The Lane took control of their world. He was composing the article he would write about this fascinating development. The women were turning these men away without bloodshed but he doubted many of the men would be brave enough to try and come into this area again for illicit purposes.

Garda Barney Collins wished he could make note of the names of some of these men but he was keeping a mental tally. His purpose here this evening, according to Mrs Wiggins, was as a deterrent. That woman would have made a great general; the armed forces lost out by not recruiting women like Marcella Wiggins. She'd organised her troops to within an inch of their lives. The women of The Lane had jumped to obey her every order.

In the back yard of the tenements Declan Johnson was so angry he was almost frothing at the mouth. He and his men had made enough noise to wake the dead but not one person had appeared to complain, still less to hand over his sisters and brothers to him. He'd drag the little bastards out of whatever place they'd found to hide – he refused to believe his useless shower of brothers and sisters had disappeared into thin air. He'd a use for every one of them this evening. It was the opening night of his big money-making business. He'd been rubbing his hands all day. He could practically taste

109

the money he would make from the idiots who would pay for cheap drink and cheaper women. He'd get the fools comfortable and, when they were good and drunk, empty their pockets. He had it all in hand, his grand plan. He'd be able to charge extra for his sisters and some of his brothers if there were any who wanted that sort of thing. He didn't care what men wanted as long as they paid good money. It was a good plan. He knew it would be a money-making venture: the flesh on sale wasn't shopworn, yet. But the bloody lot of them were missing. When he got his hands on them he'd soon teach them who was boss around here.

Abandoning their search at the back of the tenements, now he and his men made their way around to the front of the block and the open courtyard.

Jem Ryan stood, with a group of men, inside the barely open doors of his livery. The men were ready for action but they'd been ordered to stay away while the women tried to move the group of visiting men along peacefully. He could almost feel the tension pouring off the men around him as they watched their women face a crowd of men looking for cheap pleasure. He kept his body still but his eyes moved constantly, seeking to find trouble before it could get out of hand. He saw three heads bobbing up and down like seals in the ocean, across at Ivy's place. He should have known that woman would never obey an order to stay out of trouble. He prayed she'd keep her head well down. This situation could turn ugly very fast.

Declan Johnson emerged from behind the end

gable wall of the tenement block and onto the courtyard. He froze in place when he saw the party fires lit. What the hell was going on? He didn't care – he was going to invite the men he was expecting into his place. He still had the two women he'd trained up in the business and there was plenty of rotgut. This was his night. He was going to show everyone that he was a force to be reckoned with. No shower of old biddies was going to stop him. He was going to be rich. He began to step out of the shadows when he caught sight of a bloody priest warming his hands by the fire. He stared into the night, squinting to get a better look. What the fuck was a Franciscan Friar doing in The Lane? He'd never get the men past a bloody monk. Jesus, was that a member of the Garda standing with that priest? He wanted to throw his head back and roar his frustration to the sky.

Barney Collins caught sight of Declan Johnson out of the corner of his eye. He turned and waited to see what that bowsie would do. He'd like to have a reason to collar that article but his hands were tied because the man hadn't done anything illegal he could prove, yet.

The women continued to stand around the fires but they were losing heart. They'd managed to run off some of the men but the remaining ones seemed to be gathering courage from each other. They showed no signs of walking away.

Brother Theo had a brain wave. He marched out into the middle of the courtyard, fingering the long string of heavy wooden beads that hung from the waist of his brown wool habit and in a loud firm voice began to lead the women of The

111

Lane in a decade of the rosary.

At the sound of the Hail Marys and Our Fathers being belted out from every female throat the last of the crowd of men turned tail and disappeared. It would be a very long time before they came back in here looking for a bit of innocent fun. They could get lectures and prayers at home.

Chapter 11

'We're off,' Bull, a tiny ferret of a man, one of Declan's hired men, grunted. They'd been promised an easy life and good money. 'You know where to find us when yeh need us.' He grabbed Skinny, a muscled mountain of a man, by the jacket and turned him in the direction of the tunnel.

Declan watched them leave, his fingernails digging into the skin of his hands he was clenching his fists so hard. He couldn't open his locked teeth enough to make a sound. This changed nothing. It was a knock-back, that was all. He was down but not out. He had a plan to make money and no one was going to stop him. He stormed back to his two-room basement. He needed to shift those two lazy bitches. He needed the money they could make yet tonight. He'd lay low for a few days, play nice while he discovered who had dared to hide his workers.

As the decade of the rosary ended, the men of The Lane pushed each other out of the way as en masse they tried to leave the livery and reach their women. It had been torture to watch them face that crowd alone.

The women were glad to see their men coming – there were quite a few felt their knees wanting to give way. They collapsed back against their men and waited.

'He's back in his hole,' a voice offered out of the darkness. 'I pity them poor cows he's got down there.'

Two women strolled towards the fire. They'd been keeping watch over the Johnsons' place, as ordered, although what they would have done if any of the men had decided to ignore the crowd they weren't exactly sure.

'Is anyone going to explain to me what was going on around here tonight?' Garda Collins had a very good idea but he could do nothing if these people didn't make an official complaint. He sighed deeply, knowing that wasn't going to happen, but he'd had to ask. At least he was aware what to look for now. That was more than he'd known earlier when he'd been explaining his problem to Brother Theo.

'What yeh don't know can't hurt yeh, Garda Collins.' Marcella Wiggins stepped forward. 'It was good of you to lend us your company but we'll take it from here.' Although what they were going to do she didn't know. They hadn't solved anything here tonight and she knew it. Ah, well – *'sufficient unto the day the evil thereof'*, or something like that.

'I'll have two of the Garda patrol the tunnel for the rest of the evening,' Barney Collins offered. 'I can't do more than that, I'm afraid. I need someone to file an official complaint before I can do more.' He waited without much hope. These people didn't tell on each other. 'I'll get along so.' He knew when to leave well enough alone.

'I'll walk out with you,' Brother Theo said. 'I have to be getting back.'

The two men turned to leave the people of The Lane to handle their own problems as they obviously preferred.

'Are you leaving, Brother Theo?' Ivy ran up her steps and stepped out into the courtyard.

'I have to be getting back to the Friary,' Theo said with a smile. 'I'll stop in to visit you next time I'm passing, Ivy.' He turned and joined Garda Collins, and the two men walked from The Lane, very much aware of the eyes of the silent crowd upon them.

'Me knees are knocking.' Marcella Wiggins leaned against the railing that surrounded the drop down to Ivy's basement. 'I wouldn't want to do that again anytime soon.'

'It won't stop the bugger for long.' Ginie put her empty jam jar on the step at her feet and walked up to join the crowd. 'He thinks he's going to make his fortune and what happened tonight won't stop him.'

Ann Marie walked slowly up the steps. She had nothing to contribute to the mutterings but she wasn't willing to go back down and baby-sit.

She walked over to join the person in the crowd she knew the best. 'Dear Lord, Jem, I'm still shaking.'

'You're not the only one!' Ivy said as she joined them.

'I thought I told you to keep out of this, Ivy Murphy.' Jem was dealing with a few trembles himself. 'Where's Emmy?'

'She's fine,' Ivy said. 'She's playing cards with Seán McDonald and, knowing her, probably cheating.'

'Some of the men are going to stay by the fires and keep an eye out for trouble. There's nothing more we can do here.' Jem looked around the crowd of people lingering in the courtyard. 'We're going to have to do something about Declan Johnson but I don't think anyone is up to discussing that right now.' He put an arm around each of the women and grinned down at Ivy. 'I'm surprised I have to say this to you, Ivy Murphy, but I could murder a cup of tea.'

'Honestly, you two!' Ann Marie pushed gently away from Jem. 'I have to get home. I hadn't intended to stay this long. Sadie will be wondering what has happened to me.'

'Sadie knows what's going on in here,' Jem said. 'John telephoned her. He was afraid she might decide to put the baby in the pram and stroll over. He didn't want her here.'

'Very smart of him,' Ann Marie agreed, 'but I really do have to leave.'

'I'll have one of my lads walk home with you, Ann Marie,' Jem insisted. 'You don't want to bump into any of the crowd that might still be hanging around outside.' He doubted any of the men were still hanging about but he didn't want Ann Marie to take any risks.

'Thank you.' Ann Marie wasn't going to refuse. She was still feeling shaky.

115

'Ginie,' Ivy called when she saw the other woman start to move, 'do you have somewhere for you and Seán to stay tonight?' They couldn't go home.

'I'm staying with yer one in old Granny's place,' Ginie said as she turned to go back to Ivy's and pick up her son. 'Seán'll like that.'

'I'll come with you.' Ivy hurried over to accompany Ginie. She didn't want the woman to help herself to anything that might be lying about.

'I'll talk to you soon, Ivy!' Ann Marie called to Ivy's back. Having seen Ivy protect her belongings from Ginie, she had a good idea what was sending Ivy into a run although in her opinion there wasn't a lot in Ivy's place that was worth stealing. Still, what did she know?

'Come on, Ann Marie.' Jem turned to go back into his livery. He'd pick Emmy up after he'd seen Ann Marie safely on her way. 'I was going to suggest sending one of the lads with you but I'm sure John would like to get home to his family. You two can leave together, keep each other company.'

'I'll be glad of someone to talk to.' Ann Marie accompanied him into the livery.

'Well, Ivy,' Jem stood in Ivy's back room, Emmy held close to his chest, 'that was something.'

'What are we going to do about all of them kids of the Johnsons', Jem?' Ivy was exhausted. 'They can't go back into that basement with Declan and those women.'

'We have no say in the matter, Ivy.' Jem wished he could do something but the Johnsons weren't the only people in The Lane huddled into a cramped space and clinging to each other. It was the only life they knew and he feared the kids would creep back home as soon as they could in any case. 'We're all reeling from tonight's happenings, Ivy. We'll sleep on it and see if we can come up with a plan.'

'Okay.' Ivy didn't know what else they could do. She walked along at Jem's side, patting Emmy's back, not sure if she was giving comfort or taking it.

'Night, Auntie Ivy.' Emmy raised her head to whisper. 'I had a good time.' She lay her head back down and closed her eyes.

'Didn't we all?' Ivy almost sobbed.

'Try and get some sleep.' Jem bent and pressed a kiss into her cheek. 'Lock the door behind me and get some rest. I'll see you tomorrow.'

Chapter 12

'Right, Ruby, that's two hair ribbons, four hairpins and a brooch.'

Ivy delighted in her ability to take note of everything passed to her by the under-servants. The joy of holding her notebook and pencil, making notes she could actually read, was a constant wonder to her. The cessation of the tension headaches that had plagued her when she was forced to keep everything in her head was a blessing.

'Are yeh sure about the brooch, Ruby?'

'Ivy, the young mistress threw that brooch at me

117

head and told me to get rid of it.' Ruby, a black knitted shawl pulled tight around her rough grey under-servant's uniform, looked over her shoulder. 'I was on me hands and knees tending the fire in her room when the bloody brooch came at me like a bullet. I think she was aiming for the fire but she got me.' She touched one grubby hand to the red scratch on her pale face. 'It seems the pin on the brooch tore a hole in the young lady's new dress. The very dress she bought on her latest trip to Paris.'

'Pity about her,' Ivy grinned. 'This brooch will fetch a pretty penny, Ruby, but it may take me a little time to sell it on. Can yeh wait or do you want me to take the first price I'm offered?'

'Get the best price yeh can, Ivy.' Ruby shrugged. 'I'll send the money home to me mammy so anything yeh get will be welcome.'

'That it?' Ivy closed her notebook. She touched her pram lightly, checking the weight. It was about time to return to The Lane. She wanted a cup of tea and a bite to eat. The day was dark and cold but the rain had stopped for the moment.

'Mrs Simpson – the young ladies' seamstress – said this lot was beyond mending.' Ruby turned and picked up the bundle she'd dropped while she conducted her own business with Ivy. She passed the tied bundle of what looked like old sheets and curtains to Ivy. 'I have to get back to work now. I'll see yeh next week, Ivy.'

Ruby opened the back door of the house she worked in and disappeared without another word.

'Bless you, Mrs Simpson.' Ivy could grin openly with delight now.

It seemed every house on the square was getting a deep-cleaning and revamp before the Christmas holidays.

Ivy was delighted with the torn and soiled fabric she'd received on her round this morning. She would put the fabric to soak in her tin bathtub, with a shaving of soap and a packet of bluing. Ivy couldn't wait to see what she had to sell. One more house and she'd call it a day.

'Hello, I'm Chrissy.' A pretty, smiling dark-haired plump girl stood in the portico of the last house on her round. The girl was wearing the grey dress and rough apron of an under-housemaid. 'Are you the one who will pay me a few pence for this lot?' The girl held up one hand. She had a rainbow of silk ribbons clutched in her dimpled fist.

'You're new here, aren't you?' Ivy felt her heart sink. Another one. Where did they find these innocent young girls to be served up on the altar of the chinless wonder that called this house home?

'I arrived in Dublin yesterday.' Chrissy Mc-Auliffe couldn't believe she was in the capital city of her nation. It was so exciting.

'How long have you been standing out here waiting for me to come by?' Ivy spoke slowly, her brain ticking over. 'Why aren't you inside going about your duties, Chrissy?' The under-house-maids were worked till they dropped. They didn't have time to be standing around. Chrissy should be inside the scullery right now standing over a sink of hot water, getting ready to scrub the break-fast pots, pans and dishes.

'The dishes aren't going anywhere.' Chrissy

119

shrugged with marked indifference. At home she could leave the dishes until her mammy lost her rag and did them herself. Chrissy hated hot greasy water.

'Where did you get the ribbons, Chrissy?' Ivy wanted to kick herself. Why could she never keep her nose out of other people's business? It wasn't her place to explain anything to this young girl. The housekeeper should be the one boxing the girl's ears and putting her in her place.

'Young Master Lawrence passed them to me.' Chrissy beamed with delight. 'He was ever so nice to me. Master Lawrence said as how his sister would never miss them she had so many. Can you imagine having all the ribbons in the world?' Chrissy admired the rainbow of silk in her hand.

'How old are you, Chrissy?' Ivy felt tired just looking at this freshfaced young innocent.

'I'm twelve,' Chrissy supplied with a pleased grin.

'What did Master Lawrence want for the ribbons, Chrissy?' Ivy wanted to throw up.

'He didn't want nothing!' Chrissy blushed. 'Master Lawrence gave me a sweet kiss to bring me luck on my first day in the big city.' She glared at the ragged auld hag trying to turn her good fortune into something ugly.

'Chrissy,' Ivy knew she was beating her head off a brick wall but she had to try, 'did your mother not warn you about the dangers of the big city before you left home?'

'Of course she did,' Chrissy huffed. Hadn't her ears been ringing from the lectures her widowed mother had poured over her head, morning, noon and night?

'And...?' Ivy stared down at the ribbons Chrissy was mashing in her hand.

'But – but – it was not a real kiss or anything like that. Master Lawrence didn't try to take advantage,' Chrissy blustered. 'It was for luck.'

'I'm sure.' Ivy shook her head before stepping up to join the young maidservant on the covered portico. She moved the girl gently out of her way and opened the door at Chrissy's back.

'Mrs Ivors! It's Ivy Murphy!' Ivy roared down the long hallway that led into the kitchen. 'Anything for me today?'

She hoped the cook would come to the door. She was a decent sort, Mrs Ivors. Maybe she could explain the danger of getting too close to Master Lawrence, the chinless lecher, to the young maid staring at her with tearwashed brown eyes.

'You need to take those ribbons back inside, Chrissy.' Ivy knew the servants in these houses knew what was going on. They might cover for the young girl ... this time. She closed the back door but remained standing on the step. 'If you throw yerself on her mercy and ask her politely, Miss Olivia's lady's maid Gladey might wash and iron them ribbons for you before they're missed.' Ivy waited to see if anyone would come out to join them on the step. 'Don't try and wash them yourself. You haven't the skill.' Gladey would probably have the young fool dancing on her hand and foot for the service but it was better than the alternative. Although, a clip around the ear now and being sent home to her mammy might be the best thing that could happen to this young madam.

121

The inner door remained firmly closed. The servants in these houses could smell problems and did everything they could to keep well out of them. Who could blame them? The house was not only their place of work but provided the roof over their heads, the clothes on their backs and the food in their mouths. They preferred not to interfere in the young master's pleasures. Chrissy would not be the first young country girl to find herself in trouble in this house. It had cost the last young girl her life – backstreet abortions could be deadly.

'But...' Chrissy started to protest. She stopped at the look of complete disgust the raggedly dressed woman sent her.

'First lesson is free, Chrissy,' Ivy sighed. 'The ribbons in your hand belong to the daughter of this house, Miss Olivia, a young woman who would have you dismissed from service for making use of her fingernail clippings never mind her silk ribbons. You're on a slippery slope. Learn from it and perhaps you'll live longer than the last young girl Master Lawrence treated to a welcome kiss.'

Ivy grabbed the handle of her pram and turned to leave. She'd done everything she could. Now it was up to young Chrissy how this turned out.

'I'd check to see if there is a key to the lock on the maidservants' bedroom door if I were you, Chrissy!' Ivy shouted over her shoulder as she made her way down the long back yard. 'Ask Gladey or one of the others about the girl who worked here before you.'

Ivy turned her pram in the direction of home.

'I want a cup of tea and something to eat,' she

muttered to herself. 'Who the feck do I think I am – the patron saint of stupid girls up from the country? It's none of my bloody business what goes on in those big houses. Fit me better to tend to me own business and let everyone else tend to theirs.' Ivy knew the young maid wouldn't pay her warning a blind bit of notice. 'I hope to God that young girl catches on to the ways of the bold Master Lawrence before it's too late.' She tried to put the young maid out of her mind. There was nothing else she could do. The city of Dublin was littered with girls like Chrissy.

Ivy rushed along the streets, planning her next step. She couldn't solve the problems of the world. She'd enough problems of her own, what with Declan Johnson skulking around The Lane with his two bruisers always at his side. The women might have put a halt to his gallop but they hadn't stopped him, not by a long shot.

In her mind she planned her actions. She'd take the tin bathtub from its hook outside her back door. Using the hot water from the reservoir on her marvellous black range she'd put the whites in to soak. She'd need to haul more water to refill the reservoir but that shouldn't be a problem. She could walk on the well-soaked items later – after she'd organised everything else she needed to get done.

She turned into The Lane, her mind ablaze with plans.

'Ivy!' Jem Ryan shouted after Ivy's fleeing back. He'd been trying to keep an eye on her. Declan Johnson was keeping quiet but it was the calm before the storm.

'Give me a few minutes, Jem!' Ivy waved over her shoulder without stopping. 'I've a few things to do and then I'll be over.' She grinned broadly to herself. She could get accustomed to having a man put the kettle on for her.

She almost turned around and went back the other way when she saw the long line in front of the outdoor tap. She didn't have the time to catch up on the latest happenings around The Lane. If there was something she absolutely had to know someone was sure to let her know. She sighed deeply and pushed her pram forward.

'Any sign of them nappies, Ivy?' Bitsy Martin shouted as soon as she caught sight of Ivy.

'Sorry, no.'

'Your pram looks loaded.' Jenny Black added her opinion.

'Miss Murphy, do you have a moment?' Betty Armstrong was standing in her open doorway. 'It's rather important.'

Betty had been devastated when Seán and his mother returned to their own home. She had need of advice. She wanted to help.

'I'm sorry.' Ivy didn't even glance over at the tall thin woman dressed all in black. 'I have to rush, perhaps later.' Well, that put the tall hat on that idea, she thought. I'll never be able to fill me water buckets in peace. I'll be there for the bloody day.

Ivy pushed her laden pram through the back door, feeling the women's eyes on her back. She pushed it through into her workroom. She allowed the black knit shawl to drop down around her shoulders and pushed her hands through her tousled head of curls. Since selling her long, long

124

hair, Ivy had been keeping to the convenient shorter length. She refused to even think that the short style suited her. That would be vanity and everyone knew vanity was a sin. She sighed loudly, resigned to the fact that she wouldn't be able to soak the items she'd collected as she'd planned.

'I'm going to have to get the water I need in the middle of the night if this keeps up. I can't tell the women that I've no time to stop and chat.' She pulled the items she'd amassed and, without checking to see what she'd scavenged, laid the bundles on her work table. She ran her hand inside the pram to ensure there was nothing she'd overlooked.

She hurried around her two rooms, checking that everything was in order. The range held glowing embers but, not knowing how long she'd be away, Ivy decided to add more nuggets of wet coal to the fire. When she knew Emmy Ryan was coming to her she normally remembered to leave some kind of stew simmering on the range. When it was just herself she couldn't be bothered. She'd have to pull up her socks or accept Jem's invitation to eat regularly with him.

Ivy checked the back door was locked firmly, then with her head held high she made her way out of her own little nest.

She walked up the metal steps that led from her basement front door to the cobbled square above. She brushed absently at her old army coat, wishing she had something a bit more attractive to wear for Jem. She checked that her shawl decently covered her head and shoulders.

'You're getting above your station, my girl,

thinking about primping yerself up for a man,' she whispered to herself when she stood with her hand on the iron gate that guarded the front entrance to her two rooms. She closed the gate with a half smile, proud of the fact that she had the only rooms in the tenements that boasted two locked entrances. Her da had known what he was about when he'd insisted on renting the basement of the second house from the tunnel.

'There yeh are, Maisie!' Ivy shouted to the woman who rented the two rooms above her head. 'Your turn to scrub the steps, I see.'

Maisie was on her hands and knees, using a donkey stone to scrub the wide stone steps leading up to the open tenement door.

'You don't know yer born, Ivy Murphy, not having to take a turn at scrubbing these steps.' Maisie leaned back on her heels, checking that her shawl was still wrapped securely around her head.

'I have to keep me own entrance steps clean, Maisie,' Ivy objected.

'I've seen yeh, Ivy Murphy.' Maisie used the end of her apron, a flour sack split and hemmed, to wipe the sweat from her brow. 'Yeh throw a bucket of water over the feckin' things and leave it at that. It's no work at all.'

'Yer a great big fibber, Maisie Reynolds,' Ivy grinned. 'You'd be the very one telling me off if I did the likes of that. The smell of stale water would be fierce.' Ivy washed the iron steps down twice a week. She did it on her hands and knees with a damp cloth in one hand and a wad of newspaper to dry them off in the other.

'True enough, I suppose,' Maisie admitted. 'One

126

thing I will say, though, you drink your sweat scrubbing these blessed steps. Ah well, I suppose on a day like this that can't be a bad thing. Here, Ivy, what's going on across the way? I've never seen such comings and goings in all me born days. Honest to God, if it's not new horses coming into The Lane, it's strange men. What's that Jem Ryan up to?' Maisie dipped her rag in the bucket of water on the step beside her. She didn't know why she was wasting her breath. Ivy Murphy would never tell Jem Ryan's business.

'Haven't a clue but if I find out anything I'll let you know.' Ivy stepped out to cross the courtyard. 'Keep your chin up and your chest out, Maisie.'

'Yer a cheeky article, Ivy Murphy.' Maisie stared across at the livery. There was more going on over there than met the eye. She'd be checking it out as soon as she finished with these blessed steps. Someone should tell that girl she needed to get the finger out if she was going to catch a man like Jem Ryan. She was a bit long in the tooth to be only starting to court. That da of hers had a lot to answer for, keeping a young girl tied to his side like that. Still, it was none of her business.

'I'll see yeh later, Maisie.'

Ivy stepped out smartly, her boots ringing on the cobbles. She hurried across the cobbled courtyard. She had a handsome man and a cup of tea waiting for her. What more could she want?

Chapter 13

'Ann Marie, will yeh for God's sake hurry up!' Ivy took Ann Marie's elbow and pulled her along the dark Dublin street. 'I've a lot to get done today.' She had so much stuff in her pram that it was difficult to push the ruddy thing along at the speed she needed. Waiting around for Ann Marie had delayed her.

'I don't know what has you in a bad mood this morning, Ivy Murphy.' Ann Marie had insisted on being allowed to accompany Ivy to the market this morning. It might be Ivy's last visit for a while. 'I didn't delay you that much – Sadie wouldn't let me.' She almost gasped while trying to keep up with Ivy's speed. 'It seems such a long time since we visited the markets together, Ivy.' Her life had become so busy since meeting Ivy and her motley crew that sometimes Ann Marie felt she was spinning in place. She intended to make time now, for the things she found important. Her house was almost as she wanted it and she had people on hand to take care of the day-to-day work.

'You better hurry up or I'm not letting you come with me again.' Ivy yanked on Ann Marie's elbow again to hurry her feet. 'I'm trying to shift as much of my stuff as I can before the panto-mime season starts. I don't think I'll be able to visit the markets twice a week when I'm freezing me parts off outside the Gaiety.'

'You spend a lot of time thinking and planning out your work day, Ivy,' Ann Marie said. 'I think you forget you have to work at friendship too.'

'What do you mean?' Ivy almost stopped in place. She was learning about friendship this year. She'd never had friends when her da was alive.

'I appreciate you're busy,' Ann Marie said softly. 'We all are but you've been neglecting your friends and I think you know it.'

'I have not.'

'Yes, Ivy, you have,' Ann Marie insisted. 'You've made no effort to walk across the Canal and visit me, have you? No,' she didn't wait for a response, 'I've invited you to spend the night, have a bath you don't have to haul water for, but you've never taken me up on the offer. That's hurtful, Ivy.'

'I don't know how to be a friend.' Ivy stared into the darkness, moisture flooding her eyes. She hunched her shoulders and continued to push her pram through the familiar dark streets.

'You need to learn.' Ann Marie was glad she was wearing her steel-toed boys' boots – the rain had left puddles in every dip in the road. 'You can't go around acting like Lady Bountiful–'

'What?' Ivy snorted. 'Are yeh out of yer mind, Ann Marie? Lady Bountiful, I ask yeh! That's for the rich.'

'Lady Bountiful is a term for someone who gives without expecting anything in return.' Ann Marie wasn't going to let the matter drop. Ivy Murphy was cutting a path for herself in life. It was as well she should learn her mistakes from the start and she was just the woman to teach her. 'That's how you act, Ivy.' Ann Marie fought to find the breath to continue speaking. Ivy had increased her walking speed and Ann Marie with her shorter legs was almost running to keep up with her. 'You give to everyone. Look at the situation in The Lane the other night – you'd have given Ginie and her son a bed for the night–'

'They didn't stay with me, did they?'

'That is not the point.' Ann Marie almost sighed with relief when the lights of the market appeared in the distance. She needed to sit down.

'Look,' Ivy stopped in her tracks, 'I want to be a good friend, I really do, but do you think you could hold off on the lecture until I get me business done? I can't be thinking about me failings when I'm trying to get the best price for me goods.'

'Fair enough, but we are not finished with this talk.' Ann Marie's glasses slipped down her nose she gave such an emphatic nod of her head.

'Right.' Ivy started walking again. 'Come on, I'll buy yeh a sausage sambo and a mug of tea.' She'd be glad of something to eat herself and Ann Marie could have a sit-down – the woman was huffing like a bellows.

The two women walked towards the lights of the market, each lost in her own thoughts. The market holders shouted greetings across the space as they worked frantically to set up their stalls. It took many hands to set them up – entire families worked to stretch canvas over their precious stock. When each stall was set up to everyone's satisfaction, most of the people gathered here now would return to their homes, leaving the stallholder in charge.

'Yer usual, twice over this morning, Ivy.' Hopalong gave his welcoming gummy grin. 'How's yerself, Ann Marie?' Behind his stall Hopalong filled two enamel mugs with tea. He put the two mugs on the wood stretched between two wooden supports that made up his stall. There was a tall enamel jug of fresh milk on the stall top to allow people to add their own milk. Hopalong kept a close eye on that milk jug but he knew Ivy wasn't one to filch milk for a mug she kept hidden under her shawl like some women. He got busy making two thick sausage sandwiches.

'Morning, Hopalong.' Ann Marie was perched on one of the hay bales set up to serve as seats for the stall. She sighed contentedly when Ivy passed her a mug of tea. She'd sit here while Ivy started the first stage of her day's work, exchanging insults and promises with the stallholders who came to this stall for their own cups of tea and something to eat. She accepted a paper-wrapped sandwich from Ivy with a nod of thanks. She hid a smile behind one half of what Ivy called a doorstep sambo, two thick rough-cut slices of white bread well filled with sausages sliced thinly lengthwise. She truly loved these mornings.

'Ivy, this stuff is wonderful.' Ann Marie fingered the bits of lace spread over the latest stall Ivy had stopped at to do business. She never could believe the weird and wonderful items on offer at the many stalls.

'Ann Marie, will you get the lead out and come along!' Ivy pulled on Ann Marie's elbow, very conscious of the stallholder's glare. It was a hard enough life standing out in all weathers without having a sightseer blocking potential customers' paths to the stall. 'I have things to do. See yeh, Sally.' She rolled her eyes in the stallholder's direction.

'Not if I see yeh first, Ivy Murphy.' Sally grinned.

Ivy had sold her a load of really good fabric. The starched white lace and ribbons Ivy offered had almost made Sally giddy. She'd make a pretty penny from some of the pieces this very day. She planned to take the ripped linen sheet and some of the lace she'd bought from Ivy home with her. She'd have her daughters turn the thick linen sheet into handstitched collars and cuffs. Her customers could cover the frayed edges of their tired old dresses with the pristine white collars and cuffs. She'd be able to charge more if they made some trimmed in lace. The best part of dealing with Ivy was that the stuff she sold was clean and in good nick.

Sally's stall was set out in sections. She had dividers down the long piece of wood that was her stall. The dividers separated items with clearly marked prices. She kept a close eye on her stall: woe betide anyone who tried to shift stuff from one section to another trying to get a better price. She knew her stock, she had to. Her regulars knew she kept the best of the stuff under her counter. Some of the stuff she'd bought off Ivy could go into the most expensive section of her counter right now. She'd be able to lay the stuff straight out on her stall. That is, as soon as Ivy and her nosy friend left. She didn't want Ivy to see the mark-up on the pieces she'd just bought. No point in giving

132

your supplier an advantage.

'I never knew yeh were one of those that would rob the eye out of a person's head and come back for the lashes,' said Sally. 'Yeh've robbed me blind this day, Ivy Murphy!' She waved her hands, shooing them away.

Ann Marie loved the give and take of the market, the insults running thick and fast. It was a fascinating world and she felt privileged to be allowed to be a small part of it.

'Good luck, Sally.' Ivy grinned, knowing the drill.

'I'll need more than luck to deal with the likes of you, Ivy Murphy.' Sally gave a gummy grin. 'I'll see yeh next week if God spares me.'

'Yeh'll be here for a long time, Sally.' Ivy knew she might not be at the market the following week but it would involve too much explanation to mention it now, so she grinned over her shoulder, shouting, 'God doesn't need the likes of you up there telling him how to run the world!'

It didn't matter if the day was grey, wet and cloudy. The market stallholders were always up for a laugh.

Ann Marie wished she had the confidence to exchange banter with the stallholders but she was afraid to open her mouth and perhaps offend someone.

'Me old man says the same about me, Ivy.' Sally's big stomach shook with the force of her laughter. 'I'm a misunderstood woman.'

'I've often thought that about yeh meself!' Tony Burke shouted from his stall along the line.

'Mind I don't come over there and tell yeh

what's what, Tony Burke,' Sally cackled. 'You be careful with that one, Ivy Murphy. He's a cute whore.'

'Yeh need to be careful what yeh say, Tony.' Ivy, with Ann Marie a fascinated onlooker, stopped in front of Tony's fruit and vegetable stall. 'Sally could flatten yeh with just a look.'

'What can I get yeh this fine winter's day, Ivy?' Tony was cold. The old sacking he wore around his head and shoulders was almost useless. It was soaking wet already but, sure, a laugh was good for what ailed yeh. 'Morning, Ann Marie, have yeh learned to cook yet?' Ivy's posh friend was a familiar figure around the markets.

'I'm afraid I still can't boil an egg, Mr Burke.' She didn't feel comfortable calling the stall-holders by their first names – it seemed overly familiar to her. Her voice with its cut-glass accent seemed out of place in this world.

'She still can't make a decent cup of tea, Tony, which as you know is a sin against God and man.' Ivy pulled the flour sack she'd doubled over and converted into a shopping bag from the interior of her pram. She passed the sack to Tony. 'I want some of yer best potatoes, Tony.' She couldn't believe the amount of goods she'd shifted today. Her pram was almost empty. 'I'll have some of those Spanish onions too.' Ivy examined the goods on offer.

Tony, his wife and sons grew the vegetables on a derelict patch of land that ran along the back of their tenement block. Tony chalked the price of his goods on a freestanding blackboard. Ivy's heart thrilled that she was now one of the people

134

able to read the big white letters on the board.

'Did yeh want carrots, Ivy?' Tony held up a bright orange bunch by their green heads. 'They came in lovely this year. This is the last of me own. I'll be buying them in soon and that will put the price up.'

'Yeah, gi's a few.' Ivy could clean them up and eat them raw. The greens too could be nibbled on while she was on her round. 'I'll have some of your curly kale as well, Tony.'

Ann Marie had walked off to examine the goods on sale. She hadn't a clue what most of the items were but she found it fascinating to see the raw ingredients for many of the meals she enjoyed laid out before her. Perhaps she should learn to cook?

'No cabbage today, Ivy.' The stallholder didn't bother to keep his eye on the posh woman examining his goods. He knew she wouldn't pinch anything. He'd a paying customer in front of him. Cabbage was Tony's best seller. His daughters, good girls who'd married lads with land, grew fields of the stuff and Tony sold everything they could harvest.

'Not today thanks, Tony.' Ivy was rooting through her pockets for the smallest-value coins she could find. She knew the value of the money she carried by touch. It would be a foolish person who pulled out money and stood examining it to make change. Some fly boy would have it out of your hand before you could blink.

'That's yer lot, Ivy.' Tony passed the heavy sack back over his stall. He took the coins Ivy had ready for him and grinned. Ivy Murphy could work his costs out to the penny before he opened

135

his mouth. Her eyesight must be improving, Tony thought. She'd always made him read his prices aloud but lately she'd been able to read the board clear as day herself. More power to her.

'I'm off,' Ivy shouted loudly. 'See yez next week. I'm off to make me fortune.'

'Goodbye, Mr Burke,' Ann Marie offered with a shy smile that, if she did but know it, endeared her to the stallholder.

'Think of us when you're rich, Ivy!' Ma Clements yelled.

'I won't be one of them snobs who forget their friends, Ma.' Ivy stepped out smartly with Ann Marie by her side. 'I'll come by and show yez me mink and diamonds.'

'You do that, flower!' Polly Ormiston yelled. 'Us lot'll have it all off yer back and on our stalls before yeh can blink.'

Ann Marie laughed softly while rushing to keep up with her friend. She splashed gaily through the suspect puddles that glimmered along the cobbles. She was getting better at keeping up with Ivy.

'Where are we going now, Ivy?' She didn't think Ivy could possibly have any remaining articles for sale in her pram. Today had been an exceptionally profitable day for her. Ann Marie had been keeping Ivy company around the Dublin markets long enough to know Ivy's routine. Today her friend had been selling her goods at a speed that rendered Ann Marie speechless. The mornings they spent at the markets spread throughout Dublin went with a speed that fascinated her. Time was different when she was with Ivy – it never hung heavy on her hands. The markets and

Ivy Murphy were better than theatre in her eyes.

'I have a few more things to pick up, Ann Marie. Then I'll be ready to head for home,' Ivy was having difficulty walking with the weight of the money she was carrying about her person.

'You've ruined me, Ivy Murphy.' Ann Marie laughed. 'I would kill for a cup of tea.'

The two women looked at each other and collapsed laughing. Still tittering they started to walk around the shops on the perimeter of the market.

The change in Ann Marie's attitude since her first visit to the markets was marked. She no longer thought of these people as life's unfortunates. They might be poor, have a tough time making ends meet, but that didn't stop them smiling and cracking jokes. Ivy called them the salt of the earth and she was right.

'Morning, Ivy, what can I do yeh for this fine morning?' Bob the Baker shouted as soon as Ivy cleared the open door of his little bakery shop. 'How's yerself, Ann Marie?'

'I'm fine, thank you.' Ann Marie didn't know what to call this man. She'd only ever heard him called Bob the Baker.

'Fine day for ducks, Bob.' Ivy didn't bother to shake the drops of moisture from her clothes. She'd be going back out in it soon enough. She stood and sniffed the air. She loved the smell of fresh-baked bread and cakes. 'I was wondering if yeh had any of yesterday's bread and rolls, Bob.'

'Ivy,' Ann Marie dropped her voice, 'why are you buying day-old bread?' Surely after the morning she'd had Ivy had enough to buy fresh bread.

'Whist!' Ivy glared Ann Marie into silence. Ann

Marie would never understand that to some people a bit of old bread was a luxury.

'Milly,' Bob called to his wife and shop assistant, 'check what we have in the back, will yeh?'

'Thanks, Bob,' Ivy grinned. 'I want a couple of fresh loaves too, please, Bob.' Ivy was almost salivating at the selection of cream cakes displayed on the counter top. Ivy couldn't resist temptation. 'Have yeh anything to pack a few cream cakes in, Bob?'

'A box, Ivy,' Bob shrugged, 'but it'll cost yeh.'

'Don't tell me how much, Bob,' Ivy grinned. 'Me friend here is liable to faint at the price.' She nudged Ann Marie. 'I can't make up me mind what I want, Bob – give us a minute, will yeh?'

'A miserable wet day like this, Ivy, I have nothing but time.' Bob wanted to check his stock in the back anyway but the market brought a lot of extra customers into his shop and he'd hate to leave the counter and miss a sale. Ivy Murphy he knew was trustworthy. She wouldn't pinch his cakes or lick any of the cream.

'Thanks.' Ivy was trying to make the serious choice between a cream slice or a cream apple sponge. 'Ann Marie, pick a cake.'

'Why don't we take the cakes back to my house, Ivy?' Ann Marie could pick up cream cakes for the Lawless family. 'Sadie could make a pot of tea for us. I'm sure she'd be glad of the company. She must get lonely in the house all day with just a baby for company.'

'I'm not refusing your invitation, Ann Marie,' Ivy said softly. 'But I want to discuss some stuff with you, private stuff that I don't want to talk about in front of Sadie. I want to get your advice. Is that all right with you?'

'This once I'll let you away with it,' Ann Marie sighed. She'd never get Ivy into her home at this rate. 'Excuse me, Bob,' she raised her voice to carry into the back room, 'would you bring an extra box for me, please? I want some cream cakes of my own.'

Bob came from the back of the shop carrying two flat cardboard boxes and a large paper bag filled with the day-old bread and rolls.

'Are yeh sure yeh want all this, Ivy?' Bob held up the bag. He'd be glad of a few pence for the stuff. 'There's enough here to feed the army.'

'That's grand, Bob.' Ivy grinned, thinking of Jem's lads. 'I've a hungry army to feed.'

'Well, far be it from me to miss a sale.' Bob shrugged. It was none of his business what people did with their money. If Ivy Murphy could pay for the stuff she was welcome to it. He assembled the two boxes and stood filling them with fresh cream cakes as each woman pointed to her selection.

'Let me pay for these, Ann Marie,' Ivy said when Bob had totted up their purchases. She gave her friend a sharp look, hoping she'd get the message. When Ann Marie gave her the nod she continued. 'You can fix up with me later.' Ivy laid out the correct amount on the counter. It was all in coppers.

'You out singing on the street last night, Ivy?' Bob asked.

'Money's money, Bob.' Ivy was glad to get rid of that much of the coins that were weighing her down.

'That's a fact.' Bob stood and watched while Ivy

packed the bag and boxes holding their purchases into her battered old pram. 'Bye now, ladies – see ye next week.'

'Goodbye,' said Ann Marie with a smile.

'See yeh, Bob,' Ivy called over her shoulder. 'Okay, the butcher's now.' Ivy grabbed the handle of her pram and pointed it in the direction of the butcher shop next door to the bakery.

'Hey, Will, is there anyone working here?' Ivy shouted to the empty shop. The meat hanging from hooks swung in the breeze from the open door. Rabbits and chickens hung by the neck from the rafters. Thank God there were no bluebottles buzzing about the place. Ivy hated the amount of flies and bluebottles that swarmed this butcher's in summer.

Ann Marie tried not to take a deep breath. She preferred her meat to be served, cooked, on a platter.

'I'll be with yeh in a minute.' The smell of roasting meat travelled from the back of the shop.

'While yer back there, Will,' Ivy shouted, 'I'm looking for a bucket of yer best drippin'.' The butcher sold the fat from the dish he roasted his meat in. The brown jellied juices that fell to the bottom of the pan and into the drippin' were delicious. Ivy thought Jem's lads would be thrilled with a chunk of bread spread thickly with fresh butcher's drippin'.

Ann Marie stood in silence, trying not to think of the germs that would breed in this place.

'While you're about it, Will,' Ivy shouted again, 'I want some of your roast beef and a few slices of your ham.' She knew most people didn't possess

140

an oven. She was very fortunate in that regard. If a family were having a party the butcher would roast the meat they bought from him, for a price.

'By jingo, missus,' Will arrived from the back, his rotund body covered by a blood-encrusted white apron, a heavy pot clamped to his large stomach, 'did yeh come up in the pools? Hello, Ann Marie, didn't know yeh were out here – this one,' he gave a nod towards Ivy, 'is making that much noise.'

'Hello.' Ann Marie smiled and tried not to look at the man's apron.

'I'm having a good day, Will,' Ivy said, grinning. 'I thought I'd spread the wealth.'

'Yeh can spread as much of it as yeh want in this direction, Ivy.' Will deposited the pot on the marble countertop. 'Have yeh something to put the drippin' in, Ivy?' Will looked at Ivy's empty hands. 'I don't supply pots, yeh know.'

'Lend us a pot then, Will.' Ivy sighed. She'd completely forgotten she'd need something to carry the drippin' home in. 'I'll send one of the lads back down with the pot tomorrow, promise.'

'Seeing as it's yerself, Ivy...' Will shrugged. 'I wouldn't do it for just anybody.'

'Thanks, Will, yer a gent.' Ivy's smile had Will sucking in his stomach. She was a rare beauty when she smiled, Ivy Murphy. She and her posh friend were a sight for sore eyes. 'I want the makings of a coddle as well, Will.'

'What's a coddle, Ivy?' Ann Marie wished she could paint sufficiently well to capture this scene on canvas. She made a promise to herself at that moment. She was going to buy one of those

Brownie box cameras and record this world Ivy was introducing her to. She wondered if anyone would mind having their picture taken. She'd ask Ivy's opinion.

'A coddle, missus,' Will answered her question, 'is a dish peculiar to Dublin. You won't find it anywhere else, missus. I should know. I've travelled the length and breadth of this country and never seen a coddle anywhere but here. It can have any kind of left-over meat in it, with sliced potatoes and onions, but usually people use sausages and rashers for it.'

'Shout out the prices as yeh go, Will,' Ivy said. 'I want to have me money ready for yeh.'

'Fair enough.' Will started shouting out prices, starting with the rent he intended to charge for the tin can with its lid that he was going to loan Ivy. He knew how good she was with numbers but she'd never keep all those figures in her head – however it paid to keep the customer sweet.

'Here yeh go, Will!' Ivy passed over a copper waterfall of coins. She wondered she didn't pass out at the amount she was spending. It wasn't that long ago since she'd stood outside this shop sniffing the air, unable to buy even the butcher's drippin'.

'Hold on a minute.' Will took a stub of pencil from behind his ear. He licked the lead and used the corner of the brown paper that sat on his counter to jot down the prices, putting his hand on each individual item as he went. He stood counting the figure up for a moment. He checked the money on his counter and blinked in surprise. It was right to the penny. How had she done that?

'That's my lot for today, Will.' Ivy waited while her goods were wrapped securely in brown paper. 'I'll send one of the lads down on his bike with the can tomorrow.' She packed her purchases carefully into her pram. She didn't want the drippin' spilling over her cream cakes. 'See yeh.'

'Yeah, I'll see yeh.' Will stared after the two women.

'Goodbye,' Ann Marie added as the two women left the shop.

Ann Marie's feet were aching inside her steel-toed boys' boots. She was dressed from head to toe in the clothes Ivy had insisted she buy. Ivy had no idea of the number of times Ann Marie, dressed as she was now, had danced around her comfortably furnished suite of rooms, giggling like an idiot at her own image in the mirror.

'Where to now, Ivy?'

'Home,' Ivy answered. 'I'm spittin' feathers, Ann Marie. I want a pot of tea, a sandwich and a cream cake.' She grinned. 'I want to put me aching feet up by the fire and dry out for the first time today.'

'That sounds wonderful.' Ann Marie giggled. The rain was coming down heavier than ever – cold drops of it were dripping off the end of her nose. She had a sudden vision of herself stepping into the street, putting her hand in the air and shouting 'Taxi!' She'd frighten the horses.

'What has you so amused?' Ivy glanced over at her friend.

Ann Marie's body was visibly shaking and it wasn't with cold.

'I was imagining everyone's reaction if I suddenly demanded a cabby.' Ann Marie shared

143

a grin with Ivy. 'Do you think we could store your pram in a cab and travel home in style?'

'I'd like to see you try that, Ann Marie.' Ivy bent over, laughing till tears fell from her eyes. 'They'd send for the do-gooders to take us away.'

'What did you want to discuss with me, Ivy?' Ann Marie asked as the two women strolled through the grimy back streets of Dublin. Ann Marie hadn't even known these streets existed until she'd begun to keep Ivy company on her rounds.

'Wait.' Ivy didn't want to discuss anything where other people could hear. 'Wait until we're home and the tea's made.' Then she added loudly so any interested persons could hear, 'The evenings close in so fast these days. It's practically dark now and it's not even three o'clock.'

'It's winter, Ivy.' Ann Marie shrugged. She didn't know why they were discussing the weather but she'd play along. 'What can you expect? I do like it though when the lamplighter comes around. There's something magical about the glowing blue flames of the gas lanterns.' There, Ann Marie thought, she'd done her conversational bit.

'That there is.' Ivy smirked in Ann Marie's direction. Her friend was learning.

They stepped out of Kildare Street onto Merrion Row.

'We're almost home,' said Ivy.

The two women walked silently and swiftly in the direction of The Lane.

Ann Marie could sense Ivy's unease but she didn't understand the cause. Ivy seemed to be checking everything around them as they travelled the almost deserted city streets. With their heads bent against the lashing rain the two women practically ran through the tunnel leading into The Lane.

Chapter 14

'Ivy Murphy,' Marcella Wiggins hurried over to stop the two women disappearing down Ivy's steps, 'have yeh anything we could cut wood with?'

'No,' Ivy shrugged. 'I don't. What's going on?'

There were people in bunches down at the far end of The Lane from the entrance tunnel. They were gathered in front of Mr Wilson's property. The old man was known to run people off with heavy blows from his big fists and if that didn't work he used his steel-capped boots.

'We're clearing away all that scrub down the end. It should have been done years ago and we used up the last of the wood we had on hand at our All Hallows' Eve party.' Marcella puffed along at a rapid pace, her face glowing red under her black shawl. 'I wanted a word,' she said quietly when she reached the two women.

'Do you want to come in for a cup of tea?' Ivy offered.

'That's good of yeh.' Marcella was tempted but she glanced over her shoulder at the crowd waiting for her. 'I can't, I haven't the time.'

'Well, I'll see yeh later then,' Ivy started to leave.

'Wait a minute.' Marcella stopped Ivy from

145

moving by placing her hand on her shoulder. 'I told yeh, I want to talk to yeh.'

'Should I go over to the livery?' Ann Marie offered in case the subject was private.

'That's all right, pet.' Marcella shook her head. 'You were here the other night so yeh know. Listen to me, Ivy Murphy,' she pushed the sleeves of her tatty jumper up her arms, showing she meant business, 'something has to be done about that Declan Johnson strutting around the place. Someone has got to go and talk to Billy Flint.' She ignored Ivy's gasp and continued. 'The more I got to thinking about it, the more I doubt Billy Flint knows anything about that blaggard.'

'I've never even met the man, Mrs Wiggins.' Ivy could see where this was going.

'I've known Billy Flint man and boy, Ivy.' Marcella stared into Ivy's eyes. The situation with Declan Johnson could not be allowed to continue. What they'd done the other night was like putting a bandage on a broken leg: useless. 'Yer planning to sell them dolls of yours out in front of the Gaiety, aren't yeh?' There wasn't much that was private in The Lane. 'You better have a word with Billy about that, Ivy Murphy, and you know it.'

'I refuse–' Ivy started.

'I don't care what you feel about it, Ivy Murphy,' Marcella interrupted. 'You go talk to the man for all of us here in The Lane. I'll get your one who took over Granny's room to go with you to see Billy Flint. But go you will.' She shook her finger into Ivy's face. She knew a thing or two about your one who was staying in Granny's room. She'd keep it to herself – for the moment.

'I...' Ivy wished she hadn't been raised to obey her elders in all things. She wanted to pull her own hair out. As if she didn't have enough problems already.

'That's my final word on the matter.' Marcella turned to go back to the crowd she'd been ordering around. They had probably been bone idle since she left them. She had to do everything herself. 'I'll be about me business now but you mark my words, Ivy Murphy.'

'Mr Wilson will do his nut when he sees what you've done to his place!' Ivy shouted after the woman. She couldn't believe even Marcella would go up against the man who ruled that end of The Lane.

'Pity about him.' Marcella waved her hand over her shoulder in farewell and hurried away.

'That woman is a force of nature,' Ann Marie said as she picked up the handle end of the pram. 'This wet weather doesn't seem to slow her down. I must admit I'll be glad to get out of the cold and rain.'

'It's all right, Ann Marie, you won't melt,' Ivy answered absentmindedly. She took her keys from her pocket, picked up the business end of the pram and began to back down her outside steps. She unlocked her front door and Ann Marie pushed the pram inside with a sigh of relief.

'We can push the pram into your back room, Ivy,' Ann Marie suggested. 'I'll unpack it onto the kitchen table – then I can return the pram to the front room.' She knew Ivy had a great deal to take care of as soon as she came through her door.

'Thanks, Ann Marie.'

The two women hurried towards the back room, Ivy pushing the pram in front of her.

'Let me get organised, Ann Marie.' Ivy began to take care of the range as she spoke. She'd banked the fire before leaving and now raked it out before adding a few sticks, the stub end of a candle and fresh coal to the burning embers. She wanted a fast blaze. She filled the kettle with hot water from the range before putting the kettle on the range top directly over the coals. The water would come to a boil in no time.

Ann Marie loved watching Ivy at work. It was an education.

Ivy removed her wet coat and shawl. She dragged one of the kitchen chairs over to the range and draped her wet clothing over it. 'Give us your coat and shawl, Ann Marie. You shouldn't stand around in wet clothes. Take off them boots. I'll find yeh a pair of dry socks.'

While Ann Marie removed her wet clothing Ivy dropped to her knees to root under the big brass bed. The two women would be warm and dry by the time the pot of tea was made and ready to pour. Ivy passed Ann Marie a pair of handknit socks then sat on the bed to put her knitted slippers on.

Ann Marie dropped into one of the ugly chairs placed in front of the range. It amused her that the dilapidated chairs were the most comfortable she'd ever sat in. She watched Ivy kick an empty bucket under the brass tap of the reservoir. She used the water directly from the tap to wash her hands while the water trickled into the bucket. It made her appreciate her own modern bathroom all the more.

Ivy cut the bread and assembled roast-beef sandwiches on the worktop of her tall cupboard. She carried a small table over to the range and placed it between the two easy chairs. She put her best dragonfly-decorated cups and saucers on the table with milk and sugar in the matching jug and bowl. The roast-beef sandwiches she put on one of her large plates. Ivy checked the table, making sure they had everything they needed before she joined Ann Marie, dropping into the stuffed chair across the range.

'You said you wanted my advice, Ivy? What about?' Ann Marie knew Ivy's pride insisted that she could do everything herself but sometimes one needed help.

'So many things,' Ivy pushed her hands through her hair. 'I don't know if I'm on me head or me heels sometimes.'

Ann Marie took a cup of tea and a sandwich and waited.

'I've spent me whole life counting pennies and squeezing ha'pennies. I could never stop me da from taking every penny I earned.' Ivy laughed gently. Her big strong da had removed the money from her hands almost before she'd come through the door. 'I never even thought of keeping the money away from him, to be honest.' She sipped her tea and nibbled on one of the sandwiches. 'Now the amount of money I made from the sale of those baby dolls made me dizzy, Ann Marie.' Ivy had bought the entire stock of Harry Green the wholesaler's naked baby dolls. With the help of the Lawless family she'd dressed the dolls in exquisite handmade, one-of-a-kind baby outfits. 'The money is still coming in from the shop owners who bought the dolls. I'm getting cheques in the post from around the country these days.' She shook her head in wonder at the changes taking place in her life. 'That's okay, that's all right, I can deal with that. You showed me how.'

'So, what is the problem?' Ann Marie nibbled on a delicious roast-beef sandwich. She'd learned there was no use trying to hurry Ivy when she was discussing her business.

'I don't know what to do with the cash money, Ann Marie,' Ivy whispered. 'The coins I deal with all of the time. What do I do with those?'

'I thought Brother Theo found you a tutor for economics?'

'He did,' Ivy nodded. 'Mr Clancy comes to the livery two evenings a week now. He's teaching me, Jem, John and some of the lads all about book-keeping. He's a wonderful teacher. I'm learning all about profit and loss.' Ivy stood suddenly and went to put another sandwich together. 'I'm learning about percentages and so many other things. I'm keeping my own accounts in a special book Mr Clancy got for me.'

Ivy hadn't known it but she'd always kept accounts. She'd simply done it all mentally, unable to write the facts and figures down.

'That's all paperwork, Ann Marie.' Ivy brought the freshly made sandwiches over to the range. She emptied the slop from their cups into a bowl she'd set out before pouring more tea. She dropped into the chair facing Ann Marie, her entire figure a picture of despair. 'What do I do with the actual money, Ann Marie, the pounds, shillings and pence?'

'I don't understand.'

'The feckin' money, Ann Marie!' Ivy grabbed two handfuls of her own hair. 'I'm that worried about the stuff. Now that I know Declan Johnson is back in The Lane I'm almost afraid to leave the house. I can't go on like this. There must be a way to keep money. A way I know nothing about.' She was almost wailing.

'Ivy, explain!' Ann Marie leaned forward and shook the other woman's knees.

Ivy jumped to her feet and hurried over to the big brass bed. She fell on her knees, her rear end sticking up in the air. Her upper body disappeared under the bed. With a lot of grunting and huffing she began to drag a selection of old cardboard boxes, biscuit tins and thick lumpy knotted socks out from under the bed.

'The money, Ann Marie!' Ivy stood, panting, and pointed her finger dramatically towards the floor covered in containers. 'What in the name of God do I do with the money?'

Ann Marie stood slowly. She walked over to join Ivy by the bed, staring down at the collection on the floor. 'Ivy, are you telling me that those,' she pointed, unsure what to call the motley items on the floor, 'are full of cash?' She was trying not to shout.

'What else am I supposed to do with it?' Ivy glared. 'I never knew having money was such a bloody headache. I spend half me time worrying about it and the other half making it. What am I supposed to do, Ann Marie?'

'You put it in the bank, Ivy Murphy,' Ann Marie snapped. 'That's what you do with it. Put it in the bank and allow them to worry about keeping it safe. That is what you have a bank account for.'

'*How?*' Ivy snapped. 'When I have enough cheques I get dressed in me best and go in to the bank to make a deposit. You taught me how to do that. But I take cash several times a week and have to walk about the bloody town with cash all over me. I can't just walk into that fancy bank in me rags. What would I do with me pram? They'd kick me out before I could open me mouth. But, if I get meself all dolled up and keep making special trips to the bank, that will get me noticed.'

'Push that lot,' Ann Marie pointed a toe towards the items on the floor, 'back under the bed.'

'That's not all, Ann Marie.' Ivy wanted to get all the information she could. 'What am I going to do with the money I collect for the Cinderella dolls?' She used her foot to kick the items back under the bed.

'That money too should be lodged in the bank – of course.' Ann Marie returned to her seat.

'Ann Marie, I'm not going to sell those dolls off cheap.' Ivy used the water in the bucket still standing under the tap to rinse her hands before sitting down.

'I know that, Ivy.' Ann Marie had listened to Ivy's views on the price of her dolls often enough.

'I'll be standing out in the street, in front of God and everyone, selling those dolls. I'll be shouting out the price I'm charging for all the world to hear. It won't take a genius to do the sums, Ann Marie.' Ivy had been sick with fear, carrying her earnings around the streets of Dublin. How much worse would it be with what she considered a small fortune in her pocket? 'The go-boys that hang around the streets trying to make a quick copper will hear me sales pitch, Ann Marie. They will watch me carefully. Watch the sales I'll hopefully make. They'll know I'm carrying a lot of cash on my person. I'll suddenly become a person of interest to people who think nothing of knocking someone around for a penny, never mind pounds.'

'Ivy, you'll be in danger!' Ann Marie gasped. The problem of the money Ivy was keeping under the bed was easily solved. But how would they keep Ivy safe while she stood openly in the street making money? She knew Ivy believed her to be an expert in all things to do with money but she'd never come up against this problem before.

'At the very least you need a bank bag and a key to the night safe so you can lodge your money safely,' Ann Marie stated with authority.

'What's them when they're at home?'

'I'm sure you've seen the clerks in Grafton Street dropping the big leather bank bags into the wall safes outside the banks?'

'I think so,' Ivy said slowly.

'I'm not completely sure how it works, Ivy.' Ann Marie had a vague idea but she preferred to be sure of her facts. 'We need to pay a visit to the bank and enquire about possibilities.'

'That only solves some of me problem,' Ivy sighed. 'It would be a simple matter to grab the bag from me hands. I don't think I could stop a pair or even one grown man intent on mischief.'

'What does Jem have to say about all of this?'

She knew Jem took Ivy's safety very seriously.

'He wants me to talk to Billy Flint,' Ivy admitted. 'Oh, and he thinks we should get married,' she threw into the conversation.

'Wait, wait!' Ann Marie threw both arms up in the air. She'd find out who Billy Flint was later. Right now she wanted to get to the meat of the matter. 'Ivy Rose Murphy, you are the giddy limit. Do you mean to tell me, Jem has proposed marriage and you are only now getting around to telling me!' It wasn't a surprise to hear Jem had proposed but she'd thought Ivy would have been more excited.

Ivy dropped her chin into her chest and whispered, 'I asked him to give me time.'

'I'm sorry – I thought you'd be happy to marry Jem – was I wrong?'

'No, not really. Jem is the only man I could ever imagine marrying.' Ivy shrugged. 'It's just that I have so much I want to do with my life. So much I'd like to achieve. When a woman gets married she's supposed to put her husband and childer before everything else in her life. I don't know if I can do that, Ann Marie.' Ivy was shamefaced.

'As an outsider looking in,' Ann Marie said, 'I think what you and Jem have is very special.'

'He'll want me to give up me round, me business, to stay home and take care of him and I can't do that.' She couldn't bring herself to mention her unnatural fear of constant pregnancy. The words were stuck in her throat.

'Did Jem say that?' It would surprise Ann Marie if he had.

'No.'

'Then how on earth do you know what he thinks or feels, Ivy?' Ann Marie demanded. 'This is just what I was trying to talk to you about earlier. Friendship, any kind of relationship should be about give and take. No one can read your blessed mind, Ivy. You have to talk to people, tell them what you're thinking, what you're feeling. You have simply got to learn to give and take, Ivy.'

'I'll try,' Ivy whispered. Perhaps Ann Marie would understand her concerns about limiting the number of babies a woman had. She'd never know if she didn't ask. Would her friend hate her? She was angry at herself. She had Ann Marie sitting in front of her and couldn't even work up the courage to ask the woman for her advice. She was going to do it...

She had opened her mouth to try and bring the subject up when she noticed Ann Marie pull a timepiece from her pocket.

'I need to leave, Ivy.' Ann Marie put her watch back in her pocket. She jumped to her feet and began to dress herself in her still damp outer clothing.

'I'll ask if one of Jem's lads will walk you home.' Ivy stood. She wanted to kick herself for missing her chance. Now she'd have to work up her courage all over again.

'That's not necessary.'

'Yes, it is.' Ivy wrapped her damp shawl around her shoulders. She picked up Ann Marie's box of cream cakes and waited. 'Declan Johnson is dangerous, Ann Marie – you don't want someone like him following you home. Let one of Jem's lads

155

walk out with you. If Conn's about, that would be great – I'd feel happier if I knew someone was seeing you safely home.'

Chapter 15

Ivy pushed her heavy pram along the street, her mind consumed with plans and problems. She simply didn't know where the time was going. Jem wanted her to go visit Billy Flint before the year got much older. If Billy Flint put out the word on the streets that she was off limits she'd be as safe as houses walking around the place. She'd be glad to know that she had protection, but how much would something like that cost her? Billy Flint did nothing for nothing. Ivy had been putting it off but the closer it came to pantomime season the more she tossed and turned at night.

A memory of Emmy Ryan at the Halloween party brought a smile to her lips. It had been a simple matter to make a black cat and a witch's hat for the little girl. She'd felt guilty because she hadn't put more effort into the costume but it seemed that these days there simply weren't enough hours in the day to get everything she needed done. Emmy hadn't seemed to mind. She'd hugged the little black cat close all evening as she ran around the place. The child seemed to be everywhere at once. She'd almost drowned bobbing in the galvanised tub for apples, her teeth had been in danger as she tried to catch an apple dangling from a string held aloft by a tall lad standing on a chair, and it was only by the grace of God that her fingers hadn't been crushed when she'd borrowed one of the workmen's hammers to open the nuts and coconuts that had been collected by the older children.

Little Seán had seemed to have the time of his life too. He'd never left Emmy's side, running around with her and jumping to obey her every command.

Ivy's mind whirled while her feet trod the familiar alleys and back lanes. She'd reduced her visits to the Dublin markets. She had too much to do. It struck her as amusing that, the less she visited the markets, the more the stallholders seemed to think they were missing out on something. She was in great demand when she did manage to make a dash to the markets.

'I'll have to make time to teach Emmy a party piece.' She took her notebook out of her pocket and wrote that down. The child needed to be able to perform some little ditty when called upon at one of The Lane's many street parties.

She'd paid a visit to the bank with Ann Marie and set herself up with a bank bag for the night safe. The weekend before the bank visit she'd counted up the money she'd had stashed under the bed. She'd almost passed out at the total she'd been keeping hidden. She'd honestly never realised just how much her round earned over a long period. She'd never had the money in her hand long enough to become aware of just how lucrative her business was. Her da had seen to that. At Ann Marie's suggestion she'd sorted the coins by type.

The bank teller hadn't counted the coins – he'd weighed the money and his total had matched Ivy's to the penny. She'd wanted to apologise to the poor man for the sheer volume of coins she'd pushed across the bank counter at him. Ann Marie had advised her to say nothing – that was what a bank was for after all, taking and counting money. Ivy had followed the expert's advice.

Sometimes she found it hard to believe the direction her own life was taking. What with a posh friend, a lovely man who wanted to marry her and money in the bank, well, it was past believing. If her da had a grave he'd be rolling in it. But he hadn't. His body had gone to the College of Surgeons for medical research.

She shook herself, then smiled when she realised what point she'd reached in her round.

'Hey, Curly, e'er a chance of a sup of tea?' Ivy called out to the apparently empty wooden shack sitting smack-bang in the middle of the alley that ran along the back entrances to the fancy houses forming one side of Fitzwilliam Square.

Ivy applied a bit of pressure to her pram. The weight of it caused her to smile in delight. Wednesday was her day for wandering further afield on her round. She didn't try and make it back to The Lane at midday, preferring to carry on until the afternoon. But she did make a point of being back safely in her own two rooms before complete darkness fell.

'That yerself, Ivy?' Curly Jones, his bald head well wrapped in old sacking, another sack around his shoulders, stuck his head around the rim of his wooden security shack. 'It'd skin yeh out there today, girl. Get yerself in here in the dry – the kettle's on.' He put his lips together and gave a shrill whistle. 'Won't be a minute till Moocher gets here.'

Ivy parked her pram to the side of the shack. The smell of burning metal was a welcome scent: it meant heat. Curly never let the fire in his galvanised bucket go out.

The tall, narrow, three-sided shack was one of many dotted around the wealthier areas of Dublin. Outside security, the men who lived in these pitiful shacks laughingly called themselves.

'Looks like yer doing all right for yerself today.' Curly gave a gummy grin and a nod towards Ivy's pram. 'The springs on that thing are about knackered, Ivy. Yeh need to see to them. Yeh have to take care of yer equipment, don't yeh know?'

'It seems like every house around the square is doing a spring clean in winter.' Ivy shrugged. It was none of her business what the wealthy got up to. She was picking up more stuff than ever from these houses. Her pram was loaded with stuff she couldn't wait to examine.

'Well, the world is changing, don't yeh know, Ivy? What with this great new Irish freedom we're all supposed to be enjoying.' He spat lustily into the bucket at his feet. The glob of spit sizzled on the flames. 'But there's some living in fear of what us wild Irish might get up to.' He shared an understanding glance with Ivy on the vagaries of people. 'There's a lot of the wealthy getting out of the country while the going is good.' He whistled loudly again. 'That Moocher, he gets slower every day.' He grinned broadly. 'But he'll be here as soon as the brew is ready to pour out. The lad's got a mighty nose on him. I swear he can smell a cup of tea from a mile away.'

'Then him and me have something in common.'

Ivy peeled back the cover of her pram. She'd baked last night with these two men in mind. They were a good sort and always had a cup of tea and hot gossip ready for her on her Wednesday trek around Fitzwilliam Square. When they could afford it they shared the grub they brought from the Penny Dinners with her. Sometimes, when her brothers were little, the food she got here had been all she tasted for days at a time.

'I brought buttered scones and milk with me.' Ivy grinned, taking a tightly sealed can of milk from the depths of her pram and then picking up a newspaper-covered parcel that was tucked down the side. 'We'll eat like the nobs today, Curly.'

'B'god, we will that, Ivy.' Curly licked his lips at the promised treat. 'Yer coming up in the world yerself these days, ain't yeh, Ivy?' He had noticed a definite improvement in the young woman he'd known since she was knee-high to a grasshopper.

'I can't complain, Curly.' Ivy took a seat on a propped-up broken chair that would end up in the bucket fire before too long.

'Well, yeh could complain, Ivy, but who would listen to yeh?' Curly thought it was a sad state of affairs that her da had to die before Ivy could blossom. Éamonn Murphy had been a good mate, always ready to buy a fella a drink, but Curly thought young Éamonn hadn't done right by his daughter. The poor nipper, out in all weathers, keeping her menfolk fed and fat. It wasn't right, not right at all.

'Here's Moocher now,' he grinned. 'Didn't I tell yeh he could smell the tea?'

'That yerself, Ivy?' Moocher, a tall thickset man, shambled into the clearing. 'I'm glad to see yeh because I have something to say to yeh. Yeh'd want to be keeping your wits about yeh, Ivy. I've seen a fella hanging about behaving "in a suspicious manner" as the Garda would say. I want yeh to mind how yeh go, Ivy Murphy.'

Ivy felt a shiver run down her spine. 'Do you know Declan Johnson, Moocher?' She'd seen Declan around the place – watching her. He made sure she'd seen him. The man enjoyed terrifying women. 'Could it be him?'

'That waste of space!' Moocher spat lustily into the dirt at his feet. 'I'd give the likes of him a feed of knuckle-sandwich if I saw him hanging around the place. If that bit of Johnson filth is bothering you, Ivy, you come to me. I'd soon sort him out.' Moocher held up one giant fist and shook it. He couldn't abide any man that abused women. 'I couldn't make out the face of the fella hanging about but he was dressed in the best, that much I can tell yeh. What's the likes of him doing around the back lanes, I ask meself?'

'Get yerself in here.' Curly was accustomed to Moocher's constant dire warnings. He'd learned to ignore them to a large extent. 'Ivy Murphy has invited us to dine.' Curly laughed so hard at his own wit he almost choked on the hacking cough that caught him unawares.

Moocher moved with more speed than Ivy had ever seen from him. He took the smaller man by

161

the shoulders, beating on his back with his strong hands.

'Give over, yeh daft ha'porth! You'll have me lungs coming out me front.' Curly pushed the younger man away. He took a soiled rag from his pocket and spat into it, then examined his spittle. 'No blood, Mooch – we're clear – no blood.' The fear of TB or 'consumption' as they called it struck terror into the heart of every man and woman.

'Sit yerself down, Mooch.' Ivy took a chipped enamel mug from Curly's trembling hand. The hacking cough had frightened him, she knew. 'We're dining in fine style today.'

She unscrewed the lid from her milk can, then opened the paper parcel to reveal scones rich with raisins and thickly spread with real butter.

'Help yourselves, lads!' Ivy took two of the scones onto her own knees, leaving ten for the men to share between them. 'Made by me own lily-white hands.' She grinned with delight. It did her heart good to be able to share her new-found fortune with people who had helped her when she was in need.

'B'god, them there's delicious, Ivy,' Curly said, crumbs dropping down onto his bristle-encrusted chin.

'A rare auld treat, Ivy,' Moocher concurred, reaching for a second scone. He'd swallowed the first one whole, not bothering to introduce it to his teeth.

'So,' Curly bit into his second scone with pleasure, 'about this queer fella yeh say yeh saw?'

'A strange sort.'

The two men took their job seriously. This was

162

their patch. They wouldn't allow any strangers to wander into their little piece of ground. The servants in these houses were their friends – they looked out for the two men and the men looked out for them. Curly and Mooch didn't give a hoot about the wealthy owners of these houses. If some swag-man helped himself to the pretties from one of the houses the men turned a blind eye. Touch anything belonging to the servants, however, and the two men would fall on you like the wrath of God.

'Like I said, he was dressed like a gent,' Moocher reported, 'but he was wandering around the back lanes where he didn't belong.' He shrugged. 'He'd be worth keeping an eye on.'

'Was he lost?' Curly passed another scone to his friend.

'Don't think so.' Moocher accepted the scone. 'He was eyeing up the entry ways. I didn't like the smell of him.' He pressed a dirty finger to the side of his nose knowingly.

'Well, keep your eyes peeled.' Curly shrugged. They had no right to question people who wandered into their area but that didn't stop them keeping a close eye on the comings and goings.

'Thanks for the cup of tea, lads.' Ivy put her empty mug on the bare ground the three-sided hut stood on. She emptied the rest of the milk from her can into the empty mug. 'That's set me up for the rest of the day.'

'We'll look out for yeh next Wednesday, Ivy,' Curly said. 'Thanks for the grub.'

'Keep your eyes peeled for that stranger, Ivy,' Moocher stopped eating long enough to say.

'Shout out if yeh need us.'

'I will, lads, thanks.' Ivy stood up, shaking her old coat out to remove crumbs. She put the empty can into her pram, took a firm grip on the pram handle and got ready to continue on her way. 'Look after yourselves.'

'See yeh!' the two men shouted together. They were more interested in the food Ivy had left with them.

Chapter 16

'Auntie Ivy, Auntie Ivy!' The little girl was almost vibrating with impatience.

'Miss Emmy, what are you doing out in the street?'

Ivy didn't like to see any child standing near the tunnel leading into the hidden square that housed the tenement block. The men leaving the pub used the place as a toilet. The women of The Lane tried to keep the place clean but it was a constant battle. The overpowering smell of urine wafted out of the tunnel.

'There's murder going on in The Lane!' The words shot from Emmy Ryan's red lips. Jem's adopted niece couldn't wait to share what she knew. Her green eyes were wide and gleaming, her long black hair bounced around her slim shoulders and the deep red wool of her coat and matching hat echoed the bright red flush on her cheeks.

'Is that a fact?' Ivy smiled fondly and waited for

Emmy to pass on her earth-shattering news. It could be something as simple as an infestation of mice or the far more regular scene of two women throwing off their shawls and getting ready to come to blows over their children.

'The Authorities are in The Lane!'

'Are they?' Ivy said faintly. She felt her heart sink. 'Did you happen to see where these people were visiting?'

'The Johnsons! Biddie Milligan was with me and she said it was the Johnsons' place,' Emmy supplied importantly. 'Jimmy Johnson came charging over to the livery. He was white as snow, Auntie Ivy, shaking and shivering. He's hiding in one of the horse stalls.'

'That's all we need around here – do-gooders.' Ivy closed her eyes tiredly. The Johnsons were a disgrace, everyone knew that, but bringing in the authorities to sort them out only made head-aches for everyone else.

'You run on ahead, Emmy.' Ivy wanted time to pull herself together.

'I want to stay with you, Auntie Ivy.'

Emmy Ryan, the child born Miss Emerald O'Connor of Galway, was loving her life running wild around the streets of Dublin. Halloween had been a revelation to the gently raised child. She'd had the time of her life dressed as a witch and begging around the streets of Dublin. Emmy loved everything about her new life. She had a new family, and no more shouting, beatings and pinches.

'All right, I'll come with you.' Ivy couldn't resist that pleading look.

Conn was standing in the open door of the

165

livery. 'Ivy, I suppose the "News of the World",' he nodded towards Emmy, 'has told yeh what's going on?'

'Some of it,' Ivy admitted. 'Give us a hand getting me pram down me basement steps, will yeh?'

'Don't want to walk past the do-gooders, do yeh?' Conn grinned. 'I can't say I blame yeh. Your uncle is looking for you, Emmy,' he told the little girl when she seemed all set to accompany them. 'You'd better run on inside now.'

They watched the little girl run into the livery.

'I want to change me clothes.' Ivy with Conn at her side pushed her pram across the cobbles. 'If I have to face a bunch of auld biddies I want to be dressed to impress.' She giggled at the very thought of her impressing the quality.

'Can't see why yeh'd bother.' Conn grabbed one end of the huge pram. He backed down the steps, taking most of the pram's weight while Ivy carried the handle end, 'Those auld biddies don't have a patch on yeh, Ivy Murphy. Yer feckin' gorgeous.'

Conn, four years younger than Ivy's twenty-two, considered Ivy Murphy, with her pale cream skin, big violet-blue eyes and mop of blue-black curls, one of the most beautiful women in the world. Not that he'd seen all the women in the world, mind, but still. Ivy was tall for a woman but Conn liked that. Ivy's long, slim, elegant figure was kept well hidden but Conn knew it was there. If Ivy ever had the chance to glam herself up in powder and paint like the society women he'd seen around the town, there'd be no stopping her. She'd take over the world, and he'd help her.

166

'Thank yeh, kind sir.' Ivy smiled gently at the compliment. Then she whispered, 'What's going on, Conn?'

'Someone reported young Seán wasn't attending school.' Conn grimaced. 'One of the nuns and a school official came to check into the matter. You'd think the sky had fallen with all the noise around here after that. People have been pouring in here ever since. They took Ginie and anyone else they found in the Johnsons' place away by force, Ivy. I didn't see Seán but he must have been there. The other little ones walked out of that basement like lambs to the slaughter.'

'That will soften the bold Declan's cough.' Ivy grimaced.

'Declan wasn't there.'

'That just puts a top hat on the whole thing, Conn.'

Ivy was disgusted. Why did people like Declan Johnson seem to escape whatever trouble came their way?

'Do we know where they took them?' Ivy asked with a sinking heart. This wasn't the first time people of The Lane had been taken never to be seen again. The first thing the do-gooders would do was separate mother and child. Ginie Johnson would do her nut.

'Ginie was screaming fit to burst your eardrum when they dragged her out of that basement,' Conn said. 'It's a hell of a thing, Ivy.'

Ivy pulled her keys from the pocket of her ancient army coat. She needed to get inside, give herself a quick lick and get changed. She wasn't going to sit shivering in her rooms waiting for a

167

knock on the door.

'Get up there and see what's going on, Conn.' Ivy didn't wait to see him leave. She shoved the heavy pram into the front of her two rooms, her workroom. She dropped her keys on the workbench and then with swift fingers she snatched up the black wool skirt sitting there. She shimmed out of the worn outfit she'd been wearing. She let everything fall to the floor of her workroom and kicked the worn outfit out of her way with an impatient foot. She decided that this was the last time she would ever wear that outfit. She had the money now to buy herself decent clothes. She needed to realise that. But she didn't remove the tweed boy's trousers she'd bought to wear under her work skirt. She'd need the warmth if she was to stand in the open air for very long. She was pleased with the fit of the black skirt she'd made from two torn skirts she'd scored on her round. The skirt reached from her waist to the top of her work boots. Ivy looked at her feet. She couldn't go out there wearing these boots. Not with God only knew who about. Ivy sighed deeply – this getting-dolled-up lark was time-consuming.

Ivy dropped to the floor and began tearing at the laces of her boots. The noise from the street continued to echo around her room. Ivy shivered, remembering the visits paid to The Lane by the Black and Tans.

Éamonn Murphy, Ivy's Da, had been terrified of the Black and Tans. Her da's fear had only deepened Ivy's dread of the lawless men. Her big strong da feared nothing and no one else. He hadn't been alone in his fear. Ivy remembered her da barricading his children behind a hastily erected defensive wall of objects whenever the warning of the Black and Tans' approach echoed through The Lane.

Ivy shook off the memories of those terror-soaked hours crouched on the floor surrounded by her brothers, her da standing like a tall oak tree waiting for whatever trouble was coming.

She kicked off the boots and ran swiftly into the back room. She gave the black range her attention, raking out the ashes and adding coal she had wet to make it last longer. Who knew how long she'd be away?

She dropped to her knees at the side of the giant iron bed. With her fingers she felt around and pulled out a pair of beige calfskin boots and a brown-paper bag holding her best blouse and cardigan.

She used water from the range reservoir to fill one of her enamel bowls. With a bit of soaped damp flannel she gave her face, neck and arms a quick swill.

'Can yeh see me, Da?' She pulled her best clothes on over her damp flesh. 'I'm using yer big mirror.' She watched the woman in the mirror grin. 'Yeh might have been concerned about my vanity, Da, but yeh weren't that fussy about yer own, were yeh?' Éamonn Murphy had forbidden Ivy the use of a mirror, claiming it would lead to the sin of vanity. 'You always liked to look your best, Da.' She smoothed our the lines of her clothes. 'I watched yeh get ready many's a time. I never realised how much feckin' work was involved. Hat's off to yeh, Da!'

She ran her fingers through her short crop of blue-black curls, then licked and bit at her lips before patting her cheeks to add colour to her pale cream skin.

She grabbed her relatively new black wool shawl. With a practised swirl she covered her head and shoulders, hiding her white figure-hugging blouse and pale peach-coloured hand-knit cardigan. The shawl covered her body to her knees. 'Right. I'm decent.'

Ivy turned away from the mirror and checked that her back door was locked. She grabbed her keys on her way out. It was time to see what was going on in the world.

'Ivy, I was coming to get you.' Jem Ryan was waiting at the gate that stood guard to the iron steps that led down to Ivy's rooms. His green eyes were glistening, his face was chalk-white, his clean-shaven jaw tightly clenched. 'Make sure your place is locked up tight. Then come up quick.' He glanced back over his shoulder, checking to see who might be paying any attention to him.

'What's going on, Jem?' Ivy shook the door at her back to check it was locked. She ran swiftly up the steps.

'Health visitors.' Jem uttered the words that struck terror into every woman in The Lane. He pulled Ivy under his arm and, with her body tucked tightly against his, hurried across the open ground that led to his livery building.

'Where?' Ivy had to fight to free her head. She needed to see what was going on.

The open ground was covered with people Ivy

had never seen before. Garda in their blue uniforms, men and a few women in white coats littered the place. A truck they must have greased to get through the opening into this hidden enclave of poverty and despair was parked in the middle of the courtyard.

'Jaysus, Jem, it's an invasion,' Ivy gasped.

'I want you to get upstairs, Ivy.' Jem almost pushed Ivy in through the door being held open by Conn. 'You don't want this lot getting ahold of you. I've told Emmy to stay upstairs and wait for you. There's a window up there you can open. You'll see and hear everything that goes on out here.' He feared Ivy would never be willing to hide away while her friends and neighbours were in trouble.

'What's the story, Jem?' Ivy dug her heels in, resisting being pushed around the place.

'Ivy, them women of Declan's...' He took Ivy by the shoulders. He held her in front of him, staring into her eyes. 'The poor mares are diseased.' He watched the colour leach from Ivy's cheeks. 'I need you to stay upstairs out of sight and keep Emmy with you.' He shook her shoulders gently to underline his seriousness. 'I want you to hide up there until I give you the all clear. Can you do that, Ivy?' Jem was working hard to improve his manner of speech. Not that Ivy noticed that at the moment.

'Okay.' Ivy was incapable of saying anything more. She understood Jem's warning. The two women that Declan brought to the Johnsons' place were diseased – probably with syphilis, a communicable venereal disease. The authorities

171

would now have the power to examine every man, woman and child in The Lane and they wouldn't be gentle about it. No wonder the place was being overrun by official figures.

'I'll take care of Emmy,' Ivy almost whispered. This could well prove to be one shock too many for the little one.

Besides, Jem didn't have to state aloud the desperate need to keep Miss Emmy Ryan hidden away from all official eyes.

'Right, I'll go up.'

Jem released her shoulders and watched her walk away in the direction of the ladder that led up to the room built under the rafters of the livery. The large comfortable room set well back in the eaves was Jem's home.

'Conn,' Jem snapped as soon as Ivy disappeared from view, 'give me a hand.' He marched over to the heavy ladder and with swift experienced hands pulled it away from the rim of the hayloft that surrounded the livery. If you didn't know a room existed under the roof, a casual glance would see only the hay, oats and bits of discarded tack.

'We'll hide this ladder behind the stalls for the moment.' Jem grunted with the sudden weight of the free-falling ladder. Conn grabbed one end and the two men wrestled it into a corner of the stable, well hidden behind occupied stalls. The horses stamped restless feet and their steel-shod hooves rattled, but they made no other sound. They knew these men.

'We'd better do this then, Conn.' Jem brushed Conn down, checking for anything that might attract attention – then Conn did the same for him.

'Those feckin' Johnsons–' Conn started to say before remembering that one of those Johnsons was hiding in the livery office. 'What are we going to do about Jimmy?' He looked at Jem, expecting him to know the answer.

'I'll handle it.' Jem sighed. It was always one step forward two steps back around here. 'I'm afraid you need to get out there,' he nodded towards The Lane, 'and let them examine you.'

'Ah Jaysus, Jem!' Conn's head almost disappeared into his wide shoulders.

'We have no choice now – you know that as well as I do.' Jem didn't want to expose his manhood to questing hands any more than Conn did but they had no choice. No one would take their word that they had never visited the whores in Johnsons' place. 'Now go on, best get out and get it over with.' He pushed gently at Conn's shoulders.

'Can't I wait for you?' Conn felt sick to his stomach. He'd never had to expose his private parts to anyone before.

'Stand in the doorway then – it will take them some time to get the canvas set up.' Jem had been through something similar before. He knew exactly how the younger man was feeling. He dreaded the upcoming examination himself. He had nothing to hide but the blow to his dignity would be mighty.

Chapter 17

Jem left Conn staring after him while he made his way slowly to the section of the livery that held the telephone exchange and office. He wanted to punch something but that would only lead to more trouble.

He stopped to pet his old horse Rosie, burying his burning face in her mane. She was retired now but Jem hadn't the heart to put her out to pasture. He thought the old mare would fret away from familiar surroundings. He heaved a sigh, knowing he was the one who couldn't bear to part with his old friend.

He stood looking around at his little kingdom. He had so many plans for change and improvement, so many exciting projects to undertake and then something always happened to remind him of his place in the world. He was glad most of the men who worked for him were out and about the city. They'd all have to be informed of this trouble but for the moment he'd enough to handle. He refused to allow today's upheaval to destroy the new life he was making for himself. They'd handle whatever came and go on. What else could you do?

With a last volley of pats against the old horse's neck, Jem pushed himself away and continued walking towards the space he'd designated the office which consisted of two wide comfortable horse stalls. The dividing wall between the two stalls had been removed and a wooden floor laid down to allow John Lawless to manoeuvre his wheelchair around the space.

Jem's business was blossoming. The demand for the services he offered increased daily. The taxi part of the business was in great demand. Then there were the people who wanted his horse and carts to help them move house. He also offered a delivery service for local businessmen that was in great demand. These were sidelines that had developed from his jarvey business. He'd been forced to put an actual telephone exchange in as the telephone calls quickly overpowered the original phone line. He now had staff trained by the GPO to handle the volume of telephone calls the business received every day.

'Well, Jem,' John Lawless sat tall in his wheelchair in front of the wide, high telephone-exchange switchboard, his big fists clenched on the arms of his wheelchair, 'this is a fine state of affairs, isn't it?'

'Where are your womenfolk?' Jem looked around frantically. He couldn't remember who was scheduled to cover the phones today. John's wife Sadie and his two daughters were often around the livery. Clare, John's eldest, was a post-office-trained telephonist.

'I telephoned the house and warned them to stay away. I was worried sick they'd walk into the middle of this mess.' John sighed, his massive chest heaving. 'I'd kill the first man who tried to lay a hand on them.'

'I know exactly how you feel. So does every man in The Lane.'

'There's going to be murder out there.'

'I know.' Jem could do nothing but agree. 'I hope you asked Sadie to warn Ann Marie to stay away.' As well as being a business advisor and investor in Jem's business, Ann Marie was conducting an in-depth study of the history of Jem's livery building. She was in and out of the place, frequently at a moment's notice.

'Of course I did, but I'm going to telephone them again. It looks like this is going to make me late home.' John picked up a long cable and prepared to insert it into one of the sockets in the switchboard. He pushed the earphones in place over his ears, plugged the cable into the socket and pushed the mouthpiece into place. He prepared to dial the number of Ann Marie's house, now his home too, on the rotary dial.

'Good man. Where's the lad?' Jem needed to talk to Jimmy Johnson. He should have been here at the secondary post before the telephone exchange.

'I'm here.' Jimmy Johnson stepped out of a dark alcove at the back of the livery office. The poor lad would be a handsome youth if he ever raised his head from his chest. Jimmy had dirty-blond hair and pale-blue eyes but his sharply defined features must have come from whichever of Tim Johnson's many 'wives' had birthed the lad.

'Have you heard what's going on out there?' Jem asked.

'Yeah.' Jimmy hung his head in shame. There was no escaping his family name, it seemed, no matter how hard he tried to improve himself.

'I have to ask you...' Jem felt the red blush running up his face. It was no kind of a thing for

176

one man to ask another. 'Have you ever laid with any of the women your brother or father brings around the place?'

'No!' Jimmy's head snapped up at the question. His blue eyes practically shot flames. He felt his stomach roil at the very thought of touching any of the unfortunate women that fell into his brother's clutches.

'Have you ever lain down with a woman?' Jem thought the flaming red that mantled the cheeks of all three men should have lit the office like a lamp.

'No.' Jimmy understood the necessity of these questions – but he didn't have to like them.

'Fair enough. Will any of your family tell them where you are, Jimmy – if they ask, that is?'

'No,' Jimmy said quickly. 'Not because they want to keep me away from trouble. They'll all keep their mouths shut because the others would kill them for telling the authorities anything.'

'I can offer you the use of the hayloft to hide in, Jimmy.' Jem sighed. 'I don't think they'll pull the place apart but, if they do, you're on your own.'

'What else is new?' Jimmy shrugged with false bravado.

'No need to take on like that, lad,' John Lawless snapped. 'We'll help you all we can but we have our own feckin' skin to cover, you know.'

'I know.' Jimmy was ashamed of himself. These men were offering him more than his own family ever had. 'I apologise.'

'No need, lad.' Jem cuffed Jimmy gently. 'We're all upside down with this malarkey.'

'I'll keep out of sight,' Jimmy promised. He'd

177

plenty of experience hiding himself away until the coast was clear.

'Fair enough.' Jem watched the lad take his seat in front of the bench they'd set up to hold the telephone equipment. 'If you see trouble coming use the hand-grips to get yourself up to the loft. I've stashed the ladder out of sight.'

The iron half-moon hand-grips served as a quick way up to the hayloft. Jem's uncle had put hand-holds in along the walls of the livery. It meant you could get up and throw hay down from anywhere around the hayloft. The lads who worked for Jem loved swinging up to the loft using the iron handles.

'I'd better get out there.' Jem looked down at John. 'This is a hell of a bloody mess.'

'All we can do is grin and bear it, Jem.' John tittered madly, then snorted through his nose, making a sound like a sick donkey.

'Jaysus!' Jem punched John's shoulder.

'Sorry, sorry, I didn't really mean that.' John's shoulders continued to shake. 'I got a sudden attack of gallows humour.'

'As long as we don't end up swinging from the gallows, we'll be all right,' Jem said over his shoulder as he walked from the office. He made his way, reluctantly, towards where Conn stood in the open doorway of the livery.

'What's going on out there now?' Jem stared out into the courtyard.

'There's going to be trouble, Jem.' Conn was sheet-white. 'It seems some bloody fool out there,' he jerked his head in the direction of the crowd, 'has decided that there is no need to take the time needed to put up canvas. It seems there's no need to spare the blushes of the likes of us.'

'They want to do it in the open courtyard?' Jem looked around the open space. This wasn't the first time The Lane had been invaded by health visitors but they had at least had the decency to erect tall canvas tents to use as examination rooms. 'Are they mad?' He noticed a man he knew – Garda Collins. 'Stay here,' he said, walking away from Conn.

Jem walked over to the police officer. 'Garda Collins,' he said, 'do you happen to know who is in charge around here?'

'Some bloody toffee-nosed twit who doesn't know his arse from his elbow.' Barney Collins forgot himself enough to state his opinion clearly. He almost groaned aloud when he heard the comment leave his own lips. Some things were better left unsaid. Still, Jem Ryan was a good sort. He wouldn't be reporting a slip of the tongue.

'What seems to be the problem with setting up the tents for their examinations?' Jem asked. 'It wouldn't be the first time this lot have set up house here in the courtyard.'

'The man in charge doesn't want to wait until the tents can be delivered and set up. He doesn't see the need for any kind of privacy.' Barney Collins left it at that.

'They can't seriously expect us to allow some ham-fisted individual to handle our...' Jem wasn't quite sure of a sufficiently polite term for a man's sexual equipment.

'Fishing tackle,' Barney Collins whispered with a blush.

'That'll do, thank you. These men can't seriously think we'll allow them to examine our "fishing tackle" in public for the world and all his neighbours to see. There are children running around The Lane, for heaven's sake! Have they no sense!'

'It would appear not.' Barney Collins had sent one of his officers running for someone with more braid on his uniform than Barney carried. It was a blessing that the Pearse Street Garda Station was only a short distance from The Lane. This lot would not deign to speak, or indeed listen, to someone like himself. He'd already tried to talk some sense into them. 'The children will have to be examined as well.' Barney saw Jem stiffen, but what could he do? The law was the law.

'They are demanding I place a police cordon at The Lane entrance,' Barney mumbled, looking away from Jem. 'The head man has demanded the census listings for The Lane and more police officers.' He pushed a finger under his collar. 'About the only good thing to come out of this is that I now have all the information I need to arrest Declan Johnson.' The Garda had removed an illegal still and quantities of illegal liquids from the Johnsons' basement. 'If you have any idea where the man is, you need to tell me.'

'If I knew where he was I'd make you a gift of him,' Jem said. Declan seemed to have more lives than a cat. The man had disappeared at the first hint of trouble.

Barney knew the people of this block of tenements. They were good, hard-working people for the most part, trying desperately to keep body and soul together. These poverty-entrenched people

180

were being treated like animals by this crowd of 'experts'. The entire matter was a disgrace to the system Barney upheld faithfully. This could have been handled with tact and diplomacy. Barney knew who to ask for details. There were women in here who knew where the bodies were buried. They'd be willing to talk to save their neighbours from this trouble.

'Thanks.' Jem turned away. He had to get Jimmy out before The Lane was locked down. And under no circumstances would he allow these men to put their hands on Ivy and Emmy. They too needed to leave. He'd get them over to Ann Marie's house – somehow.

Chapter 18

'Jem, do you think there's any chance them fools out there would listen to anything but the sound of their own voices?' Marcella Wiggins walked into the livery, her face paper white.

'I don't know, Mrs Wiggins,' Jem sighed.

'I live over the Johnsons, you know that, Jem.' Marcella wanted to sit down and cry. She'd never seen anything so sad in her life as all those poor childer being driven from their home, poor as it was. 'I'm willing to put me hand on the bible and swear that nobody living in The Lane ever did business with anyone in the Johnsons' place. In fact, no one would step foot in the place.'

'Conn!' Jem shouted. 'Slip out quietly and ask

Garda Collins to step inside, discreetly.'

'Right away,' Conn said.

Barney Collins wished he could bang a few heads together. He was fuming in frustration at the blatant way this crowd of officials were ignoring the orders issued by himself and his men.

'Officer Collins,' Conn whispered, 'would yeh step over the way for a minute?'

'Doyle, move this along.' Barney Collins knew Conn Connelly – he was a good lad. 'Let's go.' Barney turned away from the mess he felt powerless to handle and followed behind Conn towards the livery.

'What's going on?' he asked when he entered. He didn't have time for polite chit-chat. He had a job to do.

'Mrs Wiggins has something she wants to ask you.' Jem put his hand on the shaking woman's shoulder.

Marcella Wiggins didn't beat around the bush. 'What can we do to help that lot on their way?'

'These people are here in an official capacity.'

'Is there no way of dealing with this matter quickly?' Jem put in softly.

'It's not my place to comment on the business of the Health Officials.' He hated feeling powerless.

'You know none of the people in here have anything to do with those women of Declan's,' Marcella snapped. 'You were here yourself when we put a spoke in Declan Johnson's wheel. We've been keeping a close eye on the bugger.'

Barney ran the fingers of one hand under his collar. He didn't like discussing such things with a female. 'It's my understanding that a number of

182

females in that ... ahh ... establishment, were found to be infected with a communicable disease.'

'Those two women were not from The Lane,' Marcella snapped as if that changed everything. 'They conducted their business away from here. I can tell yeh that for a fact. That Declan Johnson walked those two women of his out of here every evening bold as brass. He couldn't get any men to come into The Lane, not after the last time.'

'Mrs Wiggins, I can't take the law into my own hands,' Barney Collins said.

'Isn't that where we're told the law belongs?' Marcella Wiggins snapped. 'In the hands of the Garda?'

'I'll see what I can do.' Garda Collins fixed his hat firmly on his head, straightened his shoulders and like a man on a mission marched out of the livery.

'By God, Missus,' Jem said, 'I think you might have started something.'

'We'll have to wait and see.' Marcella wasn't willing to relax until she'd seen that crowd of officious twits drive back out the way they'd come.

'Can we go down now, Auntie Ivy?' Emmy's whisper carried around the livery.

'Stay up there for the minute, both of you!' Jem shouted. He'd known Ivy and Emmy were lying on their stomachs looking down into the livery. At least they'd had the sense to keep out of sight but trying to keep them safe was his responsibility.

'There's ne'er a biscuit nor a drop of milk up here to go with a cup of tea, Jem Ryan!' Ivy called down.

'Hold yer whist, woman.' Jem grinned. Trust Ivy to have a pot of tea on the go. The woman was a terror for her tea. 'I'll have one of the lads climb up with a packet of biscuits and a jug of milk. If you're very good I'll even promise to buy you a cream cake. Now, for the love of God, will you both keep your heads down?'

'Ivy, do as Jem suggests,' Marcella barked. 'The situation down here could still get ugly.' She watched one of Jem's lads climb up the iron hand-holds, a can of milk clutched by the thin metal handle in his mouth. She could see the promised biscuits peeking out of his jacket pocket.

Ivy waited at the rim of the loft for the milk and biscuits. 'The situation, as you call it, is ugly enough now, Mrs Wiggins,' she said, 'but I'll stay up here with Emmy. We'll keep each other company.'

'Keep out of sight!' Jem shouted with a helpless shake of his head and a shrug. Ivy Murphy did things her own way and she'd not allow the likes of him to tell her her business.

'May I come in?' a soft voice called from the still-open main doors of the livery.

Betty Armstrong, the woman who had be-friended young Seán McDonald, stood framed by winter sunlight. The woman's tall upright frame seemed to be carved from ice until you noticed the pain in her eyes. The severe bun she had pulled her dark hair into showed off razor-sharp cheekbones. The bitter twist of her full-lipped mouth prevented her from being beautiful.

Betty Armstrong couldn't believe the horror that had been visited upon the people she now called

184

neighbours. She'd simply enquired about the need for Seán to attend school. It would appear she'd opened a can of worms. What kind of world had she come to? Didn't these people know it was almost 1926, for the Lord's sake? The world had fought a war – a war that the experts claimed was going to change society radically. Surely Ireland too was going to change?

'What can we do for you, Missus?' Jem almost sighed. What now?

'If you would allow me to use your telephone, I believe I may be able to help,' she said in a soft hesitant voice. She waited a moment but, when no one spoke, continued. 'I wish to place a call to Billy Flint. I thought to ask him to use some of his contacts, people in the know, and get these people shifted out of The Lane.'

'I think that's a fine idea,' Marcella said before anyone else could react. 'I'm sure he'd be glad of a reason to help you.' She gave the other woman the evil eye, letting her know she wasn't fooling her.

'It might be for the best.' John used his strong arms to push his wheelchair over to the open livery doors. 'It doesn't look to me as if Garda Collins is getting much done with that lot of eejits. Let the woman telephone Billy Flint – if he can move this lot along, the price, whatever it will be, will be worth it.'

'Conn,' Jem ordered, 'take the lady into the office and give her any help she may need.' He didn't want to leave his place at the door. Garda Collins appeared to be rounding up the health visitors but they were objecting. The situation could drag on forever if something wasn't done soon.

'If I wasn't so scared, I'd laugh,' John Lawless said. 'It's like those reels of film they play in between the big pictures at the Pally. What are those policemen called?'

'The Keystone Cops.' Jimmy Johnson often escaped to the local cinema.

Jem didn't find anything funny about the situation developing out in the courtyard. 'Mrs Wiggins, do you think you could get the people standing around out there to return to their own homes?'

'Leave it to me.' Marcella pushed up the sleeves of her jumper and prepared to begin issuing orders. She'd soon shift everyone. She had faith in Billy Flint if no one else did – and, besides, she knew something about yer one that no one else was aware of.

Marcella was as good as her word. She organised the unsettled people with a few suggestions. She soon had the younger children filing into one of the tenement houses with the promise of a special storytime. She reminded the women fortunate enough to have men out working that they needed to begin preparing a meal for the workers. It wasn't fast but it was efficient.

In the livery, the sound of the ringing telephones and the swift responses by the men working to answer them was the only sound heard. Jem worried about the effect this was having on his taxi business. The lads on their bikes should be flying in and out of here carrying messages to the carriages waiting in the rank around Stephen's Green. He hoped someone was giving an explanation for the delay in the service he offered. He tried to shake off the worry; there was nothing he could do about it right now. Everyone was on edge. Those not occupied with some chore simply stared out the door ... waiting.

Then a motorised bicycle seemed to explode out of the tunnel: it was a Garda messenger. The noise of the motor attracted the attention of the squabbling officials. Barney Collins hurried over to the messenger, hoping against hope that this was good news. He received freshly printed orders from the messenger's leather-gloved hands. He read the written orders and with a sigh of relief hurried over to put them into immediate effect.

The people of The Lane were keeping an eye on the situation. They watched, some from behind their windows, others keeping watch from their open doorway, as the Garda officers almost pushed the health visitors towards their vehicles. They wanted to see what was going on, now that the danger to themselves seemed to be over. It would take nerves of steel to drive that unwieldy truck out of here. When one man ran to take the crank shank out of the back of the vehicle, the sigh of relief that ran around The Lane could almost be felt. The noise of the sputtering engine as the man almost jumped on the handle to turn it more swiftly was music to Jem's ears.

Chapter 19

'Officer Collins seems to be heading in this direction.' Jem stood in the open livery doors well out of the way of a swarm of messenger lads peddling their bicycles out of the livery and into the tunnel. He was back in business.

The people would calm down now that The Lane was being cleared of official visitors. They would return to the courtyard now, needing to express their very vocal opinions.

'Come on in, Officer Collins, we're dying of curiosity,' Jem said when the red-faced Garda reached his side. He turned to lead the way to what was quickly becoming the hub of his new business, the tearoom.

'Can we come down now, Jem Ryan?' Ivy's voice drifted out over the stable yard.

'A voice from above,' Barney Collins quipped. 'That's all we need.'

'You keep a civil tone in your voice, Officer Barney Collins.' Ivy laughed. 'I've been sequestered away up here and now I want to know what the heck is going on.'

'Far be it from me to keep you away from the action, Missus.' Barney Collins admired Ivy Murphy.

'We ladies need a staircase, Jem Ryan,' said Ivy as Emmy giggled with relief.

For a time there Ivy had been terrified. The situation had been resolved somehow, but how? Had Billy Flint been responsible for that Garda messenger? Was the man really that powerful? That influential?

'Are you too proud to lend a hand, Officer Collins?' Jem walked over to where he'd hidden the heavy wooden ladder.

'For however you managed to get those orders sent out I'll suck up me pride – and don't bother denying it – someone took a hand in that situation and my money's on you.' Barney Collins joined Jem in lifting the heavy ladder and they wrestled it over to its previous location. Jem gave an experienced jerk and the ladder dropped into place.

'Your staircase, m'lady!' Jem grinned up at the two females he'd come to love.

'Thank you, my man,' Ivy quipped and without a moment's delay turned her back and began to throw her leg over the loft rim.

'Eyes right!' Barney Collins barked, blushing furiously.

'It's okay, Officer Collins,' Ivy giggled. 'I'm wearing a pair of lads' trousers under me skirt – me modesty's safe.'

'Would you get down out of that, Ivy Murphy!' Jem grinned. Ivy Murphy would always have an answer.

Jem stood and watched as the woman and girl climbed down into the livery, ready to catch them should they slip. There was no need. The two females came down the ladder as if born climbing up and down wooden rungs.

'Yeh promised us cream cakes, Jem Ryan,' Ivy said as soon as her feet touched the ground.

'So I did,' Jem grinned. 'Conn, grab a bike, will you?'

'I live to serve.' Conn grinned his relief at the peaceful resolution of the recent problem.

'Oh, if only that were true!' Jem cuffed Conn gently, glad of the younger man's attempt to add levity to the situation. 'Here.' Jem reached into his pants pocket and pulled out a florin. 'Get cream cakes for ten, will you, please, Conn?'

Barney Collins was now standing slightly to the right of the main livery door. He was watching the people pouring out of the houses and into the courtyard, judging the mood of the crowd. He couldn't believe he had managed to calm the very dangerous situation that had been developing out there.

Jem took what felt like his first easy breath of the day. He'd been sure blood was going to be spilt. He'd worried about protecting 'his' people, the most important two of whom were now laughing and giggling, teasing the young lads congregating around the livery floor. He shook his head and looked around the livery as people bustled around getting back to whatever work they'd left when the trouble began. He had spent years living alone after his uncle's death. He'd been in danger of becoming a hermit. The changes in his own life over the last year still had the power to amaze him and never more than just now.

He wondered where your one was, the woman who had offered to telephone Billy Flint. That had been a turn-up for the books. Had that man really been responsible for shifting the do-gooders from The Lane? The thought sent a shiver down Jem's

190

spine. He'd been looking for someone who could give him information on the bold Billy Flint. It seemed he might have an expert close to hand. He looked towards the office he'd set up: he hadn't seen your woman leave.

'Emmy,' Jem softly touched the thick black mane of his adopted niece, 'why don't you run upstairs and get your coat and hat on. I'll have one of the lads take you across the way and you can join the other children for storytime. I'll call you when Conn gets back here with the cream cakes.'

'All right!' Emmy couldn't wait to see her friends and hear their views of the goings-on. It had been very exciting but frightening too. Emmy didn't like it when she didn't understand something. The older kids would explain it to her.

'I don't mind telling you,' Barney Collins said when Jem walked over to join him at his watching post in the livery doorway, 'there were times out there that I was worried we'd have murder committed. This is not the end of the matter. We can't allow the spread of infectious, communicable diseases – you both have to realise that.'

'We know – everyone in The Lane knows that. We don't want that filth any more than anyone else would.' Ivy dared to touch Officer Collins gently on the shoulder. 'I don't think anyone in The Lane would object to being treated like a human being. We'll co-operate with a delicately handled health examination – it won't be the first time.' The attitude of the group of health-care workers had angered and offended her. 'However, the next time that lot,' she nodded towards the tunnel leading into The Lane, 'come in here like a conquering army they'll find themselves facing an angry mob. Someone needs to inform them of that.'

'I'll have none of that, Ivy Murphy.' Barney turned to glare at her.

'And we'll have none of a crowd of toffee-nose twits trying to lay their dirty hands on us without a lick of common decency,' Ivy snapped. 'Respect works both ways, Officer Collins.'

'We can't solve the problems of the world right now,' Jem said, supplying the voice of reason. 'Let us leave everybody out there,' he nodded to the courtyard, 'to calm down in their own time. I'll put the kettle on.'

'I have to get going, Jem, Ivy.' Barney Collins needed to think about what had almost happened here today. The walk back to the station would calm his nerves. 'I'll take you up on the offer of a cup of tea another time. Right now I have a report to write.' He wanted to find out who had issued those orders that had arrived in the nick of time. He also needed to put out the order to arrest Declan Johnson on sight.

'You're welcome to stay for a cup of tea.' Ivy felt guilty. She hadn't meant to run the man off – he was a decent sort, for a Garda.

'Thank you, Ivy Murphy,' Barney Collins pulled his uniform jacket straight, 'but I need to get on.'

'You are welcome here any time,' said Jem. He understood. The man found himself in a very difficult position. The world around them was changing. He for one couldn't wait to see what the future would bring. He did not, however, plan to be as helpless and frustrated as he'd been in this situation today ever again.

'I'll be on my way then. A good evening to you both.' Barney Collins touched the tips of two fingers to the brim of his helmet before stepping out of the livery, very aware of the eyes that followed his every step.

'I'm going to see my friends.' Emmy, her hat and coat pulled on any old how, ran through the livery.

'Hold up, young lady!' Jem grabbed at the fleeing child. 'I said I'd send someone with you.'

'Oh, Uncle Jem,' Emmy rolled her big green eyes in disgust, 'I'm only going across the courtyard.'

'Nonetheless, young lady,' Jem said in a very plummy tone, much to Emmy's delight, 'I must insist you have an escort.' He shouted to Pete, a tall strong young lad standing nearby and instructed him to take Emmy across the courtyard.

'See you, Uncle Jem, see you, Auntie Ivy!' With her hand firmly gripped in Pete's, Emmy pulled the young man through the open doors and across the cobbled courtyard. It was easy for her to see which house the children were in; the door stood wide open and the stairs were packed with seated children. She hoped she hadn't missed too much of the story.

'She doesn't seem to be too upset,' Jem said wryly.

Ivy stood with Jem for a moment. She wanted to kick something, scream, pull her own hair from her head. She felt her nerves twitching under her skin. Today had frightened the life out of her. She hated feeling so powerless.

'Come on.' Jem threw his arm around her

193

shoulders and turned her in the direction of the tearoom. 'Let's get you a river of tea.' He gently nudged her with his hip. 'We'll start with a cup but you know you'll feel the better for it.'

'Jem...' Ivy stopped walking and stared up into his strong familiar face. She stepped away from him, took his hand and pulled him with her in the direction of one of the vacant stalls. They couldn't stand in the main body of the livery with people brushing past them constantly. She didn't care who saw her pull him off to one side. She didn't care what gossip this would cause. Ann Marie had advised her to ask for what she needed. She hurt and this man had the power to ease some of that pain.

'I need something far more than a cup of tea,' she said.

They were standing tall in an empty stall, clearly visible to the lads rushing around the place pretending not to see, the smell of fresh hay and horses all around them.

'Let me feel your head.' Jem looked down into her worried face. 'I never thought I'd see the day Ivy Murphy refused a cup of tea.' He didn't know how he could help her.

'I need one of your hugs, Jem.' Ivy stepped forward until her head rested on his muscular chest. She put her arms around his waist, stepped as close to his warm body as she possibly could and held on tight. 'I need this more than a cup of tea, Jem Ryan,' she whispered into his chest as his strong arms closed around her. She snuggled her head into the space between his shoulder and chin. She fought the tears that wanted to fall. She would not allow her situation in life to reduce her to tears. *She. Would. Not.*

Jem stood with his arms wrapped tightly around Ivy's trembling figure, taking his own comfort from her nearness. He rocked his body gently from side to side, offering and taking comfort. 'It will be all right, *alanna*,' he whispered, bending slightly to press a kiss into her hair, closing his eyes, willing to stand here all day if that was what she needed. The business of the livery went on around them as they held tight to each other, content to just be.

'Is there anyone going to drink this bloody tea!' John Lawless' voice echoed around the livery building. 'I've the arse burned off the kettle.' He knew what was going on – there was very little that went on around here that he didn't know – but now was not the time nor the place for Ivy and Jem to stand there like two ruddy statues. They'd been standing there so long the lads were beginning to nudge each other and giggle. Time to put a stop to all that nonsense. They could kiss and canoodle behind closed doors like the rest of them.

'Our master's voice.' Ivy tightened her arms around Jem's waist for a moment before stepping reluctantly away. She stared up into his green eyes, a slight smile on her lips. She raised herself on her toes and whispered, 'Thank you,' then pressed a delicate butterfly kiss onto his firm, lush lips. 'I needed that,' she said, dropping to her heels and stepping away.

'It was my pleasure entirely, Miss Murphy.' Jem pulled her back into his arms for a deeper kiss before he released her with a deep sigh. 'We'd better go before John sends someone to drag us away.' He put his arm around her shoulders and they slowly stepped out of the stall.

The lads pushing brooms, grooming horses, polishing tack, all seemed to be looking away from them. Jem grinned widely. He'd take a lot of teasing for this but he didn't care. Ivy Murphy had kissed and hugged him. Let them talk.

Chapter 20

'It's about time the pair of yez got over here,' John Lawless snapped as they approached him. He'd been keeping company with the woman who had telephoned Billy Flint. The darn woman just sat there staring around at everything. It was making him nervous. 'I've the arse boiled out of the kettle waiting for yez.' John refused to allow his lack of mobility to hinder him. He'd do everything he was capable of doing and then some. 'I thought we were going to be graced by the presence of a Garda officer? I suppose the pair of yez put the poor man to the blush and he ran off?' He busied himself making a fresh pot of tea in a galvanised teapot big enough to serve a battalion of thirsty soldiers. 'I offered this poor woman a cup of tea and she's still waiting.'

'It was good of you to telephone Billy Flint.' Jem didn't know what the woman was doing sitting in his tearoom but he wanted to pick her brain – not at the minute – but soon.

'Betty.' Ivy nodded briefly to a woman who made her uncomfortable for some unknown reason. She walked over to John and, with her hand on his shoulder, said, 'No need to be jealous, John.' Ivy refused to be embarrassed. She'd desperately needed that moment of sanity in a world gone mad. She was learning to ask for what she needed and, by God, it felt mighty. She'd do it again. 'You know your Sadie loves yeh. I'm sure she'd give you a bit of a kiss and a cuddle if you asked her.'

'You're a cheeky article, Ivy Murphy.' John smiled up at her. 'I'll thank you to mind your own business. What me and my Sadie get up to is our own business.'

'Give us that cup of tea you were roaring about.' Jem carried one of the wonky wooden chairs that sat in the tearoom over to Ivy. He tested the chair before seating her with a fond grin and stepping away.

'Mr Lawless suggested I waited here until things calmed down outside.' Betty Armstrong wondered how in the name of God she'd landed up in this place, sitting on a wonky chair in a stable of all things.

'Who's tending the telephones?' Jem asked.

'Jimmy Johnson and one of the other lads are handling things.' John's heart was still somewhere around his tonsils. Truthfully, he wouldn't mind a kiss and a cuddle with his own woman right now.

'Fair enough.' Jem opened a nearby freestanding cupboard and began to remove cups and saucers for the women, enamel mugs for himself and John.

'I'll be glad when Jimmy can get around to making a sturdy table to go in here.' Jem looked around the space he'd set up for the people he employed. The lads he was training up had practically moved in here. When not out and about on their business around the city the lads congregated in this space. The area offered more comfort than most of them found at home. It shocked Jem to think that he, Jem Ryan from County Sligo, was an employer.

'If I might offer a suggestion?' Betty Armstrong said softly.

'You haven't been backward in coming forward so far, missus,' Jem said. 'Why start now?' He was willing to go along with any conversation that didn't touch on what had almost happened out there in The Lane. They all needed a chance to catch their breath before tackling the underlining problems. He heaved a deep sigh: if it wasn't one thing it was another.

'Thank you.' Betty ignored the quip. 'I've noticed on my travels around the town that a lot of the people who openly supported British rule are leaving.'

'That's a fact.' John filled the cups Jem held in his hands. The two men thought nothing of serving tea to a pair of ladies. This was their work space – if they didn't do it, who would?

'The Grafton Street furniture dealers are rubbing their hands in glee at the stuff being offloaded.' Betty took the china tea cup and saucer from Jem with a smile. 'It's my understanding that the houses here in Dublin have been second homes so there is an abundance of furniture people have no intention of taking with them.'

'I can only imagine.' Jem passed Ivy her tea. He smiled down at her bent head and waited until she looked up at him before releasing the saucer. He gave her a wink and a grin, bringing burning colour to her pale cheeks. 'But what has that to do with the price of eggs?' He stepped over to take the can of milk from the bucket of cold water it sat in.

'Those Grafton Street dealers want only the front-of-house stuff.' Betty allowed Jem to add a dash of fresh milk to her tea. 'I believe one of those huge tables cooks use would be ideal in here – a table and a couple of the benches that the house staff use as seating would finish this place off.' She was willing to chit-chat until the moment was right to ask the question that most concerned her.

'I can't say as I'm familiar with the fixtures and fittings of fancy houses,' Jem admitted. He looked closely at the woman sitting, sipping tea. It was obvious she knew what went into these houses. What was a woman like her doing living in The Lane?

'There's an avenue yet to be explored, Jem,' Ivy offered. 'I think the idea of getting one of those big old kitchen tables is marvellous.' She shrugged when he looked over at her with a smile. 'The kitchen table in Ann Marie's aunt's house would seat twenty. The thing is huge, with drawers on both sides. It would be ideal in here.'

'So, Ivy Murphy, you expect me to knock on the doors of the fancy and ask if they happen to be shifting?' Jem grinned, imagining himself, hat in hand, his horse and cart at his back, knocking on the doors of the 'quality'. 'I'd like me job.'

'Jem, yer not thinking,' Ivy snapped. 'I'm talking about presenting yourself to the dealers in Grafton Street and offering to shift the heavy goods for them.'

'They must have their own means of transport.' Jem shook his head.

'Not all of them.' Ivy was thinking hard. 'You know, there may be a chance to make a few bob there. I'll have to think about it.'

'Look out,' Jem grinned. 'She's thinking!'

'Would the pair of you settle down!' John hit the arm of his wheelchair. 'You two are worse than the lads.'

Betty Armstrong could wait no longer to raise the question she wanted answered. She needed to get about her own business. The telephone call she'd just made to Billy Flint had re-opened a chapter of her life she'd thought to keep closed.

'I was wondering if any of you know what will happen to young Seán now,' she said. 'I've become extremely fond of the little rascal. Would I be able to visit him, check that he is well and happy?'

The shift in the atmosphere was alarming. Betty could almost feel ice forming.

'What? What did I say?' Betty drew back, shocked at the expressions of the people around her.

John beat at the arms of his chair with clenched fists, Jem's jaw was clenched tight, and Ivy simply stared.

'I haven't seen as much of this sort of thing as some.' John Lawless spoke first, giving the other two time to organise their thoughts. 'I heard about it from the men I worked with but this was the first time I witnessed one of these snatch-and-grabs meself.'

'You have no idea what will happen to the Johnson children, have you?' Ivy stared at the other woman.

Betty simply shook her head.

'Jem,' Ivy held out her cup, 'give us another cup of tea. That one passed over me teeth and tongue without a minute's notice.' She was just buying time.

'I'm going to take my tea into the office with me.' John Lawless had nothing to add to this conversation and he'd had enough drama for the day. 'Shout out if you need me.' He turned to make his way into the office, then closed his eyes in frustration. How the heck was he supposed to carry his mug of tea and use his arms to push himself? He'd been so involved in the goings-on around him he'd forgotten his own limitations.

'Come on.' Jem picked up John's mug of tea and without further comment carried it through into the office.

'I appear to have run everyone off,' Betty Armstrong whispered.

'They are good men frustrated by a situation they can do nothing about,' Ivy offered. 'They just didn't want to hear me say aloud what we all know. We will never see Seán again.'

'What?' Betty Armstrong surged to her feet, almost dropping the empty cup and saucer she held. 'I refuse to accept that. I want to know where the lad is, how he is. I'll not let anyone keep me away from checking up on that young boy.'

'I hope yeh can swim.' Ivy shrugged.

'I beg your pardon?' Betty sat carefully back down on her shaky chair.

'In cases where no crime has been committed, the good nuns and priests of the local charities have the final say in what happens to the people who are removed from their own homes for whatever reason.' That was the most polite way she could think of saying that the clergy thought they knew better than everyone else. 'In almost every case, that I know of anyway, men and women are separated from each other and their children. The nuns remove the children from their parents' care. They decide the children would have a chance of a better life elsewhere.' Ivy could see Betty wasn't pleased but she didn't care – the woman asked what would happen to Seán and she was answering that question. She didn't make the rules – all she could do was tell this one what was what.

'The children, that we here in The Lane have been able to find out about, are taken to an orphanage in Wexford.' Ivy sighed tiredly. 'It's close to the harbour, makes it easier to move the children onto the boats. The children are taken, as far as we've been able to discover, under the guidance of a nun for the girls, a priest for the boys, to Canada and Australia. They never see home again.'

'I refuse to believe that!' Betty snapped. How much of a fool did this woman think she was? 'Seán has a mother, a family, bad and all as it is.'

Ivy simply shrugged; there was nothing more she could add.

'Thank you for your time.' Betty almost smashed the delicate china tea cup and saucer onto a

202

nearby chair. 'I believe I'll check into this situation. I simply refuse to believe something like this goes on in this day and age. It's positively primitive.'

Ivy had a feeling Jem had wanted to talk to the woman about Billy Flint, but that could wait. She sat and watched the ramrod-straight back of the woman as she almost stormed from the tearoom.

'I'm back from me travels. I've climbed mountains, crossed ravines, wrestled alligators but I'm back with cream cakes in hand!' Conn shouted aloud with a laugh in his voice. He had no wish to discuss the woman who just passed him with her chin so high in the air it was a wonder she didn't fall over her own feet.

'Yeh must be knicky-knacked after all that travelling. You poor thing! Grab yerself a mug of tea.' Ivy welcomed the release from tension. What the heck were they going to do? The nuns wouldn't leave this place alone now. They'd be over with their rosary beads and holy water, dipping their noses into every nook and cranny of The Lane.

Jem appeared in the open door of the office. 'Where's your one gone? I wanted to talk to her.' He walked out of the office.

'You can catch her later, Jem.' Ivy felt as if she'd aged a hundred years. 'She left with a bit of a bee in her bonnet.'

'I got cream buns for us lads,' Conn said. 'They're the cheapest and we won't know the difference. I got a few cream dainties as well.'

'Good lad, but we need to figure out what we're going to serve the things on.' Jem was happy enough to concentrate on trivia for the moment.

The large flaky fresh cream cakes broke apart as soon as you bit into them. They needed something to catch the pastry flakes and cream so they could enjoy every bit of the treat. 'I don't want spilled cream and that powder sugar all over the floor in here. The stuff will stink and stick to our feet.'

'Newspaper, Jem,' Ivy grinned. 'The answer to most of our needs around here – old newspaper, you can't beat it.'

'Good enough,' Jem shrugged. 'Conn, grab some of the old newspaper from that cupboard.'

Old newspapers were a treasured commodity amongst the poor of Dublin. Newspaper was collected and hoarded carefully by everyone. The paper served a multitude of purposes.

'Jimmy, come out of there!' Jem shouted over his shoulder towards the office. He hadn't liked the look of young Jimmy earlier. It wasn't the lad's fault his family had once again brought trouble to The Lane. 'There's tea and cream cakes going.'

'You called me?' Jimmy Johnson stood uncertainly in the doorway of the break room. His eyes remained glued to the floor while he appeared to want to disappear into the flooring.

'Come in, lad.' Jem knew the last thing Jimmy wanted to do was join in a social occasion but the lad needed to learn. 'Conn, pour Jimmy a mug of tea and give him one of those cream buns.'

'What?' Jimmy's head snapped up. He was sure he hadn't heard right. He'd never had a cream cake in his life.

'I promised Emmy I'd call her as soon as Conn got back with the cakes,' Jem said to cover Jimmy's unease. 'It's getting dark out there. The lamp-

204

lighter hasn't been around yet.'

'Leave her for a minute, Jem,' Ivy suggested. Emmy heard entirely too much of what went on around here. 'We'll save her a cake.'

'Sit down, Jimmy.' Jem waved towards a nearby chair. 'Conn, my good man,' he then said in an affected accent, 'see to my guests.'

'Certainly, sir.' Conn bowed from the waist and presented Ivy with a fresh cup of tea and a cream dainty on a china saucer, all he could find to put it on. He wasn't going to give Ivy Murphy her cake on newspaper. Conn used part of the lid of the cardboard box to carry a cake in to John Lawless in the office. He hurried back out, John's mug in hand and refilled it from the giant teapot sitting on the fire. Conn never broke character. He kept his nose in the air, his back impossibly straight.

Conn presented Jem with a mug of tea and a wad of newspaper with a large cream slice sitting elegantly on top. He didn't even crack a smile. His brother and sister weren't the only ones in the family who enjoyed playacting.

'If Sir's guest would care to take a seat,' Conn gestured towards Jimmy, continuing his role as tag-tailed butler, 'I will be with him momentarily.' He turned to fetch two mugs of tea and cream buns for himself and Jimmy.

The two lads attacked the cream buns. The cakes disappeared so fast Ivy wondered how they managed to even taste them. She remembered her own first taste of a cream cake. She'd been to afternoon tea at Bewleys restaurant with Ann Marie. She'd found the cakes a nightmare to eat, the darn cream seeming to leak out of twenty

205

places at once. She'd been extremely uncomfortable but she'd loved the taste of them. Now it gave her a little thrill to pick up a cream cake from the bakery to accompany a cup of tea in her own place. Sitting here in a wide open space attached to a stable, surrounded by friends, the cakes tasted better than at Bewleys. She could lick her lips and use her fingers to scoop up the cream. There was no one to glare at her in horror.

'Conn, grab another couple of cream buns for yourself and Jimmy.' Jem grinned at the look of stunned delight on the faces of the two lads. 'Better get them into yeh quick.'

'But, but, the others?' Conn didn't really want to question his right to a second cream bun.

'What the eyes don't see the heart will never grieve over, Conn,' Jem said and laughed when Conn almost launched himself in the direction of the box of cream cakes sitting proudly on the cupboard.

'I suggest you two eat the cakes slowly this time.' Ivy grinned. 'Give yerselves time to taste the feckin' things.'

'Uncle Jem, it's getting really dark out.' Emmy strolled into the livery. 'Storytime is over.' She crawled up onto Jem's knees, sure of a loving welcome.

Conn quickly supplied the child with an enamel mug of creamy milk and a cream dainty sitting prettily on one of the spare saucers.

'Well, I'm glad to see everyone is still in one piece.' Ann Marie Gannon walked into the livery. She was dressed in her shiny black second-hand suit. She lowered herself down onto the chair

Conn offered her. Without a blink she accepted a cup of tea and a cream cake from the vigilant Conn.

'Ann Marie,' Jem grinned, 'make yourself at home – you're in your granny's.' He had never used that particular expression before but it seemed to suit the occasion.

'John telephoned the house – he told Sadie a little of what has been going on in here,' Ann Marie said simply. 'When he telephoned to tell us the situation had returned to normal I couldn't stay away. I hope you don't mind.'

'Ann Marie,' Ivy said swiftly, 'I don't think you've met Jimmy Johnson, have you?' She knew Ann Marie would have seen Jimmy about the place. 'It was Jimmy's home that was invaded this afternoon.'

'How do you do, Jimmy.' Ann Marie offered her hand, almost causing poor Jimmy to swallow his tongue. He wasn't accustomed to social niceties. 'I've seen you around the place but we've never been introduced.' She'd got the message. They couldn't discuss the situation with this young man sitting before them like a whipped puppy.

'Jimmy built all the furniture in this room,' Conn offered while he surreptitiously gave Jimmy a push in Ann Marie's direction. The poor woman's arm must be aching she'd been holding it out so long. 'He's even created something special for Ivy's dolls.'

'How do,' Jimmy muttered. He gave a quick shake to Ann Marie's hand before dropping it as if scalded.

'You are certainly turning this space into a

207

delightful little tearoom, Jem.' Ann Marie settled into exchanging polite chit-chat with Ivy and Jem. Serious conversation would have to wait.

'I don't mean to be rude, Ann Marie, but I need to get this young lady settled,' Jem said eventually, pushing to his feet with Emmy in his arms. The little girl was wearing a milk moustache and a sleepy grin.

'Quite understandable, Jem.' Ann Marie smiled at the image of the tall man with the young girl clasped so protectively to his chest.

'I'm going to finish my cup of tea, Jem,' Ivy said. 'Then Ann Marie and I will go over to my place, get out of your hair.'

'I'll see both of you later then.' Jem knew Ivy understood what he meant. They needed to talk but not in front of Emmy and the lads.

Jem carried Emmy in the direction of the ladder leading to his loft. Without breaking stride he threw Emmy over his shoulder in a fireman's lift while reaching for the ladder. The sound of Emmy's delighted laughter rang through the stable. The horses didn't react. They were used to the sound of laughter.

'So, Conn,' Ann Marie smiled at a young man she was becoming extremely fond of, 'how are your brother and sister getting along? I haven't seen them in ages.'

'I have more than one brother and sister, Ann Marie.' Conn knew what was needed. Jimmy was sitting like a scared rabbit, afraid to move, afraid to open his mouth in case he said the wrong thing and terrified he might be asked a question. 'But I know which pair you mean.' It seemed to him the world and his brother knew about Liam and his shenanigans. 'Liam and Vera are doing really well.' He could see Jimmy's shoulders drop as he relaxed and accepted the fact that no one was going to question him about his family. 'I don't know if you've heard but they're appearing, with the dogs, in the Gaiety pantomime.' Conn grinned. 'Me ma and da are telling the world and his brother about that.'

'I'm glad things are working out for them.' Ann Marie finished her tea and cake. She passed the soiled dishes to Conn without thinking. Ivy stood and put her own dishes back beside the cardboard box.

'Come on, Ann Marie.' Ivy smiled at the two young men. 'Let's be having yeh.'

'Thank you for your hospitality, gentlemen.' Ann Marie smiled sweetly and stood to follow Ivy from the livery.

'"Gentlemen" – did yeh hear that, Jimmy?' Conn grinned and pushed at Jimmy's shoulder with enough strength to shove him off his seat. 'She called us gentlemen.'

'Shows what she knows,' Jimmy grinned.

'Any chance of a bit of help in here or do you two gentlemen plan to lead a life of leisure from now on?' John Lawless leaned out of his wheelchair to shout around the office door. 'Conn, it's nearly time for a shift change. We'll have returning men and horses in here soon. You need to take care of the dockets.'

'Coming!' Jimmy and Conn jumped to obey their master's voice.

Chapter 21

'You need a light on these steps, Ivy.' Ann Marie hurried to follow Ivy down the steps leading to the basement rooms.

'Chance would be a fine thing,' Ivy answered absentmindedly. She took her keys from her pocket and unlocked her front door. 'Here, give us your hand.' She dropped the keys back into her pocket before putting her hand behind her. With Ann Marie's hand in hers, Ivy led the way into her dark basement.

She sniffed the air like a hound, checking to see that everything was as she'd left it. She knew every inch, sound and smell of these two rooms. She didn't need light but Ann Marie didn't have that advantage.

'You should carry a Vesta case or gas lighter with you when you go out, Ivy,' Ann Marie suggested.

Ivy ignored her friend. It was either that or snigger. Ann Marie meant well but the woman hadn't a clue. A Vesta case, I ask yer sacred pardon! Ivy shook her head. I suppose I should get a solid-gold Vesta like the lighter Ann Marie carries, she thought. A solid-gold match box – wouldn't that make the cat laugh?

After locking her door, with Ann Marie's hand still gripping hers Ivy made her way into her back room. She took the time to guide Ann Marie to one of her two wooden chairs placed at the big kitchen table.

Ivy hurried to light a spill of newspaper from the glowing embers in the range. In moments she had the two gas lamps lit and the fire stirred to a blaze. A warm welcoming glow filled the room.

'So, Ivy Murphy,' Ann Marie put her bent elbows on the table and dropped her chin into her hands, 'are you going to tell me what went on around here today?'

'You know, Ann Marie,' Ivy ignored the question, 'for only the second time in my life I don't want a cup of tea – but I'm going to make us a pot anyway. It'll give me something to do with my hands.'

'You're making me nervous.' Ann Marie stood and walked over to sit in one of the two large battered, ugly stuffed chairs in front of the black range. 'I thought the world would have to end before Miss Ivy Murphy refused a cup of tea.' She watched Ivy bustle around the room in a very un-Ivy-like fashion. She didn't seem to be able to settle. For a moment it even looked as if Ivy couldn't remember how to make a pot of tea – an impossibility – but she finally got it made and left the teapot warming on the hob.

'Do you know anything about booze, Ann Marie?' Ivy was on her knees now, her bottom stuck in the air, the top half of her body buried under the brass bed.

'I beg your pardon?' Ann Marie wasn't absolutely sure she'd heard correctly. Ivy's voice was muffled by the behemoth of a bed she was currently trying to crawl underneath.

'Does booze go off?' Ivy was backing out from

211

under the bed. 'I mean does it go bad or what?'

'I have no idea.'

Ivy used the side of the bed to push herself to her feet. She clutched a clear glass bottle of her da's precious poitín in her fist. No matter what the circumstance, someone in The Lane always had enough potatoes to make the strong spirit. 'Doesn't matter. I'm going to put a drop of this stuff in our tea.' She held the bottle aloft. 'Me da always claimed it was good for what ailed yeh.'

'What is it?' Ann Marie asked.

'You don't want to know, Ann Marie.' Ivy poured the tea then added a few drops of the clear liquid in each dragonfly decorated teacup. 'Just get it into yeh.' She held out the cup and saucer to Ann Marie, her eyes daring her to refuse.

'You, Miss Ivy Murphy,' Ann Marie took the cup and saucer with a grin, 'will be the death of me.'

'Bottoms up!' Ivy dropped into the chair facing Ann Marie across the range. 'If we die tonight, Ann Marie, sure we'll go together.' She giggled.

'That's not very reassuring, Miss Murphy.' Ann Marie took a dainty sip of the laced tea. 'Sweet Lord!' She felt as if she'd swallowed a burning ember. 'That will certainly clear the system of every parasite known to man.'

'So me da always claimed.' Ivy too gasped at the first taste of the liquid in her cup. 'Sweet Jaysus! Well, if it doesn't kill us, Ann Marie, it'll cure us.'

'As you say.' Ann Marie took a second sip. It went down more smoothly than the first.

The two women sat in silence, sipping their laced tea and staring into the glowing embers of the fire in the big black range. The darkness

212

outside the single window in the room deepened.

'Would you care for more tea, Ann Marie?' Ivy's voice broke the comfortable silence.

'Thank you.' Ann Marie passed her cup and saucer over. 'I'd prefer straight tea this time, though, Ivy. That liquor holds quite a kick. I'm afraid my head is already spinning.'

'We're a pair of lightweights.' Ivy felt her own head turn when she stood up. She'd added very little of the poitín to their teacups. She couldn't imagine how her da had managed to guzzle the stuff.

'Are you ever going to explain what went on out in The Lane today to me, Ivy?'

'It's a feckin' mess, Ann Marie.' Ivy passed the refilled cup to Ann Marie before taking her own seat again. She didn't feel capable of even thinking about the problems the discovery of a contagious disease would bring to The Lane. She'd have to handle whatever came ... only ... not tonight. Still, Ann Marie was concerned and deserved an explanation.

'I'll tell yeh a story.' Ivy smiled sadly, remembering the game her da had played with them that started with those words. 'When I was about six or seven years old,' she sat back in her chair, 'before my mother left home...' Ivy's life was divided into two sections, before her mother Violet deserted the family and after, when the fate of her family rested firmly in Ivy's hands. 'It wasn't the first time the do-gooders came to call but it's the first I remember.' She closed her eyes. 'I didn't understand the entire situation at the time. I only knew The Lane was in an uproar.'

'Ivy…' Ann Marie hated to see her friend hurting. She reached across and touched Ivy's knee gently, reminding her that she was not alone.

'Our neighbours – the Keegans – a lovely family…' Ivy felt tears roll down her cheeks. She wouldn't be drinking that feckin' poitín again any time soon. It left yeh feelin' all soft and sentimental, 'I knew the two youngest girls. Maura and Molly were around my age so we played together in the courtyard. We sat together on the stairs listening to the storytellers. Molly loved storytime almost as much as me.'

'What happened?' Ann Marie prompted when the silence in the room was almost touchable. She didn't know what this story had to do with the happenings in The Lane today but Ivy obviously needed to tell it.

'Mrs Keegan had a bad fall in Grafton Street.' Ivy didn't know if she remembered the facts or if the story had grown over the years. 'They took her to hospital. She'd broken her foot and needed to be in a plaster cast. When Mr Keegan went to visit his wife, to see what was going on…' Ivy took a deep shaky breath, 'the do-gooders came, supposedly to look after the children. They decided that the two older ones could be left alone but they took Molly and Maura away with them. They were going to take care of them, they said, until Mrs Keegan was back on her feet.' The situation in The Lane today had brought up memories Ivy would prefer to forget.

'Mr Keegan went mad when he got back from the hospital and discovered what had been done.' Ivy remembered the shouting and screaming.

214

'He went to the convent and demanded the return of his children but was turned away.' She had to stop to swallow the tears that clogged her throat. 'The neighbours got involved. Me da went to the priest and asked him to help.'

Ann Marie sat silently, waiting for Ivy to continue in her own time.

'The two girls were never seen around here again,' Ivy offered eventually. 'Mr and Mrs Keegan have never stopped trying to find the two girls. It's because of them we know what happens to the children that are taken from The Lane.'

'What, Ivy?'

'Molly and Maura were separated and sent to Canada,' Ivy said. 'The do-gooders insist that the two girls are living with loving families. The girls, the do-gooders claim, have been placed with wealthy couples that want children.'

'The family know at least that their children are loved and well cared for,' Ann Marie offered quietly. She could understand wanting to take young children out of the abject poverty of The Lane. It broke her heart to see the children running around in badly fitting clothing, their feet naked and blue from the cold cobblestones.

'Oh, Ann Marie, grow up!' Ivy almost snapped.

'I beg your pardon!' Ann Marie said. It was obvious that she'd once more missed the point.

'I'm sorry.' Ivy remained silent for a moment. 'I overheard my mother and me da talking. Me da thought the same as yourself.' She remembered the scorn in her mother's voice. She'd never heard that disdain directed at her da before. Her mother reserved that tone for the people of The Lane. 'It

215

was my mother's considered opinion that the children taken from The Lane would be sold into a form of slavery.'

'I can't believe that, Ivy,' Ann Marie gasped.

'Think about it for a minute, Ann Marie – you've seen something of it yourself.'

'I most certainly have not.'

'I suppose you think young Davy, your aunt's boot boy, is leading a full and exciting life?' Ivy snapped. 'The lad sleeps in the fireplace and is treated like a dog by every passing servant. You didn't even know he existed until I took you into the servants' quarters.'

There was a long wounded silence between the two women, their awareness of the differences in their social standing almost a living presence in the room with them.

'I'm sorry.' Ivy took a deep calming breath. It wasn't Ann Marie's fault that life was unfair. 'I'm sorry, Ann Marie, that was uncalled for. It's just sometimes I get angry about "me station in life".' Ivy mocked the words she'd heard all of her life.

'After the happenings of this day, Ivy, I can't blame you for needing to lash out.' Ann Marie had never felt so helpless in her life.

'It's still not fair, Ann Marie, but then who ever said life was fair? It seems to me I have more understanding of the difference in our station because of my mother.' Violet Bruton had married very far beneath her own station in life. Her family had cut her off completely, refusing to acknowledge either her marriage or her children. 'Perhaps that's why I'm not willing to settle. The people of The Lane accept their lot in life. I can't, Ann

Marie. I simply refuse to be treated like a piece of substandard trash.'

Ann Marie was lost for words.

'I shouldn't take my frustration out on you, Ann Marie. Today knocked the stuffing out of me.' Ivy stood to take care of the range while she spoke. 'I can't bear to think of young Seán being locked away. He'll never accept the separation from his mother. And the thought of what the do-gooders will do to Ginie Johnson will keep me awake at night.'

'How can I help, Ivy?' Ann Marie was completely out of her depth and she knew it.

'I wish I knew, Ann Marie.' Ivy fought the tears that wanted to fall. What was the use of crying? 'I wish I knew.'

Chapter 22

Ivy cut through a tunnel that led to the service area of the tall buildings that lined Fitzwilliam Square. This lane would be her last stop before turning around and making her way home by a different route.

She felt all at sixes and sevens today. Jem was still insisting that she should talk to Billy Flint. He seemed to believe that your one, Betty Armstrong had a strong 'in' there and could introduce Ivy to the man. He'd offered again to go with her to see Flint but she couldn't bring herself to make that move.

'Afternoon to yeh, Ivy!' Curly called out as Ivy pushed her pram past his hut.

'Hello, Curly, how's yourself?' She knew she really didn't have time to visit but it cost nothing to be polite.

'Can't complain, Ivy – the rain's keeping off – so, can't complain.' He stood up from his perch on an upturned bucket and leaned out of his shed. 'That pram is riding terrible low today, Ivy. You need to do something before the auld thing collapses on yeh.'

'I'll do that.' Ivy wasn't really paying attention to the old man's words – her mind was buzzing with things she had to get done.

'Have yeh time to stop for a mug of tea?' Curly asked. 'Moocher wants a word with yeh. He's out walking his beat but he wants to talk to yeh.'

'I can't stop, Curly.' She was chasing her own tail today.

'Moocher says that well-dressed fella is hanging around the lanes again today.' Curly stepped out of the hut and put his hand on the handle of her pram. He could see she was ready to run off. 'Moocher is worried – he says the fella only turns up the days you're passing. You need to keep your eyes open. The fella could be up to no good. Shout out if you need us.' He stepped back into his hut. It was too cold to stand outside for long.

Ivy heard the words the old man said but she didn't take them in. She'd so much to think about, so much to do. The days were passing so quickly. It was almost time for her to start selling her Cinderella dolls. Every time she stopped to think of that her stomach knotted.

That The Lane was still under close scrutiny by the local health authorities didn't help matters. The nuns had, as she'd feared, taken it into their heads to visit every single dwelling in the tenements. To top everything off, there was still no news about Seán and Ginie. The Johnsons had disappeared into official hands and that was all anyone could discover about the situation.

The servants of Fitzwilliam Square knew to watch out for Ivy every Wednesday. It didn't surprise her to see someone further along, stepping onto the packed earth of the lane that ran along the back yards of these houses. It was probably one of the under-maids – with a bit of ribbon or lace she wanted Ivy to sell on for her. Then the figure disappeared and Ivy turned her pram into the nearest back yard.

These houses had short walled yards that insured privacy to each dwelling. She walked slowly past the servants' outdoor 'necessary' – sometimes one of the younger servants hid in the toilet waiting to pass on items they wanted her to sell. Today no one stepped out. She continued on past the cement-block hut that was used for storing coal and household supplies – it was locked tight.

She was startled to see Mrs Quinn the housekeeper suddenly appear in the open back door of the house in front of her. Mrs Quinn never came to the back door – it was beneath her dignity. Ivy always dealt with one of the maids at this house.

'Here, Ivy.' Mrs Quinn shoved a thick newspaper-wrapped parcel into Ivy's hands. 'I haven't time to talk.' Then she whispered, 'Young Hetty from next door left a message...' The message had been passed along to the housekeeper as was only right and proper. 'They're needing a word.' She slammed the door in Ivy's face, leaving her staring open-mouthed at the tightly shut wooden panel.

'What the heck was that about?' Ivy wondered aloud to herself.

She turned and went back down the yard. She stepped out onto the alleyway that connected the back yards. For a moment she imagined she caught a glimpse of the man Moocher had warned her about. She stood for a moment to check, then when she saw nothing further she wanted to kick herself. She went on her way, shaking her head in disgust at her own foolishness. She'd be jumping at her own shadow soon.

'Ivy, I've been watching for yeh – I thought you'd never get here!' Hetty Allan stepped out into the alleyway. She grabbed Ivy and, almost pulling her arm out of its socket, pulled her into the yard of the house where she was employed and towards the back entrance.

'So I see.' Ivy tried to shake her arm free. 'Will yeh let up, Hetty – you're going to pull me arm off!'

'Oh, I'm sorry, Ivy,' Hetty wailed. 'I'm that nervous.'

'What's wrong?' Ivy could see that Hetty was upset. It wasn't like the placid woman Ivy knew. Hetty had come up from County Cork to work in this grand house. She'd been here for about six years as far as Ivy could remember. The gentry who owned these big houses didn't employ Dubliners, fearing they'd be murdered in their beds by a people who refused to recognise their place.

220

'It's old Nanny Grace,' Hetty whispered with a frightened glance over her shoulder. She'd thought she'd caught a glimpse of a gent following Ivy. It must have been her imagination. The good Lord knew things were so up in the air at the minute nothing would surprise her.

'What about her?'

The old woman had been a part of this house since before Ivy's mother was born. She'd been kind to Ivy through the years, making sure she was given the clothes her young charges grew out of. Ivy's brothers had been dressed like little toffs thanks to old Nanny Grace. Ivy wouldn't forget that.

'She wants to talk to yeh,' Hetty whispered.

Poor Hetty, Ivy thought. She couldn't be more than eighteen. She'd come to Dublin a fresh-faced farm girl but the years of service had taken the flesh from her bones and the bloom from her cheeks. She was now pasty white and painfully thin. 'She wants to talk to yeh in private, Ivy.'

'All right,' Ivy said, simply for something to say.

'She wants to talk to you, Ivy, up in the nursery.' Hetty stared, waiting for the penny to drop.

'What?' Ivy barked. 'Me, go in there – me, go upstairs – in there?' She felt lightheaded, her blood tingling with nervous excitement. She'd never been past the back door of any of these houses.

'That's what Nanny Grace wants.' Hetty, now that she had Ivy in her hands, felt almost weak with relief. She'd been so afraid she'd miss Ivy. The woman went down these back lanes at a speed that would frighten the horses. She'd been keeping watch for what seemed like ages but it had been worth it. She'd promised Nanny Grace she'd deliver Ivy Murphy up to see her and by God she was going to do just that.

'What'll I do with me pram?' Ivy wasn't willing to leave her well-stocked pram parked out for anyone's hands to riffle through.

'Yeh can leave it in the butler's pantry.'

'Old Misery Guts Parker,' Ivy named the family butler, 'would have a heart attack.' She wasn't willing to get into trouble. She needed the goods she received from the houses on Fitzwilliam Square. If she was caught taking liberties at this house it would lead to nothing but trouble for her. The news of her presumption would travel around this square at the speed of light.

'It was Mr Parker who suggested you leave your pram in his pantry,' Hetty said in tones of wonder.

'Lead the way.' Ivy was dying of curiosity now. What in the name of all that was good and holy was going on here?

'Yeh'll have to take off your boots,' Hetty said over her shoulder while leading Ivy through the warren of servants' rooms in the basement of this house.

Ivy was aware of the furtive glances she received from the servants gathered in the kitchen but no one passed a remark.

'In here.' Hetty pushed the door of a room open. 'Mr Parker left it unlocked for us. I almost don't dare put on a light, Ivy – can yeh see all right?'

'I can't see a bloomin' thing, Hetty,' Ivy snapped. Was all this secrecy really necessary? The masters of the house never descended to the servants' level.

'Shhh!' Hetty was shaking in her shoes. 'Get in.' She pushed Ivy into the butler's pantry. The pantry was a room she'd never entered in all of her years serving at this house. 'We have the electric power.' She daringly pushed a button with justifiable pride in her own elevated position – not everyone was allowed touch this newfangled electric.

'I've heard of this.' Ivy stood staring up at the bright naked globe hanging by a wire from the ceiling. She was so fascinated by this modern wonder she never thought to check out the butler's hidden lair.

'Don't touch!' Hetty screamed when Ivy reached up to touch the light source. 'You don't want to break it, do you?'

'Fair enough.' Ivy would think about this new wonder later. She chanced a quick look around. There seemed to be an awful lot of dark shelves and nooks stuffed with 'things'. She could spend hours in here nosing into everything.

'Take those ugly boots off yeh, Ivy.' Hetty had to get Ivy up the servants' stairway unnoticed. The noise those boots would make would wake the dead. Not all of the house servants knew about the events taking place here, and Hetty didn't want to give anyone room to gossip or carry tales. 'Here,' she grabbed Ivy by the thick ugly black shawl, 'let me give yeh a hand getting out of this thing.' She pulled so hard on the back of the shawl she was in danger of breaking Ivy's neck.

'Get off!' Ivy pushed Hetty away from her. 'I'll take me own stuff off, thank you very much, Hetty Allan.' She loosened the belt of her army coat. She used the belt to keep her shawl wrapped tightly around her. This helped to keep out the cold and preserve her modesty.

'I was only trying to help.' Hetty was actually wringing her hands tightly together now. 'We need to hurry, Ivy. Nanny Grace is waiting.' She knew Nanny wanted Ivy gone before the children returned from an outing with their tutor. Ivy didn't need to know that, however.

'Give us a sec for God's sake, Hetty.' Ivy dropped to the floor, still wearing her big coat as protection against the chill of the floor and any dirt that might linger there. She quickly untied the laces of her boots and pulled her long thick hand-knit socks up her legs. She tucked the hems of the boy's trousers she wore under her long black skirt into the top of her socks.

'In the name of God, Ivy Murphy, what are yeh wearing?' Hetty gasped at the glimpse she'd received of what appeared to be gentlemen's tweed trousers.

'They keep me warm, Hetty Allan,' Ivy snapped. She'd not apologise for her need to keep warm as she walked the streets in this cold, wet, winter weather. It was none of feckin Hetty Allan's business what she wore. Ivy was doing the woman a favour. She'd remind her of that fact.

Ivy pushed herself to a standing position. She removed her shawl and coat, dropping the two garments onto the top of her pram. The old socks she used as gloves she pushed into the deep pockets of her skirt. She didn't want to misplace them – it was perishing cold outside.

'Will yeh for the love of Jesus hurry up, Ivy

Murphy?' Hetty was dancing in place. She'd have to run down the yard to the privy if Ivy didn't get a move on.

'Wait.' Ivy bent from the waist and with a practised move shoved her fingers through her mop of blue-black curls. If she was going to walk through this house, she'd do it in style.

'Well, in the name of God, Ivy Murphy,' Hetty stared with her mouth and eyes wide open, 'look what you hide under that pig-ugly outfit!'

Chapter 23

The well-dressed man who had been watching the two women cursed loudly and fluently when he saw the woman he'd been ordered to follow disappear into the open doorway of one of these big houses. He'd followed the two women down the yard, hiding behind the outbuildings, waiting for his chance, but he couldn't follow the bloody woman into the house. Besides, the back of the house would be lousy with nosy servants.

He'd never in his life had so much difficulty laying his hands on someone. The bloody woman was like a bee, buzzing all over the place. All of this would be so much easier if he could give the woman a 'tap on the noggin' – that would take care of the problem. He'd have her well in hand then.

He thought he'd had her earlier. He'd been creeping towards her on swift and silent feet when he saw that maid standing in the alleyway, obviously waiting for something or someone. He thought for a minute he'd been spotted as something seemed to have spooked the woman he was following. But she'd gone about her business with no bother and he'd been able to breathe a sigh of relief.

He'd been hoping to nab her today. He had to get his hands on the darn woman as his chasing her around the back lanes was becoming something of an embarrassment to him. He wasn't looking forward to the lecture he'd receive if he didn't succeed soon. He'd been so close.

The man pulled the collar of his expensive coat up around his face. While pulling on the brim of his hat, he raised his eyes to the grey overcast sky as if seeking divine intervention.

Glancing at his watch he groaned. He had to leave, now. He wanted to shake his fist at the sky and curse, but stifled the impulse. If any of his old cronies ever heard about this he'd never live it down. With one more angry glance around the deserted yard, he sighed deeply and prepared to return and report yet another failure.

He carefully stepped out from his hiding place. Who knew how long the bloody woman was going to spend in the nobs' house? He'd work of his own to get back to. He made his way unseen down the back yard and out onto the lane.

Hetty couldn't believe what she was seeing. Ivy Murphy stood before her, an Ivy Murphy Hetty had never seen before. Why did the woman walk the streets looking like a beggar when with a bit of effort she could be a knockout?

Hetty almost felt her knees go weak with relief. She could relax. Ivy Murphy, in her long black skirt, spotlessly clean white lace blouse with its demure collar, and a hand-knit black cardigan, looked like she could be one of the upper servants in this house. It would be one less question Hetty might have to answer later.

'Well, I thought you were in a hurry, Hetty Allan?' Ivy was secretly pleased at Hetty's compliments.

She thought of the ugly coat, shawl and boots as her uniform. Underneath, however, she'd been making changes. She no longer needed to wear rags. It had been hard at first but she was gradually beginning to spend some of the money she earned on herself.

'Follow me,' said Hetty.

The two women crept up the servant's stairway without encountering anyone. Ivy had to wait several times until Hetty checked the coast was clear. There was no one about. They eventually reached the floor underneath the servant's attic. The top floor of the house held the nursery wing and its staff.

'Nanny, it's me, Hetty.' She pushed the door of the main nursery open slightly.

The old woman had taken to spending her days in this room, lost in her memories. The house servants kept the rooms clean. They carried coal and kept the fire going. They brought the old woman's meals to her on a tray.

'Come in, child, don't linger out there in the corridor,' Nanny called out softly. 'Is Ivy with you? Did you find her?'

'Are yeh sure about this, Nanny Grace?' Hetty almost whispered.

'I'm here, Nanny,' Ivy pushed the door open and strode into the room. They'd be in the hallway for the rest of the day if these women kept dithering. 'I hear you want to see me.'

The old woman, dressed all in black, gently rocking on her chair placed by the side of the fire, seemed to suit the room somehow. A cloud of snow-white hair pulled back into a soft bun and covered with a lace bonnet framed her kind face. Ivy tried desperately hard not to stand and stare around the large room. She'd never in her life seen anything like it. It held a world designed to appeal to children.

Ivy wanted to jump onto the back of the tall grey rocking horse. The animal stood proudly in the corner, its red-tinted nostrils flaring. Her heart leapt with excitement at the sight of the toy with its white mane and tail. She imagined riding into the sky on its broad back. One wall held a collection of doll's houses that she longed to touch. There were dolls and prams, games and strange items she didn't recognise. This place was a wonderland.

'Come and sit down, Ivy Murphy.' Nanny noticed the wonder on Ivy's face. It was a terrible shame the children this room had been designed for had never felt that overwhelming joy. 'Hetty, you'd better get back downstairs. Cook promised to have a tea tray ready to send up. Perhaps you would be good enough to carry it up for us?' Even after all of the years she'd spent in Ireland

228

Nanny Grace's English accent had never faded.

'I'll see to it immediately, Nanny Grace,' Hetty said with a quick dip of her knee. She left the room, closing the door behind her.

'What's going on, Nanny Grace?' Ivy had to force herself to take a seat across the fire from the old woman. She didn't want to sit down. She wanted to jump to her feet again and examine every item in the room. When would she ever get the chance again?

'The family have decided to leave the square, Ivy,' Nanny said after several moments had passed. 'To leave Ireland.' She didn't think she was giving away secrets. Ivy Murphy wasn't in a position to reveal Nanny's employers' intentions to their social set.

'I hadn't heard that.' Ivy was surprised – news like this normally flashed around the streets in minutes. The servants knew everything that went on in this high-priced square.

'The family do not wish the world to know their plans.' Nanny stared into the fire. She'd believed she was a trusted retainer of that family. It was true what they said: there is no fool like an old fool.

'Well, good luck to them,' Ivy said to break the silence that had fallen.

'I wish...' Nanny stopped speaking at the brisk rap on the door. She stiffened in her seat before relaxing at the soft sound of Hetty's voice.

'That girl must have wings on her feet. Open the door, Ivy, would you, please?' Nanny smiled. 'Your legs are younger than mine.'

'Cook had everything in hand, Nanny Grace.

She was pouring the boiling water over the tea leaves when I got back downstairs.' Hetty bustled importantly into the room. There was more excitement around the house these days than ever before in her working life. 'Would you grab that table, please, Ivy?' She gave a nod of her head towards an occasional table sitting against one wall. Hetty didn't think she needed to be all prim and proper at this moment.

Ivy wrestled the gate-leg table over to the fire. Hetty waited while Ivy opened the table and settled it firmly in place, then she lowered the heavy silver salver she carried onto the table top.

'I can't stay, Nanny Grace,' Hetty whispered. 'Can yeh manage without me?'

'Ivy will no doubt be able to handle everything.' Nanny smiled sweetly.

'I'll be back to take Ivy down later. Ring for me, Nanny.' Hetty hurried in the direction of the door. With a swish of her lace-edged petticoat she left the room.

'See what they've sent up for us, Ivy.' Nanny waved one blue-lined, age-spotted hand in the direction of the table.

'You can tell me what's going on while I set the food out for us.' Ivy was unconsciously using her 'posh' voice.

Nanny's eyebrows rose in surprise but she said nothing. She had a great deal that needed to be said – commenting on Ivy's improved diction would simply delay matters.

'I can't stay long. It's not that I'm not delighted at this opportunity to see how the other half lives,' Ivy said over her shoulder, 'but I do like to get home before dark and these nights it gets dark so early.'

Besides, she wanted to be home for Emmy when the little girl got back from school. Emmy was coming to Ivy's today. They would eat together and do their homework together. Emmy took Ivy's education very seriously. The little girl had a brilliant mind and was years ahead of her age group at school.

'I'll try not to keep you too long, Ivy.' Nanny accepted the teacup and saucer from Ivy's hands. The old woman watched while Ivy prepared a plate of savoury delicacies before placing them on the table close to her hand. Where had the ragged urchin she'd watched for years disappeared to? Who was this young woman? Nanny wished she had the time to figure out this mystery.

'What is it you want, Nanny Grace?' Ivy knew the old woman wanted something from her. She just couldn't begin to imagine what.

'I've mentioned the family are leaving Ireland.' Nanny closed her eyes briefly.

'What about the young lads?' Ivy knew twin boys of about five lived in this house. She'd been collecting their torn and stained clothing for years.

'The boys are being sent to boarding school in England.' Nanny fought the tears that tried to well in her eyes.

'What about you, Nanny Grace?' Ivy was beginning to see the light.

'I am to be let go,' Nanny bit out between her teeth. 'The family no longer have need of my services. It was mentioned that by the time the twins were of marrying age I would be long dead.' Nanny could almost feel the ice cold of the ghost-knife that the master had unknowingly put into her heart with his callous words.

'Well,' Ivy bit into a roast-beef sandwich and stared across the fire at the old woman, 'that's probably the truth.'

'You always were a cheeky monkey, Ivy Murphy.' Nanny was surprised into a laugh. Had she really been expecting sympathy from this young woman?

'What do you want of me, Nanny Grace?' Ivy wondered what the woman's name was. She'd never heard her referred to as anything but Nanny Grace.

'Your expertise,' Nanny answered.

'I'm surprised to hear I have any expertise.' Ivy swallowed the final bite of the tiny sandwich.

Nanny took a stern hold on her emotions. 'As I said, the family are not taking me to England with them.'

'Wait a minute.' Ivy held up a hand and stared. 'Didn't you come with the family from England? The least they could do is take you back to your own country.'

'I came to Ireland almost sixty years ago as under-nanny to the present Earl's grandfather.' Nanny wondered where the years had flown.

'So,' Ivy shrugged, 'they should still take you back with them. What do they expect you to do here in Dublin? You don't know anyone outside this bloody great house, do you?'

'No.' Nanny left it at that. It was her own fault. She had no friends, no family. She had devoted her life to a family not her own and this was the

232

thanks she received. She was to be cast out in a country not her own amongst a people she'd never come to know or understand.

'What about the rest of the servants?' Ivy wondered aloud.

'Some of the younger staff have elected to travel to England with the family. And there will be a small staff kept on here to oversee and caretake the house.' The rest of the staff would be in the same position as herself – homeless.

'Right.' Ivy didn't see what the problem was. Surely the old girl would be allowed live out the rest of her days in this house? It wasn't like she was going to be in anyone's way. Still, it was none of her business. 'What exactly are you looking for from me, Nanny Grace?' She needed to move this along. She wanted to get in behind closed doors before total darkness descended.

'I need you to use your contacts to sell some items for me.' Nanny felt the words lodge in her throat. She coughed politely. She couldn't allow her pride to choke her. She had never indulged in the petty pilfering that was rampant in these big houses. She'd disdained the additional pennies and shillings that could be amassed this way. She'd proudly donated the children's discards to Ivy and before her, her mother. 'I've been offered the contents of this room and all other rooms on this floor.' Nanny waved her hand around the well-used luxury items. The young master, a man she'd raised from his first day of life, had offered her the room's contents for her grandchildren. Nanny had reeled from the knowledge that the man staring down at her so coldly had no idea of her life outside this room.

'I hope to goodness this isn't your pension.' Ivy stood and slowly walked around the room in a wide circle, touching and examining the room's contents. The items were magical to her eyes but they held no great financial value.

'A pension was never mentioned,' Nanny whispered sadly.

'I thought...' Ivy shouldn't be surprised at the callous attitude of the wealthy.

'So did I.' Nanny understood Ivy's surprise. It was generally understood that old retainers would be homed for life. It wasn't the law of the land but common decency should dictate that having served the same family for fifty-eight years Nanny should have been well set up for the rest of her days.

'Did you receive the fixtures and fittings of this room?' Ivy wanted to change the subject. She had no right to voice her opinion here.

'I received the entire contents of this floor for my own use.'

'If they are leaving staff to take care of this place, surely you would be able to stay?' Ivy asked.

'The family are to take the children and their personal staff on a Christmas holiday in warmer climes.' Nanny had been surprised to hear that she would not accompany the family on their annual visit to their estate in Italy. 'This house is to be locked up, dustcovers throughout. It is my understanding the caretakers will lodge in the room off the kitchen. I was not given an actual date to vacate the premises.' Nanny didn't think her heart could take any more pain. She had no time to

234

wallow in self-pity, however. She had to be realistic and plan some kind of future for herself.

'Right.' Ivy was frantically trying to shift her days around in her head. She had a routine but it wasn't set in cement. She sighed deeply. The offer of these goods for sale came as a big surprise. Perhaps she should be ready to hear something similar from other servants? She'd like to help this old woman out. Nanny Grace had been good to Ivy through the years. She'd like to help but where was she going to find the time?

'I'll have to leave soon, Nanny. I really don't want to be out on the streets in the dark.' Ivy took her seat again.

'Can you at least advise me, Ivy?' Nanny didn't want to beg but she desperately needed help. 'Give me the name of someone who might be interested in these things.'

'I'll do better than that, Nanny Grace,' Ivy owed this old woman a great deal. She believed in paying her debts. 'I'll come back and discuss the matter in detail with you. We need to take stock of what you have. We want a better idea of how you're fixed. That will all take time I don't have right now.'

'Thank you, Ivy.' Nanny Grace smiled sadly. A young ragamuffin she'd thrown some crumbs of mercy to over the years was going to help her more than the family she'd devoted her life to.

'I'll come back.' Ivy held her head in her hand for a moment, trying to organise her thoughts. When did she have a spare morning? She had the schedule she kept to for her round, she couldn't change that. She didn't like to let people down.

'It will have to be early Saturday morning, Nanny Grace. Does that suit you?'

'That will suit me admirably, Ivy.'

Ivy stood abruptly. Time was passing, shadows were deepening outside the small windows that ran along the outside wall of this room. 'In the meantime you could get a start on making a list of the goods stored in these rooms. You need to make note of everything and I do mean everything, Nanny Grace. The smallest item must be accounted for. That would be a great help.'

'I'll do that, Ivy.' Nanny pulled the embroidered cord hanging by her chair. 'Hetty will be here in a moment to guide you out.'

'I'll see you Saturday morning bright and early, Nanny Grace,' Ivy promised. 'We'll go over your list, get a better idea of what's what, see how you are fixed.'

'Thank you again, Ivy.' Nanny nodded towards the door when the sound of knuckles rapping sounded. 'There's Hetty now. Have a safe journey home, Ivy.' Nanny watched the young woman hurry from the room. The children would be back soon from their visit to the museum with their tutor. She was alone for the moment. She could allow the tears to flow.

Ivy practically ran around the back streets of Dublin, frantically trying to make up the time she'd lost with her visit to old Nanny Grace. The wheels on her pram were in danger of locking. The sheer weight of the goods she'd received today excited and delighted her. She couldn't wait to examine everything. While smiling cheer-

236

fully and exchanging remarks with people she passed, Ivy's head was whirling. She had so much she needed to get done.

Chapter 24

'Is that you, Johnjo?'

'Who else would it be?' Johnjo Smith responded while removing the key from the door that opened into the Regency Suite of the Shelbourne Hotel.

If the Moocher had been there he'd have recognised Johnjo as the man he'd seen loitering in the back lanes of Fitzwilliam Square.

'What happened?' The man now known as Douglas Joyce walked out of the hotel bathroom, a towel around his waist. He was rubbing his wet blond hair with a second towel.

'I almost had her!' Johnjo Smith wanted to curse. He hated to fail at anything this man asked of him. He owed Douglas Joyce ... everything. 'I was just about to nab her when she was invited into one of those bloody great houses. I couldn't wait until she came out of there.'

'Impossible.' Doug turned to go back through his bedroom and into the bathroom again. 'Ivy is never invited inside one of those houses. She knows her place. She stands outside in all weathers like a good little beggar.' Doug's voice echoed faintly back through the bedroom and into the lushly furnished lounge. He reappeared, wearing a dragon-embroidered, padded, black satin dressing gown. He had one of the hotel's towels tucked under the collar of the robe. His bare feet sank into the thick carpet that covered the hotel-room floor.

'Well, she was invited inside today,' Johnjo stated. 'In fact I got the impression that her visit was important to someone inside that house. There was a bloomin' maid practically dancing in the alley. She's the reason I wasn't able to nab Ivy today. She almost dragged her into one of those fancy houses with her.'

'That's a turn-up for the books.' Doug grimaced. He'd hoped to have the chance to talk to Ivy. He'd been in Dublin for weeks but events had conspired to halt the plans he'd made for his own personal business. 'The situation may have changed anyway.'

'What did you find out?'

'Brace yourself.' Doug took the towel from around his neck and began rubbing his hair. He wasn't sure how he felt about the news he'd uncovered this morning.

'Did someone recognise you?' Johnjo had feared something like this happening. It was ludicrous that this man thought he could pass himself off in public as a penniless dock worker. On a stage Doug could get away with it, but in natural light he doubted it. Even standing wearing nothing but a towel Doug's long leanly muscled figure gave the impression of breeding and wealth.

'No, give me some credit.' Doug dropped the towel around his neck again. He held both ends of the towel in white-knuckled fists. 'I've learned a few things about passing myself off as something I'm not over the years.' Today had been the first chance he'd had since arriving in Dublin to get out and do any investigating for himself.

'So, what did you find out?'

'It seems me da is dead.' Doug dropped into his childhood accent automatically when speaking of his father. He had no idea how he felt about the death of his parent – was that normal?

'Yeh what? How? He wasn't an old man.'

'It's true none the less.' Doug had control of himself again. 'It would appear there is a great deal of speculating about the bold Éamonn Murphy's passing. The gossip around the pub was that Éamonn drowned on New Year's Eve. There was no funeral, the body having been lost at sea or in the Canal depending on who was telling the story. They did say that our Ivy gave him a wake fit for a king at the local pub.' Doug was sick, thinking about what his sister might have had to do to get the money needed for the bloody royal send-off.

'Well, that changes things, doesn't it? No need for grabbing her off the streets if the old man is gone.' Johnjo felt almost weak with relief. He hadn't wanted to do it. He'd feared he might have to knock her out or something. He was a dab hand at stealing inanimate objects, but not people.

'I think I'll have to pay a call on Billy Flint.' Doug turned to go back into his bedroom. 'That man has his finger on this city's pulse, we both know that. I need more information.'

'But–'

'I want more information!' Doug snapped over his shoulder. 'I need to get ready. I'll need my black suit, Johnjo.'

The sudden demanding peal of the gilded black telephone rang out.

'Get that,' Doug ordered. 'That will be Her Ladyship as you insist on calling her.'

Johnjo walked into the bedroom after his employer. He shrugged at the loud bang the hotel bathroom door made as Doug slammed it shut behind him. He removed his employer's black suit from the depths of the wardrobe, ignoring the demanding peal of the telephone placed on a dresser by the side of the bed.

'Tell her I'm not here!' the man listed on billboards as Douglas Joyce shouted through the closed door. 'I've taken the first ship to the moon.'

'That, sir, would be such an obvious lie.' Johnjo Smith continued to pay close attention to the brush he was passing over the shoulders of his employer's black jacket. He was both official dresser and friend to the man.

The telephone began to ring again.

'Answer the bloody phone, man. You and I both know she won't give up!' Doug roared.

'Very good, sir.'

Johnjo hung the suit carefully back into the wardrobe. He crossed the thick bedroom carpet. The luxury of his surroundings amused him. He picked the phone up from the nightstand. A nightstand, I ask your sacred pardon, he thought. It's far from it we were raised.

He knew well what was coming. Doug was right: only one person knew they were in Dublin and staying at this hotel.

In his snootiest voice he gave his employer's name.

'Put my son on the telephone,' a well-bred female voice snapped out of the instrument. The demand was barked over Johnjo's polite little refrain.

'I am terribly sorry, Your Ladyship,' Johnjo gave the woman on the other end of the line a title she didn't possess, 'but my master is not here at the moment.' Johnjo was not telling a lie. Doug was still in the bathroom. Johnjo would never state it aloud but it gave him great pleasure to put a spoke in the wheel of this woman.

'Have there been any developments?' the voice demanded. 'Do not try to tell me you don't know, Mr Johnjo Smith.'

'I'm afraid I really couldn't say, Your Ladyship.' Johnjo allowed his displeasure to show in his voice. He would not give this woman any information.

'Have my son telephone me!' Her Ladyship almost shouted.

Johnjo was glad she couldn't see the grin on his face. The woman was capable of scratching the eyes out of his head.

'I'll pass your demands along.' Johnjo gently replaced the telephone receiver.

He stood for a moment, looking around the room. They'd come a long way from grotty boarding rooms smelling of boiled cabbage and nights when any rough kip was a blessing. Doug had insisted on booking this suite – two bedrooms and a sitting room plus private bathrooms. He'd been adamant that they would stay at the Shelbourne Hotel.

Johnjo shook his head and shrugged. Who would have believed that he would one day stay

241

at this hotel?

'Well,' Doug stood in the open bathroom doorway, 'what did she want?'

'Her Ladyship wished to speak with her son,' Johnjo delivered deadpan. He might not have been able to make a living on the stage. That didn't mean he was entirely without talent.

'Nice to be recognised.' Doug grinned wryly. His mother had been horrified that a son of hers should take to the stage. She'd ignored him while he struggled to survive. She'd recently changed her tune when he'd started to make a name for himself.

'Her Ladyship requested an update on the situation here,' Johnjo said mildly.

'One of these days she's going to let you have it for calling her "Her Ladyship" in that snotty tone,' Doug warned. 'Meanwhile, next time she telephones, you can tell her from me that she can go–'

'Soak her head,' Johnjo put in quickly. He'd noticed their return to Dublin had also brought about the return of fluent cursing in his employer's speech.

'That'll do.' Doug closed his eyes in disgust. His mother had that effect on him.

'You need to get ready to leave, sir.' Johnjo reminded his employer of his responsibilities.

'Stop calling me "sir" in that supercilious tone, Johnjo Smith,' Doug barked. 'I've enough to put up with without your cheek.'

'I don't even know what the word *"supercilious"* means, sir.' Johnjo grinned. 'I didn't have the advantage of your education.'

'Oh, put a sock in it.' Doug smiled in spite of

242

himself. 'As you've pointed out, I'll be late to the theatre and that would never do.'

Doug wondered, yet again, what had possessed him to agree to this theatre date. He walked over to the chest-of-drawers and removed his pressed and carefully folded underwear from the depths of a drawer. Johnjo insisted on serving as his dresser these days but there were some things a man did for himself. He'd be plucked before he'd allow another man or woman to pull on his underwear for him.

He dressed quickly in his black pants and white dress shirt. He sat on the side of the bed to put on his socks and highly polished black shoes. The headliner for the Gaiety Theatre had broken his leg in three places. In the lead-up to Christmas, the busiest time of year in the entertainment calendar, few successful acts were available to step in and rescue an established show. Doug had been free only because he'd been planning to put his affairs in order before taking a long-overdue holiday. He'd been working all the hours God sent for the last four years. Fate and the obscene amount of money offered had tempted him to step into the suddenly vacant top spot at the Gaiety.

'Your jacket, sir,' Johnjo held the black dinner jacket aloft.

'Tell me again what insanity possessed me when I agreed to accept this offer. I've even agreed to play Prince Charming until they can find someone else, for god's sake.' Doug slipped his arms into the jacket and stood patiently while Johnjo arranged the fit and ran the brush over the fabric a final time. He knew the answer to his

243

own question. He'd been unable to resist the chance to return to Dublin – one final visit home.

'I'll fetch your hat and coat, sir.' Johnjo knew Doug wasn't expecting an answer to his familiar ranting.

He walked to the cupboard placed just inside the main door of the suite. He removed his employer's dark-grey cashmere coat from the depths of the cupboard. The matching trilby hat and a long white silk scarf he took down from the high shelf of the cupboard.

'I don't know why I put up with your impudence.' Doug allowed Johnjo to drape the white silk scarf around his neck. He put his arms into the sleeves of the coat Johnjo held open for him.

'Yes, you do, sir.' Johnjo took the bristle brush he kept in his pocket and applied himself to brushing his employer's broad shoulders.

'I should have had you arrested when you tried to steal my wallet.'

'Fat lot of good that did me,' Johnjo grinned. 'You had even less of the readies than I did. It was embarrassing to a man of my standing in the thieving community. I ended up feeding you and giving you somewhere to stay. I had to get out of that life. I'd never have been able to live down the shame.'

Johnjo had taken an injured, homesick, lost young man under his wing. He'd attempted to teach Doug how to 'snatch and grab' but the lad simply wouldn't learn.

Doug wanted to go on the stage. He'd heard there was money in it and travelled to London to seek his fortune. They'd formed an unlikely partnership. Together they learned to survive in

244

the cut-throat world of variety theatre.

Johnjo hadn't the skill or the looks needed to make a living as a leading man. He'd always be a bit player. He did however know a great deal more than Doug about the world at large. It was Johnjo who learned the rules and regulations of the world Doug desperately wanted to enter. He watched out for the young lad and taught him the rules of the game. It was Johnjo who had planned out the quickest routes to run from one theatre to another so Doug could repeat his spot several times a night and drag in the money they needed. They had barely survived at first but eventually they'd flourished.

'Your hat, sir.' Johnjo passed the trilby to his employer, having applied the brush with swift efficient strokes.

'Thanks.' Doug crossed to the mirror sitting proudly on a nearby table. He put the hat on his shining blond hair. He examined his face in the mirror with a sad smile. Vanity. How many times had he received a crack around the head for the sin of vanity? 'Is it raining?' he asked as he continued to examine his image.

Doug didn't see the sorrow in his own violet-blue eyes. He saw only the image he wanted to present to his public: a dapper young man about town, one gifted with an excellent tenor voice that brought him to the top of the bill in every theatre he played in these days. He'd come a long way in a relatively short space of time. He was about to step out into the unknown again as soon as he finished up his Dublin dates.

'Amazingly,' Johnjo broke into Doug's troubled

thoughts, 'it would appear that the rain is keeping off.'

'Right, I'm set to go.' Doug saluted his image in the mirror. The Great Pretender. He was ready to step out onto the stage of life and delight his admiring fans.

'We need to hurry.' Johnjo took his own coat from the closet. It was really unnecessary to leave this early but Doug preferred to be the first to arrive at the theatre and the last to leave.

'I want to walk slowly today, Johnjo, take in the scenery.' Doug stepped through the door Johnjo held open for him. News of his father's death seemed to have shaken him more than he had realised. He waited in the long hotel hallway while Johnjo locked the door to their suite. 'Haven't you heard? I'm the headliner now. I don't have to be at the theatre before everyone else.'

'You never did have to be but that never stopped you being the first there.' Johnjo put his hat on and prepared to walk down the stairs and through the lobby.

'Sometimes, Johnjo, the theatre was the only roof we had over our heads.' Doug had quickly learned that each theatre had a 'hidden' spot. He'd explored until he knew exactly where the two of them could safely hide during the dark hours of the night.

Doug ignored or didn't notice the intense feminine interest he received as he walked through the richly appointed hotel lobby. His tall, wide-shouldered, slim-hipped masculine appearance alone would have attracted attention but his growing fame as a singer and entertainer ensured he would never pass unnoticed. He'd spent all of his spare time during his weeks in Dublin feeding the publicity machine at the theatre manager's demand.

'We'll take a turn through the park.' Doug gave a brisk nod of his head to the uniformed doorman holding the hotel's main door open for him. He ignored the man's fulsome greeting. The same man had boxed his ears and on occasion kicked his arse for begging from the wealthy patrons of this hotel. Doug hoped he wasn't expecting a generous tip from him.

He stepped out to cross the road towards Stephen's Green. He wanted to collect his thoughts now that he finally appeared to have some spare time. This trip to Dublin was far more emotionally challenging than he'd ever imagined it would be. 'We have time.'

'Very good, sir.'

Johnjo Smith matched his stride to his employer's and, each lost in his own thoughts, the two men strolled through a park that held memories for both of them.

'I can try to nab Ivy tomorrow,' Johnjo offered softly when the long silence became uncomfortable.

'Not unless you're willing to go into The Lane. Tomorrow is Thursday. Unless the sky has fallen and no one told me, Ivy's routine is set. She stays home and checks out her takings tomorrow, getting ready for her turn around the markets on Friday.'

'I could follow her around the markets Friday – try to nab her then.'

'You'd be lucky.' Doug smiled. 'I don't fancy

your chances of keeping up with my sister when she puts the speed on.' He elbowed his friend and employee. 'You're out of shape, old man.'

'I'm ten years older than you,' Johnjo snapped, his vanity stung. 'We can't all be fresh-faced twenty-year-old twits.'

'Shh!' Doug winked. 'Don't you know I'm a mature man of twenty-six?'

'So your billboards say,' Johnjo shrugged. 'You're the only actor I know that increases his age instead of reducing his years.'

'If I'd given my real age in the beginning I'd have been taken on as a juvenile lead. You know what a honey-trap that is.'

'Yeah,' Johnjo said as they approached the opening in the railings that surrounded the park. 'You never get taken seriously after that.'

'I'll have to give more thought as to how I'll contact Ivy, Johnjo,' Doug said as the two men stepped out of the main park gates. They turned as one in the direction of Grafton Street and the theatre. 'With my old man dead, well, it changes everything. I get a shiver down my spine just thinking about walking back into The Lane. I don't imagine you want to revisit the place any more than I do.'

'That's a fact,' Johnjo sighed.

The two men entered the Gaiety Theatre at the side. They exchanged greetings with the man on the stage door. As usual there were a great many private messages for Doug who was fast becoming a much sought-after social prize to the leaders of Dublin society. Johnjo took those with a sigh – there would be the usual pack of women issuing

248

invitations to romantic rendezvous. Women seemed to go crazy over Doug's handsome face. The two men made their way to the star's dressing room.

Chapter 25

'Home sweet home,' Ivy sighed when she turned away from the Grand Canal with its covering of hungry swans. The tunnel into The Lane came into sight. She was having a great deal of difficulty getting her pram to roll along. The weight of her takings on the springs was pushing the undercarriage down onto the big wheels.

'Far be it from me to complain about the amount of stuff I got on me round today,' Ivy said aloud to herself. 'I won't half be glad to get indoors and put the kettle on. Me mouth feels like I've been eating feathers.' She put all of her weight behind the handles of her pram and pushed.

'Need a hand, Ivy?' Jem Ryan stood in the open door of his livery, keeping an eye on two of his lads walking one of his new horses. The horse was being trained to ignore noise and sudden movements.

'Please, Jem.' Ivy tried to avoid going around the tenement block these days. She didn't want to bump into any of the do-gooders that still swarmed in The Lane, sticking their noses in where they weren't wanted.

'Auntie Ivy!' Emmy Ryan, her black hair

bouncing on her little shoulders, keeping well away from the young horse ran over to greet Ivy. Emmy's cheeks were apple-red, almost matching her coat and hat. 'I'm having a game of balls with my friends.'

'Fair enough but I'll be calling you in soon.' Ivy grinned down at the little girl. It had been arranged that Ivy would keep the little girl with her this evening. Jem wanted time to settle some horses that had just arrived. 'It will soon be too dark to see the blinkin' balls anyway.'

Ivy had purchased the rubber balls from Harry Green. They were a great success – the children of The Lane weren't accustomed to store-bought toys. Newspaper rolled tightly and tied with string were the balls usually used in games.

'Come on – I'll help you get settled.' Jem grabbed the handle of Ivy's pram. 'Begob, this thing is heavy, woman!'

'I know.' She'd spend the evening sorting through the pram. Tomorrow she'd separate, wash and fix up anything that needed doing. If she had the time to spare for a visit to the markets, she'd have a lot to sell. If not she'd store the stuff in one of her tea chests for later.

'You'll not be lifting this thing down those steps, Ivy Murphy.' Jem put two fingers to his lips and gave a shrill whistle. He was pleased to note that the new horse put her ears back but didn't react in any other way. 'Take her in, lads,' he shouted to the two young men with the horse. 'Brush her down carefully before you put her in her stall. I'll be in to check on your work shortly. In the meantime, tell John I'll be in with Ivy if he wants me. I need a hand here, send someone out when you go in.'

'Who needs a telephone?' Ivy remarked. 'The bush telegraph will have that news around The Lane in seconds, Jem Ryan.'

'Never mind,' Jem grinned, totally unrepentant. He'd watched Ivy struggle alone for years. He'd never again stand back while she tried to kill herself doing everything alone. 'You go on down and get the place opened up. I know you'll want to get the kettle on. I'll mind your stuff.'

'Have you time to have a cup of tea with me, Jem?' Ivy could feel the blush travelling from her toes to her ears. The snatched moments she and Jem managed were becoming a mite too tempting. Just the thought of his kiss was enough to put her to the blush. 'I've something I want to discuss with you.'

'No problem – put the kettle on, Ivy.' Jem could afford to take a little time out now and again.

Ivy hurried down the steps to her basement. It felt odd to be able to walk down without anything in her hands. She unlocked the door and, leaving it standing open behind her, hurried inside. She had the gas lamps in both rooms lit and the kettle sitting on the black range top by the time Jem and his helper wrestled the heavy pram into the front room. Jem's young helper left without a word, closing the door behind him. They listened to the sound of his boots tramping up the outside steps.

'This pram is on its last legs, Ivy.' Jem knelt by the side of it, examining the thick leather straps that held it to the heavy-duty springs. 'I don't think it will get you much further.' He knew how

251

important this pram was to her. 'If you'll empty it now I'll take it away with me when I go. I'll see if I can fix it up for you. You don't want the thing to collapse in some back street when you're out and about.'

'Is it really bad, Jem?' Ivy stood in the doorway separating the two rooms. She'd removed her heavy coat and shawl. The two items of outer wear were draped over her bed. They served double duty by keeping Ivy warm at night. 'Curly, one of the old men I meet on me round, has mentioned several times that the pram was in a bad way but I didn't pay much mind to him.'

'The man knows what he's talking about.' Jem stood up, brushing his knees to remove any dust. 'I'll give it a good going-over but you might want to start looking around for a replacement.'

'Well,' Ivy sighed deeply – yet one more thing to worry about, 'the old thing doesn't owe me anything. It's older than me after all.' Her da had bought the pram second or third hand.

'I'll use some of the old horse-harnesses to replace the leather straps,' Jem promised. 'That will hold you for a while I've no doubt but it wouldn't hurt to keep your eyes open for a replacement or something that could be used for parts to fix this one up.'

'I'll do that. The good Lord knows I can't be without me pram.' Ivy hurried to take the boiling kettle off the hob and pour the steaming water into the warmed teapot. She had the tea leaves already in the pot. 'Sit down a minute, Jem. I want to talk to you.'

'Is this something Emmy shouldn't hear?' Jem

needed to have someone look after the child if Ivy wanted to speak privately.

'I don't think so.' Ivy smiled. He was such a conscientious stand-in parent. 'I want to pick your brain about some things but nothing earth-shattering.'

'Fair enough.' Jem sat down on one of Ivy's two wooden chairs. He knew she and Emmy would be doing their homework together at the kitchen table. He'd move to one of Ivy's orange crates if needed.

'I've had a strange day.' Ivy brought two cups of tea to the table. She sat down and stared at Jem. 'Dublin is in a state of chassis, Jem.'

Jem sipped at his cup of tea. This wasn't news to him. The whole country was in an uproar: times were definitely changing.

'Let me tell you about my day.' Ivy began to describe her day to Jem in detail. She wanted him to understand what Nanny Grace meant to her. The old woman had been adamant that first Ivy's mother and then Ivy herself received the torn and stained garments and discards from the nursery. Nanny had often made up the packages herself. On many occasions Ivy had found items of food wrapped carefully within a package from Nanny. The old woman deserved better than she was receiving.

'Poor old woman,' Jem said. 'She's to be left behind in a country not her own, along with the rest of the outdated rubbish. That must be hard for her to understand.'

'Nanny Grace – and I don't know her real name – no one calls her anything but Nanny Grace – she served as under-nanny to the present Earl's grand-father when he was a toddler for heaven's sake!' Ivy couldn't imagine surrendering your entire private life to someone else. 'She has been responsible for the upbringing of four generations of the same family.'

'Makes you glad you weren't forced into service, doesn't it?' Jem shook his head. The quality were different, everyone knew that.

'It's not only her, Jem.' Ivy tried to explain what she'd felt walking around the elegant houses of Fitzwilliam Square that day. 'I don't go into the houses on my round, Jem, you know that. I stand at the back door and wait to see who comes out to talk to me or pass along the discards.' Ivy shrugged. 'But, today, I can't explain it, Jem, but it felt as if every house was in an uproar. The staff were gossiping about the changes taking place. I got a lot more big items from every house than I ever have before and almost every house promised more next week. That's not normal, Jem.'

Ivy was aware of the political change in the country. You would have to be dead not to notice. The streets were free of gangs of soldiers in their red coats for the first time in Ivy's memory. The Black and Tans no longer terrified people. Ireland was free – but free to do what, that was the question.

'Well, Ivy, I've said it to you before,' Jem said. 'Ireland is changing and we have to change with it.'

'Jem, are yeh saying you think I'll lose me round?' Ivy was horrified. The round she'd built up over the years was her bread and butter. She needed it to survive. Even if she married Jem, although that was becoming *when* she married Jem, she would still want to have her own income. They needed to discuss this. The income she made from her round allowed her to gamble on other things.

'I don't think you're in danger of losing anything, Ivy,' Jem quickly reassured her. 'There will always be rich people. The round will just change, that's all.'

'Jem,' Ivy dared to bring one of the subjects she feared into the open, 'if we were to marry, would you expect me to give up me round and be like the other women around The Lane?' She meant stay home, look after their rooms and children.

'Why would I want you to change?' Jem shrugged, not understanding the importance of the subject. 'I understand that your round, your independence is important to you. I'd never expect you to wait on me hand and foot. I don't want to take over your life, Ivy. I want to share it. I want to marry Ivy Rose Murphy, big ideas, ever-thinking head and all.' He grinned, having no idea of the magnitude of her relief.

'Jem Ryan, you are the only man in Ireland that I would ever want to marry.' She grinned widely, almost faint with relief. He didn't expect her to turn into one of the grey women who crept around the place after their man. Thank God. Now if only she could work up the courage to question Ann Marie about the quality's ability to control the number of children they had. Whatever secret they possessed, she needed to know it.

She stood suddenly – the tea could wait. She walked around the table and took his hand in hers. With very little effort she pulled him from his chair and gently pointed him in the direction of the soft chairs by the range. When she had him situated to her satisfaction, she dropped onto his knees and laid her head on his chest.

'I've been that worried,' she whispered into his chest.

'I really don't think you're in any danger of losing your round, Ivy.' Jem pressed his lips into her hair. He relaxed back into the chair, pulling her with him.

'No,' her head shook back and forth on his chest, giving Jem a thrill, 'I don't mean that.' She pushed away to stare into his face. 'At least, not just that. I've been afraid you wanted me to change, Jem. Be something and someone I could never be.'

'I told you: I don't want you to change.' Jem smiled down at the woman he'd watched grow from an adorable child into a force to be reckoned with. He would never be fool enough to think he could change Ivy Murphy. 'Get that into your head.' He lowered his head, unable to resist the temptation any longer. His lips brushed hers, inviting her to relax, invite him in. When Ivy's lips trembled open he took full advantage and sank into a deep intimate kiss that had both of them shivering and shaking.

'Enough.' Jem pulled his head away from the temptation of her lips. He was panting like one of his own horses. He pushed her gently off his lap and, with his hands on her waist, waited until she was standing steady on her own two feet. 'I'm only human, Ivy. I can only take so much.' Did she have any idea what he wanted to do to her, with her?

'Jem...' Ivy's lips were throbbing, her head spinning. She wanted to crawl back into his lap and have more of those kisses.

'Pour yourself a cup of tea, Ivy.' Jem let his head drop onto the back of the chair. He closed his eyes to lock out temptation. 'I need a minute to catch me breath.' He needed to dump his overheated body into one of his horse troughs.

'I wanted to talk to you about the stuff Nanny Grace wants to sell on, Jem.'

'Give me a minute.' Jem held his hands up in the air without opening his eyes. 'Sit down at the kitchen table, have a cup of tea. I'll join you in a minute.' He needed to wrestle his body back under control.

Ivy did as he asked. She could see Jem was fighting some kind of internal battle. If the truth be told she needed to get her own breath back too. She poured a fresh cup of tea and carried it over to the table.

She took a chair ... and waited.

'Right.' Jem opened his eyes and stared across the room at Ivy sitting waiting at the table, her big violet eyes fixed firmly on him. He almost groaned aloud. Did she have no idea how bloody tempting she was? He was no saint, for God's sake! 'Tell me about this stuff.' He put his elbows on his knees and dropped his head into his hands. Maybe thinking and talking about something else would calm him down.

'There's a lot of stuff, Jem,' Ivy began, wanting to fill the uncomfortable silence that had fallen between them. 'Nanny Grace has been given the entire contents of what I suppose you'd call the children's floor, including a load of furniture and fittings. I tell yeh, Jem, some of the stuff is things I've never seen before.' She had tried to make a mental note of everything she'd seen. 'The stuff will sell, eventually, but I don't know anyone who would give her a decent price for it. They'll know she's desperate and things are worth only what someone is willing to pay for them. She's going to get gypped, Jem.'

'What are you thinking, Ivy Murphy?' Jem raised his head from his hands and stared. 'I know that look.'

'I want to help that old woman.' Ivy shrugged. 'But that's not all. I think with all the changes taking place around us, there is the chance of a moneymaking opportunity here for us. I haven't worked out all the details in my mind yet. I need to concentrate on getting ready to sell my dolls for the moment but there is an opportunity here. I'm sure of it.' She laughed. 'Even if I don't know what it is yet!'

'Ivy,' Jem dropped his head back into his hands and groaned dramatically, 'I'm running in place with all of the new business opportunities I'm taking up already.'

'I'm only saying, Jem. I'll have to spend more time thinking about everything. Anyway, Nanny has to come first. She hasn't been told when she has to leave the house. With the grace of God, we should be able to get through Christmas and the New Year before any decisions have to be made about her stuff. I couldn't take on something else right now meself.'

'I know you, Ivy.' Jem shook his head ruefully. There was no holding Ivy back when she got a bee in her bonnet about something. 'I know I haven't heard the last of this.'

He wanted to ask her about them. He wanted to say 'What about us?' But he felt too raw right now to bring that subject up. He was still reeling from the close call they'd had on this bloody chair. They needed to get churched. And soon.

'Being in that room with Nanny Grace made me think about Emmy.' Ivy looked over her shoulder as if expecting to see the child standing behind her.

'What about her?' He dragged his mind away from where it wanted to wander, forced his eyes away from the big bed standing so close and forced himself to think of the innocent child he'd taken responsibility for. A child, moreover, who could be knocking on the door at any minute. He'd given no thought to Emmy when he'd had Ivy locked in his arms.

'It occurred to me when I was talking to Nanny ... when I was sitting in that big room full of toys and wonders ... I began to think about the house Emmy grew up in. That house probably has a room very like the one I was in today.' She sighed deeply.

'Ivy, spit it out,' Jem prompted. 'Emmy will be coming in here soon. You know what she's like. She hears everything you don't want her to.'

'Jem, we need to see that Emmy gets the education she would have got if her aunt had never tried to throw her away.'

Emmy's aunt had been a passenger in Jem's

cab. She'd had a fatal accident along the route but not before letting Jem know that she intended to drop her niece off at Goldenbridge, a home officially known as a trade school but in reality a workhouse for female orphans.

'I don't understand your worries, Ivy. Emmy is getting a good education. You of all people know that. Emmy's teachers say she has the brightest mind they've ever come across. The child is able to teach you.'

'That's not the kind of education I'm talking about, Jem. That's book learning and that's important. It's the other things she needs to know.'

'What other things?'

'Emmy needs the kind of education Ann Marie Gannon got when she was growing up. Things like music and art appreciation. She'll need to learn to handle her own money or "finances" as the nobs call it. She'll need to fit into her own society, Jem. We can't teach her that. We don't know how. We never learned.'

'I still don't know what you mean, Ivy.' Jem was doing the best he could by the child he'd taken into his home.

'Emmy needs to learn to play the piano or the harp or something.' Ivy was thinking of the musical instruments standing in that room with Nanny. She hadn't recognised the half of them. 'Little girls in her social class learn to paint.' She shrugged. 'For all I know they learn foreign languages.' Ivy couldn't imagine the magic of speaking several languages. She could only make a stab at Irish and English herself. 'They learn to ride horses.' Ivy was trying to think of things she

260

herself would love to learn how to do. 'They have dance classes. They learn to mingle socially.'

'Emmy is only seven, Ivy.' Jem shrugged. 'She has time to learn anything she needs to learn.'

'She has to start now, Jem,' Ivy insisted. 'I was thinking we might ask Ann Marie for advice.'

'I thought we were going to keep Emmy and where she comes from a secret between our-selves, Ivy?' It was vital that the accident that killed Emmy's aunt was kept secret.

'I don't want to send her back to her own world unprepared, Jem. They'd snigger at her behind their hands. She'd be an outcast. We can't allow that to happen.'

'I don't know anything about high society, Ivy.' Jem sighed and pushed his hands through his hair. Trust Ivy to think up a list of problems.

'I know that, Jem. I don't know anything much myself. I listened to my mother telling tales of her life before she married me da. It was like some-thing from another world. Ann Marie would know what was needed. She knows how to move about in society. She doesn't have to learn. She never makes a fool of herself.'

Ivy fell silent, staring ahead, a hopeless expression on her face.

'Ivy...' Jem stared at her. 'What's the matter? What's going on?'

'She's challenged me, Jem,' she said with a shrug.

'Come again?' Jem stared.

'Ann Marie Gannon has issued a challenge to me.'

'I don't suppose you're talking about pistols at

dawn,' Jem said slowly.

'It's me own fault. I was praising her on how well she was beginning to fit in around here.'

'And?' Jem prompted.

'She invited me to take tea with her at the Shelbourne Hotel. She dared me, Jem.' Ivy jumped to her feet. She grabbed her cup from the table. She had to do something, move, or she'd be sick.

'Well, Ivy Murphy, no one can say you're not coming up in the world.' Jem shook his head in admiration.

'Jem,' Ivy wailed, 'I can't go into the Shelbourne Hotel! I'd die of fright. You've seen those sour auld doormen that guard the place. Can you really imagine me, Ivy Murphy, all fur coat and no knickers, going into a place like that?'

'You have to go, Ivy.' Jem grinned widely. 'You can tell the rest of us what it's like inside. Ivy Murphy, you owe it to your friends. We'll never get the chance to put a toe inside that place. You've been talking about Emmy learning to be social. B'gob, woman, it looks like you might be the one to teach her.' Jem roared laughing at the look of complete and utter horror on Ivy's face.

'Mind yeh don't choke,' Ivy said sourly. She'd thought Jem would be on her side. She couldn't do it. She could not, simply could not, step inside that big fancy hotel as if she belonged in the place. She'd drop dead of fright on the spot. 'I'm sorry I told yeh now.' Ivy glared. Didn't he understand? She'd walked past the Shelbourne Hotel so many times in her life. The look of sheer disgust whichever sneering doorman on duty directed at her almost pulled the skin from her bones. Some of

262

the doormen kept a collection of stones to throw at those they considered lowered the tone of the street in front of the hotel. She remembered every bruise she'd ever received that way.

'You got yourself all dolled up and went into that fancy toy shop in Grafton Street to do business and the sky didn't fall. That turned out really well for you as I recall.' Jem grinned widely. It was good to know something intimidated Ivy.

'I'm glad I could amuse yeh, Jem Ryan.' Ivy suddenly realised she was standing here like a fool with a cup and saucer in her hand. She put the dishes on the table then she slapped both hands on her hips and glared down at Jem. 'Anyway, we were talking about Emmy, not me. We can't help Emmy prepare for her place in society, Jem. Ann Marie is the only person I can think of that could help.' Ivy didn't want the matter of her visiting the Shelbourne raised again. She was sorry she'd ever mentioned it.

'We would have to tell her the whole story.' Jem grimaced. 'Ann Marie would have to know everything about Miss Emerald O'Connor of Galway. I don't know if I want to open that can of worms, Ivy.'

'We can think about it, Jem. We have a bit of time but we do need to start thinking about Emmy's future.'

'I suppose.' Jem heard the clatter of small feet on the outside steps. 'Here's Emmy now, Ivy.'

'I'll let her in.' Ivy was delighted at the interruption. She hurried into her front room. She had the door open before Emmy could knock.

'Auntie Ivy, I had the time o' me life.' Emmy

danced in place, delighted with herself. 'I made sure to get me balls back, Auntie Ivy.' She held up both hands, a colourful rubber ball clutched firmly in each little gloved fist.

'I beg your pardon, Miss Ryan?' Ivy said in a posh accent. That's all they needed, Emmy Ryan with a flat Dublin accent. 'I'm afraid I didn't understand that last sentence.'

'I do beg your pardon.' Emmy stuck her nose in the air. 'I had a wonderful time with my friends, Aunt. And I made sure of the safe return of my rubber balls.' And she giggled with wild delight.

'Much better.' Ivy opened the door wide and Emmy skipped through.

'Just for that, Auntie Ivy,' Emmy giggled, 'I'm going to be really cross with you if you make any mistakes in your homework.'

'Oh mercy me!' Ivy cried dramatically. 'Not that! Spare me!'

'Will you two giggling females get in here!' Jem shouted from the back room. He loved to hear Ivy and Emmy twitting each other.

'Uncle Jem!' Emmy screamed and ran towards the sound of his voice. 'I didn't know you were here. No one told me.' She threw herself at him.

'You must have missed the news broadcast.' Jem laughed and pulled Emmy up onto his knees.

'What are we having to eat, Auntie Ivy?' Emmy demanded. 'I'm hungry.'

'Duck under the table,' Ivy said, giving the Dubliner's standard reply for having nothing to eat in the house.

'Auntie Ivy!' Emmy giggled. 'You always say that. Now, really, what are we having to eat?'

'We, Miss Ryan, are having a fry-up.' Ivy grinned. 'Does that meet with your approval?' She hadn't had time to make what most would consider a cooked meal. To Dubliners, if the meal didn't include potatoes it wasn't a meal. It was a snack. She had brown soda bread from her recent baking – that, with sausage, bacon, egg and tomato would suffice for a filling snack.

'Am I invited, Ivy?' Jem allowed his lower lip to tremble, sending both females into hysterics.

'I don't see why not,' Ivy said. 'I bought plenty of food. Are you sure you wouldn't like to go and announce it to the world that you're staying for a bite to eat? You could even announce the menu.'

'I'll pass on that, thanks.' Jem sat back and watched Emmy jump around, getting the dishes from Ivy's tall cupboard. Emmy insisted on setting the table whenever she ate with Ivy.

Jem sat back in the soft chair, crossed his legs and dreamed of a time when this scene would become an everyday part of his life.

'Oh, Auntie Ivy, I forgot to tell you.' Emmy held her fork frozen between her plate and her lips. 'The sad boy gave me a message for you.' She had insisted on calling Liam Connelly 'the sad boy', ever since she'd first met him.

'When did you see Liam?' Jem asked.

'He and his sister went past when we were playing ball.' Emmy put the piece of sausage on her fork into her mouth and chewed happily.

'What was the message?' Ivy sat back and waited, expecting Emmy to simply pass along a social greeting.

265

'He wrote it down.' Emmy dropped her fork onto her partially consumed plate of food. ''Scuse me,' she muttered before jumping down from the table. She ran to where her coat was lying on the nearby bed and searched in her pockets, then returned to the table, climbed back on her chair and passed a folded piece of white unlined paper across the table to Ivy.

'Ivy?' Jem watched in almost morbid fascination while every piece of colour seemed to leach out of Ivy's face, turning it as pale as the paper that trembled in her hand. She dropped the note, shoved her plate of food out of the way and dropped her head down onto her folded arms on the tabletop.

'I can't breathe.'

'Auntie Ivy?' Emmy moved to leave her chair.

'It's okay,' Jem assured the child. Ivy could be overly dramatic at times. He prayed to God this was one of them. 'What's the matter, Ivy?'

'Look!' Ivy raised her head and stabbed a finger at Liam's copperplate script. *"An invitation-only gala evening of theatre"!'*

'Is that what's upset you?'

'Read it,' Ivy mumbled as she sank her head onto her arms again.

Jem picked up Liam's note and began to read. 'Ivy, this is marvellous!' He grinned broadly.

'Have you read all of that thing?' Ivy's head snapped up again. She reached across the table and grabbed the note from Jem's loose grip.

Emmy watched the exchange with delight while she continued to eat the food on her plate. She was hungry – running around after bouncing balls had

266

worked on her appetite. She looked between the two adults and simply sighed. Life was so good.

'It says here,' Ivy shook the paper in the air, 'that they are putting on a special preview of the pantomime starring that fella Conn told us about who stepped in as top of the bill. The one that everyone's talking about!'

'My word, Ivy Murphy, you know all the fancy terms now, it seems.' Jem couldn't resist pulling her leg. She'd given him quite a turn – it was only fair he should get his own back. He grabbed the note back and pointed to one part of it. 'Liam says it will be a chance for you to sell your dolls! It's marvellous.'

'Oh yeah, marvellous, you bloody ... *man.*' Ivy grabbed at her hair and almost shrieked. 'Did you look at the date? No, you didn't! It's *tomorrow!*'

Jem stifled a grin. He exchanged a laughing glance with Emmy who hid her own smile behind her two little hands clapped in front of her face. 'Well, Liam does say he only just found out as he and Vera won't be a part of it.' He spread his hands wide. 'Nice of them to make it on a Thursday.' He collapsed laughing at the look of horror on Ivy's face and Emmy giggled until she hiccupped.

'A "preview", Liam calls it.' Ivy grabbed the note back – at this rate the thing would be in flitters before they left the table. 'He says that the show is for an invited audience of bigwigs.'

'But, will there be little children there?' Jem wondered.

'Liam,' Ivy consulted the note again, 'says that there will be lots of children attending.' Then she added, a sparkle at last coming into her eyes, 'He

267

says only the children of the wealthy – that the theatre bosses are trying to attract people with money to back their shows.'

'It's a great opportunity, Ivy,' Jem said. 'It'll give you a chance to sell your dolls before pantomime season. You can learn what will and won't work for you. See if you'll have any problems.

'Yes,' Ivy whispered over the lump in her throat. 'Great ... but ... *tomorrow!*'

Chapter 26

She didn't think she'd ever been so cold in her life. She gritted her teeth behind her frozen smile and accepted the money being handed to her. Her feet, inside her well-worn steel-capped boys' work boots felt like blocks of ice. She shivered as the wind found every exposed inch of her flesh.

'Girls, please remember you are ladies – you have a position in society to uphold,' the sour-faced nanny snapped at her overexcited young charges.

The two girls dressed in matching red-wool coats with white fur-trimmed collars, fur muffs and hats danced in place. Their little laced black ankle-boots rapped a sound of joy on the cobbles under their feet.

Ivy stared at the two young girls, wondering what their lives were like. The two were dressed like young princesses but she'd learned appearances could be deceptive. The nanny looked like a bad-tempered pincher to her. She wouldn't fancy being under her thumb.

'Your father was kind enough to allow his driver to return us to the theatre with the coins to buy these dolls. You are fortunate indeed that we live so close. Now, do you ladies think that bouncing around in this very unladylike fashion is any way to repay your father's great kindness?' Nanny Willis wanted out of this freezing cold. The wind whistling down this street would skin a body. What a palaver over two dolls that cost more than she earned in a month!

Ivy wished the two young 'ladies' would stick their tongues out at the old biddy. Could they not be allowed to enjoy their new toys?

'The price is outrageous.' Nanny Willis sniffed and turned away from the doll seller in a huff. She grabbed each little girl by the hand and tugged them towards the waiting carriage, then pushed the two girls in front of her through the door being held open by a servant.

'Do you think the toffs cook up those auld biddies in a mad scientist's lab somewhere?' a familiar voice drawled over Ivy's shoulder.

'Jem, what are you doing here?' Ivy stamped her frozen feet and turned to greet him with a smile. He'd made the effort to come down here to meet her – she would not let him see the terror she was feeling. The whole enterprise had been a disaster. She needed time to think about everything.

'I wanted to see how your dolls were selling.' Jem grinned, his teeth sparkling in his clean-shaven face. He replaced the hat he'd removed in greeting and bent to press a kiss into her frozen cheek. 'Begob, woman, you're fair frozen.'

Ivy forced her fears to the back of her mind and admired the view. The man was good-looking. Why should he hide it? Jem's well-cut tweed suit was tailored to accentuate his broad shoulders and slim hips. The dark cashmere overcoat he wore complimented his virile form. The soft hat that was all the fashion for the man about town was tilted to a very rakish angle. Jem Ryan was really coming out of himself, Ivy thought, staring into his handsome green eyes. He was looking very prosperous.

'Jem, I've hardly sold any of me dolls.' She could tell him that much at least. 'It seems a lot of the quality don't carry cash around with them.' Ivy wanted to cuddle into his warmth and just nestle. 'Least, not when they get all dolled up to go out on the town. I've had me job stopping them from being offended when I won't charge the ruddy dolls to their accounts. I never thought of something like that. In any case, it seems most of the children come with their nannies and none of them have any money at all.'

Ivy was wearing so many layers of clothing it was difficult to move. She'd made an effort to keep the outer layer respectable. She wore a bright red paisley shawl which Pa Landers, a contact of hers, had found for her. She'd paid more for the shawl then she'd ever spent before in her life on an article of clothing but it was class and looked it. The quality and bright colour of the shawl made her stand out from the other street sellers. She'd draped it over her head and wrapped it tightly around her front. The shawl travelled down her back before being belted over her black jumper, high-neck lace blouse, and the thick black wool skirt that reached her feet. No one could see the tweed men's trousers she wore under her skirt. It was a very old-fashioned look for nineteen twenty-five but it served a purpose. She'd only recently learned presentation was everything. She was standing outside the Gaiety Theatre and it was important to present a refined appearance.

'I didn't expect you to be here so late.' Jem Ryan looked around the bustling crowd. 'The show's over. Why are you still standing here?'

'I was ordered to wait here by some toff who has something to do with the Gaiety, while "staff" of the families who live nearby returned with the required coin. But I'm ready to leave now.' Ivy had been tempted to ask some of the staff who'd hurried back to buy her dolls for the addresses of the houses they worked in. Chances were she'd visited their back doors in her time. 'I didn't know what to do, Jem. The children wanted the dolls and made no bones about demanding what they wanted but neither the parents nor the nannies had enough cash with them to pay. What am I going to do?'

'We can discuss this later, Ivy. It's too bloomin' cold to stand here worrying. Where did you park your pram?' Jem admired the attractive wooden display case that Jimmy had made for Ivy on the model of a cinema-usherette's tray.

'There's an old man, Peadar, who has the watchman's gig here.' She turned to walk towards the lane at the side of the theatre. 'He seems a decent sort so I left me pram with him. He says he'll keep an eye on me pram when the pantomime season starts. I can't let that be seen out front.' Ivy shivered – it wouldn't be long now.

'You never stop thinking and planning, Ivy.' Jem grinned, falling in beside her. 'Does this Peadar know how much you're charging for those things?' He gave a nod towards Ivy's presentation case. He knew there was many a one who might think of helping themselves to her profits.

'He'd have to be deaf and blind not to.'

'Come an' get a heat!' called Peadar as they approached. He was sitting in the open front of his wooden hut – the hut looked like a snail's shell on the old man's back to Ivy. A galvanised bucket filled with coal sat on the bare ground between his feet. The bucket had holes punched in the sides through which bright red embers gleamed. Ivy held her hands in their fingerless gloves out to the flames.

'Is that yourself, Jem Ryan?' Peadar grinned, showing his toothless pink gums. 'I would have thought you'd be picking up fares around here not walking out like a toff. Have yeh made your fortune then, Jem, and given up the taxi business? Unless Ivy here has ordered a taxi home?'

'I've come to walk my best girl home,' Jem said.

'It's shank's mare all the way for me, Peadar,' said Ivy.

She went and quickly counted the dolls in her pram parked nearby. Everything was as she'd left it. She put the display case and its remaining dolls into the pram. She'd been glad of Peadar's offer to keep an eye on it and understood the old man expected to be passed a few coins for his trouble.

She didn't mind – it was the way of the world.

She then took a thick leather bag from the bottom of her pram. It never failed to give her a thrill to realise she had a bank account. She, Ivy Murphy, the beggar that people looked down on, had a bank account like the toffs. She'd had Ann Marie teach her how to fill out a deposit slip but it wasn't necessary for this money. Ivy planned to put her takings in the security bag and drop it into the night safe at the Bank of Ireland. It would be a trial run before she started selling her dolls nightly outside the theatre. She needed to know how the system worked.

'Did yeh make a fortune then, Ivy?' Peadar was watching every move Ivy made. There were a lot of people interested in young Ivy Murphy lately.

'Not so I noticed.' Ivy shivered. 'I'm glad to be going home. I'm blue with the cold. I want a pot of tea and something to eat.'

'Yeh should have said, Ivy.' Peadar showed his gums again. 'I'd have kept yeh a sup of tea from me last pot.'

'Thanks, another time.' Ivy had her pram packed carefully. 'I've got a handsome escort this evening.' She grinned at Jem. The money she'd made was locked away in the leather bank bag and tucked under her clothes. She passed the old man a threepenny piece, grabbed the handle of her pram and, with Jem keeping step with her, turned it to walk in the direction of the street. 'I'll see yeh!' she called over her shoulder as they hurried away.

'You need to think about your own safety, Ivy,' Jem said softly. 'I can't walk with you every evening.' Having recently started up his own business, he was beginning to understand that having money was more of a headache than they'd ever realised.

'I'll think better with me feet in front of the fire and a cup of tea in me hand. I'm fair frozen, Jem. I'm nearly done for the night but I want to leave me takings in the night safe. Get a feel for the thing.' Ivy pushed her pram towards Grafton Street. She wasn't comfortable walking out boldly on one of Dublin's main thoroughfares. She normally used the back alleys. She was one of many struggling to survive in Dublin's inner city and had been invisible for most of her life. She knew every back street and lane in the sprawling city but she didn't dare travel her normal route, not with cash on her person.

'You need to see if yeh can use that bank on the corner, Ivy.' Jem nodded his head towards the branch of the bank sitting nearby.

'Do you think you can do that, Jem?' Ivy asked. 'Use another bank, I mean. Don't you have to put your money in the same one every time?'

'I don't think so, Ivy,' Jem shrugged, 'but I'm not sure. You'll have to ask.'

'Thanks for coming down to pick me up, Jem.' Ivy was aware of the people walking past. The elegantly dressed crowd were glaring daggers at her. She couldn't bring herself to care. She had as much right to walk these streets as they did.

'I thought we could enjoy an evening stroll.' Jem pushed his shoulder gently against Ivy's.

She rolled her eyes ironically at him.

'The lads have picked up some whispers on the street,' Jem said while passing Trinity College.

'What kind of whispers?' Ivy stared at him, worry in her big violet eyes.

'Your da was fond of entertaining his pub mates – boasting about the good life he lived on his daughter's earnings.' Jem, not for the first time, mentally cursed Éamonn Murphy. The very least the man could have done was have the decency to keep his big trap shut. He bit back the words of abuse he wanted to heap onto the dead man's head while they crossed the main road, heading towards the bank. He returned the waves from several of the jarveys passing on the busy street. 'There has been a lot of talk in the pubs about "Éamonn's money" and who is going to spend that money now!' He looked down at the woman at his side, his mind wrestling with the problem of protecting her. He couldn't be with her all the time. She had to be made to see that talking to Billy Flint was the safest option.

'You know, Jem, sometimes I get to wondering – how come other people have an inheritance – something precious when their relatives drop dead? What do I get? Bloody headaches.' Ivy wasn't unaware of the danger she was in while out and about the streets of Dublin. It stuck in her craw to have to consider paying protection money to some man she'd never met. She didn't want to admit she'd been stiff with fear standing out in front of the Gaiety shouting out the price of her dolls. She had been very aware of the interest some of the men hanging around the streets were taking in her activities.

'That's the way of the world, Ivy.' They'd reached the tall imposing building that housed the bank.

'Easy for you to say, Jem.' Ivy wanted to bite the words back. It wasn't his fault that his uncle had left him the livery. She wouldn't let it make her bitter that Jem had inherited a roof over his head that belonged to him and a way to make a living. 'Sorry, I don't mean to bite your head off.' She rose on her toes and pressed a kiss of apology into his freshly shaved cheek.

'You'll be the death of me, Ivy Murphy.' Jem gave her a one-arm hug before releasing her. He thought she had more reason to complain and moan than a lot of people. 'It's all right – today has been difficult for you. But, Ivy, we need to do something about keeping you safe.' Jem stood with his back to the wall safe while Ivy used her key to open it before removing the leather bag from under her clothes. 'If you don't go talk to Billy Flint soon, I will.'

Jem didn't like the open position of the wall safe. Too many streets led away from this place. Trinity College across the way would give a watcher somewhere to hide. It would be easy for someone to grab Ivy's takings and disappear into the night. Jem's eyes checked the street constantly. He wanted to know if anyone else was keeping an eye on Ivy.

'That's it.' Ivy sighed with relief. Her takings were safely behind locked doors.

'Come on then.' Jem waited to see which street Ivy would take. 'I'll walk you home.'

'Thanks,' Ivy understated. It gave her a thrill to walk along with the tall handsome Jem at her side.

Jem took Ivy's elbow in his hand. 'Ivy, you need to carefully plan what you're going to do over the pantomime season.'

'Jem, I'm sorry I've been such a worry to you. You were right all along. I'll go see this Billy Flint.' She crossed the road towards Trinity College and Nassau Street. 'I don't want to, but I could feel the eyes on me tonight. If I'd taken as much money as I was hoping to I'd have been nabbed.'

Jem let the subject of Ivy's safety drop for the moment. They could discuss this further in private. You never knew who was listening. The dark early nights made living easy for the resident fly boys that flourished in the inner city. The nights, lit only by the soft gas streetlamps, made it easy to snatch and run.

'Today was a learning experience, Jem. I'm glad I got this chance to check out how the business could be done.' Ivy was fighting the feeling of despair that threatened to cripple her. She needed to think – plan. 'I thought I had a fair idea of how it would be. You know, selling the dolls and all.'

'And?' Jem was listening for the sound of footsteps behind them. One good thing was that it was almost impossible to walk across the cobbled streets silently.

'Me dolls are so expensive.' She felt guilty about the price she was asking. However, she'd seen how the other half lived now, and she knew that what to her was a small fortune was a mere pittance to them. 'Well, that nanny you saw, well, that was typical of what happened. The childer see the dolls but the nanny doesn't have enough money to pay. I never thought of that.' Ivy fought the feeling of failure that had begun to sink into her very marrow as she stood trying to sell her dolls. She had to figure something out. She had too much depending on this venture.

'I've every faith you'll come up with a plan.' Jem nudged her gently with his shoulder. 'If we put our heads together, there's nothing we can't do.'

Chapter 27

Johnjo Smith sat in the rear pew of Westland Row Church, wondering what in the name of heaven he was doing there. What had possessed him to crawl out of his warm comfortable hotel bed? What version of Irish melancholy had made him take that ghostly walk through the back streets of Dublin first thing this morning? Why did he feel compelled to catch the first Mass of the morning at a church that featured heavily in his waking nightmares? He stared at the backs of people's heads, wondering if he'd know any of them. The faithful – people who wouldn't dream of missing the six o'clock Mass every morning of their lives – packed the front pews.

Johnjo sighed and tried mightily to ignore the familiar Latin refrain running through the church. The smell from the incense burner the altar boy swung with such diligence turned his stomach. He'd come such a long way since his days as a battered and bruised altar boy. What had dragged him back to this place this morning?

Ivy Murphy sat in the pew nearest the rear door of the church. She'd come to Mass this morning because she needed the connection with her past. It had been a long time since she'd attended Mass at this church. She usually preferred the tranquillity of an empty church but this morning she needed the soft familiar Latin chants, the comforting smell of wafting incense. She'd been dragging herself around the place. She felt bruised and disheartened after the fiasco with her dolls. She was also hoping for inspiration.

Ivy reacted to the ebb and flow of the attentive congregation, standing, sitting, bowing with them but not a part of them. She refused to beat her chest and chant 'Mea culpa'. Brother Theo had insisted on teaching Ivy the language of the Mass. He'd explained that 'Mea culpa' meant 'My fault'. Well, she might have a lot of her own sins to account for but she wasn't taking the sins of the world on her shoulders.

Ivy knew the rhythm of the Mass. It was almost over. People were shuffling, getting ready to stand and receive Communion. She'd be able to slip out. Every devout person here would want to be sure the priest noticed their attendance. They'd kneel along the altar rails to receive Communion, with lowered eyelids, presenting an image of holy purity.

A large percentage of them were probably mentally calling down the fires of hell on their neighbours. Those waiting in line to kneel would be examining the feet of the communicants, mentally making notes of who had holes in the soles of their shoes. That shame would be discussed at length throughout the day.

Johnjo was pulled from his own thoughts by the

sudden movement of the kneeling figure along the pew from where he sat lost in his memories. It was her, Ivy Murphy. Talk about divine intervention! Doug had been frantically busy, rehearsing for a pantomime preview the theatre bosses had insisted upon. The man had been stretched to the limit. He hadn't been able to arrange to meet Ivy and now here she was in front of him. It must be a sign. He could nab her today, now, and give Doug a welcome surprise. None of this lot would take notice of a woman in distress. They were too busy trying to impress the priest and ensure their reserved place in Heaven.

Ivy moved stealthily along the wooden bench in the direction of the marble font nearest the door. She wanted to bless herself in the holy water on offer there. She hadn't managed to have a chat with her da this morning. Although why she'd expected her da to have any words of wisdom, even in death, about making money was a mystery to her. Éamonn had been a dab hand at spending the ready but he'd never been much cop at making money. Still she did love to light a candle and kneel while chatting away to her da.

Ivy dipped her fingers into the font and blessed herself – then, with a quick glance over her shoulder to check that none of the congregation had seen her, slipped from the church. The misty morning was cold and damp. The miserable weather suited her mood this morning.

'Ivy Murphy, I didn't expect to see you here this morning.' Brother Theo, the hood of his brown woollen habit pulled up over his head, his hands shoved into the wide sleeves, stood on the

280

church steps.

'Good morning, Brother Theo. I wasn't exactly expecting to see you here at this hour of the morning. Do you not get enough preaching and praying at your own church?'

'You, Ivy Murphy, are a cheeky article.' Brother Theo found this young woman fascinating. He'd written well-received papers about the world of struggle and sheer human determination that this young woman had introduced him to. The papers had been published in prestigious religious journals. Ivy and her circle of friends supplied a source of constant conversation around the friary table.

'I'm here to visit with Father Flanagan as a matter of fact.' Theo was in fact here to go through the papers of Father Leary, the previous parish priest. He needed information about that man's activities. Father Flanagan was very willing to assist him in his search for proof to use against the man. Theo did not want that man to be returned to his parish. He could not be allowed to continue to hound Ivy Murphy.

'Have a nice time.' Ivy gave a brief jerk of her head and hurried away. It was too cold and wet to stand around chatting.

'God go with you, Ivy.' Theo watched the well-wrapped figure hurry away before turning to enter the church.

Johnjo Smith had stepped back into the church as soon as he viewed the scene outside. He'd wait. He knew where she was going. He'd follow along. The shadows of the morning would hide him. Now he emerged and began to follow her.

'Morning, Ivy!' a voice called out of the dim

morning light. A ghostly figure pushing a pram passed under the nearby gas lamp at the entrance to the Pearse Street Tenements, moving along at a fast clip. 'What are you doing down this way this morning?'

'Morning, Sheila!' Ivy shouted as their paths crossed. She'd recognised the voice of a dealer friend. 'You're a bit late getting started this morning, aren't yeh?' Ivy didn't want to explain her actions to anyone. Sheila was a nice woman but she loved to have the latest bit of gossip to pass along and who could blame her?

'With this weather, Ivy,' Sheila's voice was moving away in the distance, 'I'd have rather stayed in me bed.'

'I hear yeh, Sheila. See yeh!' Ivy turned away from the road. She'd reached the gap she was looking for and without a thought turned into the dark alley that divided the back entrances of the south-side city shops and houses.

'Ivy Murphy, a word.' The deep velvet female voice drifted out of the floating smog – like the voice of God.

Ivy wanted to curse fluently and with feeling. How could she have been so bloody stupid? She should have remembered that this lane led to the back of the convent. She was in for it now.

Johnjo Smith couldn't feckin' believe it. What was the woman? The bloody Oracle of Delphi? Did she never walk along unnoticed? Who the heck wanted to talk to her now?

Johnjo wished he hadn't been so bloody quick to question when he heard Ivy's next words. Her polite words of greeting sent ice skittering down his spine.

'Mother Columbanus, good morning.' Ivy watched the tall stately figure appear out of the mist.

The nun was of a height with Ivy but the heels of her tightly laced black shoes added height to her tall, slim figure which was enshrouded in a navy-blue nun's habit. Mother Columbanus, Mother Superior of the French Sisters of Charity, had it all. She frightened the life out of anyone she turned her attention upon. The final bit of intimidation was to be found in the floating white wings of her coif. The nun stood easily six and a half feet tall in her habit. With thick rimless glasses stuck onto the end of her nose, she struck terror into the hearts of all sinners.

'Ivy Murphy, you have been making enquiries concerning the Johnson family and their disposition,' Mother Columbanus stated in iced tones.

Johnjo froze in place, desperately wishing himself miles away.

'You will cease and desist, is that understood?'

The frigid tone of Mother Columbanus's beautiful speaking voice allowed Ivy to understand that she was an underling, a lesser mortal, unworthy of the great woman's attention.

'I simply want to know what happened to Ginie Johnson and her son Seán.' Ivy gulped when the nun seemed to glide forward. The whisper of starch from the nun's habit sounded like batwings.

The nun continued forward until the two women were standing toe to toe.

'Did you not understand my words, Ivy Murphy?' Mother Columbanus looked down her long beaked nose at Ivy, daring her to comment further. The icy stare had reduced novice nuns to hysteria.

'Do you have some information, Mother?' Ivy expected the ground to open up and swallow her. She had seen raptor birds in the Museum of Natural History in Kildare Street. Mother Columbanus could give lessons to those killers.

Johnjo had to take his hat off to Ivy Murphy. She wasn't taking any rubbish off a nun who regularly caused young boys to pee in their pants.

'I really don't see that it is any of your business, Ivy Murphy.' Mother Columbanus gave the heavy sigh of the burdened. She'd stepped out here hoping for a moment of peace. She had more important things to do with her time than talk to this urchin. However, if it would stop the annoyance of constant demands about the Johnsons she supposed she could spare a minute. 'What is it you want to know?' Mother Columbanus imagined she could feel the Lord's instant blessing upon her for her forbearance.

'What is going to happen to the youngest Johnson children, Mother, do you know?' Ivy had a pretty good idea of the fate of the children but she wanted to hear the answer from this woman's lips. She felt the blood leave her head at her daring.

Johnjo Smith, concealed by mist and shadow, held his breath.

'The youngest children of that unfortunate family have been sent to new homes in the colonies,' Mother Columbanus was pleased to announce. The shipping of orphans and those with undesirable parents to the New World was surely one of the Lord's true blessings. The donations made by the grateful families wishing to adopt were much appreciated. These donations financed the growth of the order throughout the world. 'The older boys,' she sighed loudly, 'have been housed in the Artane Home for Boys, where they will receive the best of education.'

'What of Ginie and Seán, Mother?' Ivy wasn't going to let it drop. She could do nothing for the older boys. Artane would either kill or cure them.

'Really, Ivy Murphy, you are becoming a pest about these people.' Mother Columbanus didn't care to repeat herself. 'I am unaware of the individual names of the young savages groomed for their new lives by the good sisters in Wexford. I have already stated that these fortunate young souls will not be returned to their poverty-ridden family. Ginie Johnson I do know something of. She is with the Magdalene Sisters. They will do the best they can with that young hussy. In time she will be brought to repent of her sinful ways. We really can't inflict someone of that nature on the kind people of the colonies.'

'I see.' Ivy – with a sinking heart – did see.

It was a nightmare. The older boys would be battered and abused. Nothing new to the Johnson lads – with luck some would survive. Seán was a different kettle of fish. He would not have gone meekly with the do-gooders. Something wasn't right. The little lad would never submit to the nuns' unthinking brutality. If Seán behaved as Ivy knew he would, this nun would have heard about it. She wouldn't be able to resist commenting on Seán's behaviour. Ginie, dear God, poor Ginie!

She'd become a 'Maggie', one of the young girls the nuns worked till they dropped – disposable slaves, prisoners of their own shame.

'Thank you, Mother,' Ivy whispered. 'I needed to know. Good morning to you.'

Ivy wanted to get away from this woman before she did something terminally stupid. She longed to give the woman the tongue-lashing she was holding back only with great effort.

'Let that be an end to it, Ivy Murphy.' Mother Columbanus bowed her white coif-covered head slightly and glared meaningfully down at Ivy. 'It really is none of your business, you know. Leave this sort of thing to those of us better qualified.'

'As you say, Mother.' Ivy gave a brief jerk of her head and turned away.

Johnjo Smith leaned against the wall at his back, glad now of its support. He felt as if he'd been sucker-punched. Some things never changed. What in the name of God was he doing here? Doug had told him he'd take care of contacting Ivy himself. He should have bloody listened. The memories the sound of that nun's voice had raised in his head, on top of the trip down memory lane in the church, had taken the strength from his knees. His shaking body was running with cold sweat. He was gasping as if he'd run a mile. He leaned against the wall, fighting the images that wanted to form in his head.

He waited until he was sure he was steady on his feet and, with his chin in the air and renewed determination in his heart, turned his feet in the direction of his fancy hotel. He would not be making any more visits down memory lane, that was for sure. They hurt too bloody much.

Ivy walked along with her eyes on her feet. She was in a worse state than when she'd left home this morning. She'd thought spending time in familiar comforting surroundings might help lift her spirits. The church and first Mass had seemed like something she'd needed. A connection with the life she'd once lived with the family she'd loved and lost. She sighed deeply, sadly.

Chapter 28

'Sadie, do you have a moment?' Ann Marie Gannon walked into the startlingly white kitchen of her new home.

The walls of the kitchen sported white tiles while every free wall space had been white-washed. The freestanding cupboards were painted white. Sadie lovingly displayed her coloured dishes around the room as decoration. The area had been completely refitted with all of the most modern kitchen features available. Ann Marie didn't like to admit the kitchen put her in mind of her former work space at the morgue. Time and constant use, she hoped, would take care of that problem. She'd been impatient to move into a home of her own. This house had been well presented and she'd been delighted that she could just move in bag and baggage. She had the freedom of choice now to do what she would with the property. She could change anything that didn't please her. It would just take time.

'Oh, Ann Marie, you timed that well.' Sadie Lawless pushed the wisps of blonde hair escaping from her bun away from her sweating face. She'd been standing over the ironing board for hours. She was using two black flat irons and had to remain near the white cast-iron range while changing the black metal irons as they cooled.

Sadie, in her long black skirt topped with a white lace blouse, wasn't aware of the improvement in her own appearance. She'd lost the careworn lines from her pretty face. Her blue eyes and soft lips had always been quick to laugh but now she glowed with health and happiness. The improved nutrition her family enjoyed gave a glow to her skin and hair that had been missing for years.

The fixtures and fittings of their new home were a constant wonder and delight to the Lawless family. They had indoor plumbing for the first time. No more standing in line for the tap and hauling buckets of water. No more slop buckets and smelly deposits. They had flushing toilets, indoors, no more freezing your parts off walking down the yard. She had a range: the sheer bliss of that would take her decades to appreciate. No more cooking over open fires for Sadie Lawless. It would take them all a long time to become accustomed to this luxury.

'Take your time.' Ann Marie walked across the flagstone floor of the kitchen. She walked past the long high heavy wooden work table sitting proudly in front of the big white range and made

288

her way over to the smaller dining table she had insisted should be included in the new kitchen. The Lawless family needed somewhere to eat and the staff dining room off the kitchen simply made more work for Sadie.

'I've just put the baby down for a nap.' Sadie took the final piece of freshly ironed bedding into the utility room. 'The two cleaning women have finished for the day.' She spoke through a mouthful of wooden pegs while hanging the freshly ironed laundry from the clothes line stretched across the ceiling of the utility room. She never thought she'd see the day when she, Sadie Lawless, had a cleaning staff. Still and all, she'd never expected to set foot inside one of these fancy houses, let alone live in one. 'I'll put the kettle on. I'm gummin' for a cup of tea.'

'I'll put the cups out,' Ann Marie offered. There was no point in her offering to actually make the tea. Her skills did not include anything to do with kitchen duties. She set the kitchen table for a tea break while Sadie put the kettle on and tidied away her work.

'Is it just a chat, Ann Marie,' Sadie asked over her shoulder, 'or is there a problem I need to know about?'

'Not a problem as such.' Ann Marie sat at the kitchen table and waited for Sadie to make the tea. She'd never had so much tea in her life as she'd had since meeting Ivy Rose Murphy. 'Where are the girls?' She looked around as if she expected the Lawless daughters to suddenly pop out of thin air.

'Clare is at school.' Sadie warmed the flowered delft teapot, smiling as she thought of her eldest daughter. 'She's doing really well at her shorthand and typing. John and Jem are that pleased with her.'

Clare Lawless worked at the livery part time. She'd taken a course at the GPO in telephone skills and was presently studying office skills at a local school and making her parents very proud.

'Dora is around the house somewhere. I asked her to check out the rooms after the cleaning women left. I can't be everywhere. I want fires set and ready to be lit in every room.' Sadie was trying to learn to run this house efficiently. She'd had long conversations with Agnes Reilly, the highly skilled housekeeper who oversaw the running of Ann Marie's aunt's home. She needed all the help she could get in this new world and wasn't too proud to ask for it.

Sadie brought the freshly made tea to the table. She checked that a jug of fresh milk, a filled sugar bowl and a bowl for the slops were on the table. 'So what's the problem?' She sat down and began pouring the tea while waiting to be told the reason for this kitchen visit.

'I'm not sure where to begin.' Ann Marie accepted a cup of tea with a resigned sigh. The new people in her life couldn't seem to function without a cup of tea in hand.

'The beginning is usually best.' Sadie waited, wondering if her family were going to be in trouble. She couldn't think of anything they might have done wrong but then they weren't accustomed to living in such a fancy place.

'I never gave any thought to visitors.' Ann Marie pushed her gold-rimmed glasses up on her nose. She tucked strands of caramel-coloured hair behind her ears and stared intently across the table at Sadie.

Sadie waited. She couldn't see the problem herself: you opened the door to visitors and put the kettle on. What more did you need to do?

'While I lived in my uncle's home,' Ann Marie said, 'I had visitors of course but the servants were on hand to handle the situation. In truth I didn't have a great many visitors calling to see me personally.'

Sadie sipped her tea and waited. She was glad of a chance to sit down.

'Well, since I've moved into this house so many people seem to want to come to call!' Ann Marie almost wailed. 'I don't know if it's because the situation here is out of the ordinary or if my friends felt uncomfortable visiting me at my uncle's house but suddenly I have so many people wanting to call on me at home.'

Sadie wished she could take her shoes off and wriggle her toes. She knew if she did that she'd never be able to get the flaming shoes back on her feet so she contented herself by turning her ankles under the table.

'In my aunt's home a visitor is greeted at the door by the butler and at least one footman is on hand to take wraps and coats.' The running of a large house was only noticeable when something went wrong. The servants knew their place and under the direction of the butler and housekeeper large homes were run like clockwork. 'Visiting guests hand their cards to the butler who takes the engraved cards on a silver salver in to a family member who will decide if they are at home to the caller.'

'You're thinking of hiring a butler?' Sadie didn't fancy having some strange man under her feet all day.

'Not in the least,' Ann Marie laughed. 'I'm just trying to think how we can handle visitors to this house. You can't be expected to run upstairs, answer the door, take the card, bring it to me, run down the stairs and prepare a tray then carry it upstairs and stand by to serve. It would be ridiculous and time-consuming. And what if it's a gentleman caller? It wouldn't be at all the thing for me to entertain a gentleman, alone.'

'I could always just bang the door in everyone's face. Tell them all to get lost.' Sadie wanted to suggest Ann Marie open the blessed door herself but bit her tongue.

'That's certainly one option.' Ann Marie held her hand over her teacup. She didn't want more tea. 'I don't want to employ a stranger.' The system she had set up with the Lawless family appeared to be working well for all of them. She didn't wish to instigate change simply to accommodate people who might drop by to visit. She wasn't actually at home that much. She enjoyed being out and about around the city. 'I hadn't given any thought to socialising in my own home, I'm afraid.'

'I don't know what's needed, Ann Marie. I'm learning as I go. I'm no fancy housekeeper with years of training behind me. I don't know how to cook fancy food either – you know that yourself – you've tasted me food.' Ann Marie ate with the

292

family. The meals Sadie produced were plain but tasty.

'I'm an unmarried female. I don't think anyone would expect me to host dinner parties. However, afternoon tea is something completely different.' She changed her mind about a fresh cup of tea and stood to fetch the teapot from the range. She was very familiar with the routine by now and there was something about sitting visiting around the kitchen table that seemed to call for tea. 'What I would like to suggest, if you agree of course, is that I make it known I am available to visitors on a certain day at a set time. What do you think?'

'What has that to do with me?' Sadie accepted a fresh cup of tea.

'I thought I could employ your Dora to answer the door to visitors and serve afternoon tea. I've noticed she is the one who answers the house phone and takes messages. This would be more of the same.' Ann Marie returned the teapot to the range. 'You would be in the kitchen preparing the tray to be carried to the withdrawing room. What do you think?'

'What's a fancy afternoon tea when it's at home?' Sadie felt her stomach sink at the very thought of having to prepare a tea for Ann Marie's snobby friends. What her Dora would say about being turned into some fancy maid, she didn't know.

'If, as I've said, we plan for stated days "at home" you could purchase "fancies" from the bakery.' Ann Marie was thinking frantically. 'We could order in smoked salmon and ham to make dainty sandwiches. You would only have to present the food attractively and that I can demonstrate for you.'

'I'm always up for learning something new, Ann Marie.' Sadie had never seen salmon that didn't come in a tin and that was for high days and holidays. She hadn't a clue what 'fancies' were. She didn't want to let Ann Marie down in front of her friends.

'We could practise.' Ann Marie warmed to the idea. 'I would, of course, purchase a uniform for Dora. I am perfectly capable of describing what is needed. We could have several practice runs. It could be fun. I'll invite Ivy and Jem to come visit while Emmy's in school. They will enjoy the experience and I can give instructions as to what's needed.'

'On your own head be it, Ann Marie.' Sadie took a deep breath and straightened her shoulders. Her family were coming up in the world thanks to this woman and Ivy Murphy. Never let it be said Sadie Lawless let the side down. She'd learn these new ways if it killed her.

'There is one more matter I wish to discuss.' Ann Marie looked down at her fingers twirling the teacup on its saucer. She was embarrassed by the subject she wanted to broach.

'Ann Marie,' Sadie felt quite daring when she leaned across the table and stopped the other woman from twirling the tea out of her cup, 'I know you have an agreement with Ivy. An understanding that you can each say what you are thinking without giving offense. Could we not have something like that between ourselves?'

'Sadie Lawless, you are a treasure. I'm afraid I

don't take the time to tell you how much I appreciate all you and your family do for me. I am happier living in this house than I have been in years. I feel part of a family again.'

'Then just spit it out, whatever it is.'

'I'd like to pay for elocution lessons for Clare and Dora.' Ann Marie watched Sadie's face carefully. Was she going too far?

The Lawless daughters were very attractive young women but, in Ann Marie's opinion, their flat Dublin accents ruined their appearance as soon as they opened their mouths. She did not want the baby, that innocent little boy, growing up speaking in the same accent. Sadie might never know that the baby she'd adopted was related to Ann Marie by blood but Ann Marie intended to do everything she could to see the child had opportunities and options as he grew to manhood.

'Ela–what?'

'Elocution, it means teaching someone to speak correctly.' Ann Marie, thankfully, could see only interest in Sadie's face. 'I believe your daughters would benefit by a course of speech instruction.'

'I ask your sacred pardon!' Sadie gasped. Whatever else?

A sharp knocking on the back door startled both women. No one was expected, and the coalman and milkman had set days and hours.

'Who on earth could that be?' Ann Marie said.

'Only one way to find out.'

Chapter 29

'Ivy Murphy!' Sadie gasped at the sight of the woman standing outside the back door.

'Ivy!' Ann Marie had been standing inside the open kitchen door, listening in case she might be needed. She hurried out of the kitchen and down the hallway to stand at Sadie's shoulder. 'Finally, you've come to visit us. Come in!'

'I didn't know where else to go.' Ivy stepped into the hall. She waited while Sadie closed the door then walked with the two women into the kitchen without speaking.

'You must have smelt the tea.' Sadie looked at Ann Marie with concern. Ivy didn't look too good.

'I've been walking around for ages.' Ivy allowed Ann Marie to take her coat and shawl. The kitchen was lovely and warm.

'Sit down, Ivy.' Ann Marie had been longing to show Ivy around her home but now was obviously not the time. Something was wrong, and the fact that Ivy had come to her in her hour of need gave her a warm glow. 'Sadie will pour you a cup of tea.' She almost pushed Ivy into one of the sturdy kitchen chairs.

Ivy waited until Sadie joined them around the table – after all, this concerned her too. 'I sold hardly any dolls.'

'Oh, Ivy!' Ann Marie reached across the table and took her friend's trembling hands. They were

296

freezing. She released them and reached for Ivy's teacup, then wrapped Ivy's hands around the bowl, hoping the tea would warm her hands. Sadie watched and said nothing. She was stunned. The Lawless family had so much riding on the sale of those dolls.

'It was a nightmare.' Ivy started to tell them about her experience at the preview show. They hung on her every word.

'You are overreacting, Ivy Murphy,' Ann Marie stated clearly when Ivy had told her story. 'Sadie, could you ask Dora to bring a bottle of whiskey from the study, please? We'll add a drop to our tea.'

'I'll get the whiskey meself.' Sadie stood quickly. 'I'll have Dora keep her ear open for the baby. She can look after him while we talk.' She hurried from the kitchen.

Ivy sat staring into her cup. She didn't know what to do or say. The silence hung over the two women.

'I overreached meself, Ann Marie,' Ivy finally muttered. She had walked the streets, trying to come up with a way of making her plan work. She'd gone to Mass seeking divine intervention for all the good that had done her. She hadn't known where to turn.

'Ivy Murphy,' Ann Marie slapped both hands on the table, 'snap out of it!'

'You don't understand.' Ivy's eyes filled with tears. She'd failed.

'For heaven's sake, Ivy!' Ann Marie sat back in her chair and glared. 'I want to shake you until your teeth rattle.'

297

'That sounds serious.' Sadie, the whiskey bottle clutched in her hand, exploded breathlessly into the kitchen. She hadn't wanted to miss a word of whatever was going on. She put the whiskey on the kitchen table and looked at the other two women.

'Make a fresh pot of tea, Sadie, please,' Ann Marie said. 'I'm about to pin Miss Ivy Rose Murphy's ears back.'

'I came here looking for comfort.' Ivy straightened in her chair. 'Seems I came to the wrong shop.'

'I've already said you're overreacting.' Ann Marie stood abruptly. She couldn't sit still and look at Ivy's miserable face. 'Sadie, hurry up with that bloody tea! That one,' she flung one hand in Ivy's direction, 'is incapable of thinking straight without a cup of her bloody tea in hand.'

'I can't make the kettle boil any faster.' Sadie looked over her shoulder at Ann Marie – she'd never heard her swear before. She thought she was being a bit hard on Ivy – after all, the poor woman had had a terrible shock.

'Listen to me, Ivy Murphy.' Ann Marie put both hands on the table and leaned down to stare into Ivy's face. 'You were extremely fortunate with your baby dolls. We all know that. You had a stroke of good fortune and I for one was delighted. However!' She slapped both hands on the table, causing Ivy and Sadie to jump.

'Here, Ivy.' Sadie poured a fresh cup of tea directly from the pot and carried it over to the table. 'It's a bit weak yet but I reckon it doesn't matter that much for once.'

'Right!' Ann Marie picked up the bottle of

whiskey, opened it and poured a healthy dollop into the cup Sadie had just set before Ivy. 'Now you have your bloody tea perhaps you'll be able to hear what I'm going to tell you.'

Ann Marie found she still couldn't sit down calmly.

'First and foremost,' she stated, stepping out across the tiled floor of the kitchen. 'I should have thought of the problem of children being brought to the theatre by servants and for that I apologise.'

'Ann Marie!' Ivy and Sadie said together.

'That's simply a fact.' Ann Marie held both hands up in the air. 'However, this is not the tragedy you are making it out to be, Ivy.'

'We all knew it was a gamble, Ivy.' Sadie cleared the table of the cups and saucers she and Ann Marie had used and replaced them with fresh ones. She poured a cup of tea for herself and without asking permission poured some of the whiskey into her own tea. She was being led into sin.

'Ivy – Sadie...' Ann Marie stormed over to the table, poured a healthy dram of whiskey into one of the cups and, without adding tea, held it in her hand as she paced. 'You are both being unrealistic.' She sipped at the whiskey, grimacing as it went down. 'You cannot expect to be an instant success every time you take a venture into business. The preview gave you an example of what to expect. Now,' and she turned to glare down at the two women sitting staring up at her, fascinated, 'you deal with it.'

'I am not lowering the price of those dolls.' Ivy's eyes were watering from the whiskey Ann Marie had dumped into her tea.

'Nobody's asking you to, you hardheaded ... Dubliner!' Ann Marie practically spat. 'If you are finished with your snit, I'll explain.'

'I'm all ears.' Ivy shrugged.

'It will take time.' Ann Marie finally dropped into one of the kitchen chairs. 'The dolls you've created are wonderful. You both know that. It may take days or even weeks but news of those dolls will travel through society. Once that happens, parents will insure that their servants carry the money necessary to purchase the bloody things.' She sat back and stared. 'That is simply a fact. You will make the dolls a desired commodity and people will fight to be the ones who can boast that their little darlings have one.'

'Do you think so?' Ivy asked.

Sadie crossed her fingers under the table. She badly wanted the dolls to sell. She had a stake in this after all.

'Yes, I do.' Ann Marie nodded decisively. 'I think they will sell like hot cakes. You will find that the house servants in and around Dublin will spread the word very quickly. I'm afraid you'll have to wait a while but you will see. Your dolls will sell. So pull yourself together, Ivy Murphy, and find your fighting spirit wherever you've left it.'

'Well,' Ivy grinned, 'you certainly told me.'

'Have we dealt with your fit of the vapours or is there something else bothering you?' Ann Marie didn't think the lack of doll sales would upset Ivy to this extent but she might be wrong.

'I've decided I'm going to have to take Jem's advice and go see Billy Flint.' Ivy sank back in her chair.

'My God, Ivy!' Sadie gasped.

'Who is this Billy Flint I keep hearing about?' Ann Marie asked.

'He's a gangster,' Sadie said, visibly shocked. 'Why on earth do you need to go see him, Ivy?'

'I was scared last night. Me knees were knocking that hard it's a wonder me legs didn't shatter. I was standing out in front of the Gaiety in full view of God and everyone. I sold a few dolls, I'm not saying I didn't, and I was yelling out the price for everyone and his brother to hear. You could see the flyboys prick up their ears. I swear I could feel their eyes on me the whole time I was there.' Ivy shivered violently. She had never been so glad to see anyone as she'd been to see Jem last night.

'I can't keep this lad quiet any longer, Ma.' Dora Lawless, a slim blonde young girl wearing a navy dress with white collar and cuffs, walked into the kitchen, a very unhappy baby on her hip. 'He wants something to eat, and he wants it now.'

Sadie stood to take the baby from her daughter but Ann Marie got there before her. She loved to cuddle the baby. It fascinated her to see the changes taking place in even so young a child. It broke her heart that she imagined she caught glimpses of her own father from time to time in the baby's face. She felt so fortunate to be able to watch this child grow. The baby the Lawless family had adopted was the result of a shabby affair between her only male cousin and a young dancer. Her father would have been the baby's great-uncle ... she wasn't too sure what that would make her.

'I'll make his bottle.' Sadie saw the look on Ivy's

face and grinned. 'You have to fight around this place to get ahold of that fella.'

'I'd never have believed it if I hadn't seen it with me own eyes.' Ivy shook her head. 'Her Ladyship,' she jerked her head in Ann Marie's direction, 'gettin' all over baby spit and not being bothered.' She laughed. 'This is one of them times when I wish I had one of those box Brownie cameras you're always talking about, Ann Marie.'

'Ivy,' Ann Marie, the baby gnawing on her expensive silk blouse, turned sharply to stare at her friend, 'you are a genius. That is exactly what we need around here, a camera to record the changes in this young man.' She caught the look of hurt on Dora's face out of the corner of her eye. She made a mental note to herself to be careful – not make too much of a fuss over the baby. It could lead to resentment. 'We can record the history of the house and everyone in it. It will be a fascinating project. Don't you think, Dora?'

'Don't know.' Dora walked over to the kitchen table and dropped into one of the chairs. 'Any tea going?'

'What did your last maid die of?' Sadie snapped. She had enough people to wait on. 'Get up and get it yourself. You're big enough and bold enough.'

'Okay!' Dora shoved the kitchen chair back with the back of her legs as she stood. 'No need to get in a snit.'

'I'll give him his bottle.' Ann Marie ignored the byplay between Sadie and Dora. She held out her hand for the bottle Sadie had prepared for the baby and dropped into the chair across the table from Ivy, a contented smile on her face. She put the teat in the baby's mouth and sat beaming around at everyone.

'That blouse will be a nightmare to clean if you don't cover it with something, Ann Marie.' Ivy grinned at her friend's absorption in the baby.

'Don't matter to her.' Dora returned to the table with her cup of tea. 'She don't wash the bloomin' thing.'

'*Dora!*' Sadie was horrified by her daughter's rudeness.

'While being unnecessarily rude,' Ann Marie looked up from the baby and around the spotlessly clean kitchen, remembering how Sadie had looked earlier, 'Dora is nevertheless correct. We need to employ a washerwoman, Sadie.' The utility room was furnished with a washing machine but she should have been aware that Sadie could not be expected to handle the sheer volume of washing, ironing, folding and putting away of laundry that five adults and a baby produced, not to mention household linens. She'd been very short-sighted there.

Sadie didn't know whether to kick or kiss her daughter. The amount of laundry in this house was a nightmare. She never seemed to finish it. Ann Marie had put a machine in the utility room to beat the dirt out of the clothes, a washing machine she called it, but Sadie was afraid of the thing.

'Marcella Wiggins.' Ivy could see the denial forming on Sadie's lips so she got in quick with her suggestion. 'The woman's a holy terror for scrubbing and cleaning.'

'Didn't she use to work in one of the big houses

303

'round the square before she got married?' Sadie almost collapsed onto one of the kitchen chairs. She glared at Dora – she'd have to talk to her about her rudeness. But the good Lord knew it would be a blessing to have someone else take care of the mountains of laundry this house produced.

Ann Marie tried not to wince as Sadie's broad Dublin accent suddenly grated on her ears. She looked at the baby in her arms, wondering if he'd grow up speaking in the same accent. 'Have a word with the woman, would you please, Ivy?'

'I'll send her over to see you,' Ivy promised, glad to be able to do something to help a woman who always held out a hand to help her neighbours. 'She'd be a great help to you, Sadie.' She ignored the panicked look on Sadie's face. 'Mrs Wiggins is not exactly backward about coming forward. She learned a lot in the years she spent in service. You could ask her for advice–' Ivy laughed, thinking of the almost overpowering woman, 'that is, if she waits long enough to let you ask.'

Chapter 30

Ivy wanted to kick up her heels and dance in the street. It was so strange to walk along these familiar streets without her pram. She'd been for a second visit to Nanny Grace. The rooms Nanny Grace inhabited were a wonderland to Ivy. She had touched diaries, mementos and what should have been precious objects. It was hard for her to understand people who threw away their family history. Perhaps it was because she'd none of her own? She didn't know, she only knew it saddened her to see that old woman sitting surrounded by the memories of others, worrying about her future.

The furniture Nanny had to sell was top class – obviously moved from other areas of the house over the years. It was well tended but Ivy didn't think anyone would pay a great deal of money for the stuff. She was tempted to buy one of the beds and some of the bedroom furniture for herself. She was running a mental list of the families in The Lane, wondering if anyone she knew could afford to buy some of the toys. They would make ideal Santa gifts. She thought Emmy would love some of the toys too. She'd have a word with Jem, see what he thought. She sighed, wrapping her thick knitted beige scarf tighter around her neck against the chill wind.

She really should have been at the market today but the thought of Nanny Grace's plight was one of the things that kept her awake last night. She was still worrying about those darn Cinderella dolls too. Listening to Ann Marie had put new heart into her but she couldn't help fretting in the dark of night. She'd been stupid to think the dolls would be snatched out of her hand. She unconsciously straightened her shoulders as she walked. So, she had problems. She wasn't the only one in the world. She'd make a success of that little venture or her name wasn't Ivy Rose Murphy.

She turned into the tunnel that led into The Lane ... right into a scene of chaos. People were running around shouting, and children were screaming and pointing towards the end of the livery. From where she stood in the mouth of the tunnel her eyes tracked Jem's long livery building, fearing there was a problem with the structure. She took a deep breath of relief when she realised that whatever was going on appeared to have nothing to do with the livery building itself – Jem was standing grinning in the open doorway.

There was a crowd of people pushing and shoving down at the end of The Lane. It seemed, from a distance, to have something to do with the bramble patch. Had they found something in the long wide gap between the end of the livery and the front of Old Man Wilson's place? She hurried her footsteps.

'What's going on, Jem?' Ivy asked.

'I was wondering when you were going to show up.' Jem threw his arm around Ivy's shoulders and began to lead her towards the gathered crowd, 'You were out and about early this morning.'

'I went by the church to light a few candles. Then I went to see Nanny Grace.'

She stared at the crowd pulling at the area of wild scrub that ran between the wide end of the livery building and what Old Man Wilson always claimed was his garden. The brambles were thick and tall, defying even the smallest child to climb through. The bushes were bare now but in September the children of The Lane risked a thick ear from Mr Wilson by sneaking in to pick blackberries and rosethorn buds from this area. 'What is going on down there, Jem?'

'You went out without your pram and the sky

306

didn't fall?'

'Eejit!' She nudged him with her elbow. 'What on earth is going on, Jem?'

The area was a hive of activity. Young men and boys were busy chopping down the small forest of brambles, women were shouting instructions. An army of children were filling their homemade wagons with the cut-down brambles and branches. There would be blazing fires in a lot of homes this evening.

'Mrs Wiggins and her army cleared a lot of that stuff away,' Jem jerked his head towards the brambles, 'when they raided the place for the bin fires, remember? Well...' He looked down at her with a grin. 'But first let me tell you the best bit: Seán McDonald has been hiding in there – ever since his family were taken away.'

'Go 'way!' Ivy turned to stare at Jem. 'How did he manage to survive in all them brambles? What's he been living on?'

'He's weak but alive, thank God. Some of the children have been sneaking him their school milk and bread and the lad's always been good at finding something for himself to eat ... and Ivy...' Jem grinned, delighted with himself, 'he's been coming and going by way of his "secret tunnel" behind the brambles!'

'My God, Jem!' Ivy stared at the busy crowd. 'Are you telling me that there's another tunnel down there?'

'So, it seems. You know, Ann Marie's a terror for reading old papers and looking through things. She has always reckoned there had to be more openings into this square. She's been looking for

307

them in my livery, banging on the walls, pulling out rubbish and such. She even sent away to some government office for papers she says I should have on hand. As far as I know she hasn't received any new documents, as she calls them, but it seems young Seán found one of those bloody openings all on his own.'

'Where's Seán now?' She looked around as if expecting the child to be collapsed on the cobbles.

'Lily Connelly,' Jem whispered under his breath. Declan Johnson was still on the loose. He wouldn't want that fella to get news of young Seán. In his opinion the man was off his rocker – who knew what he'd do? 'She's the one who followed one of the little kids, wondering what they were getting up to over here. She has Seán stashed away at her place.'

'What's going on over here?' Maisie Reynolds was standing behind them, her arms holding her shawl folded over her chest as she examined the situation.

Ivy had to leave it to Jem to explain. She was having a hard time understanding how something as important as an entrance tunnel could be kept hidden from the people who needed to know.

'Yer telling me that there's a way in and out of this place hidden behind that lot?' Maisie asked when Jem had explained, pointing her chin at the bramble-choked plot.

'So it would seem.' Jem grinned. He knew how much a new entrance would mean to the people of The Lane. No more marching in your best shoes through the questionable liquids and whatnot of the Tunnel. No more walking past drunken louts

308

hanging around outside the pub.

'Are they going to open up all of this today?' Ivy stared at the area she'd known all of her life. She'd been one of the children running in there to pick berries.

'We're going to give it a ruddy good try,' Jem said.

'We'll need some of that lot,' Maisie jerked her head towards the disappearing scrub bush while pushing the sleeves of her jumper up to her elbows, 'for the party fires. The workers will need a drop of tea to keep them going. Where's Marcella?' She turned around, looking for the woman who could always get things done.

'In the thick of it as usual.' Jem nodded to where Mrs Wiggins was locked in a verbal knock-down drag-out argument with Mr Wilson. The man had come home for a bite to eat and found his property had been invaded. He was shaking his fists in Marcella's face but the woman wasn't moving.

Jem took stock of the situation between the two old neighbours. It wouldn't come to blows and they didn't need him here for a moment. 'I'm going to have a few of the lads search the livery and see if we can find any old tools stashed around the place.' He nodded his head towards the gang of youths hacking into the scrub, 'I gave that lot everything I had on hand but it would help if we had more.'

'You go do that.' Ivy gave him a gentle nudge. 'I'm not budging from here. I want to see what's behind all that lot. I'll give the lads a hand while I'm waiting for you to get back. Don't be too long.'

'I'll be as quick as I can – you're not the only

one wants to know what's been hidden.' Jem gave her shoulders a squeeze before stepping away.

'Right, folks!' Marcella had said all she was going to say to Fred Wilson. If that man wanted to call the Garda that was his prerogative. She was getting stuck in while the going was good. 'We need to get organised, work in turn. It makes no sense for all of us to be pushing and shoving.'

In no time at all she had a team of willing workers of all ages and sizes organised into a relay work force.

'Maisie, get them party fires lit!' Marcella shouted. 'The older kids will be home from school soon and they can lend a hand getting some of the sticks and bits over to the fires.' She looked around to plan out the best use of her work force. 'I suppose the women with childer coming in from school will want to stop work to get them something to eat.' She sighed at the thought of any delay.

'There's too much work here for us to stop, Mrs Wiggins.' Ivy wiped her sweating face on the arm of her jumper. She'd thrown off her coat and shawl, and taken the back of her long skirt and pulled it up between her legs to give her room to move. She felt like a child again. 'Why don't you ask Jem Ryan to organise a few lads to pick up something from the Penny Dinners? We can have everyone in The Lane working on this.'

'We can't ask Jem to feed The Lane, Ivy.' Marcella was tempted though. It would mean they could keep working. She couldn't wait to see what was behind this load of old scrub.

'Jem Ryan!'

The female voice booming out of the tunnel stopped Jem in his tracks.

He'd been hurrying back, a load of old tools in hand, to join in the work of clearing the scrub. He jerked back around, wondering what it was that would bring Ann Marie Gannon charging down the tunnel like a hooligan.

Ann Marie practically exploded out of the tunnel, waving a large brown envelope in the air like a demented woman, the grin on her face stretched practically ear to ear.

'You won't believe what I've discovered!' she yelled, still madly waving the brown envelope in the air. 'You simply will not believe it, Jem.'

'Just a minute, Ann Marie.' Jem looked around – this looked like it might take some time. 'Baldy!' he yelled at a youth with a mop of curly hair making his way down to the area of activity at the bottom of The Lane. 'Take these tools down with you, will you?' He passed the load over to the lad with a sigh. He'd have to see what had Ann Marie so excited.

'Where's Ivy?' Ann Marie had been so intent on passing along her news she hadn't noticed the crowd at the end of the cobbled square. 'She'll never forgive us if we don't share this news with her.'

'She's down there.' Jem grinned as he pointed.

Ann Marie's eyes almost popped out of her head at the large crowd she'd failed to notice... Maybe she needed new glasses? 'In the thick of things as per usual. We think a new tunnel into The Lane has been discovered. I was headed down there when you caught me.'

'Talk about divine providence!' Ann Marie waved her hand in the air to stop Jem saying whatever he'd opened his mouth to add. She opened the large brown envelope she carried and ruffled through the papers inside. She pulled a thick, many times folded, large sheet of paper from the envelope. 'I think this is the one I need,' she muttered almost to herself. 'Yes ... this is it. I need somewhere to spread this.' She looked around as if expecting a table to suddenly appear from thin air.

'Ann Marie, what are you doing here? Are you the one keeping Jem Ryan from doing his bit?' A sweating Ivy was taking long angry strides down the exterior length of the livery building towards them. 'There's work to be done!'

'Ann Marie has something to show us, Ivy,' Jem shrugged.

'We haven't the time for whatever it is, Ann Marie,' Ivy said when she reached the other two. 'We have too much work we need to get done.'

'This is important, Ivy.' Ann Marie waved both hands in the air. 'I believe whatever you're doing down there has something to do with what I ran over here to share with you and Jem.' She dropped both document-laden hands to her hips.

'It never rains but it pours around here.' Ivy sighed. 'Give us a minute, Ann Marie. Jem, I offered your money to buy a few buckets of food from the Penny Dinners. I know you won't mind. There's just too much work to be done down there,' a jerk of her chin in the direction of the activity underlined her meaning, 'and we can't have everyone stopping to get their family something to eat. Some of them lazy buggers will forget to come back to work.'

'If something can be organised, I'll gladly pay for buckets of stew and for gur cake.' Ann Marie was familiar with the Penny Dinner menu by this time. 'But I must insist you two give me your full attention. You need to know what I've discovered.'

'Can't it wait, Ann Marie?' Ivy looked back towards the people working at clearing the scrub. She wanted to be there when they discovered whatever was hidden behind that lot.

'No,' Ann Marie was adamant. 'I believe what I've discovered in these papers will help with the work you've been doing down there. I really must insist you hear me out.'

'Let's take it inside, ladies!' Jem took each woman by the elbow and turned them towards the livery doors. 'It would appear we need to hear what Ann Marie has to say, Ivy.'

The threesome headed into the livery.

Betty Armstrong stood in the opening into The Lane, wondering what on earth was going on. She'd been about the town all day and now returned to find a hive of activity with people swarming about. She was about to approach Ivy and her friends when they turned into the livery, their heads bent in what appeared to be earnest conversation. She didn't want to interrupt. She looked at the packages in her hand and wondered about dropping them off in her own room before approaching the crowd at the far end of The Lane – then with a shrug she began walking slowly in that direction.

'May I do anything to help?' she asked when she reached the woman who appeared to be in charge of the controlled madness that surrounded her.

'The very woman.' Marcella's jumper sleeves signalled her satisfaction: they were pushed up as far as they would go. 'Do you know Lily Connelly?' She couldn't mention Seán and his whereabouts aloud.

'I don't think so.' Betty wondered what that had to do with anything.

'Fair enough.' Marcella took the woman by the elbow and gently towed her away from the crowd. She pointed to one of the houses and told her which rooms the Connellys rented. 'I need you to ask Mrs Connelly to organise the tables and such for a street party.' Marcella knew this woman had been scouring the town for news of young Seán. She'd bet money she would be willing to nurse Seán and let Lily, who'd be far more of an asset, join in the work to be done in The Lane. That would be the best use of everyone.

'I'll be on my way.' Betty had no idea what was going on. She'd go take care of the chore set before her, drop off her packages and return to find out what the commotion was all about.

Her departure went unnoticed by the crowd of people willingly pulling decades of wild scrub from the ground. This sudden explosion of activity gave the people something to do together – and helped them stay warm on a cold day. There was much shouting back and forward while the crowd got stuck in.

'Mrs Wiggins, look!' Bitsy Martin pointed with a

314

shaking finger towards the naked red-brick wall being slowly exposed.

Everyone stopped to stare – unable to believe what their eyes were telling them. Almost as one the fascinated crowd of women and children followed after some of Jem's lads as they walked towards the wall they'd uncovered. The hole Seán had made to climb inside and hide clearly showed.

'In the name of all that's good and holy!' Marcella and her workers stood staring at the newly revealed wall. 'Get back, everyone!' she suddenly shouted. 'That wall could come down on our heads. We need experienced men and more hands than ours to handle this.'

Chapter 31

While the excitement went on outside, Ivy and Jem were staring open-mouthed at the map Ann Marie had spread on the wonky table in the tearoom.

'I ask your sacred pardon,' Ivy gasped.

Jem, standing at her shoulder, was still as a statue, his mind refusing to believe what his eyes were seeing.

'As I've always thought,' Ann Marie's well-manicured finger traced over the map, 'there is another entrance to this building. It never made sense to me that a throughway from side to side of the livery did not exist.'

Her words were wasted on her listeners. They

were having a difficult time understanding these startling new developments.

Jem, without a word to anyone and walking like someone in a daze, left the two women and walked slowly over to his tack room. He reappeared in moments, a large mallet and what looked like an iron spike in his hands.

Exchanging glances, Ivy and Ann Marie hurried after him. Ivy stood for a moment in the long wide aisle that divided two sections of the long livery building, looking at the familiar wide-open double doors. She gave her body a shake and hurried over to stand at Ann Marie's shoulder and watch Jem force the iron spike – with powerful swings of the mallet – through what they had assumed was a solid brick wall.

'I've chalked and whitewashed this wall for years.' The sound of Jem's grunts and the groaning from the large hole he was making were almost smothered by the restless movements of the horses in their stalls. 'This section isn't bricks at all but daubing.' He recognised the wattle and daub material – Lord knew he'd made enough of these walls in his time. He pulled handfuls of old material from the newly created hole. 'It was well done – you would never see the difference once the wall had been daubed and whitened.'

According to the map they'd just been examining there was a second opening to the livery directly opposite the entrance they all knew. It was hard to believe. Jem grunted and muttered, straining to remove a section of the age-old materials, as the two women looked on wordlessly.

'That's about as much as I want to do now.' Jem

316

stood back, panting, covered in white dust and pieces of straw. 'If your maps are right, Ann Marie, and there is an entrance hidden behind this lot – I'll need men and tools before I can open up a section of my back wall.'

'I reckon if there really is another entryway it was blocked up long before any of us was ever born.' John Lawless had come to see what was upsetting the horses. He'd rolled his wheelchair silently up behind them.

'This place has been blocked off for years. We need to know what's behind this wall before we go any further. I need to make a hole big enough for me to be able to look through. First I'm going to get a sheet of wood we can use to cover the hole afterwards.'

Jem turned and walked slowly across the width of his livery, past the double rows of stalls, on either side of the main aisle, some holding curious horses standing with their heads over the half doors. He was having a hard time believing the evidence of his own eyes. His world was being turned on its head. Still, you had to deal with what life threw at you. He probably had a sheet of wood in his tack room he could use.

'Is that hay?' Ivy put out her hand to touch the stalks sticking out of the wall.

'I wouldn't,' John Lawless snapped. 'I'm no expert, you understand, but from my reading I think I learned that daub was made with urine-soaked straw and manure. You might want to wait for Jem to get back.'

'I should have known your curiosity would be killing you, Ivy Murphy.' Jem came up behind them. Two lads followed him with a sheet of wood and a handful of tools. 'Stand back.'

He used the iron spike to break through the wattling and daub, trying to carve out a space as large as a window. It was dusty work and clouds almost smothered him. He pushed the decaying materials out through the hole in front of him. When he was finished he put the tools to one side and cautiously stuck his head and shoulders through the hole he'd made.

'Dear merciful Lord!' Jem pushed back into the livery and simply stood staring with his mouth agape.

'What did you see?' Ivy rushed forward and pushed her head and shoulders through just as Jem had done. She hung there, simply staring at the strange world in front of her. The area in front of the newly opened window appeared to be long and wide. As far as she could make out it stretched the entire length of the livery and then some. The area was a tangled wilderness that had lain undiscovered for many years.

'I believe,' Ann Marie almost whispered when she too had taken a glimpse through the newly opened 'window', 'that what we have uncovered is the original front entrance of the livery.'

'Jaysus, Jem, how did we never know that place existed?' Ivy gasped. 'All the times me and me brothers ran in and out of your place. Through all the years and all the kids over all those years, kids who climbed and played around the livery. How the feck did we never see this? It's like the secret garden from that story.'

'It's a mystery all right.' Jem took Ivy's hand

318

and they stood, silently staring and wondering, for a moment. It would be a lot of dirty work removing that daub wall and he would need something to cover the opening – a carpenter to cut doors if it turned out that this was really another entrance to his business. He'd need to know a lot more before he could go any further.

'Let us get your lads to cover this opening back up for the moment,' Ann Marie suggested. 'We need to examine another of the maps I've had sent to me. I really believe we have more yet to discover.'

While Jem, Ivy and Ann Marie tried to remove the dust from their clothing, John sat in his chair and instructed the two lads who were grunting and struggling to cover the hole in the wall. He waited until it was finished to his satisfaction before sending the two lads about their business.

'Right.' Ivy wiped her hands together to remove the dust. 'I need a pot of tea before any more news that's going to take me breath away.' She took the handles of John's wheelchair and began to push. 'What about anyone else?'

'You and your tea, Ivy Murphy!' John looked over his shoulder to grin at her. He didn't mind being given a helping hand now and again.

'Wait, Ivy! There's more!' said Ann Marie.

'More?' said Jem. 'You mean there was something else of importance in my uncle's papers?' He shook his head, remembering Ann Marie sitting in his stable studying the papers he'd given her.

'No, Jem – in fact there was nothing about the second entrance in your uncle's papers. I found mention of it in one of the articles I received in the post today. I didn't know what else I'd find so I took the time to examine everything before I came over to share the news with you. And I discovered more! Drum roll, please!' She rolled her arms in glee, shaking her hands in a phantom drum roll. 'The area that your Mr Wilson claims as his own is, in fact, a public byway according to the papers – delivered to me today – that have been buried in a dusty government archive somewhere for years!' Ann Marie shook her head and grinned. 'I need to spend more time looking at the maps but there was mention made of tunnels being blocked up by the British in order to keep what they called "undesirable elements" from coming and going freely.' She giggled. 'I think you would be among those undesirables.'

'Uncle Jem, I'm home!' Emmy Ryan shouted as she ran into the livery. 'I have to change quick and get back out – what have we to eat? – there's something going on in The Lane, did you know?' She hadn't even paused for breath. 'Auntie Ivy! Ann Marie! Mr Lawless!' Emmy grinned widely at them as they began to walk towards her but she didn't stop her movements, swinging her schoolbag off her shoulders and onto the floor. 'Do you know – did you see?' She waved one arm back towards the opening.

'Dear Lord,' Jem shoved his hands through his hair, 'is it that time already?'

'Now then, folks,' Marcella Wiggins walked into the livery, 'I've the women setting up the fires and tables and things but the time got away from us and there's not bit, bite nor sup for the childer coming home from school. There was mention

320

made of a run to the Penny Dinners?'

'What's going on?' Conn, returning from a message run, stopped his bike and simply sat there on the saddle, staring around. 'What's happening down the way?'

'My nerves are shot,' Jem declared dramatically.

'Time to gird your loins, Jem, me auld flower.' John Lawless grinned widely. 'I'll put the kettle on.' He began to roll his wheelchair towards the tearoom. 'Them lads better have left plenty of fresh water in the buckets or there will be wigs on the green.'

'Me stomach thinks me throat is slit, I'm that hungry, Jem,' Ivy admitted.

'We need to study the other maps, Jem,' Ann Marie said softly.

'Right!' Jem shouted, feeling under siege. 'Emmy, run up and change out of your school clothes. Take your bag up with you – it doesn't belong in the middle of my stables.' He pushed his shoulders back when the little girl ran to obey. 'Conn, keep the bicycle out – we need you to make a run to the Penny Dinners – Ann Marie has offered to pay. You might need to take someone with you – it will be a lot of grub. What else needs doing?' He seemed to be asking the air around him.

It was dark now but it seemed every man, woman and child living in The Lane was still out in the courtyard. Tables had been pulled out of homes and the party fires burned brightly, giving additional light. The hungry crowd were diving into the stew from the Penny Dinners. The sound of enamel plates being scraped clean could be heard echoing around.

With the help of Ann Marie's many maps two new tunnel entrances into The Lane had been discovered. The Lane was buzzing with the news. It would change all of their lives. The work on completely clearing the ground before the first tunnel had gone swiftly when the working men returned home with their tools. While Ivy and Jem were busy organising the food supply for the crowd, Ann Marie had taken Nat Taylor, a skilled carpenter, with her to examine the two sites she'd discovered on the ordinance map. Together they had examined the newly exposed entrance to the tunnel that Seán had discovered. They had then turned their attention across the entire length of the square to a wall the children used for playing ball. Nat with Ann Marie and a curious crowd at his back had walked over to the wall and with a few heavy blows of a borrowed sledgehammer he'd knocked several red bricks from the wall, revealing a second hidden tunnel.

There was a great deal of work still to be done but the workers had stopped to eat. The women had big black kettles of water boiling over specially constructed hangers on each bin fire. The need for a constant supply of tea was in hand. The skilled labourers among the men were at one table, plotting the best use of the labour to hand and the jobs that needed doing. The people of The Lane were determined to get both tunnel entrances cleared and ready to use before a new day had dawned.

Chapter 32

'Well, this is nice.' Ann Marie put her arm through Ivy's. 'I'm glad you asked me to come along with you today.'

They were coming from a visit to the College Green bank where Ivy, with Ann Marie's silent support, had questioned the bank teller. She'd established that, yes, she would be able to use the night safe of the bank on the corner of Grafton Street and King Street. She was snootily informed that it was a branch office of her bank. To her relief she'd learned she'd also be able to make future deposits at the Grafton Street bank. A lot of street vendors used that branch of the bank, she knew. She wouldn't feel so out of place in her old army coat in the less ornate bank building.

Ivy was still nervous about walking into the bank on College Green. She kept expecting to be kicked out for even daring to set foot into that august establishment. Having Ann Marie by her side relieved a lot of the social pressure she felt stepping into the place. The people in the bank almost fell over themselves trying to be of service to Miss Gannon.

'I'm glad we didn't bring the automobile.' Ann Marie sighed. 'It's so pleasant to walk along the city streets.'

'Ann Marie, it's an education watching you in action.' Ivy looked at her friend who was wrapped from head to toe in fur and thought it was well for her. She couldn't feel the sharp bite of the wind slicing into everything it passed.

'I want to stop by the Gaiety Theatre booking office, Ivy.'

'Fine!' Ivy was wearing her good tweed suit, her best boots and a hat that had once belonged to Granny that Ivy had battered into shape. The thick handknit scarf and gloves kept her warm but the wind seemed to find every break in the thread. Hopefully the tall buildings of Grafton Street would reduce the wind factor considerably.

The two women strolled along College Green, avoiding the shouts and demands of the street hawkers. The clip-clop of the passing horses was soothing to Ivy's ears. From time to time one of the jarveys would raise his hat to the two women.

The Trinity College students were easily identified. They strolled along, heads close together, discussing the serious business of changing the world. The lack of redcoated soldiers, even after several years of absence, was a relief. The city had a different feeling to it these days.

'I thought we were going to stop for coffee at Bewleys?' Ivy remarked as they approached the elegant Grafton Street exterior to the coffee shop.

'I'd prefer to visit the Gaiety booking office first, if you don't mind? I'll be able to relax when I've that chore completed.'

'That's fine with me.' Ivy refused to think of the packages sitting unopened on her work table at home. The stuff she got from her rounds was going nowhere. It would wait until she was ready to deal with it. Ivy was forcing herself to learn that she didn't have to do everything alone and instantly. The world wouldn't end if she took the occasional day off.

The two women continued to stroll along Grafton Street, stopping from time to time when an item in a shop window attracted their attention. Ivy sometimes felt as if she was standing outside of herself looking at her own figure strolling along this street with the nobs. She was living two lives. She was finding both lifestyles suited her.

They turned onto King Street and walked in the direction of the Gaiety.

'I want to look at the billboard, Ann Marie,' Ivy said when the two women stood on the street outside the Gaiety Theatre. 'I didn't get a chance to see anything the other night but I heard enough. The women were sighing over that fella who's going to play Prince Charming. I'd like to be sure of the starting date and time as well.' Ivy had checked the newspaper advertisement for the show but it didn't hurt to be sure. She was still having nightmares about her failure to sell as many dolls as she'd expected at the gala evening. That had been a bruising setback but she was determined to apply herself – and succeed.

'I shouldn't be too long.' Ann Marie was glad Ivy wasn't about to accompany her inside the theatre building. She'd telephoned ahead. She intended to purchase the use of a theatre box, over a period of several days, perhaps for the Christmas Season. She wanted to be able to invite Jem and Ivy and some of her other friends from The Lane to join her in an evening at the theatre. She knew the cost of such an extravagant gesture would horrify Ivy.

The women separated. Ann Marie walked through the door being held open by a uniformed doorman. Ivy made her way towards the tall billboard with its information and glossy black-and-white photographs arranged to catch the attention. The thrill of knowing she was capable of reading whatever might be written there brought a wide smile to her face.

Doug Joyce, Johnjo Smith at his side, strolled along King Street. He wanted to arrive at the theatre early. He'd had some new music by an unknown writer delivered directly to the theatre for him to study. He found it easier to concentrate on new tunes when he had a piano available to him. The bustling noise of the theatre energised him. If the music pleased him he'd buy it and add his own topical lyrics before using the music in his act.

'It's Her Ladyship!' Johnjo Smith barked suddenly. He grabbed Doug by the elbow, stopping his forward movement.

'What?' Doug had been so lost in his own thoughts it took him a moment to process what his friend had said. 'Where?'

'There.' Johnjo pointed rudely at the tall woman staring so intently at the billboard. 'Are you blind?'

'Where? I don't see her,' Doug knew Johnjo intensely disliked the woman he called Her Ladyship but this was the first time he'd ever imagined seeing her in the street.

'She's standing right in front of the billboard,' Johnjo said. He wanted to grab his friend and run.

'That's not my mother,' Doug almost whispered, suddenly white to his lips. If it wasn't his mother it could only be one other. 'Ivy?' He had to cough to clear the lump that threatened to cut off his breathing. 'Ivy?'

Ann Marie was waiting for her payment to be processed and her reservation docket to be written out. Rather than staying to watch the clerk work she walked over to stand behind the glass doors of the main entrance to the theatre. She saw the two well-dressed men stroll into view. Their disparate appearance amused her. Their differences were almost comic-book perfect. One man tall, slim and blond, the other shorter, muscled and dark. Although both were dressed expensively the blond man wore his clothes with a casual elegant perfection. The shorter dark man looked like a bad-tempered boy forced to dress in his Sunday best. She wished desperately she'd bought that box Brownie camera as she'd promised herself. This was an image she'd love to capture. She determined to purchase a camera that very day.

She was curious when the two men stopped in their tracks. She looked up and down King Street, trying to see what had attracted their attention. She didn't see anything out of the ordinary. She realised with a start that she knew the identity of one of the men. The incredibly handsome blond man was Douglas Joyce. His handsome face had been featured on almost a daily basis in the newspapers. She assumed the shorter man was a bodyguard. He possessed the build of a pugilist.

Douglas Joyce, Ann Marie knew, was making a name for himself in Dublin society. He was becoming known as a man of mystery, a much-sought-after individual. Every hostess in Dublin longed to be the one who managed to attract him to one of her social events.

Then Ann Marie realised the two men were staring at Ivy who was studying the billboard, lost in a world of her own.

'*Ivy!*' the blond man called loudly.

Ann Marie felt almost as if she were a silent witness to a train wreck. She saw Ivy's head turn in the direction of the two men. Her heart broke for her friend Jem Ryan when she saw the expression on Ivy's face. She'd never looked at Jem like that. Ivy looked as if she'd seen the face of a god, something otherworldly. Her entire face lit up. The smile that creased her face illuminated her with an almost blinding beauty.

'*Shay!*' Ivy forgot all decorum as she flung herself at her brother. She didn't care who was looking on. This was her baby brother, come home to her.

The force of Ivy's hug knocked Doug's hat from his head – neither noticed Johnjo catch the hat before it hit the ground. Only the hatpins stuck firmly into Ivy's hat saved it from hitting the ground too. The man and woman stood in the street hugging each other tightly, their aligned bodies swaying in place. They were completely unaware of the fascinated people that strolled slowly past, trying to get a good look at these goings-on.

'Ivy, I need to breathe now,' Doug Joyce croaked. His sister had her arms wrapped so tightly around his neck he was in danger of suffocating.

Ivy stepped back slightly. She took her brother's face in her two hands and stood staring up at this familiar stranger, completely enthralled to see the passage of time written so clearly on his handsome face.

'Shay Murphy, where have you been?'

'So many places, Ivy.' Doug looked down at the woman who had been his true mother ever since his seventh birthday. Ivy's phantom voice in his ear over the years had egged him on, encouraged him whenever he faltered. She'd been his guardian angel most of his life.

'What, you broke all your fingers?' Ivy wanted to wrap Shay up in cotton wool and take him home with her. 'Is that why you never wrote to me?'

'You can't...' Doug glanced around. He wouldn't shame her by mentioning her illiteracy.

'I can now.' Ivy grinned in proud delight.

'Well, well, well, Miss Murphy, you've certainly come up in the world.' Doug took her glove-encased hands from his face and pushed her gently away from him. Still holding her two hands in his, he stood examining every inch of her fashionably attired figure.

'Shay, you're here – in Dublin. Why didn't yeh come home? Yeh know yer always welcome. Did yeh hear about me da?' She hated to start this first meeting after years with sadness – but this needed to be said.

'I heard,' Doug said simply.

'Sir.' Johnjo Smith broke into the siblings' fascination with each other to pass Doug his hat. The pair couldn't continue to stand out here attracting attention.

'Ivy, come back to my hotel with me.' Doug returned the hat to his head with careless ele-

329

gance. 'We have so much to talk about.'

'Which hotel?' Ivy was impressed by her brother's casual acceptance of the other man's help. It looked like her little brother was coming up in the world.

'I have a suite of rooms at the Shelbourne,' Doug replied in a toffee-nosed voice with a huge grin on his handsome face.

'Go 'way! You've lost the run of yourself completely, Shay Murphy!' Ivy gasped. 'The Shelbourne, I ask yer sacred pardon! It's far from it yeh were raised!'

'Seriously, Ivy.' Doug grinned to hear Ivy use his old name.

He felt far removed from the sixteen-year-old Shay Murphy who left Ireland. He'd taken nothing of his old life with him. He had only the money in his pocket that this woman had shoved in there at the last possible moment. He'd hardly noticed as he boarded the boat sitting waiting on Dun Laoghaire dock. The sight of Ivy sobbing as if her heart was breaking, her arms wrapped tightly around his younger brother Petey, almost broke his own heart. That image was etched in his heart forever. It had driven him on to succeed.

'Come on. We can sit in the lobby and talk in comfort there. I'll order up all the tea you can drink – promise.' Doug pulled gently on the hands he held tightly in his. He knew his sister's big heart was fuelled by gallons and gallons of tea. 'I've had poor Johnjo here,' he indicated the man standing to one side, 'chasing around the back streets of Dublin trying to catch up with you.'

'Were yeh not going somewhere?' Ivy looked

around in a daze. She had a hard time remembering what she was doing here.

Doug grinned. Trust Ivy not to notice his famously handsome mush sitting in the top right-hand corner of the billboard she'd been examining, framed for all the world to see. 'I'll have you know, Miss Murphy, I am the headliner at this august establishment.' He nodded towards the towering edifice of the Gaiety Theatre at their backs.

'Would yeh go way!' Ivy gasped.

'Come see.' Doug released one of Ivy's hands and began to tow her back towards the billboard. He pointed to the eight-by-ten black-and-white glossy photograph at the very top of the tall billboard. 'There you are, missus, me in all me glory.' Doug dropped effortlessly back into the language of his youth.

'The state of you and the price of best butter!' Ivy elbowed her brother in the ribs, her heart swelling with pride in all he'd apparently accomplished. He'd been away from home for four years. Look how well he'd done for himself!

'Come on, Ivy.' Doug shook the hand he held. 'Come on back to the Shelbourne with me. We've years of catching up to do.'

'Ivy!' Ann Marie, her business completed, walked through the door being held open for her by the uniformed doorman. She automatically gave a little head-bow of acknowledgement for the service but all of her attention was fixed on Ivy and the company she was keeping.

'Ann Marie!' Ivy closed her eyes and shook her head. She didn't know if she was on her head or her heels. How could she have forgotten all about her friend!

Ann Marie approached, unsure of her movements under the circumstances.

Ivy, still holding tightly to her brother's hand, grinned widely and gestured her friend over to her side with a wave of her free arm. Ann Marie was going to get her own way again. It would appear Ivy was going to step into the Shelbourne Hotel after all. If she didn't think about the matter she'd be better off. Otherwise she'd be found running screaming through the streets of Dublin.

'Miss Ann Marie Gannon,' Ivy had a smile so wide on her face she was surprised her face didn't split in two, 'allow me to introduce you to my brother–'

Shay squeezed the fingers on the hand he still held. 'Douglas Joyce at your service, Miss Gannon,' he interjected quickly before Ivy could blow his image completely. He raised his hat from his head before settling it back into place.

He wanted to know what this obviously upper-class woman was doing with his sister. The woman was wearing a small fortune in furs on her small slim person. Where had she met Ivy? How had his sister earned the money needed to buy the fancy outfit she was wearing? Doug had a lot of questions he wanted answers to from his sister. He graced Ivy's friend with one of his famous grins, flashing the pearly whites to great effect.

'Allow me to introduce my companion to you both: Mr Johnjo Smith. I'm afraid in the surprise of bumping into my sister all of my manners appear to have deserted me,' Doug said, very much tongue in cheek. He grinned when Ivy and

332

Johnjo both snorted quietly. Far from it they were raised indeed.

'Ladies,' Johnjo raised his hat.

'Mr Smith, Mr Joyce – enchanted,' Ann Marie said faintly. She examined the man standing next to Ivy with great interest. Apart from the difference in hair colour and obvious gender differences, the two could have been twins. This was certainly a turn-up for the books. This man was one of Ivy's missing brothers?

'I've invited Ivy to join me in taking tea at the Shelbourne, Miss Gannon. Perhaps you would care to join us?' Doug didn't want anyone listening to what he had to say to his sister but the presence of another woman would add an air of respectability to Ivy spending time in his company. He had no wish to announce their relationship to the world at large.

'Mr Joyce, you are apparently the "wild horses" needed to drag Ivy through those doors.' Ann Marie had listened for hours to Ivy stating wild horses couldn't drag her through the doors of the hotel.

Doug grinned. 'Miss Gannon, Miss Murphy, if you would allow my companion and me to escort you to our nearby hotel, I would be delighted.' Doug issued the invitation in a style that would have delighted his snobbish mother if he did but know it.

'Miss Gannon, if you would allow me?' Johnjo, introductions completed, placed the hat he'd raised in the presence of a lady back on his head and offered his crooked elbow to Ann Marie.

'Mr Smith.' Ann Marie accepted the offered

elbow and as one they turned to walk back down King Street in the direction of Stephen's Green.

Johnjo Smith bit back a grin. He'd had some adventures since he'd joined his lot to Doug Joyce but this – walking out with a high class cutie on his arm – this took the biscuit.

Chapter 33

Shay/Doug watched his friend walk away with a smirk on his face. He had a fair idea what was going through Johnjo's head at this moment. He allowed a small space to grow between the two couples.

'Miss Murphy,' Doug used the hand he still held to bend his sister's arm and thread her arm through his own, 'allow me to escort you.' He grinned and stepped out to follow after the other two.

'You, Shay Murphy, are shovelling horse shite.' She used her hip to knock him slightly off balance. 'You'd think butter wouldn't melt in your mouth.' She looked up into the eyes that so exactly matched her own. 'I'm scared spitless, Shay,' she said in a low whisper.

'Pretend yeh own the feckin' gaff!' Doug/Shay bent his head to whisper in Ivy's ear.

'Why didn't yeh want me to tell Ann Marie yer real name?'

'I'm not that person any more, Ivy.' Doug had created an image for himself. One he had worked hard to establish. 'I'm Douglas Joyce, man about town, these days. I like who I am now, Ivy.' He knew he didn't have to explain to Ivy what he meant.

'I'll have a hard time remembering to call you "Doug".'

'Only in public, Ivy – call me Doug in public, please. In private I will always be your brother Shay.' He felt a lump form in his throat. He couldn't believe Ivy was walking along these posh streets at his side. 'Jaysus, Ivy, would yeh look at the state of us!' He grinned hugely.

'It's a turn-up for the books right enough.' Ivy understood completely. 'I've been having a lot of moments like this since me da died.'

'Who's your woman?' Doug asked the question that had been on the tip of his tongue ever since he'd seen the company his big sister was keeping.

Ivy began to explain and the brother and sister walked slowly along the Dublin streets trying to catch up on years of news. They had a lot of things they wanted to say to each other without other ears hearing.

Ann Marie wanted desperately to ask the man at her side a million questions about Ivy's brother but she refrained. Ivy would tell her whatever she wanted her to know. She would not intrude on this private moment for her friend.

Johnjo Smith wanted to whoop with glee and dance madly in the street. He wanted to shout out to the passing strangers that three of the people they were examining so minutely had run around these streets with bare feet, naked arses, runny noses and hungry bellies. Look at us now,

335

he wanted to shout. Have a good feckin' look at how we've come up in the world. Instead he strolled along, raising his hat to passing ladies and exchanging polite chit-chat with the upper-class woman on his arm.

The bowing doorman at the Shelbourne Hotel didn't even blink as he opened the hallowed portals for the two couples climbing the entryway steps.

Ivy went up on her toes to whisper into Shay's ear. 'Shows what he knows! How many times do you reckon that sour-faced auld besom kicked us away from these doorsteps?'

'Thoughts like that, Ivy,' Doug/Shay whispered back, 'are what make moments like this so enjoyable.' He led the way towards the opulent lounge. 'Every time he opens that door for me I think of the times that man sent us kids away from here with a flea in our ear. I almost gave him a heart attack the other day.' He nudged her gently. 'I stocked up on thrupenny bits and on Halloween night I threw them to all the hungry kids begging on the steps.' He walked in the direction of a table for four situated in front of a window overlooking Stephen's Green, his giggling sister on his arm.

'I believe I'd like a moment to freshen up,' Ann Marie said when all four of them stood by the table in the lounge. She wanted to leave her furs with the cloakroom attendant but she wasn't willing to leave until she'd forced Ivy to remove her hat.

'If you would pass me your outer wear, I'll leave them with the cloakroom attendant,' Johnjo said to Doug. He didn't call him by the title that amused both of them. If he called Doug 'sir' in present company his position amongst them would be changed in a way that could give offence. He didn't think the woman in furs would be amused by knowing she'd walked the Dublin streets on the arm of a man who might be viewed as a servant.

'Thanks, Johnjo.' Doug shrugged out of his cashmere coat, revealing a charcoal suit that screamed the skill of the tailor who'd fashioned it to his body. The pristine white shirt and pale grey tie were elegance personified. There were hints of gold revealed at his shirt cuffs. His solid-gold tie-pin twinkled in the light from the crystal chandeliers hanging from the ceiling. 'On your way past the reception desk, Johnjo, order up afternoon tea for four, would you please?' He passed his coat, scarf, hat and gloves over to his friend.

Ivy stood there, wondering what to do with herself. She wasn't willing to take off her suit jacket. The tweed jacket was tightly fashioned to her waist before swinging out and falling to her knees over the matching long skirt. She hadn't planned to take the jacket off. She refused to sit in this august hotel in just a skirt, blouse and thin jumper and the thought of removing her hat, revealing her uncovered head in public, horrified her. She looked to Ann Marie for guidance.

'If you would pass me your hat, scarf and gloves, Ivy, I'll leave them with the cloakroom attendant.' Ann Marie waited, knowing Ivy still clung to the old-fashioned notion that women simply did not reveal their uncovered heads in public. She couldn't allow her friend to sit in this

337

lounge in that perfectly dreadful hat sipping tea. It simply wouldn't do.

'You've cut your hair!' Doug gasped, while Ivy stood sticking the hatpins back into the hat she'd reluctantly removed from her head.

The ice was broken. Johnjo stepped away to carry out his duties. Ann Marie grabbed Ivy's items and hurried away in the direction of the cloakroom. Doug pulled the heavy leather chair nearest the window away from the table. He waved away the assistance of a waiter approaching from the direction of the nearby restaurant. Ivy sank into the comfortable chair being held for her by her brother and simply beamed up into his smiling face.

'Let me tell you about my hair,' Ivy said as soon as he sat in the chair across the table from her. She leaned in his direction and to his complete fascination began to tell him about the day she'd sold her hair. The day of her first real venture into 'high society'.

'Jaysus, Ivy,' Doug took her hands in his on the tabletop, 'I'd never doubt yeh. You really sold the hair off your head and me da's body as well!'

'I had to, Shay.' Ivy stared down at their joined hands on the table. She was afraid to meet his eyes, afraid he'd look at her with disgust. 'He'd left me without "bit, bite nor sup" in the place. You know how he was.'

'I know.'

'Are yeh ashamed of me?' Ivy had to ask.

'Ivy, I'm that fecking proud of yeh I'm in danger of bursting the buttons off me vest.' He sensed Ivy needed him to be as he'd been before he left home – for a little while anyway.

'Shay, will yeh come home?' Ivy couldn't feel comfortable in these surroundings. She wanted to visit with her brother, catch up on the years of separation, but not here.

'I don't want to go back into The Lane, Ivy,' Doug said simply. He refused to walk past the men hanging around the public house. He would not soil his shoes walking down that piss-soaked tunnel. He'd come a long way from that ... he wasn't going back.

'Are you ashamed of where you come from?' Ivy switched into her posh voice when she noticed two waiters approaching their table.

'No, Ivy, never that.' Doug watched the waiters place the folding legs of an occasional table to one side of their table. He waited until the occasional table was set up, a tablecloth and accessories placed on it, and the two waiters hurried away. 'I'm not ashamed of where I come from, Ivy. I'll never deny what and who I am but such things are private. Doug Joyce is someone I created – he's me now. Shay Murphy – that lad is part of my past. I won't lie about him if asked but I won't exactly shout where I come from to the world either.'

'Fair enough, but our two friends are standing out in the lobby. I think they want to give us time together. They've been standing under one of them pig-ugly black-and-gold statues pretending an interest. They're beginning to attract attention and look like ornaments themselves. I'm afraid someone will start polishing them soon if they don't move.'

Doug laughed, released Ivy's hands and turned

to look into the lobby. He grinned and waved at the two people trying to pretend an interest in the tall black statue holding a gold-painted lamp aloft.

'We need to talk, Ivy.' Doug hadn't touched on any of the things he'd needed to discuss with her. He had the chance of a great new life in front of him. He couldn't move on without apologising to his sister. He needed to make reparation for the way he and his brothers had taken her for granted.

'I know.' Ivy reached for her handbag, a gift from Ann Marie. 'Let me give you a telephone number where I can be reached.' She lowered her eyes, knowing the shock she was giving her brother and delighting in the matter.

Doug came to his feet politely as Ann Marie approached the table.

'What did she say? Is she coming with us?' Johnjo asked.

'Johnjo, you have a bigger mouth than the town crier.' Doug closed his eyes and shook his head. 'I haven't even mentioned the matter yet. Now help Miss Gannon into her chair then sit down.' The 'shut up' was silent but Johnjo heard it.

'Miss Gannon...' Johnjo held the back of the chair closest to Ivy.

Ann Marie sank into the chair beside Ivy's and prepared to be fascinated.

They sat making polite chit-chat while a group of waiters hurried around importantly, preparing and presenting a 'high tea' for them.

'That will be all,' Ann Marie said to the waiters. She wanted to hear what these people had to say. The tables in this lounge were set far enough apart for privacy. But they'd never get anything accomplished if these waiters continued to hover over them. They could return to the glass-walled restaurant or tend to some of the other people in the lounge, all of them staring under their eyelids in Doug's direction. 'We will serve ourselves – thank you.'

'Well done!' Doug grinned in admiration at the way Ann Marie had dismissed the waiters.

'It comes from being one of the upper class, don't you know?' Ivy grinned. 'She was born with a silver spoon in her mouth. What can you do?'

'Oh really!' Ann Marie blushed.

'Seriously, Doug,' Ivy finally began to sip the tea from the dainty cup one of the waiters had placed before her, 'you can say anything you like in front of Ann Marie. And I recognise Johnjo.' If the man wasn't a Johnson she'd eat her hat. Still, if her brother's friend wanted to remain incognito she'd no problem with that.

'I have so much I want to discuss with you, Ivy, but I have a show to do this evening. I'm going to be tied up in rehearsals for the bloomin' pantomime as well.' Doug glanced at the gold wristwatch he wore. 'I want to spend time with you. I don't want our time together to be rushed.' He never ate before going on stage. His stomach would rebel. He'd drink the coffee and watch the others eat. It wouldn't be the first time. 'We have an awful lot of catching-up to do.'

'Do you ever see the others?' Ivy couldn't wait any longer for news of her brothers and mother. She'd tried to question Shay in the street but he'd avoided giving her any answers. She pointed towards her empty teacup and silently asked Ann Marie to serve her. Her hands were shaking too much to lift that heavy teapot.

Doug wanted to curse at finding himself in this position. He'd hoped to avoid telling Ivy how matters stood but that was unrealistic. She deserved to know. 'Ivy, I telephoned our mother as soon as I found out about me da's death. The lads live with her in London.' He could almost see her body flinch from that blow. 'I left it up to her to tell them about da.'

'I'm glad she knows.' Ivy gratefully accepted the cup of tea Ann Marie placed into her shaking hands. She took several sips of tea, trying to control her reaction. She failed. She gently put the cup back on its saucer.

Then the other three people at the table watched as Ivy simply fell apart. She'd wanted news of her family. She'd never imagined how much it would hurt to hear that they had all been living together – without her.

'Ann Marie, would you oblige me by changing seats?' Doug stood abruptly. What did he care what these feckin' strangers staring at them thought? He'd paid a small fortune to rent the suite here and this tea didn't come cheap. Let them look. 'My shoulders are a great deal broader than yours.'

'Allow me!' Johnjo jumped to his feet and quickly rearranged dishes and chairs. In minutes they were all once again seated around the table, ignoring the stares of the curious staff members and guests.

The maître d' hurried over, followed by two

waiters carrying a silk screen between them. They placed the screen around the area for maximum privacy.

'Thank you.' Doug bowed his blond head graciously. 'I appreciate it. My sister has just been given disturbing news.' He offered that titbit of gossip as it would keep the staff busy passing it along to the curious.

Doug pulled his chair closer to Ivy's. He knew his sister. He picked up the cup of tea and offered it to her. He put his long strong fingers to the base of the teacup she clutched between shaking hands and helped her carry it to her lips.

'Ivy,' he said, 'we are not worth your tears.'

He took a pristine white handkerchief from his breast pocket and tried to dab at the tears rolling silently down her chalk-pale cheeks.

Ivy tried to bury her face in her teacup. 'I'm makin' a show of meself.' She lowered the empty cup, mortified.

'You most certainly are not,' Ann Marie snapped past the lump in her throat. How many knocks was this woman supposed to take without breaking?

'Tell her everything quickly.' Johnjo wished he could punch someone. 'It will be easier on her to take it all in at once.'

'Have some more tea, Ivy.' Ann Marie refilled Ivy's teacup.

'I'm not going to collapse, you know.' Ivy almost smiled. The other three were looking at her as if she were an unexploded bomb.

Doug was heartily ashamed of himself. His sister didn't deserve the treatment he and his brothers had subjected her to.

They had always known where their mother went after she left home. They'd received letters and packages from her which a neighbour had passed on. The arrangements had been made before their mother left. The secrecy had been presented as a delightful bit of fun by their mother. Why had they never questioned it? They deserved to be horsewhipped for their treatment of a woman who'd done nothing but love and protect them. He dreaded telling Ivy of the luxury his two brothers and their mother lived in.

'I'm not being overly dramatic to say that our brothers and mother have sold their souls to the devil.' Doug heard his own words and wanted to groan. He meant every word, however.

'Could you put it any worse?' Johnjo snapped into the heavy silence that had fallen over the table.

'Violet was never a loving mother, Ivy,' Doug said slowly. 'The only person beside herself she ever loved was our da. That's a simple fact of life.' He paused, not sure how to go on. 'She's a hard cold woman and leaving Éamonn broke something inside her. I can't explain it to you, Ivy, because I don't understand it meself but she's empty inside.'

Doug accepted a cup of coffee from Johnjo. He sipped slowly while looking at the elegant young beauty at his side. He wondered how much of his mother's attitude was driven by the fear of someone outshining her.

'The lads?' Ivy croaked.

'Violet has the uppercrust belief that only a male

344

child will suffice. In the eyes of her new ultra-snobbish society friends she has supplied an heir and a spare to the man she calls her husband. The lads seem willing enough to go along with the deception. As far as I can see the two of them are revelling in a life of total uselessness. I mean no offense to you and yours, Ann Marie.'

'None taken.' Ann Marie looked at the table spread with sandwiches, cakes and assorted goodies. It was all completely untouched. She intended to scandalise the staff by requesting they pack it up to be carried away. She knew people, Ivy being one of them, that could use this food. Doug would be billed for everything anyway. 'I'm afraid I know people like those you describe.'

'Our Éamo has changed his name,' said Doug. 'As soon as he arrived in London they enrolled him in a posh school as the eldest son of a returning Anglo-Irish family. He is now more English than the English. He has settled into the lifestyle of "Little Lord Fauntleroy" with an ease that is embarrassing.'

'Well for him.' Ivy shrugged.

'No, Ivy, it's not,' Doug said seriously. 'Our brother is ruled with such a rigid hand by our mother's consort it's a wonder to me he doesn't suffocate. He has been forced to change everything about himself – nothing he does is enough. There is too much of the old man in me. I wouldn't accept the rules and regulations set down by an upper-class British chinless wonder. Our mother and brothers live in a fancy house with a very fancy London address. Violet's been known as that man's wife since the day she left us.

I suppose they'll be able to make it official now.'

He didn't mention his own reaction to the man his mother lived with. He'd recognised the look in that man's eyes on first meeting him. Doug and his brothers had always been 'pretty boys'. His da made sure his sons knew what that could mean. Éamonn had taught his sons to use their fists. He'd encouraged them to walk away from a fight whenever possible. However, if you had to fight, as his son you'd better feckin' win. Doug had been dodging men with seeking hands all of his life. He wasn't about to move in and live with one. He'd taken to his heels.

'Ivy,' Doug caught the grimace on Johnjo's face as he checked his watch, 'I'll have to leave soon. We can go into all of this another time. Give me that phone number you were boasting about.' He grinned when she looked like objecting. 'You were, you know. Anyway, give me the phone number. I have gifts for you from the lads.' He didn't mention he'd shamed his brothers and his mother into contributing them. 'I'll be in Dublin through Christmas and the New Year. We'll meet up and discuss our lives past, present and future.'

'I'll get our coats.' Johnjo stood and left the lounge without waiting for a response.

'I want to instruct the waiters to pack up this food.' Ann Marie too stood and left the lounge, obviously once again wanting to give brother and sister time to themselves.

'Ivy, I have to tell you.' Doug grabbed her hands, turning her to face him. He stared into her eyes, eyes so like his own. He hadn't imagined telling Ivy his news in this hurried fashion. It couldn't be helped. She deserved some time to think about the life-changing decision he was about to ask her to make. 'When I've finished up here in Dublin I'm going to America.' He could feel the shock travel through her body. 'I've been offered a chance at a life in the "fillums". I don't know if you're aware, but they are going to start making talking pictures. The big boys out in America have been looking for people with "pleasing" voices. Apparently I sound "just wonderful on record", according to the talent scouts I've talked to anyway.'

'In the name of Divine Jesus!' Ivy prayed, staring at her brother. What could she say? Was he out of his mind? From the looks of things he had a great life as top of the bill here and now. Was he really going to take a chance on a wild-hare dream like 'talking pictures'? Surely to God something like that would never catch on?

'I want you to come to America with me, Ivy.' Doug leaned over her to underline his seriousness. 'I'll be able to give you a much better life than the one you have now. Come away with me, Ivy. Somewhere no one will judge us by where we came from or who we come from. It will be a whole new life for you and me. I'd take care of you the way you always took care of me.'

'I can't...'

'I'm not asking you to make a decision now,' Doug said. 'I want you to think about it. Just think – California, sunshine and happiness. We'd be on the pig's back, Ivy.'

'Me head's spinning, Shay.' Ivy thought the room was spinning too.

Doug saw Johnjo enter the lounge. 'I've got to

go, Ivy. I want you to think long and hard about what I've said. It would be a new life for all of us, a fresh start. We'll be in a strange world where no one knows anything about us. We can be anyone we want to be. A new life, Ivy, think about it. I want you to come with me, share the wealth.'

'You've given me so much to think about I have a headache. I'll think about everything you've said. But before you go I want you to promise me you'll telephone and let me know when we can meet up again. Promise!' Ivy squeezed her brother's hands, staring into his eyes. She couldn't let him leave her here without that promise. He'd walked out of her life without a backward glance once before.

'I promise.' Doug stood and accepted his coat from Johnjo while admiring the way Ann Marie commanded the hotel staff to pack up the food on the nearby occasional table. She did it in a charming manner but none the less the staff hopped to obey.

'We won't lose touch again, Ivy,' Doug bent and pressed a kiss into his sister's lily-white cheek. 'I promise, no matter where I am or what I'm doing. We will always be brother and sister.' Doug felt a lump in his throat at the thought of the pain he'd caused to a woman who'd been nothing but loving and caring towards him. He was heartily ashamed of himself.

Chapter 34

'Jem!' Ivy felt as she imagined a homing pigeon must feel as she made directly for the livery. Ann Marie had insisted they take a horse-drawn taxi from the Shelbourne. She had stacked the boxes of food the waiters packed for her onto one seat of the carriage and almost hauled a still stunned Ivy home with her. They'd taken the foodstuff in to Sadie. Ann Marie wanted Ivy to stay with her but she couldn't. She'd needed to get away. She'd left the food parcels with Ann Marie. She was going to use the fancy foodstuff to show Sadie how to present a high tea. She might as well – they'd never touched it.

She stood in the middle of the livery and shouted. 'Jem!'

'He's upstairs in his own place.' John Lawless put his head out of the office to shout. 'He said he was sick of the sight and sound of us lot so he took himself off for five minutes of peace.' He grinned. 'He must have known you were coming, Ivy. He said he was going to put the kettle on.'

'Thanks, John.' Ivy crossed to the wooden ladder and climbed the rungs swiftly, thanking the fates that Jem would be alone.

'Jem Ryan!' she called when she was halfway up the ladder. 'Fancy a bit of company?'

'If it's only you, Ivy.' Jem appeared in the open door of his home. 'You're welcome but if any of those hairy lads are with you I'm kicking that ladder away.' He was only half joking. The antics of the lads today had almost driven him demented. There was so much to be done clearing and preparing the new entrance to the livery.

'There's a rumour going around The Lane ... that you have the kettle on.' Ivy continued to climb the ladder. She accepted the hand Jem held out to help her over the rim of the loft.

'Did you get your business done at the bank?' Jem asked.

Ivy went blank for a minute. It seemed such a long time ago that she'd left the bank with Ann Marie, weeks instead of hours. So much had happened.

'What's wrong?' Now that she was standing closer Jem noticed the look on her face.

'Let's go inside.' Ivy didn't answer, she couldn't, not yet.

'What's wrong, Ivy?' Jem closed the door at their back and simply stood waiting to see what she would do or say.

Ivy looked around the room with dazed eyes. Jem had only one soft chair in his room. That was all right – they only needed one. She pulled the hat from her head, took off her suit jacket and turned to look at Jem still standing staring at her as if waiting for her to collapse. She must look as bad as she felt.

'Jem...' She held out her hand to him.

He walked slowly over to take it. He was shocked by the chill of her skin. She pushed him towards the soft fireside chair and he allowed himself to fall into it. She dropped down onto his knees and

350

simply folded her body into his.

'Ivy?' He ran his hand up and down her back, wondering what on earth had brought his Ivy to this state. He didn't think it could have anything to do with the business of the Cinderella dolls that she'd been fretting about. She'd been full of plans about those before she'd left to meet Ann Marie.

'I saw our Shay.' Ivy finally let the tears that had been tearing her apart inside free. She shook with the force of the sorrow and shocks she'd sustained.

Jem didn't say a word. He didn't need to ask who Shay was – he knew. He didn't try to stop her tears. God knows if anyone deserved a good cry it was the woman shivering in his arms. He was content just to sit there holding her.

'I'm getting you all over wet and making a fool of meself,' Ivy muttered at last through her blocked-up nose. She hid her head in his neck, not willing to let him see the mess she must have made of herself.

'I've been sitting here so long I'm spittin' feathers,' Jem quipped. 'I'm gummin' for a cup of tea.'

'Oh, you!' Ivy gave him a gentle punch.

'Can you tell me about it?' He pushed her away from him slightly while he fought to remove a clean handkerchief from his trouser pocket. He pressed the linen into her hand and grinned when she blew her nose with gusto. She moved around on his lap, obviously trying to get more comfortable, but bringing a sheen of sweat to his brow.

'I saw our Shay.'

'You said...'

'He's a big noise now, my little brother,' Ivy whispered. 'Headliner at the Gaiety no less. Prince blinkin' Charming, if you wouldn't be minding. Off to America to make his fortune in the fillums.'

'Ivy,' he pushed her away from his chest to stare down into her face, 'what in the name of God are you talking about?'

'Shay.' She shrugged. 'Only he's not my Shay any more – he's the big noise Doug Joyce, your man everyone has been talking about for ages. You remember Conn told us all about yer man, the one who has been packing the audiences in for weeks now. He's been in all the papers, Jem. I've been so busy I haven't been reading the papers from cover to cover but still, you'd think I'd have caught on before this. I felt like an eejit.'

'Doug Joyce is your brother Shay, the middle lad?' Jem was beginning to understand. 'I read the papers myself, Ivy. I never noticed it was him either. I suppose it's because it would never occur to us.' He shrugged. Who would have thought that a star of the stage was one of Ivy's brothers?

'He took me to tea at the Shelbourne Hotel no less.' Ivy twisted the soaked handkerchief in her hands.

'Did he?' Jem tried to lighten the mood. 'So you finally got to take tea with the toffs.'

'He's going to America, Jem.' Ivy couldn't joke. 'Going to make his fortune in the fillums out there. The talkies, he called them – have you heard about that?'

'I've read something about them in the papers.' Jem, always fascinated by the changes in the world around them, had been intrigued to read about

352

talking pictures and couldn't wait to see one.

'He wants me to go to America with him.' Ivy stared into Jem's eyes as she said this. She saw the shock register, felt his body stiffen against her. 'He wants me to become a lady of leisure, let him look after me.'

'What did you say to that?' Jem felt his heart break. Nothing he had to offer her could compare to a life in the sun with film stars.

'I didn't say anything. We had no time – he had to get ready to go on stage this evening.'

Jem simply waited. There was nothing he could say. He would not be the one to stand in her way if she wanted to accept this chance of a lifetime.

'It breaks my heart that he's going so far away,' Ivy offered, 'and I think he's going to be left penniless. Talking pictures, I ask your sacred pardon, what will they think of next?' She couldn't bear the look of silent suffering on his face. She'd made her mind up already. It hadn't been a hard decision to make. 'I'm not going anywhere, Jem Ryan. I have too much to do right here.' She slapped her hand on his chest. 'Someone has to be around to keep you in line.'

'I'm glad,' he understated, pulling her back against his chest while the relief that went through him made him weak. He'd almost lost her.

'He told me the lads are living with my mother in London,' Ivy whispered when her face was once more safely hidden against his chest. 'She has a fancy man in London, has had from the moment she left here.'

Jem remained silent, his teeth clenched. He wanted to curse the lot of them but they were her family and Ivy was funny about such things. They didn't deserve her.

Ivy sighed after a long silence – so much emotion was exhausting. 'Oh, I forgot to tell you – we're invited to high tea at Ann Marie's: you, me and Emmy.' She pushed away again to grin up at him, letting him see the emotional storm had passed.

'Is that a fact?'

'Yes, it is. Ann Marie wants to use us as guinea pigs for Sadie to practise on.' She shrugged. 'I didn't get the full ins and outs but I will.'

'That's nice,' Jem pulled her back down against his chest, fighting the temptation to devour her. She was so precious to him. She had no idea how much she meant to him. She had no idea how much he feared losing her.

'I'm going over to Ann Marie's later.' Ivy felt her bones melt. She could stay here for the rest of her life without moving. 'They want to see the outfit I put together to sell my dolls. You and Emmy can come over when she gets home from school.' She pushed away for a moment. 'You have to get dressed up, Mr Ryan.'

'I'll wear me good suit.'

They sank into a contented silence, disaster averted.

Chapter 35

'You were out early this morning, Ivy.' Maisie Reynolds, two galvanised buckets at her feet, stood in the queue of people waiting to use the outside tap.

'I went to early Mass,' Ivy said. She'd wanted to light a candle for her da and for Granny.

'Not turning into one of them Holy Marys, are yeh, Ivy?' Pete Winters grinned gummily.

'I'm thinking of becoming a nun, Mr Winters,' Ivy said.

'Oh, aye,' Marcella Wiggins grinned, her many chins wiggling. 'You'd be a fine nun, Ivy Murphy. Where none are feckin' wanted.'

'The story of me life, Mrs Wiggins.' Ivy shoved her two buckets with her feet as the line moved forward. She'd gone to Mass, hoping for divine intervention. She had a great deal of thinking to do, questions she needed answers to, but if the Good Lord had an opinion on the woes of one Ivy Murphy he was keeping them to himself.

'That new Father Flanagan is a pleasure to listen to.' Mabel O'Rourke gave one of her children a quick slap around the ears when the boy kicked one of her many buckets. 'I wasn't sure at first, what with poor Father Leary being taken bad like that and having to go away, but this fella is all right.'

Ivy kept her lips firmly locked. She could never

oice aloud her joy at the news that the Parish Priest was taking a long holiday after his retreat. The recently departed Father Leary appeared to think it was his life's mission to make Ivy's life miserable. The man's absence from his parish meant that Ivy could return to Westland Row, the church of her youth, to pray in peace.

'Not that I understand a word that new priest says, mind,' Mabel laughed, 'but I could listen to the sound of his voice all day – it's like music.'

'Father Flanagan is from Cork, Mabel.' Rita Harper joined the chat. 'They sing to yeh down there, don't yeh know? It sounds great and not understanding a word he says can only be a blessing.'

'PJ!' Ivy shouted when the young boy looked like kicking his mother's buckets again.

The lad hunched his shoulders and glared sulenly in Ivy's direction. Mabel cut all of her children's hair herself. Boys and girls received a quick shave around the pudding bowl. It made for a very unattractive look when combined with a snotty nose and sullen glare.

'Come here, I want yeh.' Ivy pointed at the ground in front of her.

'Go on, ye were supposed to be sick yesterday, now look at yeh!' Mabel O'Rourke gave PJ another clip around the ears, just because. 'He wouldn't get out of the bed to go to school yesterday, then this morning he's up with the bloomin' larks. I'll have the bloody do-gooders around if this fella doesn't pull up his ruddy socks.'

'What do yeh want?' PJ wiped his runny nose on the frayed cuffs of his hand-me-down jumper.

'I want to know if yer strong enough to carry two full buckets of water.' Ivy looked down at the boy, wondering why she'd never thought of paying to have her water delivered. It would save her a lot of time and energy.

'Course I am!' PJ pushed out his little chest in indignation. 'I carry four for me mam.'

'Oh, aye, when?' Mabel O'Rourke shouted from her place at the front of the line. 'If I had a camera I'd have taken a picture of that.'

'Ah, Mam, you know I'm strong as an ox.' PJ squirmed. 'Me da says so.'

'I'll pay yeh to haul water for me,' Ivy said softly. She should have shouted. A whisper made everyone in the line pick up their ears. 'I want four buckets – full ones, mind – delivered to me back door. Can yeh do it?'

'How much?' PJ couldn't believe his luck. He'd have to come out to the water line with his ma more often.

'A farthing a full bucket delivered to me door,' Ivy offered.

'Done.' PJ spat in his skinny little hand like he'd seen the men do and held it out.

'Throwing yer money around, Ivy Murphy, aren't yeh?' Mabel O'Rourke felt faint. An extra penny on a Saturday morning – she wouldn't know herself.

'She'd have a few extra pence now,' the Widow Casey muttered to no one in particular. 'What with no man waiting for her with his hand out for every penny she earns. That da of hers must have been an expensive bugger to keep.'

'Now, now, ladies, do yeh mind?' Ivy ignored the

357

slander of her da. It was only the truth they were speaking. 'I'm conducting business here.' She spat in her own hand and shook the little white paw offered. 'Right, PJ,' she stepped away from her two empty buckets, 'you take my place in the queue.'

'You can count on me, missus.' PJ puffed out his eight-year-old chest. He was going to earn money, real money. He couldn't wait to tell his da.

'I'll be waiting.' Ivy stepped out from the long line of neighbours. She was acutely aware of the storm of whispering that followed her. She didn't care. She hadn't the time to stand in line waiting for her turn at the tap.

'Miss Murphy, do you have a moment?' Betty Armstrong's voice froze Ivy in place as she reached to take her galvanised bathtub from its peg outside the backdoor. She almost closed her eyes and dropped her head onto the bottom of the bathtub.

'Let me give you a hand.' Betty hurried forward to lend a hand in getting the heavy bathtub from its high hook.

'Thanks,' Ivy sighed. There went her bath. She'd have to get rid of this woman before she could get started on the work that was piling up around her. She'd been spending every minute she could with her brother, moments snatched from both their busy lives. They had years of catching up to do. The change in her schedule meant she wasn't keeping up with her own chores.

'What can I do for yeh, Miss Armstrong,' Ivy asked while the two women dragged the tub into Ivy's back room.

'Betty, please.' Betty Armstrong knew she was as welcome as the plague. She sighed deeply. It couldn't be helped.

'Betty then.' Ivy stood and brushed her hands off. 'What can I do for yeh?'

'I'm sure you're aware I'm sharing in the care of young Seán. He's staying with the Connelly family.' Betty dropped into one of the wooden chairs she pulled from its place tucked under the table. 'The little lad is fretting about his mother.' The poor child was so unhappy, Betty didn't know what to do for him. 'I'm keeping you from your bath, it looks like.' But Betty didn't make any attempt to move. She needed answers and Ivy Murphy might be able to help her. She'd exhausted her own contacts. 'I was wondering if you heard anything about Seán's mother?'

'I'll put the kettle on.' Ivy suited action to words. 'I talked to someone a few weeks ago about Ginie.' Ivy had put the kettle on and was now wriggling underneath the big bed that took up so much of the space in her back room. She found the packet she was looking for and began to wriggle backwards, trying to clear the bed frame.

Betty wondered what on earth Ivy was up to but didn't like to ask. She was on shaky enough ground as it was.

'Ginie is with the Maggies.' Ivy unwrapped the bleached flour sacks to reveal her white summer suit. She took time to spread the long skirt and lace jacket on top of the bed. She'd have to give them a belt of an iron. She wanted to see if she could wear the outfit in this weather or perhaps dye it. It was one of the things she'd planned to do today. She'd have to ask Sadie to take pity on her and let her have her bath at their house. It would save her a lot of time and work.

'The Maggies,' Betty gasped. 'Do you know which one? We have to get her out of there.'

'I'd be glad to hear any idea you might have.'

Ivy made a pot of tea, then carried the dishes she needed over to the table and set them out. 'Ginie could walk out of the place. It's not a prison, so they say.' Ivy, like most people in Dublin, knew once girls went through those doors the nuns didn't like to let their unpaid workers go. It sounded good to say the women were free to leave but it was only lip service to anyone nosy enough to ask. 'But Ginie would need somewhere to live and a way of earning a few bob.' The women of The Lane had been racking their brains trying to come up with a way to help Ginie.

'Billy Flint,' Betty offered. 'He'd be able to get her out of there, no problem.'

'Everything in my life lately seems to come back to Billy Flint.' Ivy closed her eyes in despair. She still hadn't been to see the man. She'd been putting it off, praying that the need to consult him would be needless but, so far no miracles.

'I'll go see Billy Flint today.' Betty slapped the table with her hands, causing the china to jump. 'I won't leave his office until I know that Ginie is on her way back to her son.'

'Wait a minute–' Ivy put out her hand to stop the woman from leaving as she obviously intended. 'Are you telling me you know where Billy Flint's office is?' That was shocking. She'd known this woman had telephoned Billy Flint about the situation in The Lane but the man was fiercely private. He didn't exactly advertise his services as far as Ivy knew.

'I'm sorry, I haven't time for tea. I have to go.' Betty stood abruptly, determination written all over her.

'I need to talk to Billy Flint,' Ivy almost whispered. 'Could you give me his address?'

'I'm afraid I couldn't do that.' Betty shrugged. 'Billy is a very private person – only a few people know how to contact him directly.' She couldn't tell this woman that Billy was a phantom, a figment of his own imagination. He'd built up a fearsome reputation and was making money off it but he was nothing like the gangster that Dubliners believed him to be.

'I really need to talk to him,' Ivy said. Now that she was being denied the chance to talk to the man, she became determined to see him.

'Perhaps I could put in a word for you,' Betty offered. 'Pour out that tea and you can tell me what you want to see Billy about. That's the best I can do, I'm afraid.'

'Right.' Ivy quickly poured the tea. 'It's like this...' She began to talk and by the time she'd explained her problem they had drunk the teapot dry.

'Well, I'll see what I can do,' said Betty.

'And then there's Declan Johnson,' Ivy went on. 'He told everyone in The Lane that he had Billy's protection. I think I've seen him around. I'm not completely sure it is him. I haven't told anyone but he scares me.'

'There is no way on this earth that Billy would have anything to do with Declan Johnson,' Betty said. 'I can state that without fear of contradiction.'

'I don't know anything about paying for protection.' Ivy wondered if the woman facing her knew that her accent and body language had changed almost completely. It was as if she'd sat down at the table with one woman and was now talking with a completely different person. It was unsettling to say the least.

'I'm going to see about getting Ginie away from the Maggies.' Betty stood. 'I'm sorry but right now that is the most important thing to me. There is a little boy fretting himself to skin and bone. I can't let that continue. I'll talk to Billy about your situation and I'll let you know what he says but, understand me, Billy would never do business with someone like Declan Johnson.'

Ivy sat at the table, staring after the woman as she hurried out of her place without another word. Well, now, what was all that about?

A knock on the door surprised her for a moment.

'That will be PJ with me water.' She jumped to her feet, hurrying to open the door.

'Here yeh go, missus!' PJ grinned with pride.

Ivy had never seen the lad with shining eyes and a smile before. He wasn't a bad-looking lad.

'I'll have the other two for yeh in no time.'

'Wait while I empty these.' Ivy took the buckets one at a time with great care. She emptied each bucket into the water reservoir on her black range and gave PJ the empty buckets to refill. The boy grabbed the buckets and ran away to rejoin the line.

Chapter 36

Twenty minutes before that, Doug Joyce had stood on the canal side of the road, completely absorbed in staring across the wide road at an opening into his old home he'd never seen before. He'd dressed down for this return visit to The Lane. His tweed suit was old and well worn. The brown brogues on his feet were scuffed. His blond hair was covered by a flat cap. He shouldn't stand out too much. However, nothing could disguise the shine of money he'd worked so hard to acquire.

Johnjo Smith stood at his side. A large brown-leather suitcase sat at their feet on the cobbled walkway.

'I can't believe we didn't know this entrance was here,' Doug said.

'Ivy said it had been bricked up by the British,' Johnjo reminded him. 'Look at the way the thing is built. With the overhanging rooms from those houses on either side covering the top and the brick blocks, it was just part of the scenery around here.'

'I suppose.' Doug picked up the leather suitcase and started across the road. 'Come on, Ivy said there's another tunnel directly across from this, I want a look at that too. Then you can get about your business.'

They had decided to take a cab to this entrance, not being absolutely sure they could find the place on their own. Doug was eager to spend a little time alone with his sister. He wanted to sit at the table under the window while she did whatever it was she needed to do.

'I can't believe your sister would rather stay here than come to America with us.' Johnjo looked around, shaking his head.

'She's making a life for herself here.' Doug sighed. 'I have to respect that.'

'Well, she can always change her mind, I suppose.' The two men entered the tunnel. 'You will remember you have a matinée performance this afternoon?'

'I'm not likely to forget.'

'Ay up!' Johnjo snorted as the tunnel opened onto the rear of the tenement block. 'You better use the front entrance. You'll never get past that crowd of nosy biddies hanging around the outdoor tap.'

'That takes me back.' Doug grinned at the sight of the crowd around the tap. 'Ivy used to make us stand in line for the water. She'd box our ears if we spilled any on our walk around the tenement block. My father insisted we use the front door – the back door led into his room and we weren't allowed into that.'

'I don't know why you wanted me to come with you. I can't say I have one pleasant memory about this place.' Johnjo could feel his head trying to shrink into his shoulders. The place gave him the willies.

'To be honest, Johnjo, I thought you'd want to see if you could get some news about your family,' Doug admitted. 'We're going a long way away in the New Year. Who knows if we'll ever get back this way again?'

'I ran away from here when I was ten years old.' Johnjo breathed a sigh of relief when they came to the two-storey houses opening onto the square courtyard. The tenement at their back blocked them from the view of the gathered women. He didn't need any of those old biddies to recognise him. 'It was a miracle I'd no broken bones to go with my cuts and bruises.'

'I don't know if I'd have had the nerve to stow away on one of those ships that come and go to the city dock,' Doug said.

'Believe me, being dumped in the sea seemed like the lesser of two evils to me.' Johnjo had put this place behind him and there he was determined it would stay. 'I never thought I'd be back here,' he added as they walked across the width of the courtyard towards the second newly opened tunnel. 'I should never have picked you up from the London streets.'

'What are you talking about with your "picked me up"? You tried to pick my pockets, you bloody thief!'

'Hey, Lord Muck, kick the ball back, will yeh?' one of the raggedly dressed barefoot kids yelled.

Doug had no doubt he was the Lord Muck the lad was referring to. A well-placed kick sent the ball of tightly packed newspaper tied up with string flying back down to the children who returned to their game without a second glance.

'I wish to God I'd known about these tunnels.' Johnjo pushed his trilby back on his head. He'd refused to dress down for this quick visit to The Lane. If he saw anyone he knew he wanted them to be aware he'd come up in the world. He was no longer one of those useless, feckless Johnsons. 'This would have been a great place to hide until my bruises healed up.'

'I'm trying to see it in my mind's eye.' Doug turned his head from side to side, checking the width of the new openings. 'Can you remember what this place looked like before?'

'It's been twenty years since I ran from here,' Johnjo snapped. 'You've only been gone for four years. With the way you talked about this place I thought it was engraved in your bloody memory.' He'd been forced to listen to a homesick lad talking constantly about his home and the sister he missed so much.

'There were tall walls here.' Doug waved his hand at the tunnel. 'Remember, almost like a box? We used to pick the blackberries off the brambles.' He almost licked his lips remembering the blackberry juice Ivy had poured over the stale ends of bread.

'Ooooh Mister, aren't you pretty?' A high-pitched voice shattered the men's contemplation.

'It doesn't matter what age the female, Doug,' Johnjo stared down at the two little girls staring up openmouthed at his friend, 'they all fall for your pretty face.'

'Where did you two ladies come from?' Doug bent his knees and dropped down to smile into the little faces.

'I'm Emmy Ryan,' a little girl that reminded Doug of his sister stated without a blush. 'And

366

this is my friend Biddy.'

'How do you do, ladies?' Doug raised his cap to the two wide-eyed children. Her accent certainly isn't from around here, he thought.

The two girls giggled delightfully.

'Where are you off to this bitter cold day?' Doug asked.

'We're going to play ball in the tunnel.' Emmy Ryan held up two hands to show her brightly coloured rubber balls – rare shop-bought balls.

'I haven't played ball in years,' Doug grinned, straightening. 'May I borrow your balls, Miss Ryan?' He held out his hands and the little girl willingly dropped the two orbs into his hands. 'Watch the case, Johnjo. I won't be long.'

Doug strode into the tunnel, the two little girls hurrying after him.

Johnjo picked up the case and followed along. He wasn't willing to stand around like a statue. That would invite the women standing in their doorways watching the goings-on to come over and speak to him.

Doug juggled the balls against the wall with a speed and skill that had the little girls gasping. As he passed the balls through his slightly bent legs, slamming them against the wall before catching each ball on the return, he chanted:

Janey Mack, me shirt is black
What'll I do for Sunday?
Get into bed and cover your head
And don't get up till Monday!

'Oooh, Mister, you're more than just a pretty face!' Emmy Ryan breathed – awestruck.

Doug dropped the balls he was laughing so

hard. He ran after the bright rubber balls before they could roll into the road.

'Here you go, ladies!' He returned the balls to the little girls, a huge grin on his face. He bent his knees and lowered his body until he was once again face to face with them. 'I think this tunnel is a bit dangerous for you two to be playing ball in.' Doug stared hard at the girls. 'The ball could roll into the road and under a passing carriage. Are you both being careful?'

'We know.' Emmy Ryan sighed deeply. Did this pretty man think they were babies?

'Fair enough.' Doug stood.

'And you call me a nag.' Johnjo Smith shook his head. 'We survived this place. They will too.' He turned to walk away. 'I'm off. Don't forget to keep an eye on the time.' His command echoed around the tunnel.

'Yes, sir!' Doug chirped and picked up the discarded suitcase. 'Ladies,' he again raised his hat to the little girls, delighting them, 'please be careful.' He began to walk in the direction of his old home.

'Do yeh want tae folla him?' Biddie whispered to her bestest friend.

'No.' Emmy wanted to play ball.

'Okay.' Biddy shrugged and looked over her shoulder at the man walking away from them. He was nice.

Doug walked through his old home place with ghosts for company.

Chapter 37

'In the name of Jesus, are me eyes deceiving me?'
Maisie Reynolds stood in her open doorway, staring down at Doug. 'Is that you, Shay Murphy?
About feckin' time one of you lads thought to
come visit your sister. It's not right a woman living
on her own like that. It isn't decent.'

'Hiya, Missus Reynolds,' Doug grinned up at
his old neighbour. The woman had always been
good to Ivy. 'How's it going? How's the family?'

'Much you care.' Maisie grinned down at a lad
she'd always been very fond of. 'Where have you
been?'

'All kinds of places, Missus Reynolds.' Doug
quickly opened the gate that led to the entrance
steps leading down to the front door of his old
home. If Maisie Reynolds managed to trap him
he'd never get away from her. The woman did
love to talk. 'See you later!' he shouted over his
shoulder as he practically ran down the steps.

He was surprised to find the front door locked.
Ivy had always left the door unlocked so he and
his brothers could run in and out of the place. He
dropped the suitcase at his feet and used the side
of his fist to beat on the entrance door.

'I don't know who yeh are but I'll scratch yeh
baldheaded for banging on me door like that!'
Ivy's voice carried through the locked door.

Doug grinned and waited for her to open up. He

369

could practically feel Mrs Reynolds's eyes drilling into his back. The woman would be all around The Lane in minutes, letting everyone know he was back.

'What do you mean–' Ivy's mouth dropped open when she saw who was standing on her front doorstep. Her eyes travelled over her brother's tall figure and landed on the case sitting at his feet. 'Are yeh thinking of moving back home then, Shay?' Ivy held the doorframe in her fist, the other hand on her hip. 'I'm afraid we can't offer you the kind of accommodation you've become accustomed to. This is no Shelbourne Hotel.'

'Let me in before Mrs Reynolds has half the place told I'm here.' Doug picked up his suitcase and pushed his sister gently out of his way. He walked into the front room and stopped in shock. 'You haven't even the fire lit.' Doug stared at the empty grate. She'd assured him she was doing well for herself.

'Move!' Ivy shoved at her brother's broad back. He was blocking her entry into the room. 'This is me work room now.' She passed behind his frozen figure and made her way into the back room.

'Jesus,' Doug took a deep breath and followed, 'I half expect the old man to appear and beat the tar out of us for daring to step into his bloody room.'

'Sit yourself down.' Ivy waved at one of the two stuffed chairs in front of the brightly burning range. 'Do you fancy a cup of tea?'

'Give us a minute, Ivy.' Doug took off his cap and stood staring around him. 'This is a shock to my system.'

He dropped the suitcase and his cap on top of

the big brass bed and slowly examined the room he vaguely remembered.

'I'd forgotten that range was there,' he contented himself in saying. He wanted to swear at the old man's selfishness. He kept his thoughts firmly behind his teeth. Ivy wouldn't allow him to say a bad word against their da.

'Where did this cupboard come from?' He stood examining the paltry few dishes proudly displayed on the old dresser. In his mind he compared it to the gleaming glass, silver and china-stocked cabinets in his mother's London dining room.

'Old Granny gave it to me before she died.' Ivy put the kettle on.

Doug walked over and sat in the chair in front of the range. He kicked off his shoes then bent and put the shoes in the range surround – out of the way. 'I have a matinée this afternoon so I can't stay too long.'

It was difficult for her to see her brother in the self-assured man about town, Doug Joyce. She'd been spending quick snatches of time with that familiar stranger. This man with his sock-covered feet held out to the fire – that was a much more familiar image to her. She felt comfortable with this man.

A rap at the back door had her reaching into the pocket of her black skirt. She had a penny ready for young PJ.

'Open the top of that range, Shay,' Ivy ordered as she hurried over to open the door.

'Which one?' Doug jumped up to stare down at the multiple circles cut into the top of the range.

'The water holder.' Ivy pulled open the back

door. 'Come, take these buckets, Shay – pour one into the reservoir and keep the other. Don't spill any of the water. I need it for tea and things.'

'Certainly, madam.' Doug grinned.

'Don't be cheeky, Shay Murphy, or I'll box your ears for you.' Ivy laughed down at the bewildered PJ. 'Here yeh go, PJ.' She held out the large brown penny. 'One penny as agreed.'

'Thanks, missus.' PJ grinned. 'Any time yeh need a helpin' hand just give us a shout.' He couldn't wait to take his first ever wage home to his ma. He'd be able to sit close to the fire tonight. He'd earned his place.

'You're paying to have water delivered now, Ivy Murphy?' Doug grinned. 'You never paid me!'

'That's the first time.' She closed the back door. 'It won't be the last. I went to first Mass this morning and by the time I got back the line for the tap seemed a mile long. I haven't the time to stand gossiping.'

'I'll give you a hand seeing as I'm here.'

'Do you remember how to dust?'

'Some things, Ivy, you never forget.' Doug removed his tweed jacket and hung it over the back of a kitchen chair. He pushed the sleeves of his blue jumper up. He removed his gold cufflinks and watch, pushing them into the deep pockets of his trousers. 'I turned skating across the floor to clean it into a spot I performed on stage for years. It was a big success.' He'd thought of her every time he'd stood taking a bow.

'Really?' Ivy frantically rearranged her morning in her head. 'Tell me about you and that Johnjo – if that man's not a Johnson he's a dead ringer for the family.' She grabbed a broom and walked into her front room.

'Johnjo saved my life.' Doug raised his voice to carry to where Ivy was sweeping out the front room. 'I'd had the stuffin' knocked out of me when he found me. He took me in hand. He'd managed to survive on his own. He had street smarts, something I certainly didn't have. He helped me get started on the stage.'

'What did he want?' Ivy walked back to stand in the open doorway. She stood with the broom in one hand, staring at her brother's bent head as he dusted around the bed.

'He wanted a chance.' Doug stood and stared at Ivy. 'When I met him he was a sometimes pick-pocket and from time to time he'd fence stolen goods.'

'Be hard to be an upstanding citizen coming from the Johnsons' warren.' Ivy returned to her sweeping.

'We learned the ropes together.' Doug refused to admit or deny his friend's identity. 'Johnjo asked around. Without being vain I knew I had the looks and the talent needed to make a success on the stage. He had the connections. Johnjo studied the business end of things while I worked on putting an act together. We're a team, Ivy.'

'You made something of yourself, Shay.' Ivy picked up the dust on a piece of old cardboard, emptied it into an old biscuit tin and carried it into the back room. 'I'm proud of you, Shay.' She'd give the floor a quick lick and a promise after he left. 'What's in the suitcase?'

'It took you a whole lot longer to ask that than

I'd figured!' Doug grinned.

'Don't be so cheeky.' Ivy put her cleaning stuff away – the dust was going nowhere. 'You're not too big to have your ears boxed, you know.'

'The suitcase is full of presents for you.' Doug looked around for a damp cloth – he knew Ivy always had one to hand. 'I'll show you.' He found a rag hanging from a hook over the range and wiped his hands.

'Hurry up.'

'Are your hands clean?' Doug grinned.

'Of course.' Ivy was so focused on Shay and his actions she didn't recognise he was using the words she'd used a thousand times around her brothers. Her nerves were shattered. It was such a rare thing for her to receive presents.

'Here, try this on.' He'd kept his back to her while opening the case. He turned and brandished a beige cashmere coat between his spread hands.

'Oh God,' Ivy sobbed. A coat ... a wonderful, beautiful coat ... how had he known? She'd been saving so hard and checking out all of the markets for a decent coat. She couldn't bring herself to spend the kind of money a new coat cost on her own back. 'Is that for me?'

'Well, it's not for me.' Doug smiled gently. He knew what a new coat would mean to Ivy. 'Here,' he shook the coat, 'try it on.'

'Oh Shay!' Ivy walked slowly over to slide her arms into the first new garment she'd ever possessed. 'It fits!' she squealed. 'Look, it fits!' She danced over to the tall mirror standing against the wall.

'So it does.' Doug didn't mention that the coat

was a shrug. It had no buttons just wide lapels that crossed over in front. It wasn't exactly a fitted garment. 'Here, try the matching hat.' Doug slipped a beige cloche hat onto Ivy's gleaming hair. 'That's a flapper's hat. It's the latest thing in London. I haven't noticed a lot of them around town. You'll stop the traffic in that outfit, Ivy.'

'I love it, Shay.' Ivy fought the tears that filled her eyes.

'You can wear it tonight when you come to see me perform.' He walked over to his jacket and pulled an envelope out of the inside pocket. 'Two box tickets for tonight's preview show.' He held the envelope up with a grin. 'I know it's a little late to be asking but I didn't think you'd mind. I want you to come see me on stage before the pantomime season proper starts.' He didn't mention that thanks to him tickets were impossible to get. He'd asked the ticket office to keep an eye open for a cancellation that he could avail of.

He walked back over to the open suitcase sitting on the bed.

'I wasn't sure of your shoe size but anything that doesn't fit should fetch you a few bob down the market. You should be able to find something to wear to the theatre tonight among this lot.'

'I'll wear me tweed suit.'

'Everyone will be dressed to the nines, Ivy. Those theatre boxes are full of toffs showing off to one another.'

'I don't have fancy clothes.'

'Let's see what's in here.' Doug started pulling a rainbow of silk, satin and feathers from the case. 'Something here is sure to do you for your first public appearance.'

'Public appearance? What are you talking about? I'm going to the Gaiety not the Queen's palace.'

'I was hoping you'd join me for a late drink and a meal after the theatre. You and Jem both.' He wanted to see his sister with her beau.

'Not a chance.' Ivy gulped. 'Every time you take a deep breath someone seems to be there to take a picture.' Ivy had already established a scrap-book of all the pictures of her brother that appeared in the papers.

'Please, Ivy.' Doug stood staring down at the silk stockings he'd packed into a soft drawstring bag. Did Ivy even know how to put on silk stockings? He'd helped many a woman out of them. He wasn't about to show his sister how to wear them.

'We'll see.' Ivy wasn't ready to promise anything. She'd see what she looked like when she was all dolled up. 'I'm going to make that pot of tea now. Do you fancy a cup and a rasher sambo? It's nearly eleven and I'm rawmin'.'

'Are you sure you don't want me to help you with some of this?' Doug waved towards the articles falling from the case. He had his fingers crossed she'd refuse. He'd be blushing like a lad if he had to show some of this stuff to his sister.

'I think I can figure it out for meself.' Ivy got busy making the tea and sandwiches. She'd ask your one next door to give her a hand. Ivy had been sweeping her outside steps when the woman was leaving The Lane a short time ago. She'd looked like a fillum star.

'I'd love tea and a sambo.' He pulled his watch from his pocket, checking the time before he put it back on his wrist. He should be safe enough – he wasn't due on stage for hours.

'They call this a bacon sandwich in England,' Doug said when Ivy put a plate with two thick slices of buttered bread stuffed with rashers of bacon on the table in front of him. He accepted the cup of tea with a smile. She'd bought herself a fancy tea set at least.

'Yeh can call it what you like,' Ivy said, putting her tea and a matching sandwich on the table for herself. 'It tastes great no matter what you call it.' She joined her brother at the table. There was silence while they both tucked into the food.

'Are you really serious about staying here, Ivy?' Doug asked when he'd half his sandwich eaten. He sipped the tea and waited.

'You're me brother and I love you, Shay.' Ivy put the sandwich slowly down onto her plate. She picked up her teacup and tried to think how to explain her feelings. 'I'd love to see this place, this Hollywood, but I don't want to live there. This is my home.' She glanced around. She never got tired of the feeling of accomplishment she got every time she sat in here.

'Think about what I'm offering, Ivy. They say California is the land of sunshine. If I make it big in the fillums we'd be on the pig's back.'

'Shay, you'll get married some day. A new wife wouldn't want an old maid sister under her feet.'

'I'm not thinking about getting married any time soon.'

'Nevertheless ... I have to think of my future.' She hated to see the sadness in his eyes but he needed to understand. 'I'm making something of myself here. I have big plans for my own future. Maybe not as fancy as being a big noise in the fillums but a life I think would suit me better. Ireland is changing, Shay. I want to be part of those changes. But I thank you from the bottom of my heart for wanting me with you.' Ivy discovered her cup was empty. She was glad of the chance to step away from the sorrow in her brother's eyes. This was for the best. He'd understand that some day.

'We'll be able to keep in touch anyway.' She put her cup on the table and took Shay's cup to refill. 'You can write to me of all the wonders you'll no doubt see. If you're in the money we can even talk on the telephone. There will be no stoppin' us, Shay.'

'I suppose.'

'Tell me a bit more about the lads.' They hadn't been able to discuss the subject very much up to now. Their meetings so far had been in public, surrounded by other people.

'You wouldn't know them, Ivy.' Doug shook his head sadly. 'I don't know if you'd want to know them.'

'Shay!'

'Seriously, they are nothing like the lads we used to know,' Doug looked around the bare room with a sigh. 'I know I've said it before but I don't know if you fully understand how much they've changed. They've become the kind of toff who looks down his nose at everyone and everything.'

'Far from it they were raised.'

'I don't like them very much, Ivy.'

'That's a shame.' Ivy didn't know what to say. 'Still, they're grown men now, Shay. What they decide to do with their lives is their business. I did the best I could for all of you. I won't say I wash my hands of them but I won't be losing any sleep over them either.'

'That's probably for the best. They have their own row to hoe. All we can do is wait and see what happens.' Doug didn't want to talk about his brothers. He was heartily ashamed of them. 'I'll have to be leaving soon, Ivy.' He rolled down his sleeves and put his cufflinks back on. 'Old Misery Guts Johnjo will get himself into a right strop if I turn up late to the theatre.'

'I'm looking forward to seeing your turn tonight,' Ivy admitted shyly as she strolled slowly towards her front door with him. She hated to see Shay leave but he'd things to do and so had she.

Chapter 38

While Ivy and Doug relived old memories, another brother and sister were catching up on the passing years.

'Well, Queenie, I have to say – you look damn good for a dead woman.' Billy Flint, tall, strong and handsome, stood framed by the light coming from the electric lamp on his desk. He was beautifully suited in dark grey, with a white shirt and red tie. He walked from behind his mahogany desk and simply stood with his arms open and waited.

'Your bloody butler almost refused to let me in.'

Betty Armstrong walked into her brother's arms. The two stood locked in a tight embrace for a few moments.

'I can't believe you bought a house on Merrion Square.' She pushed away, using her gloves to wipe the tears from her eyes. 'Trying to rub their noses in it?' She walked to one of the two green leather chairs pulled up to a blazing fire and sat down. She removed her gloves, dropped them into the hat she'd taken from her head and let it fall to the floor at the side of her chair.

'Brandy?' It might be a bit early for some but he needed a drink. He held a cut-glass decanter over two balloon crystal glasses while his blue eyes took in every detail of her appearance. She looked prosperous.

'Shouldn't your butler be doing that?' She gave a sharp nod of her head. She needed a drink.

'No need for sarcasm yet – sister dear.' He poured brandy into two glasses and, cradling a glass in each hand, walked over to join her before the fire. He passed her one of the glasses before taking the chair opposite, 'It's good to see you, but I know you wouldn't be here if you didn't want something.'

'You knew I was back in Dublin before I telephoned you.' Betty sipped at the brandy, glad of the warmth that flowed through her. 'There's very little goes on in this town that you don't know about.'

'You thought I should stroll into that stinking tunnel and pay a visit,' he bit out before taking a sip from his glass. 'What the fuck are you doing living in The Lane of all places, Queenie?'

'I go by Betty now.'

'William.'

'The story of our lives: we don't even know what to call each other.' Betty sighed.

'You're not here to beat your breast and chant "poor little me", are you?' William Flint Armstrong said through clenched teeth.

'No,' Betty stared into the fire. 'I like to think I've grown up – finally.'

'What's going on, Qu– Betty? Why did you come back? You let us believe you were dead all of these years, lost when the *Titanic* went down. We grieved for you and suddenly you telephone looking for my help with no word of explanation. A bit hard.' William was fighting to control his own feelings. He'd thought her dead for so long. Looking at her now sitting across the fire from him was ... difficult.

'I need to make some important decisions about my life,' Betty said slowly. It was difficult to put her thoughts and feelings into words. 'I came back to Dublin with the intention of either staying, starting a life here or if that didn't work out, saying goodbye – properly – to the old life.' She didn't know how to explain it better than that. She'd been foolish to believe she could walk back into his life demanding help for Ginie and Seán, then walk back out again. What had she been thinking? She hadn't thought, she'd reacted, just as she had before. She had thought she'd grown out of that.

'Do you have money?'

'It always comes down to that, doesn't it?' Betty sank back against her chair and stared across at the man facing her. It broke her heart that their conversation was so stilted, almost like strangers. It was her fault – this divide between them – and she knew it. 'But to answer your question. Yes, I have money. I'm not in need of rescuing, big brother.'

'Then why live in The Lane?' He couldn't imagine willingly living in that place.

'I wanted to see Ivy,' Betty admitted. 'I needed to see how she was doing. I'd wild thoughts of dragging her away from Éamonn and introducing her to the big wild world. Crazy thoughts.'

'Éamonn – Jesus,' William closed his eyes and sighed, 'that was a hell of a shock. I thought at first that he'd been knocked off but it was just as they said – stinking drunk and taking a header into a horse trough – hell of a way to go.' He'd thought he'd lost both of his siblings and it had been hard to deal with. His brother had cut all ties with the family when he'd changed his name and become a man he was ashamed of – a man who allowed his young daughter to support him ... but he'd still been his brother.

'Why didn't you help Ivy?' She knew they were skating around the subjects they needed to discuss but she didn't talk about her years away – not to anyone. Betty had tried to suppress every memory of arriving in New York. Everything she owned had gone down with the *Titanic* – she'd been penniless, friendless and wearing the clothes someone had managed to cobble together for her. It was the lowest time in her life.

'No one thought to contact me. As Éamonn fucking Murphy, our brother, lived and died.' He took a healthy sip of his brandy. 'Anyway, the bloody woman handled everything herself.' William raised his glass in the air. 'I was bloody proud of her to tell the truth. The girl's got spine. It would seem you found your spine while you were dead.' He'd had enough polite chit-chat. The woman sitting opposite him was a different creature to the one who'd left Ireland swearing never to return again.

'When you've lost everything – seen almost everyone around you die – you grow up in a hurry.' Betty remembered the faces of every servant woman who'd refused to board the lifeboats because it 'wouldn't be right for them to go before the gentry'. They had died each and every one of them. 'I was alone for the first time in my life. I had no big brothers to ride to the rescue, no parents pulling strings.'

'You made that choice,' William stated. 'It would only have taken one telegram to any of us and you know it.'

'I'm sorry, Billy.' Betty felt the tears flow down her face and didn't try to stop them. 'Sitting here in front of this fire with you, the past seems another lifetime ago. I was so angry when I left Ireland, so hurt. I think I lost my mind for a while. The *Titanic* felt like God's judgement on me.'

William ignored her tears. 'Trust you to make a disaster that took countless lives all about you.'

'Yes,' she sobbed and laughed, wiping the tears from her cheeks with her hands, 'it did sound very dramatic, didn't it?'

'Here.' He reached over to pass her the handkerchief he'd taken from his pocket. 'You never remember to carry a bloody handkerchief.'

'I intended to stay with you when I arrived in Ireland, you know.' Betty wiped her cheeks. 'I went to your house in Baggot Street ... there was a woman there.'

'Yes.' He simply stared.

'Oh, Billy, do you really intend to repeat history?'

'There will be no children.' He glared. 'We are in a new age. What goes on between me and the women in my life is none of your business but I can guaran-damn-tee that there will be no bastard children. I will never visit that hurt upon a child of mine.'

'How are they?' She asked after their parents, the elephant in the room.

'The old man had a seizure when he heard about Éamonn.' William sighed. They'd have to discuss their parents, he supposed. 'He had the first seizure when we received news of your fate.' He let that sink in for a minute before continuing. 'Éamonn's death almost finished him off. He's a cripple.'

'Do they let her in to see him?' Betty hated the fact that her mother had been her father's mistress for years. The two had expected both of his families to carry on as if it were nothing out of the ordinary, bringing hurt to everyone they touched.

'Someone has to wipe his arse.' He shrugged. 'They allow her to be his nurse.'

'Jesus!'

'Are you not over that shit yet?' he practically shouted. 'You're a fucking grown woman! Get over it!'

384

'I haven't thought about the situation for years.' Betty had almost forgotten that the man she'd loved had allowed his family to cancel their wedding when the word 'bastard' had appeared stamped in large letters over her birth certificate. 'It's being back with you that's raising those old ghosts.'

'Well, leave them decently buried, for fuck's sake!'

'The way you have by buying a house two doors down from Daddy Dearest?' she snapped.

'Yes, you were right – I like to rub their noses in it.' He stood and with his arms out, glass in hand, gave a slow twirl before sitting back down again. 'I love the fact that I'm taller, more handsome, better formed and much, much, richer than his weak-chinned legitimate son and ... I still have all my own jet-black hair, not a hint of grey.'

'And so modest and retiring on top of it.'

He gave her his devil's grin and melted her heart. She couldn't deny his claim: he was a hunk of a man.

'Are you going to try and see them?'

'I don't know.' Betty would give it more thought.

'Are you planning to disappear from my life again?'

'No.'

'Are you ever going to get around to telling me what brought you here to my lair?'

'Jesus, I can't believe I nearly forgot!' Betty gasped. She settled in to tell him everything she knew about Ginie and Seán.

'Getting her away from the Maggies won't be much of a problem.' William shrugged. 'I'll send my butler and chauffeur in the Rolls Royce down there. The nuns respect money. But what are you going to do with her when she does get out?'

'They can have the room I'm renting now.' Betty had been giving the matter a great deal of thought while sharing Seán's care with the Connelly family. 'I'll take care of that. I'll take care of getting Ginie a job, too. I think I know exactly where and how she can earn a living. I'll discuss it with her once she's free.'

'I don't like the gleam in your eyes.' William couldn't take much more of this polite conversation. He needed time alone to process the emotions that seeing his sister had raised. He had to decide if he really wanted to open his heart to her again. 'Well, if that's it?'

'We haven't discussed Ivy.'

'What about her? I keep an eye on her. She's doing okay, isn't she?' He grimaced. 'I hate to admit how much better she looks since our brother died.'

'She's having problems with someone claiming to be under your protection ... and that's not all.' She sat back to tell him about Ivy's fear of being robbed in the street.

'Declan Johnson, that arse-wipe!' William was furious the man claimed even a passing acquaintance with him. 'I'll have my men find him and bring him to my office for a "come to Jesus" meeting. Then I'll have to think some on how to let Ivy know she's safe as houses walking the street. Is that it?'

'Thank you.' Betty didn't know how she was feeling about being around this powerful brother of hers. It was obvious to her that he had places to go, people to see. She'd been lucky to get this time with him.

'Do you have time to meet my wife and sons?' William grinned like a bandit, knowing how much she would disapprove of his lifestyle as she imagined it. He had no intention of being unfaithful to his wife. The woman in the Baggot Street house simply needed somewhere to live ... but he didn't intend to tell his sister that – not yet.

'I think I'll pass on that for the moment, if you don't mind.' She'd had all the emotional upheaval she could take for one day.

The Connelly family had been sharing the care of Seán with her but today she'd left Jimmy Johnson looking after him. She wasn't worried ... exactly ... but she needed to get back. For the first time in her life she had a child she needed to get back to.

Chapter 39

'Ivy Murphy asks if you'll drop in to see her,' Jimmy Johnson said as soon as Betty opened her own door.

'She was real excited about something,' a pale-faced Seán offered.

'I just got back.' Betty was torn. 'I was going to prepare something for you two to eat.'

'I'll look after Seán,' Jimmy offered. 'Him and me is pals. Ivy brought us stew from the Penny

Dinners and now we're going to play cards.' He looked at the woman from under his eyebrows, hoping she didn't mind him offering an opinion, but if Ivy wanted to see her, then Jimmy would help in any way he could.

'I'll go see Ivy then.' Betty could plainly see both youngsters wanted her to see what Ivy wanted. 'You know where I'll be if you should need me.'

Ivy looked around her room, trying not to hyperventilate. The bath she'd pulled indoors with Betty sat empty in the middle of her room. The suitcase of clothes Shay had left was open but she'd been afraid to touch it. Some of the stuff inside was top class. What was she going to do with all of that? She'd been running around like a chicken with her head cut off. Where was your one from next door? Jem Ryan was going to wear his new suit to take her to the theatre tonight. She had to look her best. She didn't want to shame Jem or her brother. She almost shouted aloud when the knock came on her back door.

'I believe you asked to see me,' Betty said as Ivy opened the door. She thought the glitter in Ivy's eyes was almost frantic.

'I need help.' Ivy pulled the other woman through the door, slamming it closed behind them. 'I have to get all dressed up and I can't wear my tweed suit.'

'Relax. And tell me what's going on.' Betty listened while Ivy explained everything in stops and starts but she got the gist of the problem.

'I have sometimes earned my living as a lady's maid. I can help you look as if you belong with

388

the quality. It won't take much, Ivy. There are just a few things you need to know. I've noticed you're working on improving your appearance. You've almost got it.'

'I thought you needed all kinds of training and references to be a lady's maid?'

'Or a quick tongue with a lie.' Betty shrugged.

'Do you really think I can look like a toff?' Ivy jumped slightly when the other woman took one of her hands.

'I'd like to trim your hair.' Betty released her hand. 'I can do it like a professional. Your hair needs to be styled. It looks like a haystack at the moment. Do you cut it yourself?'

Ivy nodded, beyond speech.

'You do a good job of keeping your hands clean and soft, always a good thing, but you need to trim and fashion your nails properly. I can do it for you and show you how to do it yourself.'

'Okay,' Ivy said slowly. 'What else?'

'You need to trim your eyebrows, use a dusting of make-up.'

'Make-up?' Ivy roared. 'I don't want to look like a trollop.'

'Don't be ridiculous,' Betty snapped. 'Do you think all those society ladies have natural black eyelashes and pencil brows? Why should they have naturally perfect pink cheeks and ruby-red lips? Think, Ivy!'

'They wear make-up?' Ivy couldn't believe it.

'Of course they do.' Betty grinned, delighted with Ivy's response. 'I can teach you how to make the best of yourself.'

'I don't have any make-up,' Ivy muttered.

'I do,' Betty tempted her. 'We have time to sort ourselves out but we need to start now. I suggest a nice long soak in a perfumed bath.'

'My brother,' Ivy loved just saying that, 'gave me a suitcase full of clothes – see!' She walked over to the bed and pulled the first dress she touched out of the case.

'I'm sure we'll be able to find you something to wear.' Betty could always loan her one of her own outfits. They were of a size. She walked over and looked at the designer label inside the flapper dress Ivy held and almost gasped. Someone had money. 'You take care of bathing yourself. I'll go next door and get the items I'll need.'

Ivy sat in the warm water of her tub and tried to plan out her evening. She had her legs bent, her knees pulled up against her chest. She wanted to loll in the bath and dream of the evening ahead. Having a deep bath in a warm room – she wanted to revel in the luxury. She sighed deeply – she hadn't the time. She reached over the rim of the tub for the shavings of soap sitting on a plate on the floor. She used the soap to scour every inch of her skin. She didn't miss a spot.

She stepped out of the tub onto the bare floor. Her skin was tingling and rosy-red. She'd left a length of linen at hand to dry herself off. She scrubbed her skin dry with the length of rough cloth. She pulled a black skirt and a loose jumper over her damp body for decency and simply stood looking around. What was she supposed to do next?

'Your one from next door said to knock on the

wall when I'd finished me bath.' She used a bucket to empty the water from the bath, simply opening the back door and throwing the bath water into the yard. She thought it was a sheer waste – she could have used the water for soaking something – but she'd no time. She wrestled the bath onto the hook outside the back door and went back in. Feeling nervous, she left the back door unlocked for Betty. She picked up a block of wood sitting by the range and rapped the block on the wall that separated her room from the one next door.

Ivy prepared to wash her hair. The temperature of the water in the reservoir was just right. She filled her enamel bowl with water and grabbed her bar of old faithful Ivory soap. She'd give her hair a couple of washes. She put a clean linen rag and a chipped enamel mug on the table beside the bowl. Then she bent and dipped the enamel mug into the water. She let the water run over her head and drip down into the basin. That done she reached for her bar of Ivory.

'*Don't use that!*' Betty Armstrong screamed from the door she'd pushed open after a brisk knock. 'Are you mad, woman? Kitchen soap? That will ruin your hair.'

'Come in, why don't yeh, missus?' Ivy stood with her hair dripping into her eyes. She glared at the woman who'd just frightened the life out of her.

'It seems I have a great deal more to do than I first thought.'

Betty put a large case and a mug of boiling water she was using to warm the oil for Ivy's hair onto the kitchen table. Betty sighed and shook her head. It was bloody primitive but she could handle it.

'Right.' She snapped open the case, revealing bottles, lotions and potions such as Ivy had never seen before.

'All that!' Ivy poked one long finger into the case and got a slapped wrist for her trouble.

'I'll wash your hair.' Betty took a special blend of hair soap from her case. 'Bend down.'

Ivy yelped when Betty's nails scraped her delicate scalp. She couldn't remember anyone ever washing her hair before. 'Would yeh go easy, missus?'

'You have to suffer for beauty,' Betty snapped. She rinsed the hair using the enamel mug. She picked up the basin and threw the soapy water out the door, then refilled the basin and brought it back to where Ivy hunched over the table.

'I brought hot oil to rub into your hair.' Betty didn't wait for Ivy's response but took the container of oil she'd put in the mug of hot water before leaving her own place. She was determined to show Ivy how to make the best of her blue-black hair. She massaged the hot oil into Ivy's hair.

'We'll leave the oil on for a while.' Betty picked up the piece of clean linen Ivy had put by the bowl on the table. She wrapped the linen around Ivy's head before pushing her into one of the wooden kitchen chairs.

Ivy sat like a statue and received an expert education in grooming. The things the woman, Betty Armstrong, did to her person took Ivy's breath away. The woman showed Ivy how to make a paste from goose fat and ash from the fireplace. She scrubbed Ivy's face with the mixture. She almost drowned her when she dunked her face into the basin of clean water. Ivy thought she'd breathed her last.

Then your one slathered her face in goose fat. She used a small spoon she took from her case to coat Ivy's eyelashes with more of the goose fat and ash. She used her thumb to curl the lashes. Who knew you had to curl your lashes? Then Betty wet more ash and used the mixture on Ivy's eyelashes, to thicken and darken them, she said. Ivy was terrified she was going to look like a streetwalker by the time the woman was finished with her.

'Sit with your head back and your eyes closed for a minute,' Betty snapped while rinsing her own hands. The dampened ash could seep into your pores if you left it. She didn't wait for Ivy to react to her order but pushed her head back herself.

'I'm going to pluck your eyebrows then give you a manicure.' Betty placed both Ivy's hands on the tabletop. 'Thankfully, here we don't have that much to do. Someone taught you excellent hand care.'

'Granny Grunt,' Ivy whispered through clenched teeth. 'The old woman who lived in the room you rent now. *Ouch!*' Ivy couldn't believe the sharp stab of pain.

'Don't be such a baby,' Betty snapped without a sprig of sympathy. She got a stronger hold on Ivy's head. 'You don't know how lucky you are. You have naturally well-shaped brows. You'd know all about it if I had to pluck a small forest from your face.'

'Are yeh sure yeh know what yer doing, missus?' Ivy gasped.

'It's a little late to be asking now.' Betty laughed when Ivy stiffened. 'Relax – I'm an expert in making the best of a woman's features. I want to get this done then we need to do something about the outfit you'll need for this evening.'

Ivy settled back to suffer in silence. She'd no idea what the woman was doing but she'd hold her whist. She'd asked for help after all. The pinches and pulls on her face hurt but she remained still.

'Do those society women really go through all this?' she asked when she thought she'd run screaming from the room.

'They spend part of every day being pampered and petted,' Betty said absently. 'I need to rinse the oil from your hair.' She emptied the water once more and refilled the enamel bowl. 'I'm afraid I'm going to have to put the last bucket of water into this reservoir.' The hot water had sputtered from the tap.

'Go ahead,' Ivy sighed. She'd try and catch young PJ and have him carry more water for her.

'Right, let us get on,' Betty said when she'd emptied the galvanised bucket into the reservoir. 'I need you to bend over the bowl again.' She applied herself to removing every vestige of oil from Ivy's thick hair. When she was satisfied, she roughly dried the hair with a cloth which she then put around Ivy's neck. 'Sit back in the chair.'

'What are you going to do?' Ivy felt like a rag doll being tossed and pushed around the place.

'I'm going to trim your hair.' Betty picked up a pair of sharp scissors and began to snip away before Ivy could comment further.

Betty knew exactly how she wanted to cut the hair. She'd been dreaming about getting her hands on it for what felt like ages. By the time she finished Ivy's hair would be trimmed into the latest fashion – a bob, they called it.

'Can I look?' Ivy asked when she felt the other woman take a step back.

Betty removed the cloth holding the clipped hair from around Ivy's shoulders. 'Go ahead, have a look.' She carried the cloth over to the range and shook the hair into the nuggets of coal sitting there in a box.

Ivy stood in front of her mirror, staring at her own reflection. She was still wearing her skirt and blouse. Betty walked over to join her.

'I'm not sure what you did to me, missus,' Ivy said to Betty's image in the mirror, 'but I can tell yeh this much. I look a step above buttermilk.'

'I only touched up what nature provided.' Betty was pleased with what they'd done so far.

'By Jesus, the state of me and the price of best butter!' Ivy touched the mop of damp curls that seemed to flatter her face. Her skin was gleaming and, to her eyes anyway, it somehow looked rich, creamy. The skin around her eyebrows was slightly red but your woman said that would fade. Her eyelashes looked like sooty brooms and her lips were wet and gleaming.

'We need to check out the clothes in that suit-case.' Betty needed to wrap up her bag of tricks. She'd excelled herself cutting Ivy's hair if she did say so herself. It was time to sort out an outfit for the evening.

Ivy began to pull items from the case and lay them on the bed – items that had both women gasping.

'That, young lady,' Betty was stunned by the articles displayed on the bed, 'is what they call quality.' She picked up a rich royal-blue-satin, heavily beaded dress from the bed and, with a deep sigh of pleasure, simply said: 'This one!' She'd already noticed the matching shoes.

'Do you think so?' Ivy hadn't a clue.

'Yes, it's perfect.' Betty examined the long-waisted dress with satisfaction. Ivy wouldn't need a corset – she could wear the tight long cotton petticoat sitting on the bed. That would hold her figure steady under the glamorous dress.

'I don't even know how to wear half these feckin' things!' Ivy eyed the smaller items the woman had separated into a pile.

'Not to worry, I can show you,' said Betty. 'You need to strip down, Ivy. We have to get a move on.'

'I'm not stripping down to me skin in front of anyone!' Ivy gasped. 'I'd like me job.'

'For goodness sake, Ivy Murphy, you haven't got anything I haven't seen before.' Betty could see the stubborn expression on Ivy's face. She began to pull articles of intimate apparel from the bed, holding them up and explaining their use to a gaping Ivy. 'I'll close my eyes tight until you tell me you're decent – how's that?'

'Fair enough.' Living in such close quarters, a promise to close the eyes was often the most privacy you could hope for in the tenements.

'When you've removed your clothes, I want you to rub this cream all over your body, Ivy.' Betty turned to take a jar of cream she'd left sitting on the table for this moment. 'Only from your neck down, mind. Then put your new underwear on.' She passed the large jar of scented body lotion to Ivy. 'I'll turn my back to you and put the kettle on and we'll have a cup of tea – give your hair a little more time to dry.'

'Thank you, Sweet Baby Jesus, I'm gummin'.'

Betty busied herself preparing a pot of tea.

'I'm decent.' Ivy had pulled a petticoat, panties and stockings on over her soft, smooth, scented flesh. She'd put her skirt and jumper back on. She had a pair of old socks on her feet to protect her new stockings.

'Come have your cup of tea,' said Betty. The girl had a fabulous figure. It was a shame she was too shy to wear the flapper dress they'd found in the suitcase. It would suit her better than most who sported the fashion. 'Drink that tea quickly, Ivy. I want to touch up your face after you're dressed. And you don't want to keep Jem standing around waiting.'

Ivy gulped her tea, delighted with everything.

'Now we must get you dressed.' Betty put her teacup down and stood. She walked over and picked up the dress. It would leave Ivy's arms bare but the strings of beads on it would drape over her shoulders and the tops of her arms.

'I can dress myself.' Ivy walked over to the bed eagerly. She couldn't wait to step into that dress.

'I'll close my eyes.' Betty couldn't wait. Ivy Murphy was going to give the young men and women of this town something to talk about when she walked into the theatre in the outfit they'd

397

selected. She stood with her eyes tight closed.

'I'm dressed.' Ivy was shaking.

Betty opened her eyes. The dress looked wonderful on Ivy.

'Let me just fix that beading over your shoulders – it should drape, see?' Betty turned her towards the mirror. The matching fabric shoes with a slight heel fit Ivy perfectly. 'Have a look.'

'I look good,' Ivy nodded at her reflection, wondering who the stranger was staring back at her. She'd never looked like this before in her life. She could hardly tell she was wearing make-up. Whatever your one had done to her seemed to accentuate her features. She nodded her head at the image in the mirror. 'Thank you.'

'I can't believe your brother picked out all of these things.' Betty was rooting in the suitcase for an item she knew she'd seen. Ivy's brother certainly knew women. He seemed to have an intimate knowledge of their requirements. 'Ah ha,' she cried, diving on something in the case. 'I knew I'd seen one of these!'

Ivy stared at what looked like a diamond-encrusted cobweb draped over Betty's fist.

'This must have come from Paris. It's the latest thing. I've seen them in magazines – they're worn to replace hats in the evening – they're designed to be worn with the new short hair styles.' Betty touched her own dark hair which was pulled away from her face into a low bun.

'Gi's a look.' Ivy decided she might as well be hung for a sheep as a lamb.

'I'll put it on for you.' Betty took the silver-and-white jewelled hat-shaped mesh and settled it carefully over Ivy's dark hair, pulling several curls out and brushing them back over the outer edge of the rimless hat. She examined Ivy's face. A quick touch-up and she was ready.

'Oh, Ivy,' Betty breathed, 'you look like you have diamond raindrops in your hair. I want you to walk slowly over to the far side of the room. Then turn around and walk back towards the mirror, examining your image in the mirror with every step you take. See what you think of the new you.' Betty stood fighting tears as she watched Ivy walk slowly away and then back towards the mirror.

'I look like a nob,' Ivy whispered in wonder, unable to believe she was staring at her own image.

'Here.' Betty held Ivy's new cashmere coat open for her to slip her arms inside. 'You can't wear a hat over that web. Lift the wide collar of your coat up to frame your face. Oh! We forgot your gloves.' Betty wanted to hit her own head. 'Take your coat off again.' She held the back of the coat while Ivy removed her arms. Then she passed the long evening gloves to Ivy and waited.

Ivy pulled the gloves on over her long delicate fingers. She admired how the black lace made her skin glow before putting her coat back on.

'I'll be getting along, Ivy.' Betty was standing at the back door, admiring her work. 'Have a great time this evening. I'll be in tomorrow and you can tell me all about it.'

'Thank you for all your help.' Ivy walked slowly over to the door. She waited till Betty stepped out onto the cobbles. 'I'd never have been able to do all of this,' she waved a black-gloved hand at her body, 'without your help.'

'You're welcome.' Betty heard the door lock behind her as she turned away to return to her own room.

Chapter 40

'Oooh, you two look wonderful!' Emmy Ryan clapped her hands and stared with wide green eyes at the two adults standing surrounded by a crowd of onlookers on the cobbled courtyard.

Ann Marie stood with Emmy who was going to spend the night at her house but neither had wanted to leave without first seeing Ivy and Jem in all their finery.

Marcella Wiggins had tears in her eyes, looking at the young couple stepping out for a big night together. 'Ivy Murphy, Granny would be that proud of yeh. Yeh look a proper toff. You too, Jem.'

The courtyard was filling up with people curious to see what was going on.

'Conn,' Lily Connelly had to nudge her son to get his attention away from the couple.

'Huh?' Conn had been dreaming of the day he might stand here wearing a fancy new suit and a toff's hat with a woman like Ivy on his arm.

'Run down to the end,' Lily said, referring to the row of houses at the end of the square. 'Get that fella that takes photographs on O'Connell Bridge out here. Tell him we want some pictures taken.'

'Oh, you're thinking, girl!' Marcella grinned.

'What do you think?' Jem smiled down at the glowing beauty on his arm, thrilled with his life.

'I've never had me picture took,' Ivy whispered. 'I wouldn't mind a photograph of the two of us all dolled up like the dog's dinner.' Ivy couldn't believe all of this. She was floating away in the clouds. She'd never felt anything like this before.

'You look very handsome, Mr Ryan, in your new suit.' Ivy admired the beautifully tailored black pinstripe suit Jem wore. The white of his shirt was almost blinding. She didn't know that the green silk tie that perfectly matched his eyes had been a gift from Ann Marie. 'You polish up real well, Mister.'

'Should I put on my new overcoat for the photograph, Ivy?' Jem wasn't accustomed to being the centre of attention.

'Why don't we get some photographs of the two of you in your evening clothes and then more wearing your coats?' Ann Marie walked over to join them. She'd had no idea this evening out for Ivy would attract so much attention.

'What's going on?' Milo Norton, carrying his big camera, with a tall sticklike lamp held in one hand, hurried to join the crowd. He made his living taking photographs of courting couples crossing O'Connell Bridge. He took their names and addresses there on the bridge. He sold the photographs sight unseen then mailed the couple their copy when he'd developed them. The people of The Lane called on him for Communion and Confirmation photographs too. If a young couple were in the money he sometimes took photographs of their wedding day or, rarely, new babies.

He developed the photographs himself in one of his two rooms.

'We need some photies took,' Marcella Wiggins said, feeling very important. She'd never been able to afford Milo and his camera. She was thrilled to be able to stand here and watch him work.

Ann Marie stood back, taking mental notes of the procedure. She listened to the people around her talk about the man and his skill with the camera. With a fast-beating heart she wondered if he would be willing to give lessons.

Jem and Ivy stood posing self-consciously. Milo was becoming frustrated. They looked too stiff and formal. He wanted to capture the light inside the couple. They were a very handsome pair. If he got the photograph he wanted he could use it to show to the couples on O'Connell Bridge. This couple would be good for his business but not if he couldn't get them to relax.

'Where are you two off to then?' Milo tried one more time to get them to forget about the camera. Pay dirt! They lit up as they talked about their plans for the evening. Milo snapped as fast as his camera would allow. He knew he had quick fingers. He had to capture as many people as possible as they tried to walk past him on O'Connell Bridge.

'Well, Ivy, how do you feel?' Jem was feeling ten feet tall. He was walking out with his best girl on his arm. They were going to the theatre.

'I don't know if I'm on me head or me heels, Jem,' Ivy admitted as they strolled through the tunnel leading into Stephen's Lane. 'I've never been on one of them roller-coasters you see with the travelling fairs but I think this is how it must feel afterwards.'

'You sure we shouldn't have taken a cab to the Gaiety?' Jem had offered to have one of his prime carriages available to them this evening.

'It's quicker to walk, Jem.' Ivy strolled along, her arm in Jem's, the gas lamps glittering like jewels. She wondered if she should confess she'd wanted to get a look and feel for the crowds arriving to enjoy an evening at the theatre.

'True enough.' Jem didn't care how they got to the theatre. He was willing to go along with anything Ivy wanted. 'It can take ages for the carriage to get close enough to the theatre to set people down.'

'Well, you would know.' Ivy was busy taking in the scene around her.

'You look lovely, Ivy.' Jem looked down at the top of her head. He didn't know what she was wearing on her head but it was pretty. 'Did I tell you that before?'

'You did, Jem,' Ivy laughed up into his beautiful green eyes, 'but it bears repeating.'

The two strolled along talking in hushed voices about nothing in particular. Jem didn't care if the short walk to the theatre took forever. He was having the time of his life and the evening had only started.

'Have you thought any more about the sale of your Cinderella dolls?' he asked. John Lawless had fretted and worried about those bloomin' dolls until Jem had to ask him to shut up. He couldn't believe he'd just asked Ivy about them now.

'I have.' Ivy gave a little skip of delight. 'I'm going to do as Mr Clancy,' Ivy was referring to the man who came by the livery to teach accounting, 'suggests.'

'What's that?'

'I divided the number of dolls I have ready for sale by the number of days the pantomime will be on,' Ivy said, delighted with herself.

'And?' Jem nudged her gently with his shoulder.

'I'm going to take twenty-two dolls with me each evening.' Ivy had been worried until she'd come up with this idea. It had been a great relief to her. 'If I'm lucky enough to sell every doll at a half crown a piece that will be five guineas a night. I'll put the money in the night safe and then I just go home.'

'Do you have that many dolls ready for sale?' Jem had done the maths. That was a lot of dolls – hundreds.

'The Lawless family have been churning out those dolls for months.' Ivy had been so intent on their conversation they'd passed the Shelbourne Hotel without her noticing. They were almost at the theatre. 'By having such a small number for sale every night I'm hoping people will come to know that you have to get in quick. I'm going to be creating a demand for my product.' Ivy giggled, delighted with herself. They were Mr Clancy's words but she liked the sound of them.

'There will be no stopping you, Ivy Murphy.' Jem shook his head, lost in admiration. What could this woman have achieved if she'd been supported as she should have been?

'Merciful Lord!' Ivy gasped at the crowd. Not so

404

much at the smartly dressed people gathered around the Gaiety – she had seen them when she'd been here the other evening – but this was the ordinary people of Dublin and they were everywhere. You could hardly move all along King Street. 'Did you know there were this many people in all of Dublin, Jem? Look at all these carriages. How do they avoid each other?' She examined the women selling flowers, oranges and chocolates from their prams. She'd be one of them soon, but not tonight. Tonight she was one of the toffs making their way through the open doors of the theatre.

Jem smiled at her reaction but said nothing. It was a familiar scene to him, though he was usually one of the drivers trying to drop their passengers down in front of the theatre before going to wait around Stephen's Green to see if they could pick up another fare.

'Ivy,' Jem put his hand over hers on his arm, 'you're pinching the life out of me. And I need to get our tickets out of my pocket.'

Ivy was now staring around at the crowd of people gathered in the vestibule. She had a death grip on Jem's arm. She was terrified of losing him.

She was breathless as they strolled across the carpet towards the uniformed man standing guard at the bottom of the roped-off steps. Jem showed their tickets to the usher. He was glad he'd asked Ann Marie what he should do, where he should go this evening. He wasn't any more experienced in places like this than Ivy was.

'Thank you, sir.' The man tore the ticket and returned half. 'Up these stairs and to your left.' He opened the thick blue rope-gate and allowed the well-dressed couple to pass.

Ivy was afraid to open her mouth. She allowed Jem to lead her up the stairs to the next level and yet another man who checked their tickets before opening a door and waving them through.

Ivy found herself standing on some sort of balcony. She looked around her, trying to take everything in. She knew the people of The Lane would want every detail.

'Let me take your coat, Ivy.' Jem stood staring around, just as thunderstruck as Ivy. He was that grateful to Ann Marie for the detailed instructions she'd given him. 'I'll take it down to the cloak-room.'

'Jem, did yeh get a look at this place?' Ivy stood staring around at the richly decorated theatre. The balcony she was standing on was just over the stage. They'd have the best view in the house. She noticed people in the other boxes staring over and wondered what they were looking at.

'Give me your coat, Ivy.' Jem stood behind her, ready to help her off with the beautiful cashmere coat.

'Are yeh going to leave me here on me own?' Ivy was terrified.

'Buck up, Ivy.' Jem was feeling pretty shaky himself. 'Remember, you're one of the nobs tonight.'

'What are those people staring over here for?' Ivy allowed Jem to remove her coat. She almost fell into the red velvet chair he held out for her.

'They're wondering about the beautiful woman in this box.' Jem put her coat over his arm and turned to leave.

Ivy had to force herself to sit still and not pull on

his coat to keep him with her. She sat like a statue, only her eyes moving as she looked around at the theatre. She was trying to ignore the stares from the people in the other boxes. She had no way of knowing that the crowd were curious about someone they didn't recognise. The Dublin upper crust was a small select group. A new face was of interest to everyone.

Jem returned without his hat and coat. He put a box of chocolates in Ivy's hands before pulling a seat over beside hers. They sat behind the balcony wall, the polished brass rail fixed on top in a position guaranteed not to ruin their view of the stage.

Ivy dropped the unopened box of chocolates and grabbed onto Jem's hand when the music rang out around the theatre. She leaned across the rail to look down into a pit in front of the stage. There were people sitting down there, in the dark, playing music. She took a deep breath and sat back, prepared to enjoy herself.

Jem and Ivy sat enthralled as turn after turn seemed to explode through the opening and closing red-velvet curtains. There were all sorts: people who juggled balls, people who danced – there were even people who came out and told funny stories. Ivy loved it. She wasn't aware of the passage of time. She sat with her eyes glued to the stage, her hand in Jem's.

'It's almost time for the interval, Ivy,' Jem leaned forward to say when the curtain closed to allow one act off and another on. He'd been afraid at times that Ivy had stopped breathing. She hadn't taken her eyes off the stage for a minute.

'What's that?' she whispered without removing

her eyes from the stage. She was afraid of missing anything.

'I'll explain later.' Jem was enjoying watching her reaction almost more than the acts on stage.

'Jem!' Ivy squeezed his hand.

Their neighbour Liam Connelly strolled non-chalantly into view from stage left, beautifully groomed in one of Ivy's best toff's cut-down suits. His sister Vera, in the pink-and-white ensemble that Ivy and the ladies of The Lane had put together, skipped into view from stage right. The two on stage jerked in shock at the sight of each other and with much waving of arms and pushes appeared to enter into a fierce non-verbal argument. When Vera appeared to notice the audience, she nudged her brother dramatically. They seemed shocked to see the audience but with sickly smiles began their act.

The pair danced and sang a clever little ditty that brought laughter from the audience. Vera dipped into a curtsey while Liam bowed deeply. A black and white collie dog ran from the wings across the red curtain and jumped onto his back, knocked his hat off his head and barked. The audience went wild.

The dog jumped off his back, grabbed the hat and ran around the stage with Liam in pursuit.

'I warned you not to bring that animal to the theatre with you,' Liam blustered.

The audience loved it.

'That animal's ruined my best hat!' Liam roared, holding his hat up for everyone to see the bite marks. 'I'm going to get rid of her!'

The dog rose up onto its back legs and ran over

to appeal to Vera.

'Scotty!' Vera called prettily while appearing distressed. 'Scotty, dear, come and get your dog! Scotty!'

Ivy almost fell over the brass rail when 'Scotty' appeared on stage. It was Seán McDonald wearing his horrible cut-down jacket. He was dressed in short trousers, jumper and shirt underneath. He was wearing socks that fell down over his shoes. She hadn't known they were going to include him in their act.

'Scotty,' Liam took the lad by the big shoulder of his jacket and pulled him to the front of the stage while shaking his finger in his face, 'didn't I tell you we couldn't have dogs in the theatre, didn't I say that?'

'Yes, sir!' Young Seán pulled his jacket free. 'You said that right enough, sir.'

Liam turned to lecture his stage partner. As soon as his back was turned puppy heads peeked out of the deep pockets and the loosened neck of Seán's old coat. The audience exploded. Liam swung around to see why the audience was roaring. The puppies disappeared before he completed his well-timed turn. Ivy noticed the supply of what she assumed was cracklin' that Seán was pulling from his 'secret' pocket to tempt the dogs to behave.

Ivy sat with her mouth open, watching three people she'd known since they were babies entertain the crowd. They had the place in the palms of their hands. She laughed, clapped and roared along with everyone else.

'Jem, it's been a day.' Ivy stood holding a fancy

409

glass, looking around the lounge bar of the Gaiety Theatre. She'd been to the toilet and almost fainted when someone had asked her where she'd bought her hair adornment. It had taken her a minute to figure out what your one was talking about. She'd smiled politely, mentioned Paris then done a runner. As if the likes of her had ever even sniffed Paris.

Her head was still in a spin from the show she'd just seen and it was only half-time. From time to time she'd catch a glimpse of Jem and herself in the mirrors that lined the room. She didn't know those people.

'That it has, Ivy.' Jem sipped his whiskey and wished for a pint. He was thirsty. 'Did you know the Connellys were putting young Seán in their act?'

'No, I almost fell over the balcony when he came out.' Ivy grinned wide in delight. 'They were bloody good, weren't they?'

'We might not be the best of judges,' Jem returned the grin, 'but I thought them the stars of the show.'

'There will be no stopping them now.' Ivy sipped the bitter-tasting drink in her hand. Jem had ordered the drink he'd heard the other men order for the ladies – gin and tonic. She'd have preferred a cup of tea.

'That's the bell,' Jem said unnecessarily. 'Time for us to return to our seats.'

'I don't know if me nerves are up to this.' She passed him the almost untouched drink. She was sorry he'd wasted good money on the thing but she wasn't drinking that stuff.

Ivy almost collapsed onto the red chair when they returned to their box, grateful to have its support.

'Buck up, Ivy, the evening's not over yet.' Jem wasn't sure about having drinks and a bite to eat with the star of the show. He wouldn't have any problem enjoying himself with Ivy's brother Shay but the big noise Doug Joyce was a different kettle of fish. He didn't know how to act around someone famous. Jem had heard all the muttering about the man around the bar. He didn't want to let Ivy down.

They sat through the second half of the show in a daze. It seemed to Ivy that the performers had more polish to them this time around. Perhaps it was just that she was relaxed.

Then the entire audience stood up and started shouting, stamping their feet and applauding. Ivy thought the place was on fire. The stage curtains were tightly closed. She couldn't see anything to cause this uproar.

'Do you have any idea what's going on, Jem?' She turned to look at Jem but he was as puzzled as she.

They sat there watching the hysteria of the crowd and waited.

Then Ivy almost fell off her chair when her brother walked onto the stage. She had no idea the music the orchestra was playing was known as his theme tune. It was time for the star of the show, the headliner. No, it wasn't Shay – this was Douglas Joyce, star. The audience continued to scream and shout. He waited for them to calm down, then;

'The girl I love is on the Gaiety balcony.
The sort of girl that you want to take home
Mother always said I'd fall in love someday...'

Doug stood tall on the stage and sang his heart out for Ivy. He was aware of heads turning to see where he was looking. He knew Ivy would want to kill him but he wanted her to know she was special to him. He'd hastily written these words this afternoon. It was one of those songs that just came to him. The catchy little tune he'd bought from an aspiring musician matched the words perfectly.

He danced across the stage, still singing his heart out. He stopped under the box Ivy and Jem sat in and went into a frenetic tap routine. The words of the song changed to allow it to be seen that the woman he was singing to belonged to another. Women in the audience reached for their hankies. Doug had them in the palm of his hand.

'I'll kill him,' Ivy whispered to Jem as Doug danced back across the stage.

'I'm glad he's your brother, Ivy,' Jem admitted. He wouldn't have a chance against someone like the fella on that stage.

'He'll be me dead brother tomorrow,' Ivy said. 'I'll kill him.'

'Don't be like that.' Jem leaned forward to whisper in her ear. 'That's your little brother down there. The lad you raised is dancing and singing his heart out for you on that stage.'

'You're right, Jem, you're exactly right.' Ivy blushed scarlet but she fairly beamed with delight. That was her Shay whatever the heck he called himself.

Chapter 41

Ivy pushed her pram along, heading for the tunnel leading to Stephen's Street. It was sheer joy not to have to pass in front of the pub whenever she entered or left The Lane. No more drunken men shouting abuse and risqué remarks. No more dreading what she was walking through. She didn't know her own luxury these days. It was a short walk from The Lane to King's Street and the Gaiety Theatre. She walked along the high iron fence of Stephen's Green, a smile crossing her face without conscious thought as she passed the Shelbourne Hotel. Who would believe that a brother of hers would ever be a guest there? Once upon a time she'd been afraid to walk in front of the hotel – now she'd taken tea there like a toff and the sky hadn't fallen in.

Who knew what she could do in the future? If her little brother could go off to America to star in the fillums then she'd have to pull up her socks to keep up with him. No better woman. She strode along with her chin in the air.

'How's yerself, Ivy?' Old Peadar was hunched over his makeshift fire, holding his rag-wrapped dirt-encrusted hands out to the flame. The fire in the holed steel bucket at his feet was miserable but it was heat.

'Not so bad, Peadar.' Ivy parked her pram by the three-sided hut. 'You'll keep an eye on me pram?'

She couldn't believe how much better she felt knowing that the word was out on the street that she was under the protection of Billy Flint. She hadn't met the man herself but Betty Armstrong had put in a good word for her. Ivy didn't know how much the man's protection was going to cost her but for the moment she was delighted with the safety she felt walking the streets. She'd face the man's charges when she had to. She'd fight to keep most of the money she'd earned but that worry was for another day.

'That I will.' Peadar offered a gummy grin, practically smothered by the grey whiskers that decorated his face. He'd been keeping careful watch over Ivy's pram every night. She slipped him a few pence for the service but she was always polite enough to ask which pleased the old man.

'It'll soon be Christmas, Ivy.' Peadar accepted the paper-wrapped parcel of coal nuggets Ivy slipped from the depths of her pram without a word. They never mentioned the gift but every evening she brought him enough coal to keep him alive another day.

'We'll all get a day off then, Peadar.' She knew the old man would get a meal from the Ivy, one of the doss houses around the city. It seemed to amuse the old man that Ivy's name was the same as the infamous doss house. She dropped her shawl on the pram before removing the usherette tray. She slipped the leather straps over her suit jacket before settling her red paisley shawl over her head and shoulders again. She wrapped a money belt around her waist under her jacket before pulling fingerless gloves onto her hands. She couldn't make change wearing ordinary gloves.

'Here, I brought a can of tea.' She offered the tightly lidded can to the old man. 'Yeh might have to pour it into yer pot and give it a warm.'

She kept a wet rag in her pram to wipe her fingers clean and without seeming to pay attention to the old man she used this rag now to assure herself her fingers and nails were clean. She took the empty can back as soon as he'd emptied the tea into his battered metal teapot. Peadar wasn't past keeping the can and selling it on for a few pence.

'Here, yeh need to know,' Peadar tapped a dirty finger to the side of his bulbous red-veined nose, 'them fancy-talkin' nanny women were talking about yer dolls.' Peadar knew he was invisible to most people. That didn't bother him – he overheard enough gossip to keep him entertained. Sometimes he heard something that made him a few coppers. 'They got to planning how they could buy yer dolls for less if they ganged together. Yeh need to mind yerself.'

'I will, Peadar, thanks.' Ivy took her carefully covered orange-box crate from the pram. She removed the custom-made cover and carefully began transferring her dolls from the box onto her tray. 'It wouldn't be the first time someone tried to get me to offer them a special price. They'll find out the same as the others that me price is set in cement.'

'A half crown, Ivy. That's bloody expensive for a doll – that's more than a working man's week's wages, that is.'

'To you and me, Peadar, but not to the likes of them out there.' Ivy gave a jerk of her chin towards the people beginning to gather outside the Gaiety doors. 'I'm taking the money from them that can afford it.'

'Well, yeh seem to know what yer doin' right enough.' Peadar shook his head at the wonder of it all. 'Yeh better get out there before they open the doors. I'll keep me eye on yeh and yer goods.'

'Here we go.' Ivy checked she had everything she'd need, put the cover over her pram, locked the brake and then with a deep breath stepped out to conduct business.

She approached the crowd of richly dressed people swarming around the entry door to the Theatre. There were two lines of people waiting for the doors to open: those with money for the expensive seats and those who'd saved and scrimped to buy the tickets to take their families to the pantomime. She took her place standing as close to the street as she dared. The horses pulling the carriages and hired cabs ignored her but she didn't fancy getting shoved in the back by a passing horse.

'*Get yer Cinderella dolls here!*' Ivy shouted when she was in position. She had to make sure her voice carried over the shouts of the other dealers and the hum of the excited crowd. The cry to buy oranges, sweets, chocolates and even flowers sounded alongside her own. She held up one of the pink lace-dressed dolls and shook it towards the waiting line of nannies and children.

'*Hand-made by the fairies in Tír na nÓg... Cinderella dolls here!*' She waited to see the usual nudges and demands from the well-groomed children to their uniformed nannies. It shouldn't take her long to shift this lot. 'Get them before they're gone!'

It wasn't long before the first of the women guarding the wealthy children stepped out of line.

Ivy settled in to do a brisk business. She held out her hand with a smile when she accepted the silver coin decorated with a standing horse. Every afternoon she feared it would be the day when the demand dried up but word of her dolls had spread around Dublin. There were now other Cinderella dolls on sale outside the Gaiety. The other dealers, seeing the success of Ivy's dolls, had quickly jumped on the bandwagon. Ivy welcomed the competition – her dolls were superior and she knew it.

'Looks to me like you're almost finished up here,' a welcome voice whispered in her ear.

'Jem!' She turned with a beaming grin. 'If I could feel my feet I'd be dancing in the street.' She used her 'posh' voice when she was selling her dolls.

'I believe I was here first,' a nasal voice snapped.

Ivy turned to find a very irate nanny standing waiting to buy the last doll on her tray. The theatre doors hadn't even opened yet and she was all sold up. She ignored the woman's glare and with a beaming smile passed over the doll with one hand while taking the coin with the other. 'Enjoy the show,' she wished the woman who'd turned away without a word of thanks.

'You can't be coming down here all the time, Jem.' She was always glad to see him but he had his own business to run.

'I have to see my best girl safely home.' Jem

followed Ivy back down the alley to pick up her pram. He nodded to Peadar and waited while Ivy removed her usherette tray and prepared her bank bag.

'You know, Jem,' Ivy said as they walked out of the alley and along King Street towards the bank, 'I never thought of young gents wanting to buy the doll for the ladies on their arms. I need to think on that ... it's a business opportunity I'm missing out on.'

'Ivy,' he took her elbow in his hand, 'I don't want to talk about business. Ann Marie is taking Emmy to her house. I thought we could drop the pram in The Lane and have an evening to ourselves. How does a picture with fish and chips for afters sound to you?'

'Music to me ears, Jem.'

Ivy dropped the bank bag in the night safe, took the handle of her pram firmly in one hand and held out the other to her best fella. They walked in the direction of The Lane, discussing the films on offer around town.

Chapter 42

'I do believe I'm a mite tiddly.' Ivy enunciated clearly in the tone of someone who finds herself surprised to be drunk.

'In that case,' John Lawless used two crutches to push himself to his feet, then stood swaying for a moment before catching his balance, 'I'd better make my toast now. I wouldn't want you to miss it, Ivy. I've been working on it.'

'Let me refill the glasses.' Doug Joyce jumped to his feet. The champagne that was turning Ivy's head was his contribution to this feast.

'I don't know how long I can remain standing on my feet,' John admitted. He'd worked very hard to stand on his own two feet for this, his first Christmas with his family in their new home.

'Then sit down, John, do.' Ann Marie looked around the table, thrilled with her new life. They were gathered around the large table in the staff dining room. She'd wanted to have this dinner in her upstairs dining room but that suggestion had been vetoed by everyone else. What would have been the servants' table was the place they picked so that was where they were.

'I want to stand for this,' John insisted stubbornly.

'Good man.' Doug had finished refilling the fancy glasses which looked out of place on the heavy wooden surface of the long table.

'You better be quick about it, love.' Sadie Lawless beamed up at her husband. She beamed a lot these days. 'I want to get all this food cleared away. I'm putting me feet up for the rest of the day.'

'You deserve to, love. You've worked like a Trojan, you and the girls. I'm proud of all of us.' He grinned. 'Now as to me toast – I want everyone to raise a glass to Miss Ivy Rose Murphy!' He didn't dare pick up his own glass. Not yet.

Everyone picked up a glass and prepared to listen. Ivy blushed furiously. She put her two hands to her face.

'Everyone sitting around this table owes something to Ivy Murphy,' John said. 'I don't think I'm speaking out of turn to say that.'

'Ivy's not the only one slightly drunk,' Sadie muttered under her breath.

'I wanted to die when that bale of hay fell on me back and took the strength from me legs,' John admitted. 'Ivy Murphy wouldn't let me. She pestered me to live and become a part of this merry crowd.'

'She has a way of doing that,' Jem interjected.

'She raised me so I'm saying nothing or she'll box me ears.' Doug Joyce looked around the long table, a table groaning with the remains of the feast they'd just enjoyed, a table surrounded by people who would take care of and love his sister when he was far away.

'Will yez let me husband speak before he falls down!' Sadie watched the man she loved sway in place.

'Thanks to the same Ivy Murphy,' John ignored the interruption, 'I can give my girls, my Clare and Dora, a better life than Sadie and I ever imagined. Thanks too to her I've a son any man could be proud of.'

'Ay up, Ivy – what's that about?' Doug knew all about Ivy's life in the last year but it was fun to joke and fool about.

'Will yeh hold yer whist?' John swayed alarmingly but remained on his feet. He was determined to get this said. 'There's not a one sitting around this table that doesn't owe the good things in their lives to Ivy Murphy.' He picked up his glass and raised it to her. 'Now, I've had me say.

The rest of yeh can do what you like.' He held his glass up, whispered 'Ivy' with a smile and drank deeply before collapsing back into the chair his wife held for him.

'I suppose it's my turn.' Jem pushed to his feet.

'Sit down, Jem,' Ivy hissed. 'You don't have to do anything at all.'

'You, Miss Ivy Rose Murphy, are a hard woman to thank.' Jem grinned down at a glaring Ivy. If looks could kill he'd drop where he stood. 'Everyone here knows the effect Ivy has had on my life for the past year. I didn't want to die like John but I wasn't really living either. I was content to let life pass me by until Ivy Murphy and Fate kicked me in the posterior.'

Emmy Ryan was having the time of her life. She'd never been to a party like this before. She hid her giggles behind her hands and stared across the table at her new friend Seán McDonald.

'I'm a changed man from this time last year,' Jem said. 'I have new friends.' He moved his glass around the table. 'I have the chance of a business that scares me yet invigorates me at the same time.'

'Them's five-guinea words you're using there, boss,' John grinned.

'Every time I turn around, these two women,' Jem tipped his glass to Ivy and Ann Marie, 'have come up with another plan or risk they want me to take. I'm proud of myself for being able to tighten me sinews and carry on.'

'Uncle Jem, are you a mite tipsy too?' Emmy Ryan's sweet young voice rang out.

'The lot of them are drunk!' Seán McDonald

crossed his arms in front of his chest like an old man. He glared around the table, disgusted at the adults. 'Why don't we take our new toys back to The Lane and show them off? Later Old Man Solomon will bring out his gramophone and his records for the street party.'

Nothing loath, Emmy asked for permission to leave the table and return to The Lane. Seán watched openmouthed as the silly female waited to be given permission to leave the table. These people were strange. One thing he would say for them though. They sure knew how to feed a fella.

The newly named Ginie McDonald, released from incarceration with the Maggies, sat silently staring around the table at these strangers who had rescued her. She didn't trust them. She didn't know what they wanted from her. That Johnjo fella who said he was a brother to her, she didn't know him. He looked enough like feckin' Declan to be his twin until you looked in his eyes. You saw the difference then but it was still a shock to the system. There had been no news of Declan for a while but Ginie wasn't holding her breath that that bad bugger was gone from her life. A bad penny always found a way of turning up.

'Ma, do yeh want to come back to The Lane with me?' Seán stood staring at his mother. Her eyes were all sad. He didn't know what to do to make things better for her.

'No, son, you go ahead.' Ginie didn't trust the people of The Lane either. She and Seán had taken over the rent on the basement room next door to Ivy Murphy. Betty Armstrong had arranged everything. She'd found Ginie a job in a 'fancy house'. She was being paid to spank grown men. She'd never known such a thing went on but she was being paid good money to do something she'd do for nothing if she could afford it. What with her earnings and the money Seán was bringing in for his work on the stage, she didn't know if she was coming or going.

'Can we take them over, Ma, Da?' Dora Lawless stood up. She wanted to go to The Lane. She wanted to show Conn her new red dress. Conn hadn't come to their house for dinner. She looked at all the food left over and thought her mother wouldn't mind if she made him up a plate. He was keeping an eye on the phones and the livery in case of an emergency. She'd be able to sit in the office with him and visit.

'I'd like to go talk to Vera Connelly.' Clare stood up and looked towards her parents.

'Clear the table and take everything into the kitchen before yez leave,' Sadie said. 'But I give yeh fair warning the dishes will be waiting for yeh when yeh get back.'

'We'll do them later.' Dora grabbed Clare by the hand and with the help of Seán and Emmy they started clearing the table.

'I think,' Johnjo Smith said, standing away from the table, 'if it offends no one Ginie and I will go for a long walk by the Canal. We have a lot of talking to do.'

'Suit yerself.' Ginie stood up with a flounce. She was wearing the clothes Ann Marie had bought for her. The long woollen dress was warm and covered her from neck to ankle. She'd even bought Ginie new boots and a new coat and hat.

Ginie didn't trust the woman.

Ann Marie watched the brother and sister leave. 'We are going to have to do something about that young woman, Ivy.'

'All in good time, Ann Marie,' Ivy sighed. 'All in good time. We've managed to get her away from the Maggies, Seán is earning a few bob with his stage work, Ginie has a place of her own in The Lane. That's enough to be going on with, don't you think?'

Having cleared the table, the young people happily took their leave, while the adults sat on with their drinks.

Betty Armstrong had been sitting back watching the action around her. She'd moved out of The Lane after she'd organised as much as she could for Seán and his mother. It nearly broke her heart to leave that little lad but Seán loved his mother. She'd wanted to keep him with her but realised that was selfish of her. She'd moved into her brother's house in Baggot Street while she arranged the next stage of her life. She'd accepted the invitation to have Christmas dinner with these people, wanting to see them all again. She'd enjoyed a fabulous feast and good company.

'And what have you got to say for yourself, Auntie Betty?' Doug drawled with what he imagined was an American accent. He'd heard a lot of American accents from visiting performers to the variety theatres he'd played in around England. With six of the people who sat down to eat having left there were gaps at the long table. He walked along the table, shifting his place to be closer to the people who remained.

'Are you practising your accent for the fillums,' Ivy grinned, 'talking all funny like that?'

But her grin faded when she saw her brother's serious expression as he stared at Betty, who stared silently back.

Ivy took a swig of sparkling liquid from her glass and simply stared between her brother and the woman she knew as Betty. '"Auntie"? Name of Jesus, Shay, did you say "auntie"?' She felt faint.

'I did indeed.' Doug stared at the woman sitting frozen in her seat. 'Why don't you come join us down this end of the table, Auntie Betty?' He waved a hand towards a chair across the table from him.

Ann Marie, Jem, John and Sadie stared at each other and waited to see what would happen next.

'Or should I call you Auntie Queenie?' Doug added.

'Auntie Queenie!' Ivy fell back in her chair. 'Me da's sister – the sister who went down on the *Titanic* – are yeh talking about that one? The one he was always crying over – that Queenie?' Ivy was in shock.

'I didn't think you remembered me.' Betty stood and moved down the table, joining the rest of the people gathered there.

'Only vaguely,' Doug admitted. 'I have vague memories of visiting you with me da.'

Ivy stared at her brother. She'd never been taken to visit anyone. Not by her mother or her da.

'No,' Doug continued, 'what made me think was seeing you the other day with Billy Flint. That got me to thinking and remembering.'

'Billy Flint,' Ivy gasped. How did her little

425

brother know what that man looked like? She closed her mouth and waited to hear more.

'Billy Flint is me da's brother, Ivy.' Doug was determined that Ivy should know everything she needed to know. There would be no more secrets. If Ivy had known she had family she could turn to when their da died, life would have been much easier for her. She deserved to know it all.

'Your father never wanted her to know about us.' Betty refused to apologise for her own existence.

'Betty, I have one day off from the theatre. Today, Christmas Day. I have no time to waste.' Doug leaned over the table. 'I'm leaving here – going to America and a new life. I've asked Ivy to come with me but she's refused. I will not leave here and allow my sister to continue on in ignorance. She deserves to know what's what and I'm determined to tell her. I never want to think of my sister completely alone again. No offence to you, Jem – you were there when those who should have looked after and protected her ignored her very existence.' Doug looked around at the shocked faces. He was bloody well going to have his say. 'I know she has friends, good friends, people who have been kinder to her than her blood relatives but she deserves to know that she's bloody surrounded by family.'

'I beg your pardon.' Ann Marie stared at Ivy's brother in horror. Ivy had family that ignored her and left her to struggle on alone? She thought of the pathetic figure who'd fainted in the morgue from hunger and sorrow the first day she met her. How dare her family allow her to go through

426

that horror alone and penniless? They should be brought to account.

'Oh yes, Ann Marie, Ivy has family,' Doug said bitterly. 'You probably know all of them. I wouldn't be surprised to learn you visit their homes on occasion.'

'Shay,' Betty said softly.

'Enough with the bloody secrets, Betty!' Doug beat the table top, setting the glasses and bottles that remained rattling.

'Shay, you don't know what you're saying.' But Betty actually agreed with him. She'd tried to keep out of Ivy's life but it had proved impossible.

'My name is Doug now.' He was not going to back down. Ivy had been abused enough. 'I will never be Shay Murphy again. My name is Douglas Joyce and I plan to make the best of the opportunities opening up to me. I might be willing to let go of my name but I will never desert my sister again. Ivy deserves a whole lot better than she's received from any of us.'

'Éamonn changed his name and made the decision to keep us out of her life.' Betty wasn't willing to say anything bad about their mother but Violet had been at the root of that decision. Violet Burton had left a trail of destruction in her wake. Betty might not be willing to say it aloud but she could think it. The woman had deserted her husband and children after all.

'I really don't care any more,' Doug said softly. 'Ivy needs to know that she has two grandmothers, two grandfathers and a host of aunts, uncles and cousins all living within walking distance of The Lane. In fact she knocks on their back doors most Mondays.'

'Me head is spinning.' Ivy took Jem's hand in hers, holding on tightly. She needed his strength. She'd known her mother had family living about the Square, family that refused to recognise them but she'd never known about her da's family.

'I regret to say this,' Ann Marie stated loudly, 'but your family does not deserve the extraordinary person that is Ivy Rose Murphy. She is someone any family should be proud to claim. I'd like a list of those family members, Doug. I will be sure to avoid them in the future. I will also be extremely happy to tell them why.'

'I'll see that you get it, Ann Marie,' Doug grinned. He knew who this woman was now. He knew just how rich and influential Ann Marie Gannon was. With her on her side, his sister would be all right. Ivy had made a life for herself. A good life surrounded by people who cared for her and would fight in her corner. She'd done it all on her own. She hadn't asked for or received help from their family but she bloody well deserved to know who they were.

'I'll just tidy the table.' Sadie stood and began collecting the dirty glasses and empty bottles. She'd been sitting there like a lump on a log, listening to the revelations. It was better than the fillums any day.

'I'll help you.' Ann Marie wanted to sit here and express her opinion. She wanted to hear everything that was about to be revealed but she couldn't let Sadie do all the work. She was trying to learn to live without servants after all.

'With the best will in the world, Ann Marie,'

Sadie grinned, 'You're feckin' useless. I'll get finished faster on me own. You sit there and listen to what's what. You can hold up our Ivy's end of the story. I'm just going to tidy these things away. I won't wash the dishes. The girls can do that later. That's their job and I'm not doing it for them.'

'I'll help you.' Jem released Ivy's hand and stood up. She'd tell him everything she wanted him to know.

'Is there e'er a chance of a pot of tea?' Ivy almost whimpered. She needed an ocean of tea to deal with these revelations.

'Ivy Murphy,' Jem laughed down at her, 'don't ever change. If the world was going to end in two minutes you'd be the one putting on the kettle.' He leaned forward and kissed her forehead. Her family might not look out for her but he would. 'You've made your own family this year, Ivy, and everyone here knows it.'

Jem went to put the kettle on. His Ivy needed her tea.

'And so say all of us!' John Lawless glared around the table, making sure everyone there knew he had Ivy's back. The Lawless family owed the woman everything.

Ivy watched the man she would marry hurry away to attend to her needs. She smiled at Ann Marie's indignant expression. Her friend was ready to go to battle for her, it seemed. She looked at her brother with loving sadness. He was leaving her again. She let her eyes examine the people around the table. Jem was right – she'd made her own family this year and they were the best in the world.

The publishers hope that this book has given you enjoyable reading. Large Print Books are especially designed to be as easy to see and hold as possible. If you wish a complete list of our books please ask at your local library or write directly to:

Magna Large Print Books
Magna House, Long Preston,
Skipton, North Yorkshire.
BD23 4ND

This Large Print Book for the partially sighted, who cannot read normal print, is published under the auspices of

THE ULVERSCROFT FOUNDATION